# HEAR NO EVIL

## TERRY PERSUN

Booktrope Editions
Seattle WA 2013

Cover Design by Renda Dodge
Edited by Janna Balthaser

*This is a work of fiction. Names, characters, places, brands, media, and incidents are either the product of the author's imagination or are used fictitiously. Any resemblance to similarly named places or to persons living or deceased is unintentional.*

PRINT ISBN 978-1-62015-116-7
EPUB ISBN 978-1-62015-106-8

For further information regarding permissions, please contact info@booktrope.com.

Library of Congress Control Number: 2013943853

*For my brother, Howard,*
*who introduced me*
*to science fiction.*

# CHAPTER 1

HE NEVER EXPECTED TO BE SHOT DOWN while on a peaceful mission — although any time an angry labor group is involved it becomes a possibility — until he realized that the lander was loaded with explosives, which only made him wonder what kind of peace they were peddling. Of course that didn't matter now. All that really mattered was to stay alive, and to keep the other two who were on board alive as well. He glanced over at Palmer and she batted her eyes before yanking the stick back and throwing them both against their seats, like she did it on purpose.

"Stay put and strap into the seat's parachute." She gave him a sideways glance and pursed her lips as though blowing him a kiss.

The last radio transmission from ground control asked the same question that had crossed Brandon's mind. "Why is a lander for the Intergalactic Peace Force weighed down with explosives and heading away from the landing strip straight for the colony's main city?"

As much as he wanted to ask that question, with a Peace Force official on board there wasn't time to waste. "I'm engaging the gunner pod," he said as he slapped the release on his harness.

"Brandon, no." Palmer banked left to avoid being hit by what appeared to be a makeshift tracer and shoved a finger at the comm unit, taking them offline. "Get into a chute," she yelled. "No heroes; trust me."

"Only slow me down," he said. Brandon dove into the rear of the lander, near the official who appeared to be praying.

After Palmer's insistence on getting into a chute, Brandon heard nothing more than garbled words from her captain's seat.

He nodded as calmly as he could to let Clark, the IPF's Peace Coordinator, know that he had everything under control.

The lander pulled left a second time, then dropped. Brandon had learned to manipulate his movements to get where he wanted under any circumstances. He grabbed door handles and leaned against electrical panels for balance as he continued toward the pod. It was easy going so far.

In the next chamber he backed against the loading zone where his weapons cuffs were waiting. He pushed his shoulders under the clamps, then slipped his hands through the fiber-armored sleeves that fit from his fingers to his forearms. He could smell a thick oilcloth odor and feel the rough interior as he pushed into them. Once his fingers were snug, he quickly engaged the shoulder clamps and let the straps tighten around his thick arms, practically making him part of the machine. He pulled loose from the loading zone. Fully loaded, his thigh muscles tightened under his uniform. The cuffs drew his body down. That was until Palmer banked again, then the cuffs tried to go where the lander's momentum led them. He forced his arms into staying put and lifted his shoulders to test the weight of the ammunition. Careful not to blast a hole into the side of the lander, Brandon swung into the gunner pod, wrapped his legs around the tower pole and used voice command to get strapped in. "Engage," he said when he was ready, and two plugs were exposed so that he could interface with the ship's weapons.

He was doubly endowed, cuffs and ship's weapons.

The pod screen opened to the dim light of the pending dusk. Grey clouds streaked the sky immediately overhead, while a crimson background glowed over the bluish rocks of the C-47 terrain. "Labor disputes," he shook his head. "When will these people learn?"

He had been trained on using weapons cuffs for years. Firing rounds, whether personal or ship's weapons, was like pointing a finger where you wanted bullets to fly or a missile to launch. The real key was a muscle twitch that triggered the device. Learning which muscle that was, and how to keep it from twitching on its own, that was the trick. The weapons were simple and difficult to use. Most cadets when they first joined any Weapons Squadron, whether for Earth Central or the Intergalactic Peace Force had such poor hand-eye coordination that they shot at everything but what they thought they were pointing at. Brandon had his own problems with the machine at the beginning, but happened to be a fast learner. His good luck, because only the best worked for Earth Central. Better pay, more travel. Until he met Palmer, that's all he wanted.

Incoming rounds whizzed past the pod, leaving a trail of fire and dust. Brandon pointed and released, pointed and released, each time knocking out another blast from nearby the colony where they had been heading. With all Palmer's evasive movements, Brandon's rounds connected on the outside edge of the makeshift missiles being shot at them, which made the missiles spin toward the ship even after being knocked out. It took a moment of focus, but he adjusted his aim and that fixed everything. He did miss a few times, whenever Palmer slowed, sped up, banked, or dove unexpectedly. It did make for a frustrating game, but he was good and deterred hits more often and faster than she could avoid them.

When the lander was grazed, it threw the ship sideways for a few thousand feet before she could pull it back into control. He imagined her wrestling with the stick, while he kept pummeling the incoming rounds. It took a lot of focus, but out the corner of his eye he saw something coming at them. Instinct told him that it wasn't dangerous, which was confirmed once he realized it was a second IPF vehicle. He didn't like what he saw. They were supposed to be alone. The mother ship wouldn't have had time to send a second lander unless they expected some sort of retaliation from the colony. That didn't make any sense. Brandon glanced down but couldn't see Clark. His seat was left of the doorway.

Palmer twisted the lander to the right and pitched the nose into the gray sky and low clouds.

"Where the hell are you going," Brandon yelled, knowing that she couldn't hear a word. He never plugged into the intercom; it broke his focus. "Hair-brained maneuver," he said under his breath. The pitch meant that he couldn't see under the lander, which was where the attack came from. She needed to pull out of her lift or he couldn't keep them safe. They were vulnerable. That's when he saw Palmer, still strapped into her pilot's seat, fly past him. He turned and caught a glimpse of her chute kicking open. He couldn't believe his eyes. She left him there to die. There wasn't time for sentiment. "Fuck." The pod's interconnect plugs snapped away as he pulled from the lander's weapons and leaped from the pod. The lander would hit a stall and drop like a rock from the sky if he didn't get to the controls fast.

Clark said something as Brandon ran toward the cockpit. His squeaky voice sounded thin. Brandon knew what that expressed. Fear. He didn't have to hear the words spoken.

Air gushed into the cockpit from the jettisoned cab. Good news. The lander was still moving. The weight of the cuffs gave Brandon a false sense of power as he grabbed for the stick and pushed the lander into a dive, hoping to gain air speed and a bit more control.

Wrong idea. The engines had been cut. There was no control.

Duty was a louder voice than personal survival, which had Brandon step into Clark's chamber. The man's eyes were wide. Brandon used the back of his hand to punch the release and get Clark out of his harness. Simultaneously he pointed and released a short-range missile into the side of the lander: the fastest way out. Wrapping his arms around Clark, Brandon jumped into the open air. Only Clark had an emergency chute strapped to his back, and Brandon knew that once it deployed he'd have to hang on to whatever he could.

"Pull," he instructed.

Clark wedged his hand between them and yanked on the chute's cord. A loud fluffing sound roared in their ears and Brandon clenched his strong body even closer to Clark's scrawny one.

The jerk, once the chute opened, wasn't so bad on Brandon, but he imagined how it must have felt to Clark. He was wearing the cuffs and the extra weight would hurt anyone's shoulders.

He searched the sky for Palmer and the other lander while praying that the colonists were bad shots. But they weren't shooting at Brandon and Clark; they aimed for the lander. Brandon saw the missile that was going to hit its target. They were still too close to avoid the explosion that was about to come. "Hold tight," he said to Clark.

The blast blew the two men sideways. Brandon took the brunt of it and with his face turned, so did his inner ear. It knocked him out. Dreamland wasn't so bad, a slow floating feeling until he woke up realizing that Clark now held onto him.

Brandon heard the man's heavy breathing and was thankful that his arms had been positioned over Clark's shoulders. If not, the frail man wouldn't have been able to hold onto Brandon loaded down with all his gear. "You're tougher than you appear," Brandon said.

"You have no idea," Clark said.

Brandon, less drowsy with every second, recovered quickly enough to know that they couldn't land together. He resumed his hold around Clark's shoulders and felt the man relax, although it couldn't have felt that good. Clark still held Brandon's weight and the weight of the weapons cuffs. As they neared the ground, Brandon said, "This is going to hurt," then pushed off, falling into a tuck and roll. He angled so that he'd land on his shoulder, protected by the cuff. Even that didn't make the landing any softer. The rocks were sharp and the thick dust, when he rolled over it, kicked up and into his lungs. When he stopped, there was no time to waste. He coughed and spit out the oddly salty dirt he'd swallowed, and searched the area for Clark who was being dragged along the rough ground at the end of the chute.

"Shit. Don't they teach these guys anything?" Brandon knew his limits, and even though he could run faster without the cuffs, he hated having to leave them. He only had one hand weapon and a knife on him other than the cuffs. Again, duty took over and he released the cuffs and ran full speed after Clark.

The chute snagged on a rock and crumpled long enough to slow it down. This gave Brandon the chance to dive over Clark and land on the cords. In no time he rolled toward the half-opened chute bringing it to a full stop. He grabbed the cloth and began pulling it in. They might need the material and the cord later. Brandon knew to save everything when in this type of situation.

Holding the chute in his arms, Brandon walked back to Clark. "You saved my ass, Buddy, but all I have for you is a thank you."

Clark didn't respond.

Brandon kneeled next to him. A puddle of blood pooled in the blue-tinted dust near Clark's head. Brandon looked up the dragline and saw all manner of protrusions. Clark could have hit his head on any or all of the rocks. It hardly mattered. Brandon reached over and touched a finger to Clark's neck, searching for a carotid pulse.

Nothing. He flipped Clark onto his stomach. The whole back of his head had been torn open, as was his jacket collar and the clothes half way down his back.

Brandon shook his head. After all that, Clark still didn't make it.

He unstrapped the chute, which he could refold later. For the time being, he stuffed it inside the emergency pack that he pulled from Clark for safekeeping. The emergency pack included water and some packaged goop that was supposed to pass as food, along with a multi-tooled knife and a compass. He quickly went through Clark's pockets, but there wasn't anything worth saving except for a few high-energy bars. No additional weapons. Not that he'd expected any from an IPF official.

From Brandon's position on the ground, the sun had fallen behind the blue hills. The air already had a chill in it, and was about to get much colder. Brandon stripped Clark of his torn jacket and shirt and stuffed them inside the pack with the chute. He scanned the area and saw no immediate danger, but wasn't about to wait out in the open for something to arrive. He knew nothing about the wildlife on C-47.

With the items he collected, Brandon jogged back to where he had let the cuffs fall. He strapped the pack to his back and lay down next to the weapons cuffs. He slipped his hands and forearm into the cuffs using the ground as a source of friction so that he could get a snug fit for his fingers. That was important. That's where directional control came from. The cuffs would be heavy to carry—with thousands of fiber bullets folded inside each one—no matter how he carried them; so he'd might as well wear them. At least that way he'd have protection for a while.

He engaged the shoulder clamps and arm straps, then lifted into a sitting position. He rolled to one side then stood. He rotated 360 degrees and, in a moment, oriented himself. He recalled flying over the main colony, which was nestled into a green and brown valley, wide fields in one direction with crops he couldn't recognize. That area rose to a height that became more barren, and on the other side of that it looked like desert, rocky canyons, and flood lowlands. He shook his head. "I had to land in the most barren place," he said to no one.

The mountains to his left, shaped like a crown, meant that the colony was a few hills south of where he stood. He wasn't exactly sure where the lander crashed after the explosion, and looked for smoke. He hoped that no one had gotten hurt in the crash. Any colony would have to be stupid to use weapons, especially homespun ones, against the Intergalactic Peace Force, he thought. He knew enough about them to understand that Force wasn't just part of their name.

Still, he knew that the colony wasn't an army, just a bunch of disgruntled scientists and their families. They probably didn't understand that the IPF often used force to settle touchy situations. Sometimes you had to kill a few people to initiate peace and get to an agreement. It was usually one bad apple who had to be taken out. That's what he'd been taught.

The temperature dropped quickly as the sun lowered. Brandon thought of heading south into the colony, but decided against it for the moment. Something strange appeared to be going on. Having been in combat situations plenty of times, he knew to stick with his gut feel.

Another thing, Palmer wasn't the type to eject and leave the rest of them vulnerable. Especially him. He hoped anyway. He thought they had started a nice relationship. But duty came above all else and he had no idea what her duty was on this excursion. He couldn't fault her for following orders. He'd mull it around for a while. And, for now, he'd head north.

He spent an hour piling rocks on top of Clark's body before he left.

He traveled along the base of the eastern mountains. The sky darkened and he began to trip over protrusions. A groundswell of insects, bugs of some kind, appeared once the temperature dropped below about 50 degrees. He waved them away for a while, but the weight of the cuffs made it difficult to keep up. Then the bugs started to bite. He stopped moving. This was as good a place as any to camp.

Brandon released the cuffs and removed the pack. It was much easier to swat at the bugs and keep them away when his arms had full motion. In the dim light, he located a large rock and threw the chute over it, yanking the cords to pull it tight along the ground. Using the cuffs, he propped one on either side so that the chute created a closed tent. In the front, he threw the emergency pack to keep it from flapping in the breeze. Using Clark's ripped jacket and shirt for a mat, Brandon sat down with his back against the rock. After slapping at a few bugs, his enclosure was fairly bug free.

In the dimness, he opened one of the bars he had found on Clark and ate it. It tasted like stale bread. He had an emergency vitamin panel on the cuffs, but he needed bulk in his stomach. For now, until he could hunt in the morning, the energy bar would have to do. The dark settled in around him and strange sounds started to creep into the area. His parachute tent smelled like plastic. He knew that sleep wouldn't come easily, but closed his eyes anyway. Before he knew it he awoke to rustling sounds outside the tent.

He continued to breathe deeply, as though he were still sleeping. The scuffling got closer and Brandon tried to decide how many of whatever-they-were were milling around outside. First thought: were they carnivorous? The things made chirping sounds and growling noises. An argument appeared to ensue, matched with scuffling noises. Then it sounded as though one of them got bit or kicked and ran off, leaving only one. By the sound of its footsteps on the dirt, it wasn't large, but Brandon knew that didn't matter one bit. Fierce always trumped big. And some of the smallest beasts were the most fierce.

For several hours the thing paced around his tent and he never knew if it was protecting its discovery or waiting to see what came out of the mound of cloth. Either way, once the sun began to lighten the area, he heard the thing scuffle off. He breathed easier.

Although he didn't feel itchy, his arms were covered with welts. Touching his face exposed several more welts. All else appeared to be satisfactory. "At least the bloody things weren't poisonous," he said. It took him a few minutes to break down camp, gather his gear, get the parachute stuffed into the pack, and check on his surroundings.

There were three-toed tracks, with what appeared to be huge toenails, all around where he had set up his tent. The feet were almost a foot long. He wished he knew what the beast was, but it was probably better that he didn't.

He had to lie down on the ground again to get the cuffs on. He opened the chamber on the inside of his cuff and popped a few vitamins, chewing their bitter flavor and swallowing them without water. He needed to save what little water he had for emergencies. The food goop too. He'd eat the energy bars as long as they lasted.

The temperature had already climbed about 20 degrees from the night before, which hadn't fallen much under 40 as far as he could tell. Since the sun was barely over the horizon, the day threatened to be hot. The sun rose in the west on C-47. There were low-lying shrubs and what appeared to be stubby trees running down the middle of the valley. Hopefully there was running water there, too. But where there's water, there are animals. He hoisted his shoulders to feel the heft of the cuffs, his security blanket for the moment.

Brandon decided to cross the valley and walk in the shade of the western hills until the sun stood overhead, then cross the valley again. Keeping cool would help him retain what little water he had in his system. He had no idea where he was headed for now, but he hoped someone came looking for him. Anyone. He thought of Palmer, but quickly put her out of his mind. What she had done bothered him, even though his gut told him that it wasn't like her to eject and leave anyone behind, especially him.

# CHAPTER 2

**PALMER CRAWLED INTO THE LANDER** with help from an IPF sergeant wearing a safety harness. She flipped her helmet off and brushed her black hair behind her ears. She took stock of the area and saw Jacobs standing near the open airlock holding to one of the security handles to keep himself steady. He wore a safety harness too, clipped to the inside of the lander.

Jacobs was the man who had hired her to escort and then abandon Clark, letting him go down with the ship, as they say. It had been a hasty job all the way around. She was called to make a quick decision, got paid plenty, and only had to deal with a small amount of guilt. Boarding the lander, she had asked Clark one question: "Do you know you're most likely going to die?" Unequivocally, he said, "Yes." She still insisted that he wear a chute even though she could see in his eyes that he meant what he had said.

"What the hell did you do?" she said between breaths. The sergeant reached over and pushed a button to close the lander off from the outside air rushing in. The area suddenly got quieter. They were already high over the blue mountains headed for the mother ship.

Palmer leaned to look out the window to see where her lander had fallen or if Brandon was able to get it back into operation. She knew he was fast and well trained. The window faced the wrong way, but she heard an explosion and the lander quaked.

Jacobs didn't show any emotion. "It's done," he said.

Palmer reached for him and he stepped back. "We had to get you out of there."

She knew he was a go-between for whoever was in charge of the operation, but he didn't have to be so cold. She hesitated and thought for a moment, then said, "That could have ripped my head off. What if I wasn't ready?" She shifted her weight around and sat on the grating, her tight-fitting, black uniform stretched easily over her bent knee. Her other leg folded under her uncomfortably. She closed her eyes for a moment and rubbed a hand across her forehead and into her hair. Brandon's face crossed her mind. She missed him. She wanted to cry, but couldn't allow herself to show unnecessary concern about him. No one could learn that the two of them were close. They weren't even supposed to be friends. But she could enquire. Regardless of what he meant to her, Brandon was from Earth Central and only recently assigned to the IPF. His safety had been put into her hands as the captain of the lander. Clark, on the other hand, had already fulfilled his duty. "Brandon?" she asked. "He was supposed to eject with me. I was supposed to initiate the ejections."

"He didn't make it. He never should have gone into the gunner pod. That wasn't supposed to happen. You knew that." Jacobs stepped closer to Palmer, still holding to the airlock's safety handle as though the safety harness wasn't enough. He bent down so that they were face-to-face. His lips quivered. "You failed. It was supposed to look like the lander was shot down without provocation."

She stared into his stern face. "You rigged the lander so that you could control the ejection. You didn't trust me to go through with it?"

"We need pilots," Jacobs said. "I couldn't have you doing something stupid…in this case like waiting until Lt. Lockhardt was back in his seat." He stood and walked away.

Palmer knew that he would have let her die, too, if her talents weren't needed.

"Let me help you," the attending sergeant said.

Palmer took his forearm and rose to her feet. She stood half a foot above him. "You're dismissed," she said.

"I'm to take you to debriefing. We'll have to stay together for now." His short-cropped hair and awkward smile made him look innocent, fuzzy headed like a newborn.

She glanced down at his nametag. "Carpenter. That's a really old Earth name. Is that even a talent anymore?"

"Not one of mine," he said.

She smiled despite herself. He didn't take offense to her quip and she liked that. "Name's Palmer." She thrust a hand toward him and they shook. "What's the deal here?" She nodded toward the direction Jacobs had exited. "What's he afraid of? The job was carried out as planned. Mostly."

"I don't know what you mean. You were fired on," he said.

So, the faked trip fooled him, she thought. "Yeah, well, that was supposed to happen. I just didn't know we were loaded with explosives."

"Explosives?" Carpenter made a face.

"Never mind," Palmer said. "Back to Jacobs. He's shaking all over."

"Maybe he's about to get into trouble. If so, he'll need someone to blame. My guess that would be you." Carpenter winked at her, making him look all the more cute. "Before you ask any more questions, you have to understand that I was just assigned and that this is my first trip anywhere. I don't even know what your mission was except to deliver something. Even that was a bit shady. The fact that you were supposed to be fired on," his face twisted into a painful look, "that's more than I need to know." He held up his hand to keep her from talking. "And I don't want to know. I've already heard too much. I'm just supposed to make sure you get to the debriefing room once we're back at the ship."

She fully understood his feelings. It was always best to get your orders and do the job. Less worry. Less guilt. And fewer problems. "Can I use the head on my own?"

He smiled. "By all means."

Palmer stepped past Carpenter and ducked into the head. The room was barely large enough for her slim body, which made her wonder how a man as wide as Brandon, or even Carpenter, could get around in there. Once inside she opened her waist pack and pulled out an ear-bud recording device. She pulled back her hair and shoved it deep into her ear. Then she checked to make sure that all her weapons were still in place. They'd take her short-range Taser and knife she figured, but they probably wouldn't find the three plastic pin-knives that had been sewn into her uniform. After she was through, she sat on the toilet seat and gave herself a moment to feel hurt. If she were any other woman, she might have cried, she wanted to, but Palmer wasn't about to be one of those women. She flushed the toilet. Then she cocked her head so that she could see her reflection in the mirror. She wet her hands and ran them through her hair. She rubbed more water over her face, then dried off. She didn't know what to expect, but for the first time during what should have been a relatively routine mission, she was about to be debriefed. Plus, Carpenter didn't know anything about the operation, which meant that it was more secret than she had thought.

A knock came to the door. "Out of there," Jacobs said.

Palmer unlocked the door and stepped out making sure that she stood her full six feet two inches so that she could look down on Jacobs like she had Carpenter. "Can't a girl primp?"

"Not that long." He turned to Carpenter. "Now stick with her."

"Yes, sir."

Once he was gone again, she asked, "Where the hell am I going to go?"

Carpenter shrugged. "I promise not to be a pest."

Palmer grinned. "No worries there. But Jacobs is already drilling into it."

After landing in the mother ship's launch bay, Carpenter grabbed hold of Palmer's forearm. He ushered her out the same passage she had come through to get on board, stepping down to the bay's noisy metal panels. The bay smelled of grease and fuel like any mechanic's shop. Palmer liked the odor, it reminded her of a well-maintained ship. Carpenter marched at her side, letting go of her arm once they stepped inside the main corridor of the ship. She meandered down the hall as though she was in charge and knew where they were going. Carpenter didn't let on like he gave a shit, and announced their turns long enough ahead that she got to maintain her appearances. The few IPF enforcers who passed them in the hall looked at Carpenter more than Palmer, probably wondering what he was doing with her in the first place. She made him look good, she thought.

"And a final left," he said as they approached a closed door. "Just walk in."

Palmer shoved the door open as though she had set up the meeting. She scanned the length of a boardroom table then walked to the only empty seat among seven and sat down. Carpenter closed the door behind her and continued on down the hall, probably to perform his next duties or get his next orders. She heard his fading footsteps as he walked away.

Jacobs was not in the room. She didn't know any of the men who were. They dressed in standard civilian code suits, no ranking insignia. "Where's Jacobs?"

"We're debriefing him in a different room," a thin man with gray hair and a slight slouch said. She noticed that he wasn't sitting at the head of the table, which meant that he was a lackey, there to answer the simple questions. She took her eyes from him and slowly brought them to the man who was really in charge and sitting at the head of the table, a balding man of about forty, wrinkled brow, squinted eyes, mouth stretched straight across his face. Not very pleasant to look at on any level. She stopped and narrowed her eyes as well. Leaning forward she said, "I have to account for an IPF assigned, Earth-trained Lieutenant who was supposed to eject with me and be picked up and taken here for his next assignment…out of here if he was lucky." She stopped for effect. "Jacobs rigged my seats," she accused. At this point she just wanted out of there and back to her own Shadow Cruiser F-9 where she was sure she had offers for another job already.

The man at the end of the table brought his hands together.

None of the other men moved. In fact, their stillness was more indication to their fear than movement would have been. The man who had spoken to her first watched the guy at the head of the table without blinking.

"We'll take care of that," the main man said.

She sat back into her chair. "Then what's to debrief? I was hired to run a decoy and allow a lander to crash. Make it look like the colony's fault so that you could buy some time. That's all I was told. That's what I know." She glanced around the room and came back to rest her eyes on the head man, at which time she smiled broadly. "Oh, and Clark was a criminal with a terminal disease who volunteered for the job." She shook her head. "I suspect his family is getting the benefit from his choice. And I can guarantee you that it was his choice or I wouldn't have run that lander into the ground."

She sat back again, closed her hands together to match her apparent opponent, and waited. They had not even patted her down for weapons. They didn't expect any trouble. Either that or every one of the men in the room except for Mister Big was armed. They could be secret service. On second look, she changed her mind. Most of them looked too soft to be in any kind of service. She smiled to herself.

After a long silence, the head man said, "We recorded your conversation with the, shall we say, dissidents."

"Expected," Palmer said even though she didn't like the term dissident when talking about the families of colonists. They probably wanted more government assistance, more supplies, and Earth Central needed time to decide what they were going to negotiate for. Or something like that, what did she care?

"They found explosives on board," the man said.

"Yeah, what was that all about? I was told it only had defensive weapons. The usual."

"We don't know what that was about, Miss..." he looked at one of the other men who sat around the table.

"Luce," one of them said. She didn't see which one.

"Miss Luce. Why don't you tell us," he said.

"It wasn't my ship. I was hired to pilot it. That's all. You guys loaded the damned thing. My cruiser is in your launch bay. And I'm probably late for another job. So, could we wrap this up?"

"That's not what my paperwork says. It says that you loaded the lander. You inspected it before leaving."

She leaned forward. "Then your paperwork is wrong. All I inspected were the engines, the safety gear, and the environmentals. Standard procedure before takeoff. Remember, you guys loaded the cargo."

The man smiled for the first time. "I'm afraid that I'm going to have to charge you with attempting to foul an IPF negotiation with the C-47 Governmental Council. Do you have anything more to say?"

She shook her head and scrunched her face in confusion. That was fast. "What?" She looked around. Suddenly she didn't feel so safe. "You hired me to fly that lander into the ground so that it looked as though it was shot down. I don't know why. And I don't give a shit why. I'm a pilot, not a politician. I've performed these types of missions a hundred times. You can't accuse me of anything but completing a mission." She yelled to be sure that what she said was on tape, as she expected the proceedings were being recorded. And she wanted it on record that she was just following orders according to the contract.

"Every time you pilot a craft you are responsible for checking it out. The IPF's equipment is no exception. Isn't that correct?" The man was already preparing to get up and leave.

"Hold it." She slapped the table. "Jacobs wouldn't let me near that lander until it was time to do the run." She was already dreading that decision. "He said that I knew all I needed to know about the top-secret procedure. I was just the driver."

The man stood and turned away. She rose and yelled after him, "I tested the engines…"

"Hold her for processing," he said before leaving.

Four of the six men left in the room pulled stunners on her. She sat back down. While she waited for them to call a few enforcers to take her away, she thought about her decision to do the job in the first place. It had been hurried from start to finish. That's what warranted the high pay, which, lucky for her, had been transferred before she started. She had hoped for a short vacation afterwards, where she and Brandon could be alone — she had recommended him for the job, too. She was going to ask him to join her after they got back.

Palmer was a strong woman and held back her sorrow with a clenched jaw. Her decisions may have caused his death. She lowered her eyes, letting out a shallow breath. She shook her head. They were both professionals. If anyone could escape that vehicle, it was Brandon. She held to that conviction. All she had to do was get to the surface and find him.

Two well-built enforcers in IPF uniform grabbed her arms and lifted her from her seat before she could react. It took a moment for her legs to catch up to them as they dragged her from the chair. The men in suits were filing out of the room first. Not a word was said as she was taken out of the debriefing room and down the hall in the opposite direction from where the suits were headed. Two doors down and the enforcers hauled her into another room. This one lay bare of furniture. The enforcers let her go with a little shove and stepped outside and shut the door. She heard them snap into position, guarding the door.

A large older woman entered from a separate door on the opposite wall. "Sorry Missy, but I'm here to confiscate your weapons."

Palmer looked around the room. "Where do I put them?"

The woman had short gray hair and weighed about thirty pounds more than Palmer even though she was over a foot shorter. "On the floor is good."

Palmer removed the Taser and knife and dropped them at her feet. "Now what?"

"Strip."

"I don't have a stunner up my ass," Palmer said.

The woman smiled as though she thought the statement was funny. "I like you. But, I'll be making sure of that."

"Jesus," Palmer said. She bent down and disengaged the tie reel on her shoes and pulled them off one by one. She removed her socks and dropped them on the floor next to her shoes. She unzipped the shirt of her pilot's uniform and removed it, letting her breasts drop slightly. The room was chilly. Then she unclasped her waistband and slid her pants and underwear off at the same time. She stood naked before the woman.

The woman put on plastic gloves and walked closer, asking Palmer to raise her arms and spread her legs. She reached up and Palmer opened her mouth automatically. The woman investigated the inside of Palmer's mouth, then lowered her hands and walked all the way around Palmer without touching her. "You can lower your arms. I'll be checking for implants." Her chubby hands, still damp, gripped Palmer's left hand and rubbed each finger individually. Then the woman used both hands to push into Palmer's skin. There were particular pockets where implants could be placed and not seen with the naked eye. The woman appeared to know where those pockets were. Palmer grimaced at one point. "This does tend to hurt sometimes," the woman said.

Palmer looked over at her. "It's not my first time."

"Sorry to hear that." The woman smiled. "Bend over. This will feel a bit intrusive." She took a small bottle from her pocket and doused her fingers with a lubricant.

"You've got to be kidding me?" Palmer closed her eyes while the woman checked her other openings. "I'm a pilot, not a soldier," Palmer said. "I have no reason to hide weapons. Think of me as the driver of the getaway car."

The woman didn't answer. When she was through, she reached inside her pocket and removed a small device that she strapped to her palm. She bent down and ran the device over Palmer's clothes one item at a time.

"Can I stand normally, now?"

"Sure," the woman said. "Make yourself comfortable."

"Not likely."

After going over the clothes with her metal detector, the older woman looked up at Palmer. "You're clean."

"I think I told you that."

The woman smiled again. "I really do like your spunk." She scooped up the Taser and knife and put them in her pocket with the metal scanner. "You can get dressed again."

"Now what?" Palmer had lowered her voice. She was more serious. She really wanted to know what was next, if the woman had a clue.

"Just doing my job," the woman said. "So, I have no idea what's next." She smiled broadly. "Probably better that way for both of us."

Palmer was beginning to see that "just doing your job" wasn't good for anyone. She had learned over the years that the fewer questions she asked, the more work and better pay she received. Now, just when she wanted answers, nobody had any. Not even her.

Palmer dressed slowly. The woman watched her every move. She had never looked into Palmer's ear or she may have seen the recorder. And when Palmer drew her pants back on, she let her hand slide over the three pin knives, still in place. Had the woman crumpled Palmer's pants she may have found them, but that didn't happen. Tightening the last lace reel on her shoes Palmer announced that she was ready to go.

The woman walked over and knocked twice on the door and the guards came in. "She's clean," the woman said.

Palmer looked at each of the men. Neither of them as tall as she was. "I can walk on my own if you don't mind."

"Sorry ma'am," the one on the right said.

"Captain," she said. "I may be a free agent, but I have rank as long as I'm on a mission."

She got no response. Each of them held to one of her biceps as they guided her back down the hall. They soon pushed through double doors that were labeled secure area. She recognized the brig when she saw it. They escorted her into a small room with a few wall protrusions that were to be used as chairs or cots. A toilet and sink extended out from the corner. Only a small opening was in the door, not large enough for her to crawl through.

The soldiers left the room and locked her in.

She didn't hear any sound after that. The room probably employed an electronic lock. She scanned the walls and ceiling for cameras, but saw none. Probably too small to see with the naked eye.

She turned around a few times and then took a seat. This wasn't going to help her get down to C-47 and find Brandon.

# CHAPTER 3

**THE ROCKY TERRAIN CAUSED** Brandon's ankles to twist in one direction and then another until the ground became sandier as he approached the lowlands of the valley. Then he relaxed and gained some speed. Eventually, the terrain became rocky again, this time smooth rocks of various colors. Only running water could make such smooth edges so he figured he traveled through a flood zone.

Brandon felt the beating heat of the sun across his forehead. Even the top of his head was sweating. No clouds, no flash floods today, he thought. He dropped the cuffs and slid the emergency pack around so that he could reach it. A small sip of water wouldn't hurt. He couldn't tell if there was a stream beyond the underbrush, but he could feel the dull ache in the back of his neck that warned of dehydration. He took a few sips of warm water and put the water bag back into the pack. He thought about breakfast, but saved the last two energy bars for later. He'd work on the goop for dinner. What he needed was to get into the shade or set up his parachute tent again. That sun was hot.

As soon as he lay on the ground to put the cuffs back on, a rustling came from inside the underbrush. The noise headed his way, so he sat up quickly and reached for his stunner. The noise stopped. In slow motion, his toned stomach flexing as he lay back down. When the sound of movement didn't come a second time, he rushed to strap his thick arms into place. The cuffs could get heavy if worn all the time, and he hadn't needed them yet. It was only a matter of time before he dumped them altogether, he thought. "Yeah, not likely," he said. He rolled to his knees, then pushed into a standing position. He rolled his neck to get it to crack and continued on. Whatever had made the noise in the brush wasn't after him or it would have jumped him while he was down.

Hefting his shoulders up, Brandon headed toward the underbrush. He expected it to be fairly thick. It would have to be in order for it to grow so tall in a flood zone. The stuff probably grew a half a foot a day. He wandered along the edge for a short while, looking for a natural entrance. He heard more rustling, like fluttering. Maybe this planet's idea of a bird. There was no wind to speak of.

He found what looked like a path and bent down to go through. The cuffs worked perfectly to keep branches and leaves from his face. And he didn't have to worry about getting scratched along his arms. He proceeded slowly and as quietly as he could, listening for unusual sounds beyond the rustling that he was already getting used to hearing, and ignoring.

About twenty feet into the brush he stepped into an opening. Thicker tree-like plants, with reddish-orange trunks and full canopies of brown leaves, kept the sun out, which made for less underbrush and cooler air. He stood straight and took a deep breath. "Nice." The area was dense with shadow, but he saw something even darker rush by to his right. When he turned to get a better look another shadowy figure scooted past on his left. He turned that way and several other moved — this time loud enough to hear their stomping footfalls — to his right again.

Brandon kept his back against the thicket he had just passed through, but moved a few steps to the left to be out of the way of the path. Keeping his face straight ahead, Brandon softened his gaze so that he could more easily use his peripheral vision. He lifted his arm and pointed his finger, ready to shoot at any threat. Nothing happened for a few minutes so he took his first step deeper into the thicket.

From behind one of the stocky trees stepped an animal about four feet tall, with a long neck, a ball-shaped head with what appeared to be three pointed ears, and an oblong body. It was covered in brown and charcoal colored fur that matched the leaves and shadows of the area, and had two long legs equal to the length of its neck, with what appeared to be a three-toed foot about the size of the prints he had seen that morning. It had no arms. He only saw the one beast, but knew that there were many others.

Testing the situation, he took another tentative step forward while simultaneously moving his hand to point at the thing staring his way. The animal took another step too. He repeated his action and the animal followed suit. Several steps from the underbrush put him in a vulnerable position. Perhaps he was being guided into the open for an attack. He brought his feet together and stood straight. "Well, now what?"

The animal responded by opening its mouth and letting out a loud, "Ekk." The thing had teeth, long pointed ones good for ripping. It was a carnivore all right. Brandon swallowed. He could only guess how fast the thing might be able to run on those long legs, and knew that once he started shooting the rest of the beasts would either scatter or attack. If they scattered, he'd be lucky, but if they attacked he wouldn't be fast enough to stop them. "Shit."

"Ekk." The animal shook its body and Brandon watched as it extended two fur-lined, wing-like appendages, one from either side, similar to pictures of bat's wings he had seen.

"So now what, Brother?" he said.

In a moment the animal shook again, then turned away as though disinterested. That's when Brandon saw the other ones, on all sides, lift up from the ground, come around trees, exit the underbrush where he had entered. They all took the lead from the one animal and turned and walked away. He couldn't believe it. Weren't they hungry? He turned his head and sniffed toward his armpit. Maybe he stunk. He took another step and another, watching over his shoulder as the animals continued to ignore him and leave. He shook his head in disbelief and ambled through the miniature forest until he came to a tiny stream about three feet wide. The water flowed very slowly over a bed of colored sandstones. Tiny brown and green grasses mixed with patches of muddy yellow moss bordered the stream.

"Perfect." He pulled the water plug on his cuff and drank the small ration embedded within the fibers. The liquid was hot, but carried additional vitamins, at least this first round. He wasn't about to remove the cuffs. Not in there.

After drinking the vitamin-fortified water, Brandon pulled the fill hose loose, kneeled down, and reached the tube toward the water. He heard a large thumping similar to native drumming all around him. He halted his movements and the drumming stopped. He needed the water, so he reached the hose closer again. This time along with the drumming one of the animals ran toward him, leaped into the air, flapped its bat wings and floated until it landed with a thump a few feet away. It stomped its foot on the ground.

Brandon hit the auto-reel button and the hose sucked back into the cuff. He stood as slowly as possible so that he wouldn't frighten the birdlike thing standing close to him. "You win. I die of thirst, you fanged son-of-a-bitch." He smiled, but got no reaction from the beast. He stepped over the small stream toward the animal.

"Ekk." Like the first one, this bird turned and walked away. The second time that happened this morning.

"So water is sacred down here," he said. Brandon didn't waste time after that. He got through the tiny forest of stumpy, brown-leafed trees and through about ten more feet of underbrush on the other side. When he stepped into the brighter light he was also still in the shade. At least the sun wouldn't be sucking the water from his body. But he was sorry that he had depleted most of the water from his cuff.

He put a hundred yards between himself and the foliage that grew along the stream. The animals didn't appear to be hostile at the moment, but there was no use taking a chance on that changing. Maybe they had specific meal times. He laughed at the thought. He did consider shooting one for dinner once his food ran out, but that could wait until he absolutely had no other choice. If they attacked, it would be all over for him. He'd only chance it if he had to.

Before the sun made its way overhead, Brandon had made good progress. The valley floor along which he advanced, lifted slowly, and the streambed of smooth rocks that were there at one time thinned and became sand and angular rocks again as he separated himself from the valley floor. Eventually, up ahead, he saw that the foliage made a sharp turn to the east. He took in his position and decided to go over the hill he was traversing. He'd only be in the sun a short while before crossing to the other side of the hill where there'd be shade again by the time he got there.

He rested briefly. The streambed ran for miles and miles along the valley floor, which appeared to twist eastward where it disappeared behind the mountain. No time to waste, he angled up the hill.

It wasn't long before he heard thumping coming from inside the oasis. Then the noise of what could only be a thousand of those animals fluffing their wings. A loud, multi-layered and simultaneous "Ekk" later and Brandon heard the stampede coming his way. "Shit." He ran up the hill as fast as he could. The stampede came closer and as he glanced back he saw hundreds of the animals burst from the underbrush. Only some of them headed uphill toward him; the rest ran along the valley floor weaving in and out of the shrubbery. The beasts ran in a close-knit band for the most part, and every time two crashed together, one would leap into the air and fly for several yards before coming back down. Dust kicked up and filled the air. Where the dust hit the sunlight, it sparkled a brilliant blue, like diamonds.

He had no choice what to do. As about thirty of the animals headed straight for him, he opened fire dropping two of them right away, enough that the others veered off to go around him. Their mouths stretched into an open and scary looking cry, the pointed teeth bared aggressively. The Ekking sounds were loud and all around him, so loud that it took a moment before he saw what had chased them into the open. Half a mile from where he stood came a large gray ground vehicle traveling at about twenty miles and hour. They'd be on him in minutes and he had nowhere to go but up. The pitch of the climb could slow them down, which would give him time to get to the top. He had no idea whether there was a plateau up there or a drop-off. If he remembered correctly, and he couldn't be sure, there'd be a ridge and steep slope into yet another valley. The slope should be steep enough that they'd have to follow him on foot.

He used his arms to pull him forward while running straight up the hillside. The beasts thinned out as they ran around him and headed back down with the herd, or flock, or whatever, he thought. By the time Brandon reached the ridge at the top of the hill, he had changed his plans. He stopped running and sat on a large rock to wait for his captors. He couldn't outrun them, and besides they could have come to rescue him. There was no reason to think the worst. After all, he wore the IPF insignia alongside his Earth Central rank, which must account for something, even at the edge of the galaxy.

When the squared-off vehicle crested the hill it broke into the air and landed with a creak, a scream, and a thud. The driver spun the vehicle around and stopped it dead, long enough for four men with homemade rifles to jump out and storm Brandon.

"Am I glad to see you guys," he said.

Three of the men stopped with their rifles pointed at Brandon while one man strolled forward, his gun lowered and held in one hand, the barrel pitched toward the ground. The man's shoulder was still tight, his forearm too, so Brandon rose from the rock and produced his hand.

"Keep them down," the man said.

Brandon obeyed, gave the man a quick nod.

"Can you remove those things?" The man's voice sounded dry and cracked. His skin looked thick, dark and yet appeared to be smooth. His eyes were friendly, but his mouth and cheeks showed control.

"I can," Brandon said.

"Then would you?"

Brandon knew not to provoke the man, but also wanted him to know that he wasn't dealing with just anyone. He looked around at the other three. "I'll make a deal," he said.

"Put down your guns," the man told the others, anticipating Brandon's request.

The three lowered their weapons in unison.

"They have a lot faster reaction time with their weapons," Brandon pushed as he stared the man down.

"We're holding the winning hand here. I think the compromise is fair enough. We could have killed you without all this talking. They'd think you died in the explosion that, by the way, you brought with you. So..."

"Understood." Brandon disengaged the cuffs and bent at his knees so that he could pull out of them and catch them before they fell to the ground. Holding a cuff in each hand, he advanced them toward his captor who nodded and two other men stepped forward to take the weapons. "Careful with those," Brandon said.

"The stunner and knife, too," the man said.

Brandon handed his other weapons over.

"You're a big guy under those things," the man said.

"Wheaties."

"They still make those?"

Brandon gave the man a slight grin, hoping that it looked friendly and not like he was in pain. "Wheat substitute. From some planet I never heard of and never been to."

"Name's Oliver." The tan skinned man approached with his hand outstretched. "I'll accept that handshake now."

"Brandon."

"We could use a guy as big as you," Oliver said. "Got a lot to protect."

Brandon shook his head. "Sorry, got a job."

"With the IPF," Oliver said.

"Earth Central, actually." Brandon pointed to the other insignia he wore. "I've recently been assigned to the IPF. A single mission project. Didn't expect this." Brandon let go of Oliver's hand.

"I didn't know Earth Central loaned their soldiers out."

"Only for about twenty years now. Especially to the IPF," Brandon said.

"Money's tight. And there's a whole galaxy to watch over," Oliver offered.

"It also helps Earth Central to keep track of the IPF. They were getting too big for their britches, I think, using more F than P is what we used to say." Brandon only had rumors to go on, but judging from this mission, the IPF wasn't his favorite group to be assigned to.

"You know about the explosives?" Oliver said.

"Glad you asked," Brandon said. "Truthfully, it surprised the shit out of me. I was escorting an IPF official named Clark. I'm the bodyguard. Nothing more."

"Your pilot ejected and left you behind. You expendable?"

"I didn't think so," Brandon said.

"Must have surprised you then." Oliver continued to question Brandon right there in front of all the rest of them, which made Brandon extremely comfortable. He didn't have to do that. He could have taken him off alone. This approach had integrity.

"Pilots are hard to come by. She makes a lot of money. Maybe she figured she had a few more years in her," Brandon said.

"You don't believe that."

This time Brandon smiled wider. He liked Oliver's direct approach. "A little fishy," Brandon admitted. "Not something I'd expect of her."

"How so?"

"I know Palmer. She wouldn't abandon ship without knowing everyone else was safe. Or without announcing it to me, a warning at least. It's not her style. At first, I was pissed, but I'm thinking straight now. Been rolling it around in my head." He lifted his chin toward Oliver for him to talk next. "What's your take?"

"That's a long story. We can talk about it when we get back." Oliver turned and told his men to return to the vehicle. "Come with us," he said.

One of the other men, a lanky man with three-day stubble and longish blonde hair sidled next to Oliver, and Brandon heard him say, "Could be a lie."

"We'll see," Oliver said. He turned his head and gave Brandon a peripheral glance.

The vehicle had been fitted with homemade missile launchers and had an open box of ammunition in the back for the rifles. The men, all dressed similarly in brown fatigues and caps, took most of the seats, putting Brandon on the floor near the ammo. Several packs lay in the back with him as well. He lifted a side flap on one of them and saw the corner of a plastic bag. Drugs, he thought, then dismissed the idea. These guys weren't on anything. The long-haired blond threw Brandon's cuffs in the back beside him. "I'll keep an eye on you," he said before getting into the vehicle.

"No need." Brandon removed his emergency pack and lay on his back with the pack under his head. He had to bend his knees to lie flat. "You might want to pick up those animals I shot before we head back. We could have meat tonight and I'm hungry."

One of the men turned around and spit off the side of the vehicle. "Eat an Ekk? Nasty. You don't want any of that."

"That bad?"

"Worse," the man said. "Besides they're probably gone already."

"Predators?" Brandon said. He hadn't seen anything else out there.

"Cannibals," the man said.

"No wonder they didn't attack me. And that's two reasons to call them Ekks," Brandon said.

The man laughed. "They don't eat anything but each other, and trust me, it ain't pretty."

"Three for three," Brandon said as the vehicle took off down the slope and back the way they had come. South, toward their camp. Brandon made himself as comfortable as possible while he mulled the situation over in his head. No one had asked him why he headed north after his near-escape from the lander. No one asked about Clark either.

It took half an hour to drive back to where the men had originated. Brandon ate dust most of the way and had to pull his shirt up over his mouth and nose to breathe. The vehicle made about as much noise when it stopped as it did when it ran. Even with the engine off, it snapped, creaked, and popped.

They escorted Brandon, hands-off, into a small cabin amidst about a dozen cabins. The room he entered was fitted with all sorts of workbenches along two of the walls, a few tables and chairs sat in the middle of the floor, and no other decoration other than mechanical and electrical pieces and parts lying on the workbenches and on the floor around the area.

"Research and development," Oliver said, answering Brandon's quizzical look. "Have a seat. Eldon, get the man something to drink."

Everyone filed into the room. "In a minute," Eldon, the lanky blonde, said. He threw Brandon's cuffs across one of the workbenches. "How do these bullet arms work?"

"Weapons cuffs," Brandon corrected. "They're specially fitted for one body."

"I'm about your size," Eldon said rolling the cuff nearest him so that the inside arm portion, where the opening was located, faced up. He put his arm next to it on the bench. His thin arms were nothing near the size of Brandon's.

"Sure, but…" Brandon tightened his lips, turned his head away, and cocked his head in question toward Oliver.

"But what?" Eldon slammed a fist down next to the cuff. "What?"

Oliver stayed calm, watching Brandon.

Brandon didn't even turn to look at Eldon. He nodded a few times at Oliver while thinking over what to say. "Had one cadet, during training, went to scratch his ear… blew his own head off." Brandon glanced over at Eldon. "You are about my size, though. Maybe you should try one on."

"What the fuck? You threatening me?" Eldon headed for Brandon with his arms coiled back and his hands balled into fists.

Brandon didn't move until Eldon was on him. Blocking the first punch by slapping Eldon's wrist as it came around, Brandon put the man off balance. Without getting out of his chair, Brandon shoved Eldon's hip, which caused him to fall onto the floor.

"Enough," Oliver said in a calm voice. He looked around at the other men, several with their weapons pointing at Brandon. "We all got the demonstration straight now? He's trained. Now let's put down our guns and get to business. And Eldon, get the fucking man something to drink."

# CHAPTER 4

ELDON HANDED BRANDON A CLAY MUG filled with cool water. He drank it to the bottom and set the mug on the table next to him, amidst metal parts and pieces, some steel tubing, and rags and cleaners. He picked up a piece of tubing. "Building an arsenal?"

Oliver pulled a chair close to Brandon's and sat across from him. "This was an attack on us masked as a peaceful mission. I don't get it. Do they think we don't know how to build a weapons' scanner?" His face grew stern. "Do they think we're stupid?"

"Is that a rhetorical question?" Brandon said.

Oliver sighed. "I'm slowly getting sick and tired of your smart mouth, mister."

"I've been tired of it," Eldon said.

Brandon gave Eldon a sidewise glance then leaned closer to Oliver until they were practically nose-to-nose. "Then get to the fucking point."

Oliver stood quickly, knocking the chair backwards. "I'll get to the point. Right now."

"Don't do it," Eldon said. The others either nodded their heads in agreement or moaned a quiet, "Don't," to echo their feelings.

Oliver looked around the room and pointed toward the door. "Someone out there already knows. I'm sure of it." He looked around the room. "We all know it's true."

"I just don't think…" one of them said. He broke off. Everyone in the room knew what he didn't think was a good idea.

Brandon fumbled with a trigger mechanism in front of him. "Maybe they're right. I'm not sure I should know anything. I'm bound to tell the truth when I get back."

"If," Eldon said.

"No, it's when." Brandon didn't even glance at Eldon, why give him the pleasure of being acknowledged. He knew the man would be fuming.

"Knock off the pissing contest," Oliver yelled. "I'm showing him. You want to see the truth? You'll see it. And hear it. Then you'll know what we're up against." He took in Brandon's face and held his gaze. "Then we'll see if the word is 'if' or 'when' you leave." Oliver promptly spun toward the entrance and started walking. He grabbed Brandon's stunner on the way out the door.

The other men shuffled around then raised their rifles toward Brandon, who got up from his chair and followed Oliver out the door.

The sun stood high and hot. The man who drove them there ran past everyone and started to draw a cover over the top of the vehicle, stretching the material across several roll bars. Two of the other men helped finish the job, snapping the cover into place as everyone else piled into the vehicle. Brandon's cuffs were thrown into the back.

"You're sitting with me," Oliver said. "We have to talk."

Brandon followed. He felt light and free without the cuffs, but he also felt naked and vulnerable. Judging from Eldon's haphazard dive toward him earlier, though, he figured he could take all five of them in hand-to-hand. If it came to that.

Oliver got into the vehicle first then Brandon slid in next to him but nearest the door. Eldon rode shotgun in a wide front seat that harbored a number of computers and controllers between him and the driver. The back seat sat three across, which meant that the last man, like Brandon on the trip in, was forced to hang out near the ammunition case and packs stuffed with God knows what.

The vehicle lurched forward. Dust kicked into the air spitting blue sparkles into the blazing sunlight. The air was dry and smelled of salty dirt.

Brandon noticed that the bug bites on the insides of his arms were gone. He felt his face and there weren't any welts there either. Must have been a short-term poison, or his immune system had worked overtime.

Occasionally they would startle a lizard- or snake-like animal, which would take off running from them as they passed in the vehicle. Everything Brandon saw so far had the same round, ball-shaped head.

They traveled ten or twelve miles before Oliver leaned over Brandon and pointed out a few small buildings surrounding the one large building they approached. Oliver answered Brandon's first question without him having to ask it. "There are several hundred people working around the pit at any one time. Then we have our main colony of about eight thousand or so, mostly scientists. A second colony needs to be built to house the overflow, but we're running short on funds."

"Pit?" Brandon wasn't familiar with what that meant.

"We were drilling to find water or fuel or both, thinking that this planet had to have something we could harvest other than what we needed to survive. All but this one look like drilling operations. We've also received allotments for the last ten years based on some early discoveries, but they didn't pan out like we'd thought." He took a breath then said, "We have a strong and growing population. Originally, we were looking for something to sell, to trade. What we're approaching is the largest pit. A mining operation settled in for a while to help us."

"You found C-47," Brandon said. "That's where the planet's name came from. Did the vein run out?"

"We thought it was C-47, but it turned out we were wrong. The mining operation was a last ditch effort to find something of value. Once they left, funding stopped, and we are basically on our own now." He shook his head. "They left in a kind of hurry."

"No funding. That mean you're independent?" Brandon said.

Oliver looked away for a moment. "No. More like abandoned. Earth Central isn't what it used to be. They can only do so much. Anyway, we put in for independence," Oliver said in what sounded like a defeated tone, like there was nothing else they could do.

"Why not appeal for additional help? Most colonies do if they can't quite make it on their own," Brandon said.

Oliver perked up and grinned at Brandon.

"Unless…you found something. Maybe something more negotiable?" Brandon said.

"Oh, we found something, but not what anyone expected," Oliver said.

Men and women dressed in similar gray and tan clothing appeared to be walking to and from the out buildings, some carried bundles or equipment, others looked as though they were on break. "Looks like a lot is going on," Brandon said. "But you don't appear hostile."

"Bingo," Oliver said.

"Then why the need for the IPF? They're only supposed to work with hostile situations, the tough negotiations. Sounds like you have everything in order," Brandon said.

"Yeah, about that," Oliver said.

"They want what you got," Brandon deduced.

"A bit more complicated than that, but that can wait," Oliver said.

"You're supposed to have your own government and be allowed to trade openly with the rest of the Earth Central Colonies even if you're not totally independent. But you used to receive government assistance, allotments you called them? That's usually for labor groups, mining for ore on planets with little else to offer."

"We arrived here as a colony well before they thought we found C-47 and renamed the planet. Earth Central reclassified us and brought in a big mining company. That's why we aren't automatically independent and had to apply. Lucky for us that there was little C-47 to mine." He shook his head. "We're scientists, not miners. We actually considered getting a permit to colonize somewhere else when they started drilling. But then the mining company packed up and left, leaving some of their equipment behind."

"That's where you got your equipment to maintain the pits," Brandon said. He sat back into the seat. "A bit unusual to leave equipment behind, but I have to say it's a wonderful story. Riveting. So now what are you going to do?"

"We found something that Earth Central wants. At least we thought we did. Eldon up there is a bioengineer. Kuhn is our physicist, Rockwell our Archeologist." The driver held up his hand and said, "I'm the chauffeur."

Oliver laughed. "Klein is also our botanist."

"The rest of the seven thousand plus?" Brandon said.

"Colonies are started by about a dozen teams of scientists. Mining operations are started by a hand full of scientists and thousands of laborers."

"Hence, Labor Groups," Brandon said, "I'm familiar."

Oliver shook his head. "Didn't mean to backtrack. The point is, we're a colony and we've been on this planet for a long time. Our secret is out. We're being attacked by every other operation out there. They all want control, but have no idea what they're dealing with."

"And you do."

"No," Oliver said shaking his head emphatically. "But we're getting there."

Brandon changed the subject, seeing that Oliver wasn't going to spill the beans anyway. "And you, what is your job here."

"I'm just the board director for the colony. I'm the great grandson of the ship's captain."

"You created a Monarchy."

"Not quite. There are seven of us who are voted in. I just happen to be related to the first captain. That's not always the case," Oliver said. "My dad was never voted in."

"Strange crew to send out to pick up a trained soldier," Brandon said as the vehicle came to a stop in front of a large metal building.

"We take every opportunity we can get," Klein said, turning in his seat. "The attacks are sporadic and we get plenty of warning, so there wasn't much danger. It allowed us to run samples, check in with a few research teams. We're surprised you didn't run into any of them, but then they hide pretty well."

Eldon got out first and spun around to greet Brandon and Oliver as they stepped outside into the heat. "I still disapprove," he said. "I think we should get a consensus before we show him anything else."

Brandon expected Oliver to ignore Eldon, but he didn't. "Fine, call the others," he said. "Let's get this over with, though. He may be able to help us."

"You can't be serious," Eldon said. "What can one man do? Secondly, why would he choose to?"

Kuhn and Rockwell and Klein retrieved several of the packs from the back of the vehicle. They came around and caught the middle of the conversation. "Why would he what?" Klein said.

"Eldon wants to have a quick council before we show Brandon our discovery," Oliver said.

Klein looked up. "I agree with him. After all, most of us haven't been down there, either."

"And the rest of you?" Oliver said glancing around at them.

"We all agree," Kuhn said.

"But we're just a bunch of research scientists. We want to tell everyone about our discoveries. You're the diplomat, the government here, you get to decide if it's a good idea or not."

"But it's my work," Eldon said.

"For Christ's sake," Brandon said. "You guys are like a room full of children. Who the hell's in charge anyway?"

They all looked at Oliver, but he didn't acknowledge them. He turned away. "Even I don't have full authority. It's a colony remember," he said as though making an apology. "Government's slow, military is fast."

"And science is loose," Klein said. "We're putting a lot on the line."

Brandon got the allusion to the IPF's involvement. They shouldn't have the right or the power to attack a colony. The whole trip and his involvement was put together much too quickly to be a government controlled operation. It was even fast for the IPF, which he understood was able to take things into their own hands when the situation called for it. But if he knew anything for sure, it was that he didn't have enough information just yet to know what was going on. Getting close though. He could smell it.

The metal building they entered, where the pit was located, had large double doors in the front and a wide waiting room inside. Brandon noticed guards at the two doors that led into the main building. It wasn't just a mining operation any longer. It looked more like a research lab even before they moved on. Something strange was going on in there; he could feel it.

Oliver guided him down the hall and into a large, white, air-conditioned room with a round table where they waited in relative silence for almost an hour. When a door opened on the other side of the room, Oliver said, "This should only take a minute now, and we'll know whether or not you actually learn anything new today."

Four women and two men entered the room from another entrance. Brandon noticed that there were guards outside that door as well. None of the guards thus far looked as though they were soldiers. They handled themselves too relaxed and their weapons too clumsily. More evidence that C-47 really was a colony filled with scientists. More evidence that they needed help if they were going to deal with the IPF.

The women were older, in their fifties and sixties. The men appeared even older than that, frail, slow. Oliver looked to be the youngest of the seven. Each of them sat around the table except Oliver. He didn't sit and neither did the rest of the scientists, so Brandon remained standing as well.

"What's this about," one of the women said.

"To the point," Brandon said.

"You don't get to talk," the woman said, waving him to shut up.

Oliver sniggered. Brandon nodded.

Eldon stepped forward. "Oliver wants to show our discovery to this man, who tried to drive that lander loaded with explosives into our facility."

"I didn't know it was…"

"And…" Eldon raised his voice, "I don't think we should. This is too sensitive an operation. We haven't learned enough from it yet. It's our job to protect them."

The woman raised her hand. "I know. It could take years to learn what we need to know. In the meantime, we've been attacked several times already and the firepower is escalating. We are not a military base, I might remind you. We can't stay these attacks for very long. We need to do something." She looked over at Oliver. "We should spend our time preparing for a full-scale confrontation with the IPF. What makes you think this sidetrack is worth it?"

"Brandon," Oliver said, "you took an oath of honesty, didn't you?"

"Yes. But as you know, I only need to tell you my name, rank, and serial number if talking with an enemy."

The woman looked into Brandon's eyes. "I believe you can see that we're not an enemy. We merely protected ourselves as any colony under attack would do."

Brandon nodded.

"Then if you thought what we were doing was wrong, you'd tell us." Oliver hesitated only for a second. "Regardless what that meant about your safety."

Oliver knew how to cut to the chase, Brandon thought. "I am bound to my oath and to my duty. I can avoid answering, but I cannot lie." Brandon cocked his head at Eldon. "That man's an asshole."

Eldon held back, but Brandon could see him tighten up.

"That man," the woman said, "has put his entire soul into this discovery. I'd be an asshole about it too."

Oliver interrupted. "He's a real soldier, Mary. I believe that once he knows what's going on here that he'll help us. He's been trained in weaponry, in combat. We need his expertise if we're going to hold tight until Earth Central gets involved. Plus, if I'm wrong about this, we'll know it right away. He won't lie. We can decide what to do with him at that time."

"You're with the IPF?" the woman asked.

"Earth Central, assigned to IPF," Brandon said while pulling his lapel tight showing the two insignias.

"Another reason," Oliver interrupted. "A link to Earth Central."

The woman looked impressed. "The real deal." She turned and whispered to the other members who came into the room with her and in less than a minute turned back to Eldon, not Oliver.

Brandon didn't expect that. He waited the long moment before she addressed the bioengineer directly.

"You are in charge of the tour," she said. "I want him exposed to our findings, but you'll be the sole decision maker as to what questions you answer. You dole out the information." She swung her gaze to Oliver. "Understood?"

"Agreed," Oliver said.

She then turned to Brandon. "We're not bad people here. You'll understand that soon. After the tour you'll be asked about your position. You must have an answer. No time. I think you'll know right away. Once we find out where you stand, we do what we must. Understand that our facilities are very nice and that you'll only be held as long as we need to do so. Once Earth Central is involved, you can go home."

"Unless you're attacked and the brig is blown to bits," Brandon said.

She didn't bat an eye. "Exactly." She stood up first and the six of them left the room. Once the door closed behind them Oliver motioned for Eldon to lead the way. Eldon took a left from that room and went down the hall where he led them into a laboratory.

Not Brandon's usual area of expertise, he wasn't sure if it was a biological lab, a chemical lab, or a zoological lab. There were small animals in cages — all with the same round-headed structure — but there were also vats of what smelled like chemical experiments. Then, there was a table with what appeared to be space suits for large turtles, wide backed, short armed. What would they need space suits like that for? The helmets were bubble-shaped and the hands had too many fingers that were also too long. Eldon was rattling on about something to do with the planet, its changes in air quality. The planet had apparently gone through several of them long before the colonists had arrived. Brandon began to listen closer.

"Bands of what used to be a hydrogen rich atmosphere were trapped under the surface. As the plant life evolved on the surface, oxygen increased. It's still a bit rich, but great for humans. But we didn't know anything about the Themalorite when we arrived. We noticed that the plants were edible and that the animal life was, too. So, we settled. It wasn't until years later that Earth Central got around to sending a mining crew to check out the ore base of the planet. Granted, we ran reports and sent them in. We thought there might be a rich vein of C-47," he said.

"It takes quite a bit of ore for the government to reclassify a planet from a colony to a mine," Brandon said.

Oliver laughed. "C-47 is used on every ship out there. You know that. I'm not sure what they found in our samples to alert them, maybe someone made a mistake, but they thought we were the mother lode and came calling. I think that's plenty of reason."

"And the first people they send in, knowing that the colony won't be happy about the change, is the IPF," Brandon said. "I can see that. But mining doesn't always rape the planet. You may have been able to stay and share it. In fact, you never said otherwise while explaining this earlier." He cocked his head, waiting for an answer.

Oliver shook his head. "Colonies don't want to be industrialized states of any kind. I'll give you that. But that's not the problem here anyway. They left." He motioned for Eldon to continue.

"What they first thought were veins of C-47 were actually hydrogenated bands of Themalorite. Although Themalorite is hardly abundant, we've found few uses for it." Eldon wandered to where Brandon stood next to the space suits.

"Hydrogen can be highly flammable," Brandon said. "I'm guessing that there were explosions and that it threatened the planet's structure."

Eldon said, "You may be smarter than you look. But that's not what this is about either."

"Enlighten me," Brandon said.

"There were explosions, but that's not what chased the mining crews away." He turned away and changed the subject. "A lot of equipment was destroyed. The rest of it we, ah," he glanced at Oliver for approval. "Let's say it was left behind. But what's important in this story is that the hydrogenated Themalorite situation created an atmosphere for the life that used to live on the surface."

Eldon turned away and said, "Early Earth had large concentrations of hydrogen, nearly forty percent. This and a few electrical discharges or photochemical reactions were enough to produce organic compounds. We discovered long ago that a hydrogen and $CO_2$-dominated atmosphere leads to the production of organic molecules." He shook his head in dismay. "The explosion killed hundreds of them." Eldon put a hand on one of the space suits.

"So you found animals underground that breath hydrogen rich air," Brandon said.

"Not animals," Eldon said. "Intelligent life."

# ChAPTEr 5

AFTER SEVERAL HOURS A FOOD PLATTER PROTRUDED
through the small window into Palmer's cell. A gruff and formal
voice from the other side of the door said, "Meal time," and let the
platter rest on the ledge. Palmer slid her food through the rest of the
way and took it over to one of the seats to eat. She picked at the
standard ration, not quite knowing what she ate: some sort of off-
world meat, probably what everyone referred to as space chicken,
and greenish vegetables, which were surely synthetic. When she was
half finished and considering whether to eat the rest or not, the door
opened. She looked up quickly.

Jacobs stepped into the room and walked over to her. "May I?"
he said before sitting next to her.

"You don't look roughed up at all," she said.

"I have a proposition for you," Jacobs edged too near for her
comfort.

"I don't do sexual favors," she said.

"I wouldn't ask."

"I'm not so sure." Palmer pushed the last perfect cube of meat
around on the plate. The chicken-like hybrid was actually raised
inside space stations positioned strategically all around the galaxy.
In a space bound society, food had to be taken to the people. Unless
traded through free trade agreements with the colonies, the government,
or independent agencies, it was bought from the space stations. It was
all big business as usual.

Jacobs reached for her hand but then stopped short and held to
the edge of her platter.

She kept a hand on the platter as well, holding it between them. Her other hand she used to manipulate her fork between the food she played with and her mouth.

As Jacobs talked he tapped the bottom of the platter. It didn't take long before Palmer recognized the tapping. It was Morse Code, unbelievably ancient, but still recognizable and useful. "What the hell?"

Jacobs smiled broadly but made no move to stop. He tapped out, "You have to agree to this. Either that or you'll be framed and imprisoned." At the same time he said, "We want to give you another chance, that's what. Perhaps someone did load those explosives onto your ship. We'll be investigating that prospect and will find the culprit. But we need you as a pilot if we're going to go back down there to talk."

"Back? So soon? That makes no sense," she said.

"There is a plan in place," Jacobs said.

"Well, use the pilot from the lander that picked me up," she said.

"You know as well as I do that we have no pilots trained for such a mission. Our pilots are trained for space. They can't handle a lander as well as you can under atmosphere, especially since every atmosphere is different. He'd be a sitting duck and probably couldn't land without killing us. Besides that, we have to act quickly, while we can, while they're vulnerable."

"While they're vulnerable? They shot your lander out of the air." She felt him tap out a second message. That they believed Brandon had made it out alive. Didn't she want to go back for him?

Palmer didn't believe for a second that they didn't have pilots who could do the job, only that, for some reason, they wouldn't suggest it. She understood that something illegal was going on from the beginning and decided to ignore it for the money, but she was just getting deeper into it.

She tried to focus on both strands of information, but got caught up in the probability of Brandon's survival. The thought of it caused her heart to race faster than Jacobs' tapping. If anyone could make it, Brandon would. But what about Clark? And what would those on the planet do if they found him? At that point, she knew she'd go, but wanted to get some answers as well. She still had the recorder in her ear. "You taped that debriefing so that you had something on me and now you want to solicit my help using that as blackmail?" She tried to sound and look as indignant as she could, but she was no actress.

Jacobs said, "Your other option is to stay here until a trial." But his tapping said, "You must insist that I go with you."

Palmer opened her mouth. She didn't exactly trust him, and now he expected to go with her. She tightened her lips and narrowed her eyes. "I don't like the feel of this."

"A decision," Jacobs said. He let go of the platter and started to stand.

"Two conditions," she said.

"Two?" He appeared genuinely surprised at her request.

She knew he would. She wasn't acting now. "You go with me. Side-by-side. Just in case this is a way to get rid of me." She looked right at him. "And we take my cruiser."

His eyes went wide. "But you are loaded with ammunition. They'll know. We need to go in with standard protection so they don't suspect what we're going to do."

"What are we going to do?"

"If you are going to force me to go with you, then I'll wait to debrief you once we get started." He stood firm.

She raised her eyebrows and cocked her head. "Those are my conditions."

He shook his head and rung his hands together. "If they attack us again, we could fail for the second time. You'll be forced to retaliate against their attack. I don't want to be in that situation."

"Take it or leave it." None of it made sense to her at the moment, but she was determined to find the truth in their actions. The last mission was a fake, but this one felt real. Jacobs wanted to be on that planet for a reason. They definitely had her over a barrel and the only way she'd get out of the brig was to agree. "Trust me," she said. "Now where do I sign."

"You just did," Jacobs said. He walked out. "We'll send someone for you."

The sending took a few hours, which gave her time for a short nap and to work up a few plans to help her learn what was really going on. A decoy was one thing, but that should have been enough to get the time they needed. Earth Central wouldn't have any real reason to show up unless called upon to do so. Yet an operation put into effect in such short time made it feel as though the IPF was worried about interference, which could only come from Earth Central. A Catch 22 of sorts.

Two soldiers showed up at her door to escort her away. They flanked her as she walked through the barren and empty corridors. She had memorized the hall system after only being inside the ship a few times.

At the launch bay, she saw that they had already connected her cruiser to external power and someone sat inside testing the ship's systems. She jogged ahead and climbed the rear ramp. Passing through the small cargo and passenger area, she noticed that the ship had been fully stocked, and that two soldiers were already strapped in for departure. "Get the fuck out of here," she said to the man in the cockpit.

A young man with a smooth face and short hair swung around as she entered the cockpit. "I was preparing your ship," he said. "Under orders."

"Well, you're dismissed."

The kid glanced past Palmer for approval.

She turned and Jacobs stood behind her. He nodded.

"Yes, ma'am," the young man said. He flipped the thruster test switch off and got out of the seat.

"Them too," she said, indicating the soldiers.

"They're going. In case something goes wrong," Jacobs said.

Palmer smiled and said, "You send me in a lander loaded down with high-powered explosives I didn't know were on board and only one guard. But you get two bouncers when you're just going along for the ride?" She didn't wait for an answer, but followed the young man as he passed by, until she could watch him walk down the ramp and out of the ship. Without turning to face him, she said to Jacobs. "I do all my own ground checks."

"We need to get going," he said.

"That's your fault for not sending for me sooner." She looked out the rear of the cruiser and yelled, "All clear!" In a few long strides she passed through the cargo bay and reached to flip the switch to close the rear ramp.

"How long will this take?" Jacobs said as she stepped around him.

"As long as it does." Palmer sat in the pilot's seat where she slipped her legs and arms into the seat extensions. "This is how it's done right." The cruiser became part of her. That's how she saw it, how it felt to her. The seat had an emergency parachute mounted into it that only attached to her while she was engaged in the seat. The captain went down with the ship until the very last second. Brandon should have been strapped in so that he had a chute too, or strapped into the chute separately. She shook the thoughts from her head and ran through her ground tests.

After a few minutes, Jacobs strolled into the cockpit and took the seat beside her. He shoved his arms and legs into the seat extensions and they closed around him. "We're about there aren't we?"

She put her headset on. "Pull external power." She watched for the ground crew to drag their equipment out of the way and for the final go-ahead. In a moment the bay doors began to open. Everyone would be out of the bay area now. Palmer slammed her hand against her harness release and jumped from her seat.

"We're leaving," Jacobs said. "What are you doing?"

"One final thing." Palmer turned a knob on a panel that stood behind her seat and removed a handheld meter.

"What's that?" Jacobs reached for his harness release.

"Stay put," Palmer said, and he stopped mid-motion. She opened her instrument panel next and snaked out a cable and plugged it into the handheld. After pushing a few buttons, she shook her head. "Done in a second." Palmer walked out of the cockpit and yanked another panel open while the two soldiers stared at her. They looked nervous and a bit scared, but she didn't have time to question them about it. Instead, she opened a tool cabinet and snapped loose a pair of wire cutters. She disconnected one cable then cut several wires and went back into the cockpit and checked her handheld again.

"What the hell are you doing?" Jacobs yelled. "We need to get out of here."

Palmer sidled into position and relaxed into the seat extensions leaving the handheld still connected but hanging loose next to the center console. The bay door began to close.

Jacobs looked alarmed. "What's going on?"

Palmer kicked the engines in, which slammed everyone into their seats. The open panels slammed and rattled as the cruiser shuttered from the strength of the engines under full thrust. She cocked the cruiser and passed through the bay doors long before they could close on her.

"What was that about?" Jacobs shook his head and stared wide-eyed at Palmer.

"Wiring test. We were tapped," she said. "Assholes were going to listen to our whole conversation."

"I didn't think…"

"Exactly. Don't even consider that they trust you any more than they trust me. Notice that they didn't give my weapons back to me." She gave him a grin. "And I can see that they don't trust you with a weapon either."

Jacobs jerked his head toward the passenger area and the two soldiers. "We have them?"

"We don't need them if Brandon is alive," she said. "He's worth about eight of those ill-trained goons."

"You've worked together a lot?"

"Often enough to know."

"I noticed unusual concern. When I told you he was alive, you perked up."

"My job is to protect good men, not let them go down with the ship while I eject. No pilot with any integrity would do that." She kept her face forward. "Isn't that what you're hoping long about now?"

"I have those guys in the back if you get out of hand."

"I'll kill them if I have to. They're not important." Palmer swung her cruiser around toward the southern end of the planet.

"We're going the wrong way. The IPF won't like this," Jacobs said.

She ignored his warning. "I want to hear it. Now. I'm not heading into another mess without information."

Jacobs turned in his seat so that he could see one of the soldiers sitting in the passenger area.

"I told you they don't matter. Now spill it," Palmer said.

He turned back around and said as quietly as possible, "They found something."

"Tells me nothing," she said.

Jacobs glanced back again. "I don't exactly know what it is, but it has stirred up the IPF, Earth Central, and every other organization you can think of including the Galaxy Marines, and the Colony Relocation Association. No one appears to know what is going on, but everyone is talking about it. Well, secretly talking about it. It hasn't been formally released."

Palmer turned some knobs and pushed a few buttons. "Hold on. We're entering the planet's atmosphere." There was a bounce and a noticeable slowdown in air speed, then the cruiser jostled as though hitting turbulence. "You're secret service?" she said.

Jacobs fidgeted in his seat and ran the back of his hand over his forehead. It was obvious that he didn't want the soldiers behind them to know that piece of information. But it was too late. "Earth Central," he admitted, "like your buddy Brandon."

"Investigating the IPF?"

"They're using force more often than Earth Central thinks is necessary. I'm supposed to find out why. See where the problem lies. I got my answer, but am afraid they're onto me. I had to get out of there."

"By why, you mean you were supposed to find out which of the higher-ups is the bad apple," she said. "So, who is it?"

"A man named Garth Killjoy. He wants whatever they have down there. He senses that whatever it is, whoever has it, has power to negotiate."

"Killjoy," Palmer said. "It's all in a name, I suppose." She vocalized what she understood so far. "The IPF wants independence from Earth Central. That's why they've been training their own goons. I can see that. The Earth Central government hires independent corporate types for their organizational expertise to run the IPF and eventually those same people want full independence. It's all happened before. Power and control. So, how'd IPF get here so soon?"

"Luck. They're here because they were closest to C-47 when the rumors started flying. Killjoy took a risk that it was something real, that this was his chance. He knew that if the colony showed any form of aggression, that they had reasonable cause to retaliate. And, he'd be able to take over. No questions asked."

"He'd be taking a chance on destroying whatever they had down there. That would be stupid." Palmer maneuvered the cruiser along a blue mountain range topped with sharp crags, the sides dropping into a lush valley on one side and scrub on the other. "I'd say he knew something ahead of time. I don't believe in luck. I believe in strategy."

"Doesn't matter. We're here." He went on. "The first trip was to gain the authority to be aggressive. We're going now to blackmail the colony. Simple as that. We have probable cause to wipe them out. And the IPF has the firepower to do it, too. This is a forceful negotiation we're going on." Jacobs said.

"There's only one problem." She saw the whole thing more clearly now. "As soon as a ship goes down, Earth Central responds. They'll send in War ships if they have to. Especially if they didn't know about the decoy."

"Yes."

"IPF wants to finish the deal before Earth Central shows up," she deduced.

Jacobs didn't answer. It wasn't a question.

"What happens when Earth Central finds out that the IPF set the whole thing up?" She already felt as though she had stepped into something she should have analyzed before agreeing to, and the conversation wasn't going well to stave her feelings about that.

"How would they find out? Garth can have all the tapes altered," Jacobs said.

"And I won't make it back alive," Palmer said. "Will you?"

He didn't answer, which didn't matter to her at the moment.

It would take a few hours before they'd be in range of the colony weapons. Palmer set her cruiser on autopilot, keying ship's location off of magnetic north, line of sight to the sun, and the omnidirectional signal from the colony's landing system.

She ordered Jacobs to stay in his seat. Then she cleaned up, putting her handheld back into its cabinet and closing all the instrument and electrical panels so they weren't slapping around anymore. The next thing she did was disconnect her seat and swing it up and to the side. She reached down and removed several weapons and strapped them on. Dropping the seat back into place, Palmer stepped into the passenger area and held a stunner on the two soldiers. "Your weapons."

They relinquished and she stored them in the cargo area under lock and key. The cruiser hit some turbulence again which jostled her around a bit while she wobbled her way back into the cockpit and plopped into her seat.

"You finished?" Jacobs asked.

Palmer engaged her seat extensions and relaxed. She looked over at him. "One more thing." She had a smile on her face as she pulled a pair of tweezers out of a compartment on the ship's console, and pushed them into her ear. Slowly, she removed the recording device and plugged it into her console to transfer the data.

"You taped everything?"

She couldn't tell if Jacobs tone meant happily surprised or worried about what she'd done. It didn't matter. "Every word," she said.

"I don't think you understand how dangerous that was." Jacobs stared at her.

"The operative word is 'was,'" she said. "It's too late. I succeeded. Even if I'm killed now, I just dumped the whole thing. The ship has multiple black box chips hidden throughout. It would take an expert to find them all." She disengaged the autopilot and took over at the controls. "And Earth Central employs experts."

Jacobs glanced out the side window then back at Palmer. "I considered it," he said.

"Considered what?"

"That I wouldn't make it back, but I hoped you'd be able to handle anything we ran into. I'm not a Peace Coordinator. I don't have the negotiation skills."

Palmer cruised along the ridge of the mountains knowing that she'd soon have to climb into the open where the colony's scanners would pick up on her weapons load. This time she'd leave her radios open to communication. She'd have to be able to convince them of her intent, while carrying a loaded gun. The idea posed its own problems. She turned toward Jacobs. "I heard you," she said.

As much as she wanted to trust Jacobs because he was with Earth Central — or so he claimed — she couldn't read him well enough to know where he really stood. She only knew that once he fell silent that he was mentally adjusting his plans to the new situation. Only so much time would go by before Earth Central war ships showed up and the IPF would be forced to relinquish control of the situation. That would make it too late to claim the prize. And if Garth still pulled the strings, Jacobs wasn't in touch with Earth Central yet.

# ChAPTER 6

**BRANDON SHOOK HIS HEAD IN DISBELIEF.** "We've been populating the galaxy for years. We've never found intelligent life."

"That's always been the assumption, that humans were literally the only highly intelligent life form in the universe." Eldon hesitated before he spoke again. "We're not." He had a disturbed look in his eyes.

"There's more," Brandon said.

Eldon patted the space suit with his hand. "We can't let them be bought and sold, used for research, or studied like lab rats. "We have to protect them."

"You mean gribs. Nobody uses rats anymore," Brandon said.

Eldon's eyes glared with fire. "Why do you always have to be the smart ass?"

Brandon didn't answer.

"You don't get it." Eldon said with a jerk of his head and quick shrug. He grinned, but it didn't look like he was used to it. "But you will. You will."

Brandon raised a hand. "Take me to your leader," he said.

Eldon swung around and walked away. He stopped next to Oliver. "I can't do this. Look at him. He's a military moron."

Brandon ran a hand through his closely cropped hair and let out a long sigh. "Okay, okay." He strolled toward the two of them. "Let's say that I'm not as convinced as you are at the moment. After thousands of years it gets easier for us to believe we're the chosen ones. There has been nothing like us out here. I don't care how many half-assed bright animals we find, how many dolphin-like species, or ape-like humanoids, nothing has come close to our abilities to transcend other animals as far as we have. We've had to populate the galaxy ourselves, which does make your story a bit hard to swallow. Plus, you've got to admit that rocks leaching hydrogen into the ground doesn't sound very hospitable."

"Show him," Oliver said. He looked mad when he said it, as though the conversation had carried on long enough. "We need all the help we can get. He's our first real soldier. We need him."

"One soldier isn't enough," Eldon said.

"It's a start." Oliver held his ground.

Eldon didn't look very happy with the situation. He pointed at Brandon. "If you make one comment I don't like, the information ends. The tour ends. You got that?"

Brandon didn't quite have it, but he nodded his head. He supposed he could keep his mouth shut for an hour, but after that, who knew. "Let's go." He followed Oliver and Eldon into a clean room where they suited up. They didn't need to put the helmets on yet, but Oliver insisted they make sure everything worked before heading to their next destination. It was evident to Brandon that their equipment had suffered their lack of funds too. It wasn't a bad idea to make sure his suit was leak tight. Oxygen hissed into his ear once he closed the helmet clamps. He tested the intercom. "Everyone there?" he said, while checking the dials and readouts on his wrist.

Eldon and Oliver acknowledged Brandon. "Follow me," Eldon said. They walked from the lab into a long hallway with a set of doors at the far end. Brandon couldn't tell how big the building had been from outside, but got an idea as they walked. It appeared that the colony must have built the building over the drilling pit. When they stepped through the doors, the place opened wide enough to land an airship. Vehicles were parked everywhere and the ground swept down where the building ended and they proceeded underground. A series of lights hung from the supported rock ceiling.

In the distance, Brandon recognized doors that led to an office of some kind, a control room for the equipment and supervisor of the dig perhaps, but that was a long way off. "How far do we have to walk in this suit?" Brandon asked.

"Quarter mile," Eldon said.

"Couldn't we drive there?"

"A car is coming from the far side. It'll be here in a moment," Oliver said. "Surely the walk wouldn't bother you."

"I'm under deadline," Brandon said. He heard Eldon scoff through the intercom and hoped he hadn't screwed up his chances of seeing the smart turtles. The bulky suit chafed his thighs as he walked. If he were running the dig, he'd have a place to suit up that was closer to where they were going.

Just as the jeep arrived a loud horn blew and Eldon and Oliver jumped. Brandon remained calm, but stopped walking.

"We're going back," Oliver said.

"An attack?" Brandon asked.

"I don't know, but we can't be down here in case they do." Oliver clicked offline.

Brandon watched as Oliver talked to someone over a private line. He appeared to be worried. His eyes widened and his mouth moved as though giving orders. He came back online. "A ship of some kind has been spotted heading this way. We're probably in a lot of trouble for shooting the lander down, but we had no choice. We had no choice," he repeated.

"You don't have to convince me," Brandon said. He jogged back to the lab, ignoring his chafed thighs. The three of them stripped down quickly. "How close are they?"

"Close. Maybe fifteen minutes. We have to see what they want. We already know that they're fully armed. Standard weapons. No bombs stuffed into the cargo bay this time. Nothing like before anyway." Oliver ran down the hall.

Brandon followed with Eldon close behind.

They emerged into the sunlight and ran for the vehicle, which was already occupied by a driver. Brandon leaped into the back with two other men who looked at him as though he didn't belong. "New recruit," he said, and they smiled to welcome him, shaking his hand as they drove off. Sweat beaded across his forehead and his upper lip.

In about ten minutes, the tower for a small airstrip lifted above the blue sand. Five hangars stood farther out, situated in a semicircle near one end of the runway. The tower looked as though it hadn't been used much, but its signs of obvious wear could have been hard winds and the blue sand battering it over the years. Tufts of pointed grasses with white and orange flowers pushed from the ground in clumps. Sand blew across the runway in a slight breeze. Two small airplanes were parked to one side. The air smelled good, fresh.

Brandon noticed how far along the colony had grown. He had seen colonies after only a few years and others after several hundred. The difference between the two was the difference between pioneers and city-dwellers. The C-47 colony was a growing and thriving community on many levels. He had noticed that while flying over with Palmer. This part of their growth appeared a bit behind. But he hadn't seen what sat inside the hangars yet. He could be surprised.

Oliver led the way up a set of spiral stairs to the top of the tower. Brandon and Eldon were next, followed by several of those who were already in the vehicle when Brandon had arrived. Three women and a man sat at consoles that lined the walls, their eyes close to video screens, their hands running across switches and buttons as though their lives depended on it. A few of the other men took similar positions in front of unused consoles. Screens lit up along every wall. "Status," Oliver said.

"It's not an IPF lander this time," the man who had been at the console when they arrived said. He looked about forty-five. His wrinkled face announced how long he'd been in the sun, but that was the only sign of age in the man. His hair lay flat and black across his head, and his body appeared strong and healthy under his work clothes.

"Is it a Shadow Cruiser, maybe a model F-9?" Brandon asked.

The man turned around. "They are more like war machines than what you'd expect from something called a cruiser. It's been running the ridge trying to stay hidden. I only glimpsed it once or twice," he said. "Enough to get a good scan though. Friends of yours?"

"Let's hope so." Brandon stepped closer to the console.

"He shouldn't even be here," Eldon said as though he had just noticed Brandon in the room.

"If they're hostile, I'm your only hope," Brandon said.

"We shot the first one down," Eldon said. "We can do the same again."

One of the women swung around in her chair. She stared at Brandon as though she had expected to know him, but realized he was a stranger. "Oh," she said. "Who are you?" She turned to Oliver. "I don't recognize him."

"Jenny," Oliver said. "Everyone." The rest of them turned around. "This is Brandon. He's from Earth Central."

"He's wearing an IPF insignia," Jenny said.

"I'm on loan," Brandon said. "But once they left me to die, I decided my contract was up."

Oliver put a hand on Brandon's shoulder. "Then you're with us?"

"Until I'm convinced otherwise," he said. He walked toward Jenny. "Can you make contact?"

"Not yet. They're still trying to hide."

"Let's get ready for an attack," Eldon said. "I don't like the sounds of it being a war machine."

Oliver raised his hand toward Eldon to shut him up. "What do you think?" he asked Brandon.

"I think Eldon's right. Prepare for the worst, hope for the best. That's what I always say."

Oliver made the order and everyone in the room began to ready themselves and their weapons.

Brandon couldn't see where the weapons had been stored or what types they were, but from what he recalled, they weren't government issue by any means. He suspected the launch pads to be hidden in the mountains where they could execute an attack without being close to the citizens or towns. Anything to keep a stray from harming anyone. They wouldn't want to fire over their own heads, though, either, so the fifteen-minute arrival must have been when they thought they'd be able to proceed with an attack if they had to. "If I had my cuffs, I could do a better job than those missiles you were shooting at us before," he said.

"Get them," Oliver said to one of the men who had come up behind them. "Klein knows what they look like and where they are."

The man turned and went back down the stairs.

"You know there's not enough time for that," Brandon said.

"For the next time. Because there'll be one," Oliver said.

"Your call." Brandon turned back to the console. He recognized the cruiser blip from time to time along the mountain ridge. "One minute," he said.

"Thirty seconds on this screen," Jenny corrected.

The second the cruiser broke over the mountains Brandon saw Eldon reach for what he could only imagine was a missile launch button. "Hold it!" he yelled, but it was too late. On screen a missile appeared to the cruiser's left. "Get him out of here," Brandon said. "You're not in charge," Oliver said.

Brandon watched the screen as the cruiser avoided the missile. He turned around. "Well, you're not taking charge, so I thought somebody should."

As Eldon reached a second time, Brandon intervened with two long strides and a backhand swing. Eldon fell to the floor. Several men moved to help him back up.

All of a sudden there were about seven homemade guns pointing at Brandon. He raised his hands. "I'm trying to help here."

"They intercepted the missile," one of the women said.

"Counter-attack," Eldon yelled.

Oliver nodded and the men and women around the tower went into operation.

"You won't win this fight," Brandon said over the hustle of the room. "The last thing you need is for the IPF to get mad." He stared at Oliver. "Let me talk with them. Let me see what they came back for. It may be that they want Clark."

Eldon and Oliver looked at each other for a moment. "Who's Clark," they asked in unison.

Brandon cocked his head, then shook it quickly. "Later," he said.

"Fine. You have three minutes," Oliver said.

Brandon yelled to Jenny to make radio contact.

"Cruiser one-niner-seven come in," Jenny said.

"C-47 Tower One, we copy. Hold your fire. Repeat, hold your fire."

Brandon recognized Palmer's voice and couldn't hold back his smile.

"We'll hold if you'll hold," Jenny said.

"Deal," Palmer said. "Why did you fire on us anyway? None of our weapons were engaged. Your scanners must have seen that."

Jenny swung around and said to Brandon, "Our scanners are primitive next to hers. We can locate weapons but can't detail them."

Brandon shook his head as he approached the console. He reached for the intercom button and pushed it down, "Baby, am I glad to hear your voice."

"Was that some kind of welcome kiss you sent my way?" she said.

"Minor error in judgment," Brandon said.

Her voice lowered. "It's good to hear your voice. How are they treating you?"

"Hospitably," he said while scanning the room for a disagreement.

"I've got an IPF Officer named Jacobs with me. I'm not sure what he wants. But he was pretty adamant about getting down there. May I land?"

Brandon lowered his head and thought for a moment. To Oliver, he said, "Can we land her near the ammo dump you first brought me to? I don't think it's safe to bring her this close to your discovery."

"You don't trust her?" Oliver said. "Then why should we?"

"I trust Palmer. I don't trust the IPF Officer she has with her."

"She can land there if she doesn't need a strip."

"Not with a Shadow Cruiser." Brandon keyed his mic. "I'll have someone give you coordinates and meet you in half an hour. Stay inside the cruiser. You'll be escorted out."

"Copy. It's air conditioned in here anyway. Looks like a hot day there," Palmer said.

"Hotter than you may think," Brandon said to her before heading for the stairs. "Let's get going. Something's not right."

"How do you know," Oliver said.

"The IPF can hear any conversation over the comm unit. She's not talkative enough to suggest that she doesn't care about that fact." Brandon was first down the stairs and out into the heat again. He squinted his eyes for the first few steps.

Oliver tagged closely behind Brandon. "You can't just take over," he said. "You've got to let me in on your plan." When Brandon didn't answer, he said, "You do have a plan, don't you?"

Brandon climbed into the back seat of the vehicle. Oliver ran to the other side and climbed in beside him, squeezing in so someone else could have the other window seat like they had done before. The others piled in as well and the vehicle took off toward the weapons research area and ammo dump, as Brandon called it. Brandon hung his arm out the window.

"Well," Oliver said.

"I don't have a plan," Brandon said. "And neither do you. Not until we hear from Palmer."

"What about this Jacobs guy?" Oliver said. "I don't know him. Which reminds me, I never heard of Clark either."

"The Peace Coordinator?" Brandon said.

Oliver shook his head. "Never heard of him."

"That doesn't sound right," Brandon said. "And it looks like we'll see about Jacobs once we meet him." He leaned forward in his seat and yelled loud enough for everyone to hear him. "Until I say so, everyone keeps their mouth shut about anything that's going on here." He pointed into the back of the vehicle, "And no aggressive acts unless I start it. Got that Eldon?"

Eldon grunted a yes.

"Better intercept Klein to leave my cuffs there. Are your missiles wired in as standard or did you guys make up your own interfaces?" Brandon asked.

"Whatever was on the pods when we landed. But that's been quite a while as you can imagine," Oliver answered tentatively.

"Do they match the control lines on the drilling equipment you fixed up?"

"Don't know?"

"They don't," one of the men in the back said. He waved to Brandon. "I'm an electronics tech. I've worked with both systems. No can do."

"Then my cuffs won't interface either. That's not a good sign." Brandon continued to look out the window. "Maybe they won't be so handy after all." He hadn't noticed the landscape was so varied before. Oases of plantlife cropped up now and again from what looked like a relative desert canyon. The weapons research and ammo dump area was well protected. He asked Oliver, "Are all your main trade crops on the other side of these mountains?"

"You noticed there's not much here," Oliver said.

"Pretty barren. And I was kind of busy the first time we showed up. I didn't get to explore the rest of the planet before my assignment. Just read reports. There must be some pretty big fields around," he said.

"The main colony is centered in what we consider smaller farming communities. We are totally self-sufficient. We don't actually need intergalactic trade. Sort of like early Earth. We haven't overpopulated yet, but we're getting close. We do get supplies, like I told you, but they are mostly scientific, things we don't manufacture here yet," Oliver said. Before Brandon could ask, he said, "Grant money."

"Yet?"

"After the discovery, we ramped that portion up a few notches. Again, the supplies have been helpful. Even the mining equipment was a lucky throw of the dice. We wouldn't be able to extract ore without it, and fuel."

"I thought you didn't find anything," Brandon said.

"I didn't say that. I said we didn't find C-47, and that was the deal."

Brandon took his eyes off the scenery for a moment. He turned in his seat to look Oliver squarely in the face. "You asked to be independent?"

Oliver looked nervous.

"That's what IPF wants, too. If they secure C-47 before Earth Central has the chance to arrive, they still have the authority to take over command. Once you're independent they don't have the same jurisdiction." Brandon waited for a reply.

Oliver held Brandon's gaze for a long while. "At one time, we thought it was our only way. But now, we have to keep them away. They'll own everything, even our discovery."

"Jesus Christ, Oliver, you asked for this. You must have realized that as soon as you put in for independence every agency looking for the same thing would be on your ass? Planets get independence faster than any space-located organizations; you should know that. The IPF would claim the planet, all its production, and use you as a resource for their own survival." Brandon laughed. "They would sell C-47 to supply all their needs. They wouldn't need the government for anything. But you don't have C-47."

Oliver finally turned his head away. "We know that now."

"If you staved off being reclassified, the IPF would figure out that there wasn't any C-47 here. When the mining company left, they probably figured it out, but you still wanted your independence. They know you have something. I'm actually impressed. You have a strong and savvy group of leaders here. And you may have gotten away with it." Brandon slapped the side of the vehicle with his hand. "Bad timing is all."

Eldon spoke up from behind them. "It wouldn't have been. They wouldn't care unless they knew something was up. We have a leak. That's what turned the tables on us."

"Your opinion," Brandon said. "I know the IPF, even though I haven't worked for them long. If they are like other organizations, they look for this type of opportunity. If they are self-sufficient then Earth Central is happy to agree to their independence. Do you have any idea how much it costs, how difficult it is for Earth Central to support all these operations throughout the galaxy? It's not pretty."

"They can't really take over? They can't use us like that?" Oliver said. "Even if they came here, we'd retain our planet."

"Only if you received independence before they took over," Brandon said.

"That can't be true," Oliver shoved at Brandon's shoulder to get his attention. "We put in the paperwork. We signed all the request forms."

"Doesn't matter," Brandon said. "If they're in control when your independence is allowed, then they are in control. That's it. You have to understand that Earth Central doesn't give a shit about this one planet unless it is feeding the multitudes. C-47 ore would have been a big fucking deal. Your farms aren't worth shit."

Oliver shook his head as though he didn't believe what he was hearing. His fingers tapped his knees. "Our discovery?" he said.

"Wouldn't be yours anymore." Brandon glanced into the back where Eldon sat. "IPF could sell this place to the highest bidder."

"Earth Central wouldn't let that happen once they found out," Eldon said.

"You'd be back to farming, but even most of that would go to IPF." Brandon saw the real situation they were in even if they didn't see it yet. They could lose their discovery, their food production, and their control, all in one fell swoop. It was complicated, but something told Brandon that Oliver knew the mess he was in. Did Eldon and the others realize how bad it was?

# CHAPTER 7

**PALMER RECEIVED THE COORDINATES** from the tower and ran the Shadow Cruiser south into a canyon on the barren side of the mountains.

"You look happy to know that Brandon's safe," Jacobs said.

She angled her head and shot him a peripheral glare hoping that he got the point that it wasn't his business.

"Just saying that any sort of fraternization is frowned upon. Isn't it?"

"I've never been afraid of frowns. It's bullets that kill," she said. "Why would you care anyway? You've got complete freedom. No frowning on your parade, as they say."

Jacobs turned his head away. "I have no family," he said. "Not in my job description."

Palmer nodded without comment. There wasn't time to get into Jacobs' personal history at the moment. She had enough to worry about.

"Where's the town?" Jacobs said while craning his neck to survey the area.

"Brandon's not an idiot, even if the rest of them are. He's got us remote from the general population in case you're running this show instead of me."

"The IPF won't like this," Jacobs said.

"They don't have to." She turned in her seat. "I'm not an idiot either."

"What do you mean by that?"

"I'm not their only pilot. I knew that when they hired me. You have got to employ at least a half dozen space jockeys. And maybe they can't maneuver well down here, but the IPF wouldn't hire outside for a mission unless it was a bit shady...and expendable. In this case, completely illegal, I'd guess? And from what I've heard, they've been pretty aggressive lately. So, why don't you tell me the truth before we get down there and I turn you over to them with a little explanation as to who loaded down that lander with enough explosives to surprise their scanners into overdrive and their leaders into an attack." She waited only a moment for him to speak. "Oh, and I might mention that since Clark wasn't a real official, you might want to inform me who he really was about now. Nothing fits into place with you people."

"You wouldn't tell them all that. I'm secret service. You know the truth now. I was just fulfilling a mission. No different from you."

"I haven't been convinced of your truth yet. And what mission are you talking about exactly?" She went back to her landing procedure as she slid in between two sheer cliffs.

"The IPF needed a reason to advance their negotiations before Earth Central arrived. They have a right to blow this planet away. It's their choice, but they have a very short window of time to do it in. A few days at best," Jacobs said.

"Blackmail," she said. "Give up the treasure or be destroyed. That's the message you're delivering down here."

"If I keep my cover and can get this all down, Earth Central can step in after the fact and take over. What the IPF is doing is illegal; you got that straight. They're manipulating the law so that they can bargain for independence," he said.

"You'll have trouble convincing these guys of all that on your own."

"You don't think they'll believe me?" His voice cracked.

There was no reason to answer. She smiled, adjusted her landing speed, and came down softly between several boxy warehouse buildings. A puff of blue dust rose into the air around the lander.

Jacobs reached for his harness release.

"One last thing," Palmer said. She did an electromagnetic scan of the buildings she had landed near. "Jesus."

"What is it?"

"There's enough firepower here to blow us all to smithereens. Good place to land us. We're not likely to cause much trouble around here." Palmer gave Jacobs a big smile. "One loose cannon could blow us all apart." She reached to shut down the engines then disengaged her extensions. While she lifted from her seat she slid the stunner from her belt. "These two have been way too quiet."

Jacobs glanced into the passenger chamber behind him. Then he looked at her again.

"Yes, they've been listening to our conversation. I'm surprised they haven't tried anything funny." She entered the passenger bay and told the soldiers to get up. "Into the rear and on the floor," she said.

They nervously did as they were told. One of the men's hands were already shaking even before she gave her orders.

Jacobs came in behind her and she stepped aside. "You too," she said, "for now at least."

"I'm on your side," he said.

"Told you. I'm not convinced." Palmer leaned against the wall and waited. "You two appear to be a bit passive about all this," she said. "I expected more from a couple of soldiers."

One of the men shook his head. Tears began to run down his face.

Palmer grabbed Jacobs by the collar and yanked him to his feet. "What now?"

Palmer shook her head and swung him toward the front of the ship. She jumped into the pilot's seat and started one engine. That's all she needed. She didn't even strap in. The cruiser lifted from the ground and she flew it across the blue soil toward the canyon opening. In the distance she noticed the welcoming party heading her way and passed low over their heads. Her piloting skills were smooth. She kept low between the mountains then banked nose up and rose toward a plateau where she set the cruiser back down gently. They were several miles from her last landing area. Hopefully enough. She lowered the rear ramp.

Jacobs sat stunned in his seat, shaking his head. "What's this about?"

"They're rigged. I don't know how or with what, but they're rigged." She ran back, but the two already knew what she was doing and were running down the ramp toward the open plateau.

One turned as he hit the dirt and yelled, "Richard Blakely and Jeff Carlson. Tell our wives we love them."

Palmer picked up an intercom and opened a channel to the cargo bay where they would be able to hear her words. What could she say? She closed her eyes. The only thing that came to mind was, "I'm sorry. I have no choice." She ran to the front of the cruiser and jumped into her seat. As she glided the cruiser over the ground, she raised the rear ramp, leaving the two men on the plateau. "Strap in," she said as she did so herself. She threw the cruiser into a turn and headed back into the canyon.

Passing over the two soldiers, Jacobs leaned to look at them and suddenly turned away. "Oh, no!"

Palmer glanced outside to see what he'd noticed just as the second soldier blew up, spreading blood and flesh in all directions. "Bastards," she said. "This Killjoy is after something pretty important."

"We're not going back are we?" Jacobs said jerking his chin in the direction they were headed.

Palmer tried to reach the tower and when she did she said, "You've got to stop your welcoming committee from going into the canyon. It's a trap."

The voice on the other end said, "What kind of trap?"

"Listen, Sweety, I have no time to explain. If you're in communication with them, stop them now." Just as she said that, her external scanner alarms went off. "Incoming," she yelled, pitching the cruiser up and away from those on the ground. She kicked in the second engine and threw the cruiser into a spin, pulling level just in time to fire a couple rounds at a missile and hitting it mid-air. "I wish Brandon were here," she said.

"Do you have a weapons pod on this thing?" Jacobs said.

"Landers have weapons pods, cruisers don't. We're made for speed," she said. "But we have enough ammo on board to protect ourselves if we need to. Plenty. But I don't think we will need much. If there's one thing I know about egocentric jerks it's that they think they're better and smarter than they actually are. That missile was meant to take us out right after those guys destroyed our internal systems. Lucky for us we weren't completely shut down like we could have been."

"One missile?" he said.

"Timed almost perfectly," she said. "Must have followed us as we skimmed the mountains. Either heat sinking or I didn't get all the bugs out of my system."

"They were going to kill me?" Jacobs said.

Palmer just shook her head. There was nothing to say to the man if he was that stupid. "They'll be sending a second lander or more. The pressure's on."

Jacobs stared at the console in front of him. "They were going to blow us away," he repeated.

"Maybe they found out about you," she said. "If those guys were loaded, they probably were hooked up with sound, too. I'll recheck my systems."

"Why would they do that?"

"This thing you've heard rumors about. What else do you know?" She swung the cruiser around again and tapped into the tower. "Did you stop them?"

"They don't have a radio, but we've sent someone from the weapons research area to intercept them." The radio broke off then.

"Weapons research?" Palmer headed away from the canyon, ducked behind a ridge, then turned quickly to head back into the canyon toward Brandon and the others.

"What was that move?"

"Those guys were bugged and loaded because the mother ship is docked on the horizon and can't see through the hills. They have no idea where we landed before. Without their beacons back there, they can't follow us. They could only track us using externals inside those two, and maybe..." She noticed that Jacobs had a blank look on his face. "They can't see us down here." She flew along the ground. "In fact, I'd say that they won't be able to see us for a while once they are on the other side of the planet."

"They could see well enough to shoot at us," Jacobs said.

"You haven't been around much, have you? I bet you've been aboard one mother ship after another, or one space station after another." She passed over the ground-running vehicle and spun the cruiser's back end in order to turn into them. For the third time she flipped switches and engaged engines and thrusters at the right amounts for her to land softly.

The C-47 vehicle slammed to a stop in front of her. Men jumped from all sides of the vehicle, rifles and stunners lifted and pointing in her direction.

She watched as Brandon climbed out of a side door of the truck. He yelled something to the others and the men lowered their weapons and stood fast.

"He probably just told them that this thing could blow them all away in a millisecond if I had chosen to do so," she said. She reached and flipped the control to lower the rear ramp. "Let's go." She left her seat, rushed through the cruiser, and jogged down the ramp to the outside. She came around the side of the cruiser where she walked out to meet the greeting party.

Brandon stood near the front of the vehicle as she approached. "You blew out without me," he said.

Palmer stopped in her tracks. "I did not."

Brandon gave her a quizzical glare. "I think that's a fact, not a question."

"I risked my neck coming back for you. Did you see what happened up there?" She pointed over his head toward the plateau.

"And you left Clark on board as well," he said as though that was a worse crime. "Pilots don't do that."

"How the hell would a common EC Lieutenant know what a real pilot does?" She stepped closer to him. "You ass."

"What?" he said.

"You know I'd never do that. How could you suspect…"

"It happened!"

"Hold up, both of you," a man said while taking a position next to Brandon. "We have something more important going on here and we'd better get going before we're fired on again."

Brandon and Palmer both said, "They're out of range," at the same time.

The man looked confused for a moment, then it dawned on him. "That's right. They're in a huge ship, stationary in space."

Jacobs stepped around Palmer and said to Brandon, "Her seat was rigged to go off automatically. It was out of her control."

Brandon turned his head to meet Jacobs' gaze. "Who the hell are you?"

"Jacobs is with the Secret Service," Palmer said.

Jacobs swung around. "I thought you weren't…"

"Changed my mind. As far as Killjoy's concerned you're dead and so am I. If we're lucky that is."

"I was supposed to complete the transaction so that Earth Central could step in," Jacobs said. "You blew it now."

Ignoring Jacobs, Brandon turned to the man next to him. "This is Oliver. He's on the governmental board for C-47." He shook his head at Palmer. "I knew you wouldn't leave either one of us like that. It's not like you."

"Then why did you attack me as soon as I got off the cruiser?"

He shrugged.

"You big goon," she said.

"Enough of that," Oliver said. "You two can make up later. I need to know what's going on. Your ejection was controlled?" he said to Palmer. "And you didn't know it?" he said to Brandon. He turned back to Palmer, "A pilot?"

"Wasn't my ride," she said.

"And an Earth Central officer?" Oliver said to Brandon.

"On assignment," he said.

"You two have more excuses," Oliver said.

Brandon had a question too. "They put their own man in danger?"

Palmer shook her head. "Clark wasn't who you thought he was. He was a decoy. He knew he was going to die when the lander went down." She reached for Brandon. "I didn't know about the explosives either."

"A decoy," Oliver said.

Palmer reached toward him with her hand, "Before we go any further, I'm Palmer Luce," she said. "Pilot First Class, Level Five."

"An independent," Oliver said. "You're wearing the IPF insignia too."

Palmer turned to Brandon. "Uniforms don't mean much anymore. It never changes the person."

Brandon said, "I heard you the first time."

Oliver took a few steps around Brandon and Palmer. "Someone's coming."

A jeep sped toward them from the weapons' research buildings. It pulled to a stop and a young man dressed in an open buttoned shirt ran toward Oliver. He held out a radio. "Sir, the IPF said that they're sorry they had to shoot down the cruiser." He stopped talking and jerked his head toward the cruiser behind him.

"Go on," Oliver said.

The young man lowered his voice. "They said that a prisoner had escaped. That they will send someone who will explain everything. Some kind of internal disruptions that they're in the process of fixing."

Oliver laughed. "I bet they're having internal problems." He swung around and yelled to his men. "Some of you guys are going to stay with the cruiser. We need to make room for our new guests."

"Not yet," Palmer said. "Now's the best time to move this thing, before they show up again. Besides, I need to be close to it in case they come fully loaded the next time."

"I'm with her," Brandon said.

Oliver nodded. "I'll go with you." He pointed to Jacobs. "Take him in the truck and have him debriefed. I'll debrief this one myself," he indicated Palmer.

Jacobs gestured toward Palmer with both palms up in question.

"Tell them the truth," she said. "Anything but that and it's your own head you're cutting off." She ran a finger across her throat to illustrate, hoping that it would put a little fear in him.

Oliver said, "Eldon, you're with us."

Palmer gave Brandon a stern look. "You didn't trust me?"

"Maybe temporarily," he conceded.

"Let's move," Oliver led the way around the side of the cruiser and up the rear ramp. "I'll copilot this time. You need to bond with Eldon," he said to Brandon.

Brandon and Eldon kept quiet.

Before entering the cockpit, Palmer looked over her shoulder at the two of them. She said to Eldon, "He can have that effect on people. Don't let it bother you. He's really soft on the inside."

"You blew my cover," Brandon said.

"You don't hide it that well," she said.

Once everyone was strapped in, Palmer started the engines. "I know your tower's coordinates. That where we're going?"

"Yes," he said. "We have several hangars there for our own planes. This should fit inside one of them. They're shielded, too. A natural result of the bluestone. We use it in most of our building materials."

Palmer lifted the cruiser from the ground and ran along the mountain for a short while. "What happened to Clark?" she said.

"Don't know the whole story," Oliver said. "You'll have to ask your man back there. But by the time we headed out the next morning scavengers had taken care of the body. We found pieces, but that was about it."

"You have some rough scavengers?"

"No more than any planet," Oliver said. "You should know."

"Not really," Palmer said. "Been a pilot since I was sixteen: innate skills." She gave him a sideways glance. "I was hoping this IPF job would pay enough for me to take a nice long vacation."

Oliver pointed into the back where Brandon and Eldon were sitting. "Doesn't he get a lot of vacation time?"

"They call it R&R," Brandon yelled from the back.

Palmer felt the blood flow into her face and avoided the obvious. "I don't think I'll be getting paid my second half for this one now anyway," she said.

"You should have a life too," Oliver said.

"That's what I tell her," Brandon yelled again.

"Shut up back there. This is a private conversation," Palmer yelled.

"Then have it in a private location," Brandon said.

Palmer raised the nose of the cruiser. "Hold on." She kicked the engines in and everyone fell into their seatbacks. "Be there in a minute," she said.

Oliver had a smile on his face as they flew over the mountains. She expected him to be more nervous about the flight. "You okay over there?"

Oliver cleared his throat. "Yeah. I'm the planet's liaison, being the youngest on the board. I've flown quite a bit. I go to all the off-world functions, conventions, whatever."

"Didn't know that," she said. "Then you've been to the IPF mother ship?"

"Years ago perhaps. I can't remember." Oliver kept his face to the side, looking out the window, enjoying the ride.

Palmer wanted to spend the least amount of time in the air and flew low over the hills and mountains. The sun disappeared over the horizon. "I remember some lush areas on the planet's surface, why are you living in this desert-like plain?"

"We're not," Oliver said. "We use this for what it's best for: a flat and solid landing strip or two, strong foundation for missile launches. These mountains are all that separate us from what we consider the most hospitable areas near here." He nodded as he spoke, knowing the colony intimately. "I've studied all the land maps and research performed prior to colonization. Once the planet was found to have the right air quality for humans, the right temperatures, and near Earth gravity, every colonizing location was checked for poisonous insects, animals, or plants; checked for flood zones, high and low temperatures, unbearable humidity. Everything is well documented before a colony chooses to settle."

"We've all heard the horror stories," Palmer said.

"Exactly. And eventually we learned from it." He leaned forward and pointed. "We're there. You can land near that hangar on the left. We'll have you towed in."

While Palmer settled the cruiser facing away from the hangar, Oliver said, "I hope you realize that wasn't the debriefing."

"I was afraid of that," Palmer said.

"They're harmless," Brandon yelled up to the front.

Oliver's face became stern. "Every debriefing is different," he said.

Palmer didn't like the sound of that.

# CHAPTER 8

**JAMES EMERSON TRAVELED THE CORRIDORS** in a rush even though he wasn't looking forward to seeing Garth Killjoy once he arrived. His plans weren't going as well as he'd hoped. Palmer stalled her takeoff and then they discovered that Jacobs was working undercover for Earth Central. All in a matter of hours. Garth could easily demote him. Or worse, place an explosion inside him and send him to the planet's surface like Blakely and Carlson. Killjoy would do anything. They all saw that now. And to think that working with C-47 was James' idea in the first place.

At Garth's door, James hesitated for a long while before he reached and pressed the call button. He didn't hear Garth announce for the door to open, but a moment later it slid into the wall.

James let out a long stretch of air and took a tentative step inside. Like all the quarters in the IPF mother ship, even the president of Section 204 had a small room. Garth's wall consoles were newer models, but that was all. James couldn't see into the sleeping area or bath, but standing there amidst the desk and chair, bare walls, food and drink dispenser; it could just as well have been his own room.

"Close," Garth said and the hum of a motor interrupted the silence until they were trapped inside together. "Well?" He held a glass in his hand. A gimlet. James recognized Garth's favorite drink. His shirt collar stood open. He seldom wore an IPF uniform, only a suit with the insignia emblazoned on the lapel. Garth spun around and walked to his desk where he sat in the leather seat. "It looks as though that bitch we hired stalled the plan," he said.

James' breathing was shallow. His shoulders muscles tightened and his elbows parked against the sides of his body. He pressed his hands over his pockets. At least Garth blamed Palmer for the delay and not him. That was a good sign.

Garth tapped his fingers on the desk. He angled the glass and swallowed the remaining liquid in several gulps. He must have been waiting for James' report.

"We received a feedback pulse from the missile that it blew. And it corresponded with the time we concluded would be their arrival," James said. His hands began to sweat so he rubbed them gently against the pockets of his uniform. He darted his eyes away from Garth's constant stare.

"Confirmation?" Garth said.

"We're almost positive," James said, repeating the response he received from the missile control operator. "All we have is the feedback pulse."

"Did the colonists appear surprised?"

"Since the first lander incident, they've remained fairly short in their responses. They acknowledged that they received our message. Then we went out of contact," James said. "They're not advanced enough to have satellites in place."

Garth took a deep breath. "And if we missed our target? Do you think the colonists will believe those two?"

"We detonated the men and sent the missile behind them. I doubt anyone's alive." James felt sweat bead on his forehead but didn't wipe it off. He rubbed his hands against his sides until he noticed what he was doing, then forced himself to stop. He knew Garth would notice, so he gripped his coat as though that's what he'd meant to do and held firm as he waited.

"If they're alive?" Garth repeated. "Will they be believed?"

"No sir. Why would they be? Everyone knows that independent pilots work for the highest bidder. She's not privy to any information. She's been isolated this whole time. And Jacobs, if he really is working for Earth Central, he's as unreliable as anyone. They've been trained to lie convincingly. It took us this long to notice."

Garth got up from his desk chair and went over to retrieve another drink. He reached into the dispenser. "What if she sides with

Jacobs and keeps his identity quiet? What if he negotiates as though he's an IPF officer?"

James had thought of that possibility as soon as he got the message that Jacobs was undercover. He had the answer. "I've already taken care of that, sir. We put it on record that Jacobs helped Palmer escape. That we fired him. It's already in the books," he said. Then he backed a step. "We can change the books, though. It doesn't have to stay," he pleaded.

Garth looked as though he enjoyed the power he had over James. He stood and waited, saying nothing, his eyes narrowing into slits.

James wanted to swing around and run from the room. He couldn't read Garth and had no idea where the conversation was headed. "We're looking into Jacobs, too. But being so far remote in the galaxy, it may take quite a while to learn the truth." He took a breath. It felt as though he hadn't breathed for minutes. "But he's dead anyway. I'm sure of it."

Garth spoke. "You did the right thing. You took things into your own hands and covered your tracks. I like that."

James' face and shoulders relaxed. "Thank you, sir."

"We have to take control of C-47 before Earth Central can stop us. We'll become part of their Independence Agreement and own those aliens down there one hundred percent," Garth said.

"If I may, sir?"

"Absolutely, go on."

"What if the aliens turn out to be no more intelligent than other classified animals we've run into? How do we know these things are the real deal and that the colony isn't using us for their own ends, for firepower in case their independence is denied?" James crossed his arms and took a few steps farther into the room. "I've been a bit worried lately. We've gotten in pretty deep. We've done some things…"

Garth laughed out loud, frightening James enough for him to step back into his previous space. "Perfect. Let the colonists think there's a possibility that they won't gain their independence and need our help. They're fools. You know Earth Central as well as I do. They don't want control of the colonies anymore. They can't afford to even cover this sector of the galaxy, let alone get involved in every damned colony that asks for help. Independence means that the colony is on its own. Through independence, the colony lets go of the Earth Central tit. And Earth Central saves trillions of dollars."

He pointed at the ceiling and his eyes narrowed. "That is until they're over-producing. That's when Earth Central wants to reconnect, produce a new trade route. That's also when the colony has become strong enough to be a threat," Garth said. "This far out, that might take years. And," he smiled broadly, "we'll be in charge by then."

James listened. He had never understood the nuances of the government's involvement. He only knew his job, and how much he wanted it to change. How miserable he felt much of the time. "If we're also working through their independence, that means we become the negotiators. Aliens or no aliens, we're in the catbird's seat," James said as he started to understand the complexities of the system.

Garth nodded, his wide-set eyes staring through James rather than at him. "Fewer than one out of twenty colonies make it at all. No one wants to finance that sort of yield." He sat down and slammed a fist on his desk. He was a big man, so there was a big noise. "We have the shit job. Every time a colony actually becomes profitable, that's when Earth Central employs our services. Reconnecting and creating peace is only the beginning. Earth Central comes in behind us, and sets up a new government, tax rules, and trade agreements. The colonies hate us and Earth Central uses us. Our hands are tied as long as we're government controlled. You saw what happened: one decision to use force and we're slammed with a fine so large that none of us will get off this fucking ship for years." He looked at James. "Do you have any idea how many IPF ships are in the galaxy?"

James felt momentarily confused. The conversation had shifted. "No sir, a few hundred?"

"Ten thousand," Killjoy said. "And in the past decade about three hundred have gone independent, most through partnering with a colony that was already in place. Some by colonizing an uncharted planet themselves. I don't recommend that."

"Why is that, sir?"

Garth sucked down his gimlet and held the empty glass toward James. "Ninety percent of them don't survive for ten years. They have a higher mortality rate than the colonies."

"And partnering with a colony?" James asked.

"No failures yet. And when Earth Central comes along they have to buy our services. Since they haven't had to pay us, or the colony, for a long time, we get to name our price. And, for all practical purposes, we offer the colony the firepower necessary to stay independent in a changing universe. They won't have to concern themselves with other agencies trying to take over, or pirates. Nothing. And for that we have access to their resources, their labor, their scientists.

"C-47 has been around several generations. They're well established. Solid. I have it on good authority that they're self-sufficient enough for independence already." He set the glass on his desk. "Worst case is pretty good, huh? We take over as the governing body, own what they own, plus Earth Central has to buy our services from now on."

"Will they allow us to step in that easily?" James said then rethinking his question shook his head. "I suppose they will now. We have the firepower to protect them," he repeated what Garth had said. "Of course."

"That, and the small matter that they appear to have attacked the IPF. That gives us the authority to wipe them out." Garth smiled, "A little incentive, shall we say?"

If the plan didn't work, James worried about being fined again, or replaced and never used again. They'd be forced to try to colonize, grow their own food, hunt local beasts. They'd be forced to be just like C-47. And didn't Garth say the mortality rate was high? James said nothing, but the look on his face must have alerted Garth to his concern.

Garth said, "Don't worry though, if their discovery is what they say it is, they'll want our help, and then we own it all."

"Earth Central would pay a lot to get their hands on something like this if it's real," James said.

"It's a win-win for us and all it took was a little positioning on our part." Garth got up and dropped his empty glass into the trash. "We gain our independence, control of a planet, and what could be the greatest discovery in the galaxy."

"So what's next, sir?"

"We have about ten hours according to our position in reference to the rotation of the planet and the abnormal pull from the moon's gravity. Call a meeting with the others and decide how and when to deploy several landers—minimal weapons—but send another half dozen fighters behind them. Keep them hidden. I'm sure you guys know how to do that."

"We can do that," James said.

"You're going down as the liaison as promised. You will be wired," Garth said.

James closed his eyes for a moment then opened them. He brushed the sweat from his brow. "Yes, sir," he said.

"Dismissed," Garth said. "Let's get this show on the road."

James swung around clumsily. He was no soldier, but he was a strategist. Behind him, Garth said, "Open," and the door receded into the wall; "Close," and it closed behind James. Once outside and alone in the hall, James let his head drop. He brought first one and then the other sleeve across his face and forehead. He breathed deeply and walked off toward the conference room. Over his wrist communicator he called a meeting. "I'll be there in five," he said. On his way, James stopped at his room and changed his shirt. He splashed water over his face. Not much longer, he thought. He would become the new head of C-47. To the man staring back at him in the mirror, he said, "Do you trust Killjoy?" The instant answer was no. He didn't have to say it.

There had to be a way for him to make sure that Garth either handed C-47 over to him or that Garth didn't make it through this alive. He well understood what Garth had told him at the beginning of their plan, that all he wanted was enough of the money to travel the galaxy without worry. But James had always known better. Garth craved power. He wielded it over people. He wouldn't be able to give that up so easily.

He looked at his watch. He'd better get moving. In the cabinet behind the mirror James removed a few Ibuprofen and downed them without water while on his way out. He felt a headache coming on.

When he stepped into the conference room, the other five were already sitting in their seats. No one talked. They all looked nervous. James knew how to work with them, though. That's why Garth put him in charge. In this position, he felt confident. "You all know what independence will do for us as individuals, don't you?"

Everyone nodded or said yes.

"We get to charge the government for our services. They can't fine us anymore. We can get back to our family lives." A hand went up. "Yes Jason," James said.

"Will we be able to opt for a place on the surface?"

Jason had a wife and three kids. Living on the mother ship must have been a burden in many ways for him. James could understand that. He too hated life in space. He smiled broadly. "You could have living space here and on the planet once we've sorted out the arrangements."

"Will it be joint?" Steve asked.

"That's the hope," James said, knowing that his hope was for something more dictatorial. Garth wasn't the only one with desires. "But let's get down to business, shall we?"

James opened the floor for some brainstorming, while edging the men toward the already decided upon plan. It didn't take long for them to get to a unanimous vote to send several delegates—James included—to discuss the partnership. "We have two days before Earth Central arrives. If they get here, after the first lander was fired upon, they can legally take over control. They can edge us out if we don't act now."

"And there's a highly probable chance that they know about the findings," Jason said. "At least as much as we do."

"Garth had direct contact with someone down there," James said in a very quiet tone. "I'd bet my life on it. And if I'm right, this discovery is bigger than any of us could possibly imagine." He glanced around the table at all the smiling faces and knew that they saw the potential as well as he did. That's all that he required for them to back him. He reiterated the plan and the men left the conference area, off to their respective duties.

James rushed back to his room to get a few hours of shuteye before having to take off in one of the landers. His excitement kept him awake for a long time, but when he finally fell asleep he had the best dreams. If it wasn't for his alarm he could have stayed asleep, but time didn't wait and he jumped from bed excited for the next step.

In the shower he worried for only a moment that Palmer and Jacobs had made it out alive. He had a redundancy plan, though, so that couldn't have happened. But he hadn't been in the security room during the operation. They could have lied to him. No. That had never happened before. The men trusted him. Before he got out of the shower he heard his door open. There was only one person on board who could get into his room without requesting it. Garth Killjoy.

James turned the water off and grabbed a towel. He hated being this vulnerable. Naked in the true sense of the word, he cracked the bathroom door. "Is this important?"

Garth stood in the middle of the room, suited up for travel.

"Are you going too?" James asked.

"I'm going instead," Garth said. "I need you to stay here and make sure the rest of the operation goes well."

"But then you'll have made first contact. They won't even know me. It'll be less likely for..."

Garth stopped him midsentence by raising his hand. "I'm aware of that. But there'll be plenty of time to introduce you once we've come to an agreement."

"Forgive me for saying this, but I'm your best Peace Coordinator. I've negotiated hundreds of situations tougher than this one," James said.

"You're a bit rusty," Garth said. "The last few times I took care of it. In all frankness, I carry a bigger stick and am not afraid to use it. This is less about negotiating and more about getting the job done quickly."

"The last time we were fined because of the way we handled it," James pressed. They both knew that was Garth's fault.

Garth glared at James. "Are you doubting my skills?"

James held to his towel. He didn't even want to come out from behind the door. "Not at all. I just thought that I'd have a chance to settle the situation with them."

"I'll bring you in when I need you." Garth smiled broadly. "You're my best backup man. Okay?"

That wasn't even a question and James knew it. "Okay," he said. They both knew he didn't mean it and that meant that Garth wasn't happy. What could he do to gain back Garth's approval? James ran through everything he could. What? What? What? "One thing, sir."

"James," Garth said.

"You're going to have to have a reason why Palmer was loaded with explosives."

"I'm listening," Garth said.

James had it. Garth would never be able to come up with lies the way that James could. Garth would get lost in the system and screw up the paper trail so badly they'd nail him in no time. That's what James had over him. He was still scared of the man, but gained confidence under some circumstances. "I've thought this through."

"Out with it," Garth was getting mad.

"Religious vigilantes."

"What the hell?"

"It's been a long time and there are plenty of humans who don't want to find that there are intelligent beings besides us in the universe. It would destroy their God concept. They're all over the galaxy," James said.

"I know that," Garth said.

"They can all be part of it, Palmer, Jacobs, Clark, Richard, Jeff, even Brandon." James stared back at Garth. He wanted the man to know that he wasn't that easily expendable.

"You're a good man," Garth said. "That's why I need you here."

"Will you be bugged, sir?"

Garth didn't answer. He left.

James dried off and got dressed. Maybe Garth told him the truth. Maybe he did trust James, and needed him to follow through on the plan. He wanted to believe it, wanted to trust, but he knew Garth too well. There would always be that tinge of doubt.

# CHAPTER 9

EAGER TO SUIT UP AND HEAD BACK INTO THE PIT to meet the turtles, as Brandon was getting used to thinking of them, he, instead, was told to rest. Not likely. He spent a lot of time inside his assigned room pacing the floor and running everything that had happened so far through his mind, organizing it, and trying to put the pieces of back story into logical order. The situation on C-47 was a complicated one. He sat long enough to eat two of the bars he had saved from Clark's pack. He wished he could have been with Palmer during her debriefing, but that was out of the question. Were they going to show her the turtles, too? He shook his head, wondering what Eldon and Oliver called the aliens. He'd have to find out.

At one point in his short travels from one side of the room to the other, he stopped in front of the wall and leaned into it, head down, fully concentrating on each turn of events. He had never met Jacobs while on the IPF mother ship, and couldn't help but wonder why. Used to the fact that mission jumping, as he'd done now for years, meant that he seldom got introduced to everyone at the top, he still got around enough to know names. This assignment had been rather secret all along. Even Palmer kept her mouth shut. He worked through the person he was assigned to. In this case, it was Palmer, and he trusted her, so he let the secrecy slide. Not the first time he'd worked for her either. They'd been on missions together often enough for him to fall for her. He tapped the wall as he thought about the last few times they'd been together: several rescue missions, two other negotiations between different government bodies, and as backup for a touchy trade agreement. Now this, whatever it was. Since his commission, he'd hardly worked for Earth Central, a testament to how frayed the system had become. There were often times that payment didn't come through for months, another indication of breakdown.

The door opened and a man he didn't recognize peered in. "Are you all right?"

Brandon stopped tapping the wall and looked at his hand. "Yeah," he said. "Can't sleep, is all."

"Would you like something to relax you?" the man said.

"Sure. You have anything resembling wine around here?" Brandon said.

The man smiled brightly. "Oh, we do. In fact I think you'll like it. It's made from local underbrush believe it or not. Stucca. It has a smoky flavor, fairly high in alcohol content if allowed to ferment properly."

"Sounds delightful."

When the man closed the door, Brandon stepped closer and heard him calling in the order. The man remained outside. So, he wasn't completely free to move around, even though Oliver appeared to have accepted his allegiance. He shook his head. "I guess a man can only be trusted so far…on either side."

The wine, delivered a few minutes later, had been chilled. He was handed a tall thin mug made from some kind of local clay he guessed. "Enjoy," the guard said.

Brandon lifted the mug in salute. "Wish me luck."

"Good luck. And have a nice nap." The guard winked, then shut the door.

The wine did relax Brandon enough that he lay down and slept for what felt like several hours. He had set his watch to C-47 time and saw that it had been only about 40 minutes. The quick buzz from the wine had gone. He had been awakened by sounds outside his room.

The door opened and the guard stepped all the way inside. One of the men who had picked Brandon up, Kuhn if he remembered correctly, the physicist, soft hands and soft voice, walked in holding Brandon's cuffs across his outstretched arms.

Brandon couldn't have been happier to see anything. "You do trust me," he said, taking the cuffs from Kuhn.

Oliver walked in behind Kuhn. "For now. We'll still have an eye on you, but we may need your help and I wanted to know that you had what you needed to provide that help."

"Makes sense. Remember, though, I probably can't tie into your weapons."

"We're working on that. No guarantees."

"What about Eldon?"

"He's slowly getting used to the decision. I think you hurt his ego more than anything else," Oliver said. "He's a proud man."

In the spirit of understanding, Brandon said, "He shouldn't let it bother him so much. I'm a professional just like he is. I could have taken all of you without losing my breath. One was like being bothered by a fly."

Oliver laughed. "I don't think that explanation will help a whole hell of a lot. We'll just wait for time to pass. How's that?"

"You're the boss." Brandon set the cuffs on the floor.

"You're not going to put them on now are you?" Oliver said.

Brandon had already begun kneeling between them. He looked up. "Oh, I suppose not. I just…"

"I can imagine," Oliver said. "Bring them with you if you like."

"We're going?" Brandon reached up and pulled a strap from one of the cuffs and snapped it into the other one. In a second he was standing with the cuffs slung over his shoulder. "Let's go."

Oliver led the way even though Brandon had memorized the layout already. When they turned left instead of right, Brandon hesitated. "The lab is this way," he said.

"We're going to pick up your friend first," Oliver said.

"Good idea." Brandon stepped in behind Oliver again, just the two of them. Although he had a guard at his door before, they must trust him quite a bit to put him into a one-to-one situation now. Yet, there were doors all over the place; he could easily be surrounded in seconds if he tried anything. He shook his head to clear his thoughts.

"What's wrong?" Oliver said.

"Just thinking too much." Up ahead stood a guard outside one of the rooms.

"We're here." Oliver motioned for the guard to stand aside, and knocked on the door.

"Open," Brandon heard Palmer's voice and couldn't hold back a smile. He stepped around Oliver and grabbed the door handle and shoved against it. "How's this," he said as it opened.

Palmer sat on a cot and shook her head. "I forget where we are," she said. "The next time I'll use the handle myself."

"It's like going back in time," Brandon said about having to turn the door knob. "How was the debriefing?"

"You were right. But the strip search was a bit more extensive than it had to be." She looked directly into Oliver's face. "You might want to check the sexual preference of your interrogator next time."

"We had to be thorough. Pilots have a reputation for being tricky, shall we say? Especially independents. They look out for themselves," Oliver said.

Brandon took her arm to get her attention. "You okay?"

She turned toward his body slowly, letting her hand find his chest. "I am now."

Her brown eyes were the softest he'd seen them in months. He knew what that meant, too. She kept them on him for a long time, penetrating. It took his breath away and he had to focus before he could say anything.

It was too late. Oliver interrupted. "I can see this might be a problem."

Palmer let go of Brandon with her eyes. "No problem. We know how to separate work from pleasure."

"You might," Oliver said, "but I'm not so sure about him."

"I'm fine if she's fine," Brandon said, wondering just how true that statement might be.

"That's exactly what I meant." He headed back down the hall. "Let's go before I change my mind about this." When they entered the lab, Oliver indicated a hook near the door where Brandon could mount his cuffs. "You won't need them at the moment."

Eldon turned around from one of the benches. "We'd better get going in case IPF deployed more landers before they went silent."

Brandon shrugged.

"What?" Eldon said.

"Let's not start this again," Oliver said, "or one of you has got to go."

"And it won't be me," Eldon said. "It's my project."

"It's nobody's project. It's a discovery." Oliver walked around Eldon toward the clean room. "Our job is to protect it. That's the only reason we're doing any of this."

"Fine. I still want to know what the shrug was about," Eldon said.

"Nerves," Brandon said.

"What's that supposed to mean?" Eldon leaned against the bench and glared at Brandon.

"If they give you something to follow—like the next lander visit— then you're busy. You're actively monitoring, following, making plans. But if they go completely silent and do nothing for a while, then all you can do is stay on alert. You get scattered: watching for something, scouring the area. You can't plan; you can just wait. That's much more nerve wracking than if you're busy. When they finally make a move you'll be stressed." Brandon shrugged. "That's when you make mistakes. That's when they have the upper hand."

"I don't trust them," Eldon said.

"That's what they want. They want you to have plenty of time to think the worst so that when they come up with something even marginally reasonable you jump at it. It's all strategy. You get so crazy waiting for something to happen that you aren't efficient. That and you get so negative that they can screw you and you think it's great." Brandon waited and then said one more thing. "While everyone down here is on alert, they're all getting a good night's sleep. Remember that."

"What's this all about anyway?" Palmer said. "What do they want?"

"Turtles." Brandon turned from Eldon and motioned for Palmer to follow him to the far bench where the turtle-like suits were stretched out.

Oliver opened the clean room door. "Let's go. Both of you into the clean room, get suited up, and I'll show you what this is all about." Without turning around, he called for Eldon to follow them.

Suited up, Brandon felt clumsy again. "In all these years," he said into the intercom, "we still haven't made these suits a whole lot more comfortable."

"Better than they used to be," Oliver said.

"Until we get breathing implants, this is it, I suppose," Palmer said. Eldon huffed.

"I heard that retort," Brandon said. "It's your turn to explain."

"The suit's an environment. Chances are if the air isn't right for us, neither is the climate, the flora and fauna, the pressure. These things have gotten as light and maneuverable as they're going to get," Eldon said.

"Makes sense." Brandon swung an arm around and slapped Eldon's back. "Lead on." He tried to be friendly sometimes.

On their initial walk through the double doors into the area where the pit opened up, Palmer stepped past Brandon. "Looks like a mining operation. I thought there wasn't any C-47 here."

"Hold your questions," Oliver said.

"Big mystery," Brandon said.

"So, you know what's down there," Palmer said. "You've seen these…turtles?"

"Never seen them. But I've been told some information. Not enough to answer any real questions."

The jeep stopped to pick them up. There were enough places for them to hold on while hanging off the side of the vehicle as it crept toward the old mining office near the end of the pit. The overhead lights brightened in some areas and dimmed in others, casting shadows low along the ground. As they approached the office, Brandon peered into the window. Three people sat around computer screens. "They don't have suits on," he noticed out loud.

"They won't be going where we're going," Eldon said.

The jeep stopped and the four of them disembarked. Oliver reached to shove the door open and hold it for the others to go through just as one of the operators swung around in his chair and pushed a button so that a door latch snapped. "Going down?"

Oliver nodded as he walked through the control room to the far door. "We have three levels to go through. This first one is just an elevator to take us down. Two minutes." He ushered them all inside.

After two minutes of silence, the door opposite where they entered the elevator opened to another room. Oliver led them through that room to a second door where he pushed a few buttons. The door opened and he motioned for them to step inside. There was enough room inside for eight or ten normal sized men or women.

"Five minutes in here," Oliver said.

He led them through the next and final airlock into a large room with a few stools to sit on. A small desk, fitted with a console, faced them. On the other side of the desk were other items, metallic but odd looking from the back. A series of cables ran between the console facing the four of them and a half dozen stools. They faced another door like the one they'd just gone through.

"They'll be here in a few minutes," Oliver said. "And please, let's not refer to them as turtles. We call them Mesoans."

"After Meso 12A, the original name for the planet," Brandon said.

Eldon nodded his approval.

"I always read the reports," Brandon told him.

"We should tell you," Eldon said, "that this may be one of the most emotional experiences you will ever have. I can't explain it completely. Only that a connection is made." He hesitated for a moment.

"Good emotion or bad?" Brandon asked during the short silence.

"It's different for everyone." He pointed to a light that came on over the door in front of them. "One minute," he said. "Pull up a stool and find a cable. There's an interface plug on the inside of your left forearm. See it?" He turned his arm over and indicated the connector.

Brandon grabbed a cable and started to plug it in.

"Not yet," Eldon said. "That's too fast for them. We all need to be in one another's presence for a few minutes before we connect. This allows them to converse with one another first, too. They have to create a symbiotic relationship with those in the room before they'll hook up."

"Symbiotic?" Palmer said. "How's that done without connecting?"

"An emotional bond," Eldon said. "You know how you can feel the anxiety in the person sitting next to you sometimes. It's not your anxiety, it doesn't belong to you, but you feel it?"

"No idea what you're talking about," Palmer said.

Brandon knew exactly what Eldon meant. He could always tell how Palmer felt. Much of the time he sensed what everyone felt. That's what helped to keep him alive and he knew it. But the Mesoans? he thought. That would be too weird.

A green light went on over the door, which opened.

"You will understand soon," Eldon told Palmer.

The suited aliens walked from the chamber on what appeared to be their back legs. They stabilized their upright position using one arm, while the second arm stretched to the person beside him or her. Their fingers touched and moved together. Six fingers on each hand.

"They are blind," Eldon whispered. "They communicate by touch and sound. We've been trying to get the suits to be smaller so that they can communicate better, but as our conversation up-world suggested, that's difficult since we have to maintain an environment. They breathe through their skin, so if the suits were too snug, they'd suffocate."

"I don't feel anything," Brandon said while watching the beasts assemble. There were only two of them and he noticed that they were not so thick and turtlelike as much as they were longer and more lizardlike. The suits added bulk, but underneath they weren't all that round.

"You haven't been connected quite yet. They are still stabilizing between themselves." Eldon sat next to Brandon and reached to get his attention. "Both of you, in a moment they'll turn on the light inside their helmets. Don't be shocked."

"Lights? I thought they were blind?" Palmer said.

"They are, but their facial expressions help us to understand them on a deeper level." Eldon picked up his connector. "Get ready," he said.

Brandon still had his connector poised in place.

The moment the Mesoans turned on their helmet lights, Eldon said, "Plug in."

# CHAPTER 10

**MANY OF THE CIVILIANS ON DUTY** during the loading were worried for Garth. James heard the comments. Those people had no idea what Garth planned. They did only what they were told to do and knew only what they were briefed about. As far as most of those aboard the IPF mother ship knew, Garth Killjoy was risking his life for their futures. They had been hammered with fines and late payments to Earth Central as well as odd maintenance and sustenance organizations. Killjoy proclaimed that he was about to change all that, which made him appear the hero. James knew better, but there was little he could say or do to change anyone's mind. The enforcers, IPF's idea of a military, on the other hand, were more privy to the reality of the civilian governmental control. It was from their ranks that men had been pulled for dangerous duty, sacrificed. That information couldn't be kept secret no matter who you were. That was probably why James sensed a nervousness emanating from the enforcers who were on duty at the time.

"Isn't this dangerous after the attack on the first ship," one of the men working in the launch bay's control room asked James as he stood by.

"It's the only way," James told him. "The colonists requested to speak to the head of our section and Garth is the man." He lied, but who would care? For the last few years the entire Section 204 of the IPF had been a lie. Ever since Garth got word of aliens on C-47, he became even more ruthless, even more driven.

"How will they know it's not another escaped prisoner?" the man said.

So that was the lie they were told, James thought. "They won't, but we have fighters getting ready for backup," he said.

"That makes me feel better," the controller said.

"And I'm going to be on one of those fighters," James said.

The man gave him a quizzical look. "Are you sure that's smart?"

"I'm not letting him go down there without me," James said, hoping to transfer some of the man's admiration to him.

"That's loyalty," the man said.

That's self-preservation, James thought, but he said, "It's my duty."

The man lowered his voice as though telling James a secret. "You know that Earth Central is on their way. Garth sent a cruiser through a wormhole weeks ago. We could wait this out. They'd have to take care of it."

James turned to him. "He sent for Earth Central? I thought a message was relayed to them, standard reporting," he said. "I wasn't aware that they were sent for."

The man shook his head. "Wormholes are faster and more direct than relaying a message across the galaxy."

"I know that," he spat out. "That's not the point. The point is that he made the request and is now heading down there to negotiate. James found it difficult not to show his anger at the new bit of news, but he couldn't just avoid the information as though it didn't matter. "You know about the fines, right?"

"Yes, sir. Of course I do."

"Earth Central is already suspicious of us. Even though Garth called on them, there's a good chance that they'll side with the colony. If we get hit with another fine we'll have no recourse but to reduce staff."

"That wouldn't be good, sir. This work is all any of us knows. We have families."

"No, it wouldn't be good at all," James said. "We're doing the right thing by trying to clear this up now. On our own. But Garth is taking a huge chance that things go smoothly."

"Isn't that dangerous?"

"Maybe he thought it was worth the risk," James said.

The preflight horn sounded and the ground crew disconnected the external electrical units from the three landers. The equipment was then checked to be sure that it was secured to the mother ship, and everyone headed out of the area.

James slipped a pair of sound mufflers over his ears. A rumbling shook the floor, only slightly audible. An orange light flared near the engine openings and the bay doors rolled opened. The trip would take at least six hours in a lander, maybe more. That was plenty of time for the colony leaders to stew over their situation and be ready to come to an agreement. If he were the one meeting with them, he'd have three options ready, presenting the most favorable for the IPF first. But not until he explained the situation with Earth Central sending war ships to sink in the need for a quick decision. He doubted that Garth had any second option in mind, let alone a third one. His way was to intimidate and attack.

As the bay doors closed, James turned to the man next to him. "I want seven fighters, fully staffed with air and ground soldiers. I want to be close behind the landers. They can't be on the ground more than a few hours before we show up."

"We only have four fighters in operation," he said. "Our funds…"

"Cannibalize what you can," James said. "I want at least five ready to go."

"I don't know."

"Five, no fewer. That's an order."

The man took a deep breath and turned away. "Five it is."

James left the control room for his quarters and decided to call one more meeting before his trip. "Be there in fifteen," he said into his wrist communicator.

On his way to his quarters, James walked through the family dorms. Children walked with their mothers or fathers, whoever wasn't working at the time, through the halls. He peered into one of the play areas. He had avoided marriage and children for long enough. But living on board a mother ship was no way to raise a family. He longed to be planet-side where he could become part of a community. He swung back around and headed for his room, where he came up with several back-up plans and what he thought would be a better option than what Garth would allow. If he could move

Garth out of the way, he'd be a shoe-in for the colony's governmental board. They'd see that James was out for their best interests. He just had to lock in a lifetime contract and he'd be off the IPF mother ship forever. Solid ground, he thought. A growing society. The excitement of planetary adventure and discovery. And a family if he met the right woman. He didn't care about the money. He didn't want to travel; he wanted to stay put. He wanted to stop traveling. His plan would allow the colony of C-47 to own their discovery, which would be better for all parties concerned.

James took a moment to straighten out his clothes and freshen his appearance by combing his hair and washing his face. He adjusted his jacket and made sure that the IPF insignia appeared straight. Stretching to his full six feet, James left his quarters and marched toward the conference room. He hated meetings as much as everyone, but this one was necessary. On his way, the general intercom came on requesting that he pick up at the nearest terminal. "What the…" James rushed to a wall terminal and answered. "James Emerson," he said into the microphone.

"Security code 3-5-9," a voice came.

James reached into his pocket and stretched a cable between the wall terminal and his wrist communicator and another wire from there to his ear. He slid the ear bud into place and punched in his private security code. "James here." He knew who it would be.

"I don't want you down there," Garth said. "Do you hear me?"

"I thought you'd want backup," James said.

"I want fighter backup, not negotiation backup. I'll take care of those people. I have this under control. Remember, James, you're not in control there, I am. Got it?"

"Absolutely, sir."

"You want your cut in this, don't you?" Garth said.

Intimidate and attack, James thought. "Yes, sir. I fully understand." Asshole, he thought.

"Over and out," Garth said.

James yanked the cables loose and shoved them back into his pocket. The man he had talked with earlier must have told someone his remark about being on board. But they wouldn't be able to get through to Garth. That could have happened only one way.

He hurried to the conference room and stopped outside for a moment, long enough to straighten his jacket again. He reached out and punched in the key code and the door slid open. He stepped to the head of the table, but didn't sit. "Who talked with Garth about my plans?" He watched their faces and knew right away who had passed along the information. They all knew. Several of the others actually turned toward the man.

Leon had been with IPF longer than Garth or James and had been bypassed for promotion several times. He was probably trying to get close to the man he thought could save his ass if anything went wrong. Kiss-ass. But James knew that Garth saw no one as a partner. Even James would be discarded, had been discarded, when it didn't suit Garth.

James opened a channel on his communicator and said, "Send guards to conference room C."

"What are you doing?" Leon said.

James said nothing to Leon. When the guards arrived he pointed.

Leon stood and the guards flanked him.

"You can't do this," Leon said. "When Garth gets back…"

"Hold him until I come for him," James said.

The guards hauled Leon out of the room and the door shut behind them.

"You all know that I'm going with the fighters," James said.

The other men acknowledged him. He knew what to say to them, knew exactly what they wanted to hear, what they hoped for but would be hard-pressed to say. "You three, like Leon, have been with the IPF longer than I have." He looked at Jason, the best of the bunch. "Much longer than Garth Killjoy."

Everyone in the room stared at him, waiting.

James waited them out. He knew who would speak first; he knew who the natural leader was in the group.

Jason said, "You can haul me away for speaking out if you like, James, but we all know that Garth's aggressive actions have gotten us into a lot of trouble." He leaned forward in his chair, glanced around at the others who stayed still and silent, and went on. "There is something fishy going on between him and those colonists. There's something down there, isn't there? And it's not C-47. We already know that."

James had assumed they knew about the discovery; that it had gotten out, but he must have been wrong. If that were the case, he wasn't about to tell them. He hardly knew anything about it himself. What he did know was that Garth had no plans of returning. And James planned to make sure of that. "Jason, you are in charge while I'm gone. And my plan is to be gone for a long time."

Jason smiled. The other men relaxed.

"You may not know this, but Garth sent a cruiser through a wormhole to Earth Central."

"A wormhole? They'll be here faster than we thought," Jason said.

"Soon, I suspect," James said.

Jason didn't look happy. "Why would he do that? Now if we don't work something out with C-47 we're in big trouble."

"Typical Garth," James said. "Everyone is under pressure to negotiate in his favor. Knowing what we know means that we have to put our trust in him, and him alone. I'm going to change that scenario. In the meantime, you get your jobs back."

"Leon?" Jason said.

"He's not a bad man, just a frightened one. I'm going to leave that up to you. Just don't let him out of the brig until this is over. We don't need him spilling any more information to Garth." James spun around and walked to the door. "I'll create a secure line for us to communicate." He reached up and punched the key code pad and left. Things were running smoothly at the moment, but he had to find out what else Leon knew before he could finalize his plans. He only had a little over an hour before he would be on one of the fighters heading for C-47.

Getting in to talk with Leon would be easy. The hard part was to have a private conversation. Security recorded everything. James stopped in to see the security officer on duty and sat down opposite his desk.

"What brings you here, sir?" the man said.

"I need a favor." James glanced around the room. Monitors stood along the wall behind and to the right of the officer. Green lights blinked on several panels. The IPF mother ship had twenty cells for over two thousand employees and the cells were often full. Since the last budget cut, minor crimes against one another had increased. James could see that Section 204 strained against the situation, and they were not about to get help from Earth Central. In fact, their arrival could only make things worse. He needed to get out of there fast, regardless what eventually happened planet-side.

"What sort of favor?" the security officer asked.

"I need to talk with Leon privately." James stared at the man.

The officer shook his head no, but said, "I can give you about five minutes."

"That's enough," James said, thinking that it went too easily. He started to rise. "Why?"

The man looked directly at James. "I don't know what's happening here, but I've seen too many people who don't deserve to be in here show up. These are good people. Leon is one of them. If you need to get the truth from him, without being recorded, I'm all for it." He stopped, but did not take his eyes from James. "And if this is some sort of test or trick, you can arrest me now. But something has to change."

The place was breaking down. James had never seen how rotten things had gotten inside the general workings of the mother ship. This indicated to him that Garth's method of running the place actually resolved to destroying it. "This is no test," he purposefully looked at the man's nametag, "Robert. In fact, it's probably long overdue."

Robert leaned over an intercom and called someone into the room. "Take James to cell fourteen and wait outside the door. He'll be in there for only five minutes." Robert nodded and James followed the other man out of the security office.

Things were getting complicated quickly, James thought. Hopefully, Leon would shine some light on the situation.

When the cell door closed behind James he strolled over to Leon and sat to be sure that they were at the same level. "I have little time to talk. We are not being recorded. I'm sorry about putting you in here. Jason will get you out in a few days at best, but first I have to know what Garth's up to. What does he have over you that you'd report everything to him?"

Leon's eyes swelled with tears. "We're not being recorded? You're sure?"

"Positive," James said.

"I'd be the first to go if we're fined again," he said. "Garth is looking for a reason to get rid of me. I thought..." He turned his head away.

"I know. You're not the only one." James reached and touched Leon's forearm. "What's up with sending for Earth Central using a wormhole?"

Leon shook his head and shrugged his shoulders.

James realized then that Leon and Garth shared a one-way communication. When Leon learned some new piece of information, he told Garth, but nothing went the other way. "Never mind," James said. It had been a wasted few minutes.

"If I were to guess?" Leon said.

"What would that be?"

"Scare the colony into a bad negotiation. If my calculations are right, Earth Central will come through a wormhole about six hours from now," Leon said. "They have to enter this solar system within a safe distance so that they don't come out inside a planet. Then they have to use standard power to get to us. That could take anywhere from a few hours to several days depending on where they come through."

"Just in time for the colony to know that they arrived, but still plenty of time before Earth Central can get close enough to do any damage," James said. "Intimidation." He shook his head. "Timed perfectly." James stood. There was something else and he knew it. He tapped his forehead with his index finger and walked toward the door. Swinging around he said, "Their independence has already been signed off."

"Most likely." Leon cocked his head to look at James. "Trust me. This is one thing I understand."

"Wouldn't they know?" James said.

Leon shrugged. "Depends."

"I'll bet Garth knows exactly." James pivoted back around. "Why wasn't I aware that the paperwork went through? Why?" He rushed over and Leon cowered. "He's playing every one of us, isn't he? Each against the other? Does Jason know?"

"I don't know who knows. I find things out, I tell Garth, and I keep my mouth shut."

James noticed the truth of his statement. The whole time he spent with Leon the man gave up no information that wasn't obvious. He confirmed what James knew, but told him nothing. He couldn't look at Leon any longer. At the door, he knocked and it opened. "Thank you," he said to the guard.

He couldn't trust anyone. That's why he decided to tell everyone that he changed his mind, that he wasn't going to be on one of those fighters after all. Then he'd board at the last minute. The only thing Garth could possibly use the fighters for was protection. They weren't the intimidation, Earth Central was, so their value just shifted. Garth was delivering fighting power to C-47 so that they didn't need to partner with the IPF. He's setting us adrift, James thought. Unless...

James ran back to his quarters and sat at his terminal. He plugged into the ship's main database and began to search the legal briefs concerning IPF involvement in planetary governments. His hands shook as he drilled down to see if there were any precedents concerning using force either for or against an established colony. It took him a while, but he found several. In the most drastic case, Section 417 of the IPF used fighters against a colony in order to gain what they hoped would be an eventual peaceful exchange of goods between the planet and the rest of the galaxy. Earth Central got involved in the fight mid-way. They thought that the IPF had overstepped the line and fired on the IPF mother ship, rendering it incapable of operation. Earth Central also sent troops to regain control of the situation and proceeded to negotiate with the planet itself. The upshot was that the Section 417 IPF mother ship was unusable for nearly a decade. Most of its staff lost their livelihoods, including all of upper management. He looked further into the situation and found what he didn't want to find. Garth was one of those managers.

James shut down the terminal and closed his eyes. "He's hanging us out to dry." He tried to relax by taking a couple deep breaths, but it didn't work. He needed help, but who could he trust? James slammed a fist into his leg. "God dammit." He clenched his teeth. If Garth were to make a deal with C-47, for him to help them negotiate their findings with Earth Central and the rest of the galaxy, he'd be set for life. The problem was that Section 204 would be punished for attacking the planet.

James put his face into his hands. He may be reading into the whole situation, but he wouldn't put anything past Garth at this point. He looked up. One other thing, it would look as though he ordered the fighters. Garth went down to work with the planet's government and, sure as shit, James would be the one in charge of sending in the fighters. But he couldn't stop now. The order had been made. The fighters were going. And if he wasn't on one of those flights, he'd be on-board the mother ship when all hell broke loose. He could only do one thing as far as he knew at the moment, and that was to make sure that he was on the ground as soon as possible.

# CHAPTER 11

**BRANDON ANTICIPATED ELDON'S COMMAND** to plug in and shifted his attention from the aliens to the cord and plug. As he slid the two together to create a connection, a low hum seeped into his headset, along with some background noise just after the initial click as the speakers were energized. An instant after the click, he heard Palmer suck in a quick breath as though she had seen something that startled her. Her surprised sound put him on alert for what he might see, something horrible, but when he looked at the Mesoans he saw that they weren't turtlelike at all.

Brandon stared into the face of an old man. He searched the face for anything that could be considered alien. Slightly slack, which indicated age to Brandon, the man's angular face looked handsome. Broad lips and high cheekbones surrounded a classically regal nose. His brow stood strong over blank eyes, a thin film of skin covering each of them. He didn't startle as Palmer had, though; instead his mind swam within the image before him, calm and pensive. And like many deep thoughts, words to explain them were difficult to find. So Brandon said nothing. He let himself be taken into the moment, letting his surroundings fade into peripheral vision, allowing the other people in the room to travel on their own, private journey.

The old man appeared instantly familiar, as though a long lost relative had come to visit. Faded memories returned, but not completely, only enough that Brandon felt comfortable with them, fond memories he couldn't bring forward and in reality couldn't have had at all. He sighed and took a deep breath. He noticed that the old man appeared to be equally enchanted even though he could not see Brandon. They both produced a slight smile at the same time. Brandon's entire body became warm.

"I don't get it," Palmer said. "Are we going to talk?"

The interruption yanked Brandon back into the room. He took a slow, deep breath and turned his gaze to the other alien, a woman. The face he observed, once again, appeared familiar. The moment he switched his attention, he lost contact with the man visually, but not emotionally. A presence remained, something he felt in his abdomen, a sense of being observed, but that was all that was left. Enough, he supposed, for the man to read his emotions as Eldon had suggested.

The woman gazed into the distance beyond those sitting in front of her, beyond the room. To Brandon her presence felt similar to what he received from the man only more feminine in nature. He couldn't express that sensation in words, but why should he? What was the meeting about but as an introduction, nothing more?

Palmer interrupted the flow of emotion a second time. "Can we get on with this?" Her obvious annoyance bothered Brandon, grated against his nerves.

Oliver said, "You have to relax more for them to settle in." He sounded irritated to Brandon as well.

"How long?" Palmer retorted.

Eldon sat silently beside Brandon, but now that Brandon had connected with the two in front of him, he felt Eldon's energy rise inside him too. The feeling took on an entirely different activity, a scientific one. Eldon's presence produced the sense of discovery and awe in a very controlled yet inspiring way. Brandon found that he liked the feeling, which reminded him more of a child than of a grown man. More of adventure than strictly scientific. If he were to label the sensation, he'd say that Eldon felt at home there.

Brandon allowed that perception to settle inside him before emotionally reaching out to Oliver. That's how it felt to him, as though he were reaching out. In any other setting, he would never have imagined contacting through an emotional tie, but here it became natural to do so. Even as he moved from person to person, all previous contacts remained with him. He literally sensed their presence, each separate from the other, yet each just as unexplainable in words.

Oliver's energy, his essence, produced a slight edge of discomfort for Brandon. He hadn't expected that. Oliver had appeared so genuine all along, but in this setting, in this situation, didn't feel quite right. Brandon didn't stay with Oliver long before he moved on to Palmer, who had already irritated him by interrupting the flow more than once. Her presence suddenly rubbed him the wrong way. And he knew why.

Palmer had spent years removing all feeling from her job as a pilot. She got close to no one, which, at that moment, included everyone in the room. But Brandon had expected something different when he connected to her. She had become close to him. Her barriers had melted away often while they spent time together. He knew and understood her better than anyone.

He considered the situation and just as he did, he sensed a tug from the male alien. Turning his awareness to that feeling—was it a tug at his side, a poke, or merely a nuance—Brandon locked his attention on the man.

The alien's mouth moved and a low, resonant moaning sound entered Brandon's ears through the suit's speakers. There were a lot of 'm's and 'h's in the language, as well as 'a's and 'o's. The speaker background noise rose and fell in what felt like a pattern, perhaps something to do with the electromagnetic transfer between the cables. Then the man reached with his hand and pushed some buttons on the console before him. The sounds were translated using a male voice. "We are pleased to meet you at this time."

Brandon wasn't ready to speak with the man yet. He wanted to be clear about Palmer. But that wasn't coming and the more he focused on the feeling, the more he experienced being off-center. So, he stopped thinking about why he sensed Palmer the way he did and turned his attention to the alien.

Before he could say anything, Eldon said, "We wanted you to interpret these two who have arrived recently."

Interpret? Brandon instantly hated that word. But he had already been interpreted and he knew it. The operation had already been completed. The violation had occurred. The aliens were being used as a built-in lie detector, or intention detector. It wasn't right that Oliver and Eldon would do such a thing without warning him and Palmer, but he couldn't muster the anger to let it bother him too much.

The alien man moaned into the speakers, reached for the machine, and the translator device said, "We are satisfied with them both."

But that didn't seem right to Brandon. Palmer was definitely a harsher energy, guarded, stand-offish. How could the aliens be satisfied with that? He wasn't satisfied with it.

"Would you be willing to provide a small bit of background for them?" Eldon said.

In a moment the translator said, "Our existence is eternal. We are the ones who live below the surface. Evolution is not so random as you have thought, not so based on need or greed."

"There are more of you on other planets?" Palmer asked.

"We suspect that is a true statement. There is one intelligence in the universe. Humans are that intelligence," the man said.

"But you're not human," Palmer said.

Brandon felt hurt by her statement. They were, in fact, human, more human than many of the men and women he'd met in his life. How could she suggest, merely because of their environment, that they weren't human? But he didn't get to talk. He couldn't talk. Words did not arrive.

After a moment of translation and contemplation, the man smiled and moaned into the speaker. "Your monitor," he said.

When Brandon looked at the monitor there appeared the image of a man and a woman, naked. Their hind legs were short and thick, and their arms were too, but they stood somewhat upright and had all the same human features he had seen before. For no reason he could detect, his heart rate increased and his eyes welled up. He sniffled. "You're beautiful," he said.

The woman spoke. Her moans could be heard through his intercom, but she did not reach for the monitor, did not go for a translation. Her warm tone was comforting.

Brandon didn't need to know what she said, only how she said it. He noticed that it worked. He calmed. A sense of security came over him: a blanket of warm cloth, a full stomach, the moment right before sleep. His tears ceased coming. The aliens were beautiful, but no different from him or any of those in the room. They were all beautiful.

The images on the screen faded as the male Mesoan went on to explain how they once lived above ground, but as the planet's climate changed and its atmosphere shifted, they were forced underground. They seldom traveled up-world any more. Their society managed a base of life, as they called it, at around one hundred thousand. They had pure water to drink, and towns, cities, all underground, under a layer of concentrated blue rock.

"The drilling?" Brandon was glad to find that he still had access to words.

"Where we live, there is nothing to drill for," the man said.

Eldon continued to answer the question for Brandon, filling in the gaps. "The mining operation saw the caverns as insignificant, and ignored areas where their equipment registered caverns. Once they opened the first one by accident, they packed up and moved out. We came down to explore the cavern and found that it had been walled up. But we weren't here looking for ore. We looked for life." Brandon then got a surge of happiness from Eldon.

"Which you found," Brandon said. "Something had to have built the wall."

"Yes. Which we found, and beyond our wildest dreams," Eldon said.

The woman and man both moaned then. As they reached for the terminal simultaneously, Brandon knew that they were saying their goodbyes. The time had gone by so quickly. He wasn't quite ready for their departure. Couldn't he stay in their presence longer?

Over the speaker came the two voices from the translator, one male and one female. "We are so happy to have met the two of you and hope to see you again soon." With that they unplugged, turned, a bit clumsy in the suits, and shuffled from the room and into the airlock.

"You can disconnect now," Oliver said.

Brandon pulled the plug and sat for a moment staring as the others got up from their chairs. Eldon patted Brandon's shoulder and said, "Let's go. We can talk about this on our way up."

Brandon turned toward Eldon and stood. "I'm not sure I can. I don't know what just happened. I do know that it can't be true. How can it be?"

"It's true," Eldon said. "Now, come on."

The four of them went into the airlock. Palmer fidgeted inside as though the tight quarters bothered her. Finally, just before the door opened, she said, "I didn't like that."

"What about it didn't you like?" Oliver asked.

"I felt raped. They probed into places they didn't belong, places that are personal, private. Why do you let them do that?" she said. "Is that always how it is?"

"That, my dear, is how it would feel if we were open and honest at all times," Eldon told her. "If we didn't, or couldn't, hide anything."

"I'm honest," Palmer shot back.

"Controlled openness, controlled honesty. You have to be that way. It's your job. I'm not judging that, I'm just saying that you also withhold. You can't do that with them in the room. Not as easily anyway," Eldon said.

"Not as easily," she repeated. "That means that with practice it's possible."

Brandon interrupted. "Hold on. Why would we want to lie to them if they're honest with us? Why wouldn't we be willing to let them in?"

Oliver motioned for them to leave the airlock and travel to the next one. Once inside, he pushed the buttons necessary to close the doors. The conversation stopped momentarily; he spoke first once it began again. "We don't know what their capacity is to hide from us."

"That's it?" Brandon said.

"That's always it," Oliver said. "There are more of them down here than us up there. If they turned hostile—he shrugged."

"They're not hostile," Brandon said. He heard Palmer laugh. "What?" he said.

"You," she said.

"Am I wrong?"

"You are more like them than you know," she said. "You are trained to do what you've been commissioned to do, and to do it with full conviction. Don't get me wrong; I love that about you. You hide nothing. But the rest of the world isn't like that. Take this whole IPF situation. They've got a plan, a big one. And you never saw it. You never would. You believe people."

"They may be able to hide their plans from us," Oliver said.

"But they're not," Eldon piped up.

"I agree," Brandon said. "They felt honorable, ethical. And let's get this straight: I'm not stupid."

"We've been talking with them for some time now, and you're going to find that we don't have a whole hell of a lot of information about them except how similar to us they are," Oliver said. "But we've seen none of it firsthand. We see faces inside helmets."

"The exact same could be said of us," Eldon said. "That's all they get to see."

As the four of them made their way from the airlock to the elevator, Brandon physically felt the shift of emotion inside him, in his abdomen as before. The conversation had put Eldon back into a state of anxiety and frustration, where it had evened out the feelings that Brandon received from Oliver. Now, Oliver felt honest and forthright to Brandon.

When he shifted his attention to Palmer, she actually turned and looked at him. Her eyes, for the second time that day, drove into him, and he sensed her softness. He liked the change, but it bothered him as well. What happened down in the meeting room and what happened now that the four of them were away from the aliens, had to be connected somehow?

The time spent in the airlock dragged on as though it took twice as long to go up as it had to go down. Brandon got a bit edgy. He pushed his way to be first out of the door when it opened. "Let's go," he said.

"Don't be in such a hurry," Oliver said. "We have plenty of time."

"Do we?" Brandon said.

When the door opened, he shot from the airlock and went for the elevator. Only a few more minutes. The others struck him as slow. "How long were we down there?"

"Only an hour or two," Oliver said.

"It didn't feel that long while we were there, but now it does," Brandon said.

"You're just in a hurry." Palmer tapped her helmet against his lovingly. "We'll be topside soon."

The gesture didn't relax him as he was sure Palmer expected. Instead he turned to self-evaluation, something that he did automatically, an operation that he'd been taught as part of his training. When placed in a strange situation, it is more important to be sure that you are focused, centered, and balanced, than to worry about what is going on around you. A balanced soldier can maneuver through utter chaos without harm. And at that moment the situation he had just left was the strangest he'd ever been in. Perhaps not chaotic, in the busy sense of the word, but definitely in the emotional sense of the word. Perhaps Palmer was right, had he given too much over to the aliens? After all, the whole time they were down there with the aliens, he was not his normal self.

As the elevator doors opened, Brandon reached and held Oliver back for a moment. "Their names?" he said. "We didn't even get their names." The fact bothered him because to Brandon, at that moment, not having their names meant that there was no closeness between them. The most elemental information had not been transferred. He thought that he had sensed them, had merged with them intimately, but without an introduction. That was what Palmer was saying earlier. He saw it now.

He placed a hand at the small of her back as they walked through the door to the office. He unlatched his helmet and removed it. "I don't need this anymore."

Oliver thanked the office workers and led everyone outside where the jeep stood by. "Let's get back and talk," he said.

The driver of the vehicle jumped in and took them to the entrance of the lab building. Brandon and Palmer followed Oliver and Eldon down the hall. During their short walk, Brandon reached for Palmer. Before he made contact she pulled away. He gave her the palms up to indicate, what's wrong?

Without sound, her lips said, "Later."

He nodded.

In the clean room, someone dusted down the suits and took them away. Glad to be free to move again Brandon rubbed his arms as though he hadn't felt them for days. "This feels much better."

Oliver made no attempt to be tactful when he blurted out, "Now's the time for you to work for us or get put into jail where you can't do any damage."

"We don't know what we're working for?" Palmer said.

"We'll pay you," Oliver said.

"I'm a pilot, not a mercenary."

"You want to go back and see what the IPF has for you? They tried to blow you out of the sky. They've already killed three people" — he looked at Brandon and said, "almost four—and probably are willing to put even more to the death just to have what we have here." He turned his gaze to Brandon. "You?"

"I work for Earth Central, am on assignment..."

"I know all that!" Oliver said. "I need someone I can rely on. If Earth Central takes over, they'll run this whole thing and we can't let that happen. Our first priority is to protect the Mesoans. That's more important than anything." His eyes enlarged and he leaned forward to drive home the point.

"You're not sure what anyone wants and you know it," Palmer said, her chin raised and her head cocked, a position Brandon recognized clearly. She doubted what Oliver said. Why?

"I'm positive. Until we're declared independent, we're anyone's game."

Palmer straightened her head and reached for Brandon. She took his triceps in her hand and gripped firmly. "We're in."

Brandon didn't know what she had up her sleeve, but he knew that she had a plan. He agreed in the most direct and positive way he knew how. He reached out and shook Oliver's hand, then turned and shook Eldon's. "What's next?"

# CHAPTER 12

**AN ESCORT ARRIVED SOON AFTER** to guide Brandon and Palmer back to their individual rooms. Neither of them needed an escort, which, for Brandon, threw the whole idea of trust out the window. That wasn't good enough. When he and his guard arrived at the door he swung around, face to face. "You're not staying, are you?"

"No, sir," the man said.

"Good. Neither am I."

"Excuse me?"

"I need to talk with my partner." Brandon smiled at the man and walked back the way they'd come. He sensed that the man stayed behind him, but glanced over his shoulder to be sure. "Besides, I forgot my cuffs in the lab."

"Cuffs?" the man said after him.

Brandon didn't answer. He kept walking. The man he thought was a guard only followed him a little while, then turned down a hallway in the opposite direction. Good. He felt better on his own. Maybe they did trust him.

The building layout was fairly simple, built on a circular pattern with cross hallways every once in a while, rather than a rambling one like the IPF mother ship. The lab lay in the center of the building along with other workrooms or conference rooms similar to the one he had met the planet's council in, he guessed. All the outside units were either offices or guest rooms—again, a guess. He turned the corner and rushed toward Palmer's chambers and almost ran into her. She stopped so abruptly that her long black hair continued to rush toward him even after her body stopped. When her hair settled back onto her shoulders, he reached for her, grabbing her arms, and turned her around. "I want to collect my cuffs," he said.

Palmer stood a few inches taller than Brandon, which he noticed only when they came into such close contact and he had to look up to meet her eye-to-eye. There was something about it that actually made him feel more powerful rather than less powerful and he hadn't figured out what that was yet. Didn't matter. He liked the feeling. That's all he needed to know.

He crashed through the lab doors and turned toward the wall to retrieve the cuffs. Palmer charged in behind him. They halted when they noticed Oliver and Eldon deep in conversation. The two men's faces displayed a seriousness of discussion that had been going on for a while. They didn't look very happy about being interrupted either.

"Now what?" Oliver said as he glared at Brandon the way he would a child. "Both of you?"

Brandon reached for his cuffs and unhooked them from the wall to smoothly swing them over his shoulder. He made a quick nod in greeting and apology.

"Should have known," Oliver said. Ignoring the two of them he turned his attention back to Eldon. He appeared to continue the conversation where he had left off.

Brandon used his free hand to swing Palmer around and shove her out the door. "Let's go for a walk." He shut the door and continued to push her along.

"Hey, I wanted to hear what they were talking about," she said.

"They're arguing. About us. I didn't want to give them another reason to put us under watch."

"How would you know that?" she said. "We were there for eight seconds.

"My job. You could feel the tension the second we stepped inside. Oliver had been talking, but Eldon was about to interrupt. Body language." Brandon felt Palmer's stride hesitate and she partially turned around. He knew what she was going to ask and answered before she got the chance to. "His lips were parted, eyes wide, and head and shoulders leaning in. Ready to say something." He shoved her forward again.

She stumbled on. "You're sure?" she said.

"Positive. And when Oliver recognized what we were there for, Eldon's eyes narrowed. I guarantee that he objected to allowing me to be armed. Taking the cuffs just made his case even more closed as far as he was concerned. But Oliver didn't have enough time to change his mind, or he was adamant and was about to tell Eldon so. I really don't care which it was. I just wanted my cuffs. In order to keep them, I sensed that it was best to leave quickly."

Palmer slowed down her pace. "Do you always notice details that well?"

Brandon moved his hand from her triceps to the small of her back. He stepped into stride beside her, but continued to guide her forward. "This way."

There were guards at the front of the building. They sat at a small makeshift counter. Two chairs had been tucked behind the counter and Brandon assumed that terminals displaying images from surveillance cameras were tucked back there as well.

Brandon stepped right up to the guards. They both stood as he approached. "Hi, guys. Would you mind terribly to watch over my cuffs while we take a walk outside?"

"Not at all, but let me check on the flies," the shorter of the two said. He pushed his chair back out of the way and bent down to press a button and look at a terminal screen. "You should be in good shape. Go ahead."

"Flies?" Palmer said.

"They bite," Brandon told her.

"They're really not flies, we just call them that. They are more like flying arachnids. Very sensitive to temperature, though. They only come out between about 40 and 50 degrees. Short time, but they can eat enough that when they drop back onto the ground, they're good until the temperature is right again."

"Where do they go?" Brandon said. Since he had witnessed their bites, he wanted to know how to avoid them.

"They burrow."

"And the bites?" he asked.

"Harmless for the most part, unless you're allergic. They mainly eat the sweat from your body. It's accumulated in these mandible type of jaws that leave behind an acidic fluid." He stopped and shrugged his shoulders. "Appears like a bite until the fluid evaporates. But they don't really…bite." He made a biting motion with his hand, bringing his fingers together.

"Fucking fascinating," Palmer dragged at Brandon's arm.

"I had plenty of those bites so I just wanted to know more about them," he said. Turning back he saw that the guard was smiling at the two of them. "Thanks," Brandon said. "Very interesting."

"No problem. I've studied them for a while." The man looked proud of his knowledge.

The air outside had fallen below forty degrees just as the guard had told them, and the flying spiders were nowhere to be seen, or felt. "I don't trust any of this," Palmer said.

"Let's walk." Brandon took the lead.

C-47's only moon rose above the mountain beyond which he had traveled through the valley. Beyond that first valley was where the settlement, the colony, was situated, surrounded by fields. From where they walked, the moon stood so large that its light brightened the entire area like a mid-afternoon sun. It lay partially hidden by the mountain, but still enough rose overhead to light up the sky and obscure the stars.

"Not much darkness around here, I suppose," Brandon said.

"Until that behemoth disappears," Palmer said. "That's when the predators show up I'm sure. So, are we far enough away yet or do you think they have microphones and cameras tucked away inside these rocks?"

"We're fine," Brandon said.

"So, mister 'I-can-read-everyone-like-a-book' what's going on here?"

"Not funny."

"I'm sorry," Palmer said. "But you seemed different after meeting those aliens. What happened to you down there?"

"Humans. Let's call them what they are," he said staring toward the mountaintop.

"If we're going to call them what they are, then let's say Mesoans. I didn't like that whole experience." She cocked her head and stepped back to look at Brandon. "But you did."

"Did," he said. "I'm still trying to figure it all out."

"What's to figure?"

"You were right about what happened. We learned nothing, or very little from them. Yet, they got a lot from us." He shook his head. "We communicated fully with them. We had no choice. We have no idea how to carry on a conversation through emotions alone. But they do, and they got what they wanted." He folded his arms across his chest and lifted one hand to his chin. "It's like you said, they didn't communicate with us through the methods we use and can control." He wandered from her and turned his attention to the giant moon. "Sure they showed us a picture and said a few things, but they didn't carry on a conversation. But I'll bet we did."

"You're pretty good at this. I'm impressed," she said.

"Don't be. We're not out of here yet." He stared for a moment before going on. "If I were Oliver, I wouldn't let us be so free and easy. He wants something from us."

"Yeah, protection. I got that much," she said from behind him. "That's the only reason he took us down there remember, to let them decide if we were trustworthy."

"If they can read emotion, maybe they can push them too. Maybe we were down there to be convinced," he said. "Either way, until we know for sure we have to focus on our talents and work together while we're here, and while we can."

"What do you mean, 'while we can'?"

"You don't have a weapons pod on your cruiser, so you don't need me up there. That means that I'm ground support. If anything gets dicey we're going to be split up." Brandon felt Palmer come up from behind and her arms wrap around his chest. He liked the feeling.

"How do we meet up again? How do we find each other?" she said.

He rotated to face her and hugged her. In her ear he said, "Let's make this look like we're not planning anything, but wanted time alone."

"Sneaky way to cop a feel isn't it?"

Brandon couldn't help but laugh. "As long as it works," he said while running his hand up her side.

She kissed him lightly across his lips. When she pulled away, she said, "Let's make it look good then." She went in for a real kiss and he let her pull close to him.

After their kiss, he said, "We'll have to decide on a place to meet eventually, but now's not the time. You'll figure that part out. I know you."

"Do you?"

"You already have a plan in your head, don't you? Been working on one since you arrived."

She didn't answer, which was answer enough.

"I notice everything. I can tell who's angry and who's not in a room full of people. I know who's controlling the conversation, whether or not they have weapons and if they know how to use them. You, on the other hand, are a strategist." He reached and touched her nose with his finger. "You walk into a room and organize how you're going to get from one point to another, who you'll have to step around, and who might get in your way as you're traveling straight for your goal, whatever that goal is." He squeezed her close. "You create exit strategies, while I'll know who wants to stop you and if they're able to."

"Tell me what you notice, and I'll adjust the strategy as we go along," she said.

"That's what I'm talking about."

"That guard back there, what do you know about him? The one who talked with us."

"Couldn't handle a weapon if he wanted to. That's the way most of these guys are. That kid is probably one of their scientists. They've drafted everyone into service for this operation, but they have no idea what they're in for," he said. "Their expertise is in farming, exploring, finding the resources they need to stay safe and alive on a planet where, most of the time, there's no intelligent life."

"None of the time until now," she corrected.

"That's still a hard concept to accept," he said. "All these thousands and thousands of years we've found no truly intelligent humanoid life anywhere. And now this. I don't even know what to make of it. It's beautiful and terrible. Exciting and frightening."

"So, who are the good guys?"

"Not sure yet, but when we find out there may not be much time to make our move." Brandon stepped around to her side, his arm around her waist as they walked farther into the evening. She snuggled closer to keep warm next to his body, and probably to be close to him, he hoped.

"It's going to be difficult to stay connected with all these people hanging around," Palmer said.

"Keep an eye on me when you can," Brandon said.

"Oh, I'll do that for sure."

From behind them the short guard yelled as he ran. "Hey, hey."

"Shit." Brandon turned around and yelled back, "What?"

The guy didn't have his gun and was out of breath from the short run. Brandon hadn't noticed that they had walked so far from the building until now. He pulled Palmer along with him and jogged over to the man.

"Someone's coming," he said. "Oliver sent me."

"The landers," Palmer said. "They told us what they were going to do."

Brandon asked the guard, "Weapons?"

"You mean do they have weapons or do we?" the man said.

Brandon had to laugh. "Them."

"Don't know."

Brandon headed back toward the building. "Let's find out."

The guard came up behind as Brandon and Palmer took the long strides as those on a mission. "See what I mean," Brandon said to her.

"Couldn't hurt a fly," she said.

"Or a flying spider." Brandon found the planet interesting.

"Once we find out what's going on, I need to check on my cruiser," Palmer said. "Make sure it's ready for this."

"Roger that."

As they entered the building, Oliver waited at the front counter. "There's a car coming for us."

"What do we know?" Brandon picked up his cuffs from the countertop.

"Armed, but standard weapons, no load of bombs this time." He looked at Brandon out the corner of his eye. "Not like you two."

"We didn't know about that," Palmer said.

Oliver nodded. "So you've said."

"So the aliens confirmed, I'm sure," Brandon said under his breath.

The three of them went outside just as a transport vehicle pulled up. Like the other vehicles on the planet it was part truck, with a bed, and part car, with enough room for five. They piled in and took off for the tower. Brandon held the cuffs between his legs.

"You can't relay communications to the pit?" Palmer questioned.

"Once in a while." Oliver sat in the passenger seat and turned around to talk with them. "In case they can tell where we are, the last thing we need is for them to knock out the pit. All this would be worth nothing then."

"All what?" Brandon asked.

Oliver stumbled for a moment then caught his train of thought. "All the hard work on the discovery. This is one of the most important finds in the galaxy."

"So you've said before," Brandon said. "Maybe too often."

Oliver glared at Brandon for his comment. "We must protect them," he said.

At the tower, the three of them climbed the stairs. The small area at the top displayed more activity than the last time they were there. "They're not hailing us yet," a woman said.

"They will." Oliver settled into a chair. He motioned to Brandon and Palmer. "Please, sit. You can set the cuffs down on that bench over there."

Brandon headed for the bench, but Palmer didn't. "Not yet," she said, throwing a hard look at Brandon.

"What?"

Palmer leaned toward him as though he had forgotten something important. "I need to check on the cruiser. Have you forgotten already?"

"That's right." He swung around for the exit. Before following Palmer back down the stairs, he said, "Got any communicators?" He held up his wrist communicator. "These things only handle certain frequencies, obviously not the ones you use."

Oliver motioned toward one of the other tower operators who grabbed a handheld and threw it to Brandon, who caught it in his free hand.

The night air had continued to drop in temperature. Palmer wrapped her arms around herself the best she could.

Brandon followed her hard pace as she raced for the large hangar where they had put her cruiser. Mid-travel she changed direction.

"Where you going?"

"I want to check the other hangars too," she said. "First."

They approached a metal building, rounded on top, and long inside. Several jets were parked there, spaced evenly from one another. Air transportation for long-distance planet trips only. Palmer walked around them pointing things out to Brandon. "Looks like they fitted several of these with missile launchers over the wings. A couple of them have machine guns mounted in the front." She pointed. She bent to look underneath. She stepped up onto a wing and looked around and inside the cockpits. "This might help. I just hope they have pilots."

Brandon noticed most of the armament, but Palmer appeared to know better where to look and pointed out guns he wouldn't have seen without her help. Not all the jets were armed. Only five of them. Four others were not fitted with any weapons. He followed her from that hangar, out the back, and a short distance to the next hangar. Inside sat two old-model landers. "Weapons pods," he said. "My cuffs could interface with them."

"Yes," Palmer ran over and rubbed her hand across the fuselage. "Let's check them out." She ran around the side and climbed up the stairs.

Brandon rushed behind her, still carrying his cuffs and the comm unit. "Musty."

"That's not good." She headed for the cockpit and sat down in the pilot's seat.

"You're not going to start this thing, are you?" Brandon said.

She flicked a switch on, and a light lit up, a red light. "Not today," she said. "We'll need ground power to get this thing up and running." She got up and went through the lander. "Stripped for the most part." She checked a control console in the cargo bay. "Still loaded with standards," she said. "If we can get them off the ground, we can use them as defense. Maybe." She nodded toward the communicator. "Ask Oliver if these things work," she said while heading out the door and over to the next one.

Brandon keyed the mic. "Oliver, we're in the lander hangar looking over your equipment. "Do these things fly?"

Oliver came back over the speaker. "Last time we tried."

"Could you get a crew ready? We'd like to try again," Brandon said.

"I want to meet all their pilots," Palmer said as she exited the second lander. "Now would be a good time."

Brandon relayed the message and Oliver acknowledged with an affirmative.

"I want to check on my cruiser now," Palmer said.

Brandon kept up with her, but it wasn't easy while dragging the cuffs over his shoulder. "You wouldn't want to slow down, would you?"

"I'm a big girl," Palmer said and she jogged ahead.

Brandon slowed to a more comfortable walk and watched as she entered the last hangar. Something dark jutted across the ground on the far side of the building. He upped his pace. He noticed the moon had dropped and only a sliver stood over the mountain. The area had darkened. "Predators?" he said under his breath as he fell into a jog.

# CHAPTER 13

**JAMES STARED AT HIS TERMINAL** for a long while before he broke through his contemplation. What had he gotten himself into? Garth had played him, just like he played every one of them. There was never a guarantee, not a word of loyalty from Garth. The suggestion of job security had been self-imposed and hopeful. James felt ashamed of how stupid he'd been, how expectant, even while the situation got increasingly worse. And now it had grown into a full-on sabotage. Shame made him hate Garth even more. He had to break the man, had to turn him in somehow. Stop him from destroying anyone else's life, even if he had to sacrifice his own.

He jumped from his chair and checked the time. The fighters would be leaving soon. He wanted to get on board at the last minute, as though it was an accident. Was that even possible? There would be pilots, enforcers, maintenance personnel all around the fighters. He rubbed his face and stared at the door. Go. Just go, he told himself. But there was one last thing to do.

James drifted to his closet and removed a high-powered membrane pistol and tucked it into his belt. He pulled his coat over it and buttoned three buttons to hold the garment closed. He took one large breath before he opened the door and rushed down the hall. James purposely stood tall and straight, trying to look as though he was on official business. His long strides made his quick gate appear smooth. A few of those he passed nodded to him, but he continued straight on path without acknowledging anyone. He refused to stop for any reason.

As he approached the launch bay, he ducked into one of the pilot debriefing rooms, knowing that it would be empty. He rounded the oblong table and chairs and rushed directly to the far-side door leading to the launch bay. It had not been sealed yet, which meant that the bay doors were still closed. There was a moment when he thought he hadn't breathed for his entire walk there. Another deep breath or two and he allowed his shoulders to relax and his head to clear. This was it. He had to go now.

James opened the door to find few workers in the area. Electricians were breaking down the external power units and securing them to the bay floor. The fighters' engines were all running. Last checks were being placed on the landing gear before the mechanics headed in the opposite direction, toward their stations behind sealed doors.

James jogged past one of the electricians and motioned for the pilot to have the side door opened for him. Each fighter was loaded down with ten ground soldiers as well as the pilot and copilot. One of the ground troopers reached to help James into the ship. "What is it, sir?"

"Close up," James said.

"But...we're leaving?" Just after the trooper said that, the bay horn blared.

"We are now," James said. "Close up."

While the trooper secured the door, James ducked and walked past the front row of soldiers to where three jump seats lay secured against the fuselage wall behind the pilot's seat. He waved to the pilot, giving him the go-ahead, then unlatched one of the jump seats, sat down, and strapped in. The membrane pistol barrel rammed into the top of his leg. He adjusted it slightly, but could still feel the presence of the cold metal poking him.

With everyone in position and the bay doors open, James felt a rush of power throw him forward. The soldiers were shoved into the backs of their seats. He heard the pilot say, "Clear," which was the signal that they were outside the mother ship and the bay doors could be closed again. They were in space heading for C-47. After a long few minutes for them to break into the C-47 atmosphere, he unlatched himself and swung around so that he could kneel between the pilot and copilot just behind the center console.

"You shouldn't be here," the pilot said.

"There may be a change of plans," James said. "Earth Central is on its way and we could be in danger. I can't explain what's going on right now, but we've got to be on the alert."

"But our orders…"

"I'm changing those orders directly." He tapped the copilot on the arm and said, "We're changing places for now."

The copilot hesitated as he glanced at the pilot who gave him a nod. "For now," the man said as he got up from his seat.

James let him pass and took the copilot's seat. He put on his headset and switched on the radio. He yelled over to the pilot, "What channel is private?"

"Two. Four is just between the fighters, and six is everyone, including the mother ship."

James switched the unit to the number two position, "Am I clear enough if I talk this low?"

"Yes, sir. How can I help you?" The pilot whispered, but James heard his voice loud and clear in his headset.

"Your name?" James said.

"Captain Stark."

"Well, Captain Stark, we have a difficult situation here at the moment."

"And what is that exactly, sir?" Stark asked.

"I have reason to believe that the lander and its crew are setting a trap for us. This is all part of a well-organized plan to make Section 204 of the IPF look as though they are endangering a strategic alliance between C-47 and Earth Central." He waited for a moment and was glad to find that Stark had no questions, that he was still listening. "There is a conspiracy going on that will affect the lives of everyone in Section 204. I can't let that happen," he said. "Any questions?"

The pilot glanced at a light on the console that blinked continually.

"What's that?" James pointed at the light.

"I'm being hailed by the mother ship." Stark pointed to a second light. "And the other fighters." He waited for a moment. "What should I tell them?"

"About me? An accident," James said. "Tell them that I had some last minute dealings with one of the soldiers and got caught inside after the horn went off."

"I'm not sure they'll buy it," Stark said.

James cocked his head. "It's all they get for now."

Stark switched his radio to six and asked what they wanted. With all channels open, several tried to get through at once. "Hold it, hold it. I know what you want to know, well...," and he told them the lie that James provided.

"We'll get in huge trouble with this kind of accident," the man at the main control room on the mother ship announced.

"It's okay," James said into the intercom. "A slight emergency. I'm sure the landers will be on the planet soon and that all negotiations will go smoothly. We're just backup and probably won't be needed. Let's look at this as a short ride through the country, a vacation." He laughed, but noticed that no one else did.

In a moment, the mother ship's control room came on the air and said that they'd have to create a report.

"I understand that. And you have my full support," James said. He knew that Garth didn't plan to return. And at that point, he didn't plan to return either. They could write all the damned reports they wanted to.

After his short talk with everyone, James settled in to enjoy the scene. Stark continued to run the engines pretty hard as they flew over the planet. Every colonized planet looked and felt familiar, in an Earth sort of way, especially from that distance. On each planet the continents were shaped differently, and the water supply fluctuated from about a third to two-thirds of the surface, but other than that there were mountains and rivers, valleys and deserts. No matter what the colors were, no matter the leaf patterns or textures, vegetation was vegetation, animals were animals. And, of course, each planet had its own weather patterns, so similar to Earth that it was no wonder people would want to live there. Years could go by and the colony's scientists would still be documenting every plant, animal, and insect. The excitement and adventure lasted for several lifetimes at least. James wanted to be a part of that excitement. "Beautiful," he said as he daydreamed living on the surface.

"It is that," Stark said. "I've made a lot of runs to planets and they're all unbelievably beautiful. Especially at this distance."

"There's a lot of blue land here," James said.

"It's from the rock, some sort of sandstone, usually clear of organic residues," Stark said.

"But the planet has plenty of plant and animal life," James added.

"It hasn't always been like that. At least not enough to discolor the rock and sand that's on the surface now."

"How do you know?" James said.

"I try to read up on the planets we work with. To know something about their makeup, their flora and fauna, even the group who chose to colonize."

James leaned to look down. "Is it dangerous down there?"

"Can be. The biggest danger comes from not knowing how the local beasts will act, whether they're carnivores or herbivores." He winked at James. "Most of the time, like everywhere else, they become scared and run. That is unless they feel threatened. That's when they fight back. That's when they're dangerous." He winked. "Or if they're hungry."

James let it stand at that. If there were that many colonists living on the planet, it couldn't be too bad a place. After all they had small towns with stores and restaurants, women and children. Just the type of place he wanted to live. He'd been cooped up on the IPF mother ship long enough to know how to survive in a limited space, it was time to change that scenario. The thought of living on C-47 came through his mind quickly and could have moved on, but the idea reminded him of Garth and how his decision to go to the planet had interrupted James' chances of remaining on C-47 as a diplomatic liaison. Well, that would change. He felt a familiar thickness rise in his chest and knew that an emotional plan would not be a good one. He had to calm down, think clearly. If he were going to foil Garth's plans, he had to be in top form. The situation could change quickly and in any direction. He tapped his fingers on his armrest as he thought. He took a few deep breaths. Anything he could do to relax he tried. Eventually, he simply stared out the window and watched the ground as they flew over.

Stark pushed a few buttons and ran his fingers over a knob. He brought his attention to James and waved, then pointed at a blinking light on the console. "It's one of the landers," he said.

"Garth." James shook his head.

"He's asking to talk with you," Stark said, "but I haven't answered yet. What do you want me to tell him? He's bound to know that we can hear him. I'll have to answer."

"I'll answer him, then," James looked around the console. "What do I have to do?"

"I'll patch you in."

James knew that Stark would be listening in on the conversation, but that might be a good thing. If Stark got a feel for how crazy Garth can get, it would work in James' favor. "James here," he said.

"I told you to stay on the mother ship." It was Garth, all right, and he sounded pissed.

"An emergency with one of the soldiers. I ran out for a moment and got caught after the horn blew," James said.

"There's plenty of time to leave after the horn goes off. That's why there's a fucking horn. No matter. It's too late now. And, I just want you to know that this will cost you. You made a stupid move, my friend."

"You can't fire me without the board's approval," James said.

"I won't need the board's approval for what's going to happen. You won't make it back," Garth said. "You won't even interrupt my trip, I'll tell you that. You're going to be surprised as hell." A short pause and Garth shouted through the speakers, "Captain?"

"Captain Stark, here."

"I want you to stay on course according to my orders. Anything less than that and you're gone. Do you read me?"

"Yes, sir."

"You're done, James," Garth clicked off.

"What were your orders?" James asked.

"I'm not sure I can reveal them to you. Especially now."

"You've got to. He's going to be there two hours ahead of us. That's more than enough time to execute whatever plan he has in place. And if my suspicions are correct, he's going to make it look as though we're on the attack. C-47 will have no choice but to fire on us," James said in earnest.

"They'll never see us," Stark told him.

James gave Stark a look of shock. "You're supposed to hide five fighters? Then, I'm right. You've got to see that you can't hide once you're in range. They're a colony, not Neanderthals. One of these fighters will get seen for sure."

"Why would he want them to fire on us?" Stark asked.

"So that we're the bad guys when Earth Central shows up." James watched Stark's face as he told him what he thought might be Garth's plan. "I don't know for sure, but when Earth Central comes through the wormhole, I'll bet it's on this side of the planet. They'll see what's going on down here even if they can't react fast enough to take over." He paused to allow his next thought through. "They'll engage the Section 204 mother ship first." He shook his head. He had no idea how strongly his decision to leave would affect him. But if he had stayed on board the mother ship, he'd be arrested and charged for the fighter attack for sure. Garth must have put the plan into place before James decided to go.

Stark's lips pushed tight and his eyes narrowed as though trying to sort out what James told him and fit it into place with his present orders from Garth. But an instant later he shook his head. "I don't know," he said. "It makes sense, but I have my orders. We stay on course. You heard him. If I deviate at all it could be my job."

"You're putting us all in danger. All five fighters could be shot down. A surprise attack."

Stark turned a big smile on James. "We're the professionals. Once Garth verifies a clear air space, we appear, land, drop off troops, and get back into the air. I've been through these missions a hundred times. Very straightforward. We can handle anything, including a surprise attack."

"You've never run a mission with me," James said. "We've never met. And I've run most of the missions for Section 204 for the past decade. And I almost never use fighters."

Stark shifted his attention back to his flying. "I came here six months ago, hired from Section 390. I've flown more negotiation mission back-ups than you can imagine." He glanced over at James. "I don't know how you operate, but that's my experience."

James sat back into his seat. "Is that how the IPF is operating now? Are their Peace Coordinators always using back-up, always expecting a fight?"

"Where I came from, that's what they do, but very few negotiations escalate to that level." He raised his eyebrows. "Probably because of us."

James put his hands over his face and rubbed blood back into his jaw. He was sure that he had turned pale. "Has it become that routine out of necessity? Have colonies become that volatile? That violent?"

"No," Stark said. "Colonies are usually more than happy to talk with us. They know the system. Negotiation means that they have access to Earth Central money and research, that they have opportunities for growth. They don't all want to be independent."

"Then why?" James asked.

"One out of ten want to be left alone. They fight back. Simple as that," Stark said. "I suppose independence can look like freedom."

"Then leave them alone. Help them apply for independence, like C-47," James said.

Stark shook his head. "Conversation over. I'm following orders." He grinned at James. "I guess you got that vacation you wanted."

"Garth has something up his sleeve and we'd better be ready for anything," James settled in for the remainder of the trip. He leaned his head against the window. "The second Garth lands on the planet, wake me. That means that we're almost in range, too."

"I can do that," Stark said.

James stared out the window and into the variety of blues that made up much of C-47. Earth had literally billions of living things that had been discovered and catalogued. Colonies got to start from scratch. Unlike a race that evolves, they start out with all the right equipment and knowledge. It's like starting over. They get the chance to make things better. James wanted to be part of something that interesting, that exciting, and this was his one chance.

"You want to be down there, don't you?" Stark said.

"What?"

"I know the look. I've seen it a hundred times."

James took a breath. "Yes. I was born and raised in a colony just like this one, on a planet with similar landmass. I miss it."

"What brought you to IPF?"

"Work. Adventure. As lead Peace Coordinator for the colony where I grew up, I got to call a lot of the shots, got to be part of a lot of negotiations. Got to spend a lot of time on the surface. Until Garth showed up. I should still be the lead Peace Coordinator. I have always been good at working things through with colonists. When I first started, the IPF told me that I'd be able to see more planets, more solar systems than I could dream of." He stopped. "You know, from up there, inside the mother ship, they all look exactly the same. As the years went by, I got homesick. I can't go home, though. You can never go home," he let his voice trail off.

"But you can start a new home," Stark said.

"I hope so." James leaned his head against the window and let the vibration of the engines lull him to sleep.

# CHAPTER 14

**BRANDON ROUNDED THE CORNER,** keeping his eye on the surrounding area. With his back against the building, he approached the hangar door, opened it, and hastened inside. He heard voices coming from the rear of the cruiser, low, in discussion. He closed the door and walked as quickly as possible toward the voices. "Hey, I was wondering where you were."

Jacobs gave Brandon a wave and went back to his conversation with Palmer.

"He's free to roam around as he pleases," Palmer said, her head cocked, obviously wondering what Brandon thought of that.

"Just like we are. A trusting group. Or at least that's what they'd like us to believe. There's something very odd, and alarming, about their nonchalance."

Palmer made a few peripheral glances into the corners of the hangar. "Exactly."

Brandon lifted the handheld and presented it to Palmer or Jacobs, whoever wanted it. "Probably don't need this," he said, indicating that he understood her reference to hidden microphones and cameras. When no one took it, he clipped it to his belt.

"We should have expected it," she said. "They have little reason to trust us."

"We were given the all-mighty okay by the Mesoans, though. That should have accounted for something. Maybe not this much freedom, but something," Brandon said.

"That may have helped them trust us, but Jacobs never met the aliens," she said.

Jacobs shook his head. "What aliens? There are aliens? That's impossible."

"Hold tight, Cowboy," Palmer said.

"It's true, or at least as far as we can tell," Brandon told Jacobs. "I thought you knew."

"I knew there was something," Jacobs said. "But something covers a lot of territory."

"What kind of secret service are you involved with?" Brandon inquired.

Palmer broke in, "I thought you connected with the aliens somehow."

"I did. But as we discussed before, they didn't provide us with much return information, shall we say. I'm starting to wonder about them. A trained monkey could have pushed a button and a prerecorded message could have been played. I wasn't watching Oliver or Eldon. And I should have known better. If my life were on the line…"

"But the way they look?" Palmer said.

"That's what I mean. These guys pumped us up so high just before the Mesoans came through the door that we weren't thinking straight. We were expecting something amazing, and that's what we got, true or not," Brandon said. "Thinking back, maybe the suits were the only things that were strangely shaped, and those images on screen. The actual people inside the suits didn't have to look like that."

"You are smarter than you look," Jacobs said.

Palmer and Brandon shot him a look and he raised his hands into the air. "I didn't mean it like that."

"Good," Palmer said. "You don't get to his job, or his rank, without passing a lot of high-level testing."

Jacobs turned back to the conversation at hand. "They looked like monkeys? Were they humanoid, then? If you connected that meant that they were intelligent. Jesus. I can't believe this." His eyes got big.

Brandon thought for a moment as he stared at Palmer. "Reminds me of the Ekks," he said.

"Ekks?"

"These birds I ran across out there. They have round faces. No beaks. I haven't seen any other animals on the planet so far, but I wonder if they all have round heads and faces."

"Faces," Jacobs said. "They have faces?"

Brandon ignored him. "If I'm right, then these aliens would be no different. Like I said, they could be a bunch of monkeys. They could actually look like what we were shown, and still not be intelligent."

Palmer looked over at Jacobs. "If we are being listened too, then they know we're figuring this out; or at least that we're suspicious. So," she searched the ceiling, her palms and eyes turned up, "what's next guys? You going to tell us the truth?"

"If they are listening, they're not going to answer you now," Jacobs said.

"I'd like to visit those things again," Brandon said.

"Can't. Not if the IPF landers are on their way," Palmer said. She turned back to Jacobs. "We're going to the tower. My cruiser checks out fine."

"That was you I saw sneaking in here, then," Brandon said.

Jacobs gave him a quizzical look. "I've been in here for a few hours. I knew she wouldn't go long without checking on this thing. It was the only way I could think to find you two."

Palmer said, "That thing is my life and my livelihood."

"Sorry. I meant no disrespect. I just meant that I knew you'd come along. So, you saw something?" he said to Brandon.

"In the shadows." He dropped his cuffs on the ground and used his foot to slide them into place.

"Watch out," Palmer said, backing a few steps.

Brandon kneeled and then lay next to his cuffs and slid his arms into place, first securing one and then the other. When he got up, he could feel their heft. They felt good. "I'm ready."

"I hope they are." Palmer led them toward the door.

"Don't care, now," Brandon said.

Jacobs ran ahead. "I'll open the door for you."

Brandon stood back and let Jacobs walk in front of him. "What were you doing on that mother ship anyway?"

"Investigating the morale most of the time. The general attitudes toward EC. A lot of IPF sections have managed to go independent through alliances with colonies just like this one. Earth Central has cracked down on them, but it appears to have made things worse. Section 204 is a mess in that regard," Jacobs said.

"You're a fucking psychologist?" Palmer said.

"Hey, don't say it like that. My specialty is in Large Base Dynamics, which can be colonies or mother ships."

"What about the findings down here?" Brandon asked.

"I only heard rumors that it was important. I had no idea…"

"Neither do we," Brandon said. "So it stays quiet until we do have an idea." He stopped a few feet from the door.

Jacobs grabbed the handle and pushed it open.

Brandon stepped through, both arms raised and ready. He stepped into the night, head low and crouched, ready to run if he had to. The darkness settled all around them. The air temperature had dropped so low that he could see his breath. Nothing unusual appeared in the general vicinity.

"Let's get going," Palmer said.

"Stay together and behind me," Brandon said.

Palmer and Jacobs followed Brandon across the tarmac toward the tower. "Shit, something scurried over there." Palmer pointed to Brandon's right where a clump of brush grew from the ground.

"Come out or I'll blow you away," Brandon yelled.

"You can't do that. What if it's one of them?" Jacobs said. "Or some frightened kid?"

"Haven't seen a kid around here since we arrived," Brandon said. He started walking toward the clump of brush.

"What the hell are you doing?" Palmer yelled after him.

"Checking it out." He took a few more steps and a thick form stepped from behind the brush. It moved on two legs and had a long neck. Brandon recognized the Ekk right away. A young one. "It's an Ekk," he said, turning his head to glance at the others.

"Ekk," the thing said.

"Ekk," Brandon said again.

"Ekk."

"Knock it off," Palmer said. "I take it they're not dangerous?"

"Cannibals," Brandon said. "My understanding is that they only eat each other."

"Hard on a species, isn't it," Palmer said.

"They've got to eat more than that or they'd die out," Jacobs said.

"Don't know, don't care. But, take a look at it," Brandon said as he advanced another slow step.

"Oh, good God," Jacobs said. "It has a face."

Brandon took another step and the Ekk trotted off into the darkness, so he turned back around and started walking to meet up with the other two.

As the two of them stood there waiting for Brandon to catch up, Palmer pointed, "Now what? What the hell is going on here? Is everyone bluffing?"

"If they are, why are they," Brandon said.

"As weird as those things are," Jacobs said, "it proves nothing about what you two saw. Let's keep an open mind. I'll be the first one to doubt that there's any intelligent life in the galaxy, maybe in the universe. But we don't know for sure."

"Why should we trust your opinion?" Palmer said.

"Don't trust it. I don't care. I'm just saying..." Jacobs' eyes lit up. "Uh, oh."

Brandon looked over his shoulder to see what Jacobs grew concern over. About thirty Ekks trotted from the darkness. Adult Ekks. "You guys start walking."

Palmer and Jacobs walked slowly away from Brandon who rotated back toward the Ekks. The tower stood a good hundred yards away and at the pace they were traveling would take quite a while to reach.

Brandon motioned for them to move faster. "Don't run, but get going." Then he stared into the flock and said, "Ekk," to get their attention.

Several of the Ekks advanced, but none spoke.

"Get going, you guys." Brandon could see the tension build in the Ekks and knew that they were about to charge. No one wanted to be in a stampede of Ekks, not even him. With no more than a turn of his wrist, Brandon put a bead on the one closest to him. "Come on, baby, just try it."

The moment the bird beast hunkered down, Brandon yelled to the others, "Run." He pulled off his first shot, dropping the bird that was about to spring into the air toward him. Just as he did, though, five others took to the air like chickens, clumsy but accurate, all wing and squawk. He picked two of them off, but another three dropped to the ground behind him and headed for Jacobs and Palmer. "Watch it," he yelled, but there was no need.

Palmer held a stunner in her hand and swung around. She dropped into a kneeling position and with both hands on the gun dropped two more Ekks. The third one shot off to their right like a frightened mouse.

Brandon had already shifted to the side to get out of the way of the oncoming Ekks. From limited experience, though, he knew that some of them would stop to gather the dead birds. Others, about half of them, ran toward the bird that had escaped both Brandon and Palmer's blasts. They curved around toward the tower as though they knew where the three of them were going. "What the hell," he said. "Are they thinking ahead?"

Palmer and Jacobs waited for Brandon to catch up with them. "You have the big guns," Palmer said. "Go first."

"Thanks, Sweetheart," Brandon said sarcastically as he passed them and headed straight for the birds.

The door in front of the tower opened and one of the controllers, a squat round man, stepped outside in front of the Ekks.

"What's he think he's doing?" Jacobs said while jogging with the others.

"He must know something we don't," Brandon said.

The little man lifted his hand to his mouth and suddenly a loud whistle pierced the air.

The Ekks stopped charging and shook their heads madly. Another whistle and they lowered their heads near a lifted wing as though trying to protect their ears. A third whistle and they began their stampede again, only this time toward the brush at the edges of the runway where they had come from.

"I could have whistled," Palmer said as the three of them approached the man at the door.

"No one told you?" The man looked surprised.

"Nope." Brandon shoved by him and took the stairs two at a time. He slammed the door open at the top. "You knew," he said to Oliver.

"They seldom attack," he said getting up from his chair to greet Brandon, but then backing away from his approach.

"That's not the fucking point you son-of-a-bitch. One of them could have been hurt out there." Brandon continued to advance until Oliver leaned backward across one of the control panels. Brandon was well aware that several stunners pointed at him, but he had his cuffs on and his finger pointing directly at Oliver. No one would dare shoot if they knew anything about cuffs, and it appeared as though they did.

"We can deal with this," Jacob said the second he came into the control room.

"I'm dealing." Brandon cocked his head. "Besides you already attempted to get rid of me. Oliver here is number two. The next person, I kill on sight."

Eldon came over to Brandon. He appeared calm, but also a little satisfied at the confrontation. He put a hand on Brandon's forearm and pushed lightly.

Brandon lowered his arm.

"He's telling the truth. Something must be riling them up. They never attack to harm anyone, only to threaten," Eldon said.

"Maybe they're hungry," Brandon said.

"We told you," Eldon said, "they only eat each other."

"Wouldn't they die out," Jacobs said, obviously holding to his position from earlier.

"Come on." Eldon patted Brandon's shoulder.

Brandon backed off and Oliver, who had kept quiet, let out a long breath of air. "I didn't expect a problem," he said.

Eldon said. "They hate loud noises of any kind: car engines, whistles, even a woman's scream can get them to run off." He glanced over at Palmer. "To answer your other question, they produce numerous eggs a day and the eggs can incubate and hatch completely on their own." He addressed Jacobs about it. "So, my friend, cannibalism does nothing but keep the population down. It works for them."

Eldon had an air of arrogance about his knowledge of the Ekks that would normally have bothered Brandon, but aimed at Jacobs, he found that he didn't mind at all. In fact, Brandon was beginning to like Eldon. He was a passionate man. Sloppy and stupid at times, but who could fault that? And, so far, Eldon was the only person who had the balls to openly oppose Oliver's command, which was something Brandon could admire.

Brandon backed off and Oliver nodded for the stunners to be lowered. Palmer hadn't said a word as the men figured out their new chain of command. Typical pilot move, Brandon thought, stand behind the highest bidder. As Brandon saw it, he had climbed the ladder a few rungs already. And so had Eldon. He stepped into the center of the room and asked, "Where are we?"

Oliver mumbled that they had just been hailed by the IPF lander.

"Who's coming?" Jacobs asked.

"The CEO," one of the operators said. "A mister Killjoy."

"That doesn't make sense. Since when does the CEO make a trip like this?" Jacobs didn't look happy.

"When he has other plans," Palmer said.

Brandon welcomed Palmer's take on the situation. After all, she'd notice a strategic move if anyone would. And his job, as he recalled their conversation, was to feel out those in the room, but that wasn't going to happen easily. He had brought the emotional tension up pretty high with his anger so, literally, the whole damned room was on edge. Dumb move. But he didn't know that when he charged up the stairs.

"Have you opened communications?" Palmer asked.

The controller nodded. "We only acknowledged them and told them that we'd allow them to land." His eyes drifted toward Oliver.

Brandon did notice the eye contact. "What'd Killjoy say? There must have been more."

The young man waited for Oliver's okay, but Oliver didn't have to give it. Eldon said, "He apologized for shooting her cruiser down."

"Eldon!" Oliver said in an obvious attempt to stop him from talking.

"We need their help. You've been pushing that all along. And if we're actually going to get it, we'd better start laying this out straight." Eldon was on a roll.

Brandon was proud of him. He must have gained some additional confidence from the interaction a moment before. "I'm with him," Brandon said. "Spill it."

"That's all," Eldon said. "We haven't responded."

Palmer rushed to the controller. "Did he say why they shot us down?"

The man kept quiet and looked over at Oliver again.

Frustrated with the slowness of the interactions Brandon lifted a finger and pointed it at Oliver's chest.

After a moment of shuffling, a dozen stunners pointed at him again.

"Just in case none of you know anything about cuffs," Brandon said. "If I'm shot or hit over the head it sends a pulse through my body called a reactive nerve response. That's the same thing I do when I fire this thing." He nodded quickly, "Yeah, I think you're getting it. Hit me with anything and my cuff will blow his fucking head off." Brandon produced a huge fake smile. "It won't look good."

The controller squeaked an answer. "He said that you," he pointed at Jacobs, "were a spy."

"No new information there," Brandon said.

"And that she was a rogue pilot."

Brandon laughed out loud at the statement. "I've known that for years. It's what I love about her."

"Earth Central frowns on…" Jacobs never finished his statement.

Brandon lifted his left hand and pointed a finger at Jacobs. "I, for one, would not miss you."

"Jesus," Oliver said. "You can't kill all of us."

Brandon held everyone's attention for the next few seconds. "I can kill all of you," he said. He lowered his arms. "But I won't." To Palmer he said, "How do we respond to Killjoy?"

Palmer leaned over the controls. "Tell them only that you got their message and that you've reconfirmed their approach."

He relayed the message.

"How long?" Palmer asked.

This time the man looked Palmer straight in the eye and didn't waver, didn't show any sign of needing Oliver's approval. "An hour or so."

"Keep me posted," Palmer said, "and open the line."

The controller flipped the switch that opened the communications line so that everyone in the tower could hear the conversation between him and the IPF pilot.

"Copy that," the pilot said. Then a second voice came over the intercom. A friendly voice. "This is Killjoy. I expected to hear from Oliver. Is he there?"

Everyone in the room turned their eyes to Oliver. "We're all here," Oliver said in a loud voice.

There was a muffled sound and a moment of silence before Killjoy came back on. "I don't have a lot of time. We need to have our meeting right away. Can you arrange that?"

"I believe we can make that happen," Oliver said. He shrugged.

Palmer acknowledged that she approved of the response.

"Good," Killjoy said.

The speakers clicked and the pilot came back on. "Fifty seven minutes to touchdown," he said.

The controller turned the speakers off and answered the pilot.

Brandon brought his attention back to Oliver. "We're all here," he said. "I wonder what that's supposed to mean."

"I answered him."

"You're sweating a bit and it's gotten chilly in here." Brandon cocked his head. "We might want to talk in private."

"There's a room downstairs," Eldon said as he made his way to the door. Oliver and Brandon followed, while Jacobs and Palmer brought up the rear.

Brandon heard her spouting orders to those in the control room as she left.

Once inside the small meeting room, Brandon remained standing while the others sat. "So," he said. "Where shall we start?"

# CHAPTER 15

**OLIVER REGAINED COMPOSURE** once he settled into a space around the table. He turned on Eldon right away. "This is a very touchy situation and you could easily have made things worse."

"Don't be yelling at my man," Brandon said.

Oliver appeared shocked by the comment. "Your man? He attacked you and you've been on each other since you arrived. Now he's your man?"

Brandon placed a cuffed hand on the table, nothing more, just rested it there. "Male bonding," he said.

"This won't go over with the governmental board," Oliver said.

Palmer sat back in her chair and brushed her hair behind her ears. Brandon liked her profile. She had strong cheekbones and chin. The slope of her face reminded him of the moon. Seeing that she wanted to speak, he easily gave her the floor.

"I see that you two are split in how to proceed. But recognize this: if you let us in on everything that's going on — the truth that is — then perhaps we truly can help. Without the truth, you're wasting our time and yours."

"Or you could screw everything up," Oliver said.

"I have a question," Brandon said. "Why give us free range, weapons and everything, if you weren't going to get us involved completely? Eventually we'd see through your lies and turn on you."

"We are involved," Palmer said. "They wanted us handy if bullets started flying. That's all. They knew that if we were in the line of fire we'd help, and that we're the best protection they could possibly have. For now."

"Oh," Brandon said.

Eldon sat forward and leaned both forearms on the table, his head staring down while he apparently organized his thoughts. "I'm here because I'm the head of the scientific community who's trying to understand what exactly we have down there. Oliver, on the other hand, handles all business and negotiations for the colony, local and intergalactic. He's one of those who are in charge of our attempt at independence from Earth Central, primarily aimed at allowing us to be self-sufficient."

"I don't like this," Oliver said. "We should call the board."

"Too late," Brandon said.

"I know," Eldon said to Oliver. "I'm not positive this is the best way either. But the board would just back you. You know that. I want a fair hearing for a change. People who aren't connected with anyone." He tapped the table a few times and sat a bit straighter. "He would have to fill you in on details, but as I understand things, Earth Central, through the arm of Intergalactic Peace Force, essentially owns the colonies and the whole planet. Typically, when they get involved, they'll send experts in to help with discovering what ores are available and profitable, what local crops can be exported, and they help with cataloging the flora and fauna of the planet. But they also send in their own leaders. They take over."

"I wouldn't like that either," Palmer said.

"Truthfully," Eldon said, "they'd shove us aside and take over all the research we've started and push us out of the loop."

"No," Brandon said. "You found the things. You have the right to continue your communications with them. To continue your research."

"They have no rights under the present circumstances," Palmer said. "I've seen it before. I'm surprised you haven't."

"EC has never been less than generous with me, even when they assign me to places like Section 204, run by slime balls. But that's not all IPF Sections. I've worked with others that would never think of sacrificing people for their own personal gain."

"The problems occur with trying to cover too much space," Oliver said. "Literally."

Palmer leaned in so that she could glance over at Oliver and then back to Brandon. "There are all manner of self-motivations we probably haven't seen yet. Worse ones than this."

"That's it, then?" Brandon narrowed his eyes at Jacobs. "It's your turn, Buster."

"I have nothing." He spread his hands in front of him then put them back together.

Brandon lifted his hand from the table.

"Don't. That won't help," Palmer raised a hand to slow him. "He's a psychologist remember."

"There's a leak," Jacobs blurted out. "Make you happy?" All eyes turned on him and he shrunk into his chair. "Fine. That's all I know. It's got to be direct from this planet to Killjoy otherwise he wouldn't be coming down here. I've met him often enough to know a few things for sure, he's a schemer. And he's greedy. And you can't trust anything he says."

"That's it? Shit, we gathered that," Brandon said.

"He'll double cross whoever he's working with down here," Jacobs said. "If he needs to, for sure, and if he feels like it as well. No morals."

"Have you met him?" Eldon said to Oliver.

Oliver gritted his teeth and took a breath. He didn't look very happy to Brandon. "He has," Brandon said.

Oliver jerked his head around. All eyes switched from Jacobs to Oliver. "You have no idea what trouble we're in," he said. "Earth Central will shove us all aside. They'll take over everything. They might even send us back out to find another planet while they rape this one." He glared at Eldon, probably for starting the whole conversation. "You won't be in charge of this anymore. You know that?"

"You told him?" Eldon accused.

Oliver stood in an angry rush and stepped back. "We applied for independence a long time ago. Nothing was happening." He bent down and slammed his fist on the table. "We needed protection. The IPF could help. They want their independence too. No one wants to be under Earth Central rule anymore. They're light years away. There is no protective body left. It's crazy out here. We're dropped off alone to see if we survive." He turned to Brandon. "And if we do survive, they come years later and take what they want."

"We signed up for this. All of us," Eldon said. His chair squeaked as he rotated it toward Palmer and Brandon. "We're under a lot of pressure." He glanced at Oliver. "Every one of us. He's not normally like this. You have to understand…"

"Pressure doesn't have to lead to betrayal," Brandon said.

Eldon softened as he continued to look at Oliver. "But it's our home now. Can you understand that? We don't want to give that up."

"He offered the protection we needed," Oliver looked scared. "The leverage to gain our independence from Earth Central. We want to stay here. We have to protect the Mesoans. They're helpless without us. I'm sure that together we can create a better society, a better way of working with one another than what Earth Central can possibly supply."

"Yeah, a utopia," Brandon said. "I've seen how that works."

"With help, protection, we at least have a chance," Oliver said.

Jacobs spoke up. "Not from Killjoy. He's the one who sacrificed Clark and sent these two to blow up your operations to make you vulnerable. If you had let them land…"

"That was staged," Oliver said.

"You put us in danger?" Eldon looked pissed.

"It's not like that. I knew we'd be okay," Oliver said. "The fighting wasn't supposed to last this long."

"Jacobs?" Brandon turned toward the psychologist as a gauge.

"My orders were to eject both of you the second bullets began to fly," Jacobs said. "I'm sorry. I felt terrible, even for Clark, even though he was scheduled for execution and volunteered for the job. I couldn't blow my cover," he protested.

"Then you knew about the load of explosives," Palmer said.

"Not until you did." Jacobs shook his head. "My undercover job was to facilitate early runs. Standard policy is to send in a fake officer to test the waters."

"We know policy," Brandon said. "But we didn't know he was the first." He looked at Palmer for confirmation.

She nodded.

"This is the first time I was briefed to provide an early ejection," Jacobs said. "Everyone would be safe who was supposed to be. When I found out about the explosives, I panicked."

Palmer took the floor again. "We're getting off course here. What I need to know from Oliver is this: Does Killjoy know about the Mesoans?"

The room got quiet. Oliver and Eldon locked stares.

"What?" Palmer said, addressing the silence between them.

"We don't know about the Mesoans," Oliver said.

"Shit," Brandon swung away from the table, took a few steps, then swung back, placing his knuckles on the wooden surface in front of him.

Eldon spoke up. "They read us. Truthfully, they could be reacting based on what they read from us. Their understanding of our technology was slow, sketchy at first."

"That would be expected," Jacobs said. When everyone turned to look at him again, he shrugged. "Even if they were intelligent. Means nothing to me."

"It didn't feel right, at first," Oliver said. "I had my doubts even though I knew that we had to protect them."

"And I've become more of a believer," Eldon said. "I want to go deeper. I want to enter their world and not just our meeting place."

"I sensed that from each of you," Brandon said. "I knew how you felt."

"You?" Jacobs said. "That's hard to believe."

Brandon ignored Jacobs. "Why don't you go deeper?" he said to Eldon.

"They won't let us," Eldon said.

"Killjoy believes too, doesn't he?" Jacobs said.

"Yes," Oliver said. "I told him our findings were conclusive. I guaranteed him. I lied to get his help."

Palmer perked up at that statement. "To a man like Killjoy, that could mean everything. He could easily sell the discovery to the highest bidder, bargain for money and supplies, negotiate independence..."

"Let's stop him," Brandon said to everyone. Then he engaged Eldon directly. "And while we're doing that, can you do anything to find out more about those things? I want to know if we're dealing with something extraordinary, something never found in the galaxy before, or are they just a bunch of monkeys reading our minds and feeding back what we give them."

Oliver jumped in. "We're not sure the best thing is to stop Killjoy. We may still need him."

Brandon couldn't believe what he heard, but before he could speak Jacobs cut in. "I'm sure," he said. "You've got to believe me. The man is not on your side."

"We'll lose our chance at independence. This is our only opportunity," Oliver yelled at them. "It's all we have."

"Enough," Palmer stood. "Listen boys, you're either with us or not. We don't have much time to prepare. So, which is it?" She pointed at Eldon for an answer.

"In," he said.

"Well, I'm in," Jacobs said.

"You better be," Brandon said. "Because you owe me big time."

"There's no killing you if we wanted to," Jacobs said with a laugh. "You've proven that."

"No humor," Brandon said. "You're on probation." He rubbed his cuffed hands together. "You need to repent for what you've been involved with so far — even if what you did seemed necessary to stay undercover." One person in the room had not answered. "You?" Brandon said to Oliver.

"What choice do I have?"

"If you try to fuck this up for a second…" Brandon threatened.

Oliver shook his head. "I won't. Even if I don't agree, I want nothing more than for the colony to survive. I want us to stay in our homes." He hesitated. "I want the Mesoans safe."

"That's it, then." Palmer headed for the door. "Assemble all your pilots in hangar one in ten minutes. Killjoy's almost here and I don't trust anyone at this point."

"Our pilots? What do you need them for? Killjoy's coming alone in a lander," Oliver said.

"We're going to be ready," Palmer said. "Pilots. Hangar. Ten." She snapped her fingers at each word. She also alerted Jacobs and Eldon to watch Oliver closely. "Any funny business and you're not a team player," she told Oliver.

"You're coming with me," Palmer tapped Brandon's cuff as she walked past him. She reached over and removed the handheld communicator from his belt and placed it on her own. To Jacobs, she said, "You're staying here so that you can report to us. Every three minutes I want to hear your voice and a one-sentence update. Got that?"

"I have it," Jacobs said.

She jerked her head toward the door and Brandon followed. "I love it when you're in charge," he teased.

She smiled back at him. "Someone has to be."

The sun lit up the morning sky behind the hills. There were no Ekks around, but the flying spiders had come out. The air warmed. Neither of them had much bare skin showing, so the spiders hung around their faces. They swatted at the spiders as they rushed toward the hangar.

Blue sand blew across the ground as a cool wind fell into the valley, probably from a more forested and hospitable place over the mountain in the west. The incoming air smelled fresh. If it wasn't for the spiders it would be a beautiful morning for a stroll.

Brandon kept his eyes on Palmer as she walked ahead of him. Her hips swayed and her hair bounced and twirled in the morning breeze. He couldn't wait until things settled down and they could go somewhere together. Then he remembered that she was supposed to be dead and if the truth didn't come out eventually, she wouldn't get paid. He couldn't afford a vacation on his salary until he saved for a few more months. "Shit."

Palmer turned around. "Shit, what?"

"I don't think you're going to get paid for this job, and I'll probably get orders out of here as soon as we're finished."

She slowed so they walked together for a moment. "I've been thinking of that, too. I was going to surprise you. They paid me up front." She grinned. "How about we stay here for a week or two. If we get through this safely, you could do that, right?" Her eyes brightened. "If not, if you're reassigned right away, we'll find another way."

"You're right. We'll make this work," he said.

Hangar one was where the jets were located. Once inside, there were no spiders. The air felt much warmer than outside, the lights still on from their earlier visit. This time Palmer took a closer look at the jets. She had Brandon drag an external power unit around so that she could hook each jet up one at a time and inspected all instruments, check the flaps and rudders, and look over the landing gear. Every three minutes the relative silence was interrupted with Jacobs' updates. She came out of the cockpit of the last jet smiling. "Good shape. They take care of their equipment."

Brandon accepted her into his arms. "I miss that smile," he said.

"You are not the warrior you think you are," she said.

"I only soften when I'm with you, Babe."

"Even back there," she said. "You telling them that you knew how they felt. That's a bit too sensitive for a brute."

"We can be sensitive and dangerous."

She kissed his forehead. "You can. But you're the only soldier I know who can."

He liked the sound of that.

"Jacobs here," the handheld said. "Twenty-eight minutes to their ETA. Nothing's out of the ordinary." His voice lowered. "I did find out that Oliver has been given full authority over all negotiations. The governmental board has put everything in his hands."

Palmer pulled away from Brandon's arms and yanked the handheld to her mouth. "Where will that be done?"

"I'll let you know in ten minutes," Jacobs said.

"He's taking this two sentence thing to heart," Brandon said.

"Or something's up," Palmer said. "Oh, here are the guys…or gals?"

Brandon turned around and saw that eight out of the ten pilots were women. Each one lean and beautiful. The men stood tall and handsome. "Hand picked?" he said to Palmer.

"Home grown," she answered.

One woman, a redhead about Palmer's height, stepped forward. "Ready for orders."

Palmer shook her hand then had them gather around in a circle and proceeded to explain how she wanted them to fall into formation, which ones would peel off and when, how they'd interact in a combat situation, and what to do if someone was hit. She had it all under control, even though every three minutes was interrupted by Jacobs' quick report. Brandon had seldom seen her in such a situation, and reveled in how well trained she was, and how beautiful she looked when doing what she loved.

He noticed that air battles weren't a lot different than ground battles when it came to organization. She did have a few tricks up her sleeve, though. Things she said reminded him that she was much more aware of the terrain than he'd realized, too. Listening to her confirmed that she was one of the best. At the end of the debriefing, Palmer headed for the door. "You coming?"

The pilots were all looking at him. He shrugged and said, "She's in charge," then followed her outside.

The spiders were gone and the air was warm. Wind had picked up slightly and whistled around the side of the hangar.

"How'd it go?"

"You were there."

"I know, but I couldn't see their faces. Did they follow you? Were they receptive? Or did they look like they didn't understand a word you were saying?"

"They heard me. And I'm fairly sure they'll retain it." She reached up and placed her hand on the back of his neck as they walked, like a friend might do. "They just didn't ask any questions. That always bothers me. There is such a thing as overly confident."

"Like me?"

"You and I are confident in situations we've got experience with. In a brand new situation, you'd be asking all kinds of questions and so would I. Unless they've been in battle before, which I doubt, they should have been asking questions. That's all I'm saying."

"I see your point. So what's that mean when you're up there?" He motioned toward the sky.

"We'll find out, won't we?"

Jacobs' voice interrupted them. "Meeting will be held in the building we were taken to first."

"The pit?" Palmer said.

"Hold on." There was a muffled sound as Jacobs found the answer.

"Yes, where they have all their meetings. My suspicion is that Killjoy wants to see the discovery," Jacobs said.

"I'm sure he does," Brandon whispered.

Palmer keyed the mic, "At least one of us will be there."

"How can we do that?" Brandon said. "We don't know who's going to be with him, who might recognize us. Shit, he might recognize us. Just because we weren't introduced personally doesn't mean he hasn't seen photos. In fact, I'm sure he has."

"One second. Let me think."

Brandon shut up.

"Let them do what they always do, whatever they've planned. Just be sure that there's an open comm line in the room. You," she slapped the back of his neck, "stay outside the door. There are two doors in there. Killjoy will have one door guarded. You'll be outside the other one. Any funny business and you step inside."

"Makes sense. Fairly standard, but what about you?"

"I'm going to be airborne the whole time they're here. I don't care if all we do is fly in circles. I've scheduled refueling times for each pilot. We're not safe until this thing's over. If Jacobs is right, we can't trust anything about this situation." She stopped before opening the door to the tower. "And if I'm right, we can't trust any of these guys, not even Jacobs."

"Not much to go on. I'm used to knowing who my enemy is." He reached around Palmer and opened the door to the tower for her.

"Jacobs stays hidden with you," she said as she passed him.

"Now your telling me I'm the baby-sitter."

# ChAPTER 16

INSIDE THE ROOM AT THE TOP OF THE TOWER, sunrays streamed through the window overlooking the runway. An electronic light shield had been engaged, but the tint wasn't enough to keep Brandon from squinting while his eyes adjusted for the first few seconds he entered the room from the darker stairs. Over the tarmac, a few lizardlike things scurried from one side of the runway to the other. Brandon leaned and stared a moment to be sure he wasn't hallucinating. "Those things…" He indicated the movement beyond the window.

"We call them geckos," one of the operators said. "They don't climb like geckos, but they make a lot of noise like them."

"Do they bite?"

"Not at all. You can chase them down and catch them pretty easily," he said. "Not fast either."

"Why didn't I see them before?" Brandon asked.

"Don't know. I suppose you have to look for them. They blend into the scenery when they're not moving. And they'll just bask in the sun all day if not disturbed."

"Hmm," Brandon said. There had been a crew change while he and Palmer were in the hangar dealing with the pilots. The man he talked with was someone he didn't recognize, smooth faced, polite. When Brandon turned back to the matter at hand, Oliver and Eldon were there, sitting at a small table. Each had the look of exhaustion on his face. "Get these guys some coffee. You gotta perk up for the meeting."

One of the controllers stood to go.

"Jasp is what we call it here," Oliver said. "It's from the bark of one of the trees. We steep it more like tea."

"Jasp him up, then," Brandon said to the gofer who rushed to a corner of the tower and poured them each a large cup.

Jacobs sat across the room from the other two, the comm unit sitting in front of him. He interrupted the short conversation. "They'll be here in no time."

Brandon told the gofer, "Him too."

Brandon and Palmer looked out the window. The lander could be seen in the distance coming toward them. "I'd better go," Palmer said as Oliver, Eldon, and Jacobs were being served their jasp.

"How do I get hold of you?" Brandon said. "We have ship's communicators, but they're open lines. I need something private."

One of the controllers swung around and got out of his chair. "I can fix that if you like?"

Palmer gave him a quizzical look.

The man was very slight, almost boyish in appearance. His clothes were too big for his small frame. He held out a smooth hand. "Let me have your communicator."

Palmer removed the communicator from her wrist and handed it to him. She jerked her head indicating that Brandon do the same.

The boy pulled a small screwdriver from his shirt pocket. "I do this stuff all the time," he said. "When I was in school, my friends and I would have our own conversations, text and voice." While he talked he removed a pair of wire cutters from his pocket and snipped a wire. "One more second," he said as he adjusted a flat-switch. He snapped the back onto the communicator and handed it to Palmer. "Yours next," he said to Brandon. In another minute he handed that one back. "Done. No one can hear the two of you talking to one another now. You have your own frequency." He went back to sit at the console.

Brandon looked at Palmer and shrugged his shoulders.

"Believe him," Eldon said. "He may look young, but he's the chief tech here."

"Chief tech?" Brandon said.

"Yeah, why?" Oliver said.

"You're not prepared for any of this, are you? You're using everyone you have," Brandon said.

"I told you we needed help," Oliver held the cup of jasp between his hands when it wasn't at his lips.

"Desperate is more like it." Palmer stepped next to Brandon.

Oliver looked as though he was about to cry, as though the tension had increased too much for him, or too fast, or both. "We have a race of Mesoan to protect. That's our primary job, whether independence is the only way for us to go—so that we can bargain for support from Earth Central—or whether we need to combine forces with Section 204 of the IPF to protected us from pirates and other outside attacks."

"Or Both. We heard you down there," Brandon said. "Really. But what if they're not…"

Eldon's eyes got huge and he shook his head while scanning the room.

Brandon realized that no one else knew that there was any doubt about the aliens. That uncertainty belonged only to a few, Eldon and Oliver for sure. But who else? Or worse yet, who didn't know: the governmental board? He shook his head at them. They had lied to their own people. The whole operation, the whole planet teetered on a dubious discovery. If they received their independence and the Mesoans weren't for real, they'd fall flat on their faces. The IPF would still retain their independence, but leave C-47 high and dry while they went out to find another more worthy colony to partner with. "You idiots," Brandon said under his breath.

Palmer touched his arm. "Look, I have to go. Stick to the plan. We'll discuss all this," she made a swirling motion around the table to include their conversation, "after our first contact is over." She looked at the other two. "Stall Killjoy so he has to stay overnight." Back to Brandon with a stern look. "We'll figure it out."

She had understood the flimsiness of the situation too, he could tell. But how would they figure it out? Brandon just nodded. There was little else to do but go along until they could regroup. He watched Palmer leave. After she disappeared through the door, he lifted his communicator, keyed it with a flick of his wrist, and said, "Be careful up there."

"Always," she said.

"They can't take off now," Oliver said. "Killjoy will see that as an attack."

"Jets," Brandon said loud enough for the controllers to hear. "If they ask, tell them they're on routine flights. Make something up."

"With weapons?" Oliver said.

"I doubt they'll be checking," Brandon said. "If they do, your guys will come up with something. For now, let's get to the meeting room." He motioned for Jacobs to join them.

"I have to stay," Oliver said.

"Why?"

"Killjoy will become suspicious if I don't greet him as he exits the lander. I'm his liaison," Oliver said, his voice shaky and cracking.

Brandon hadn't thought of that, and obviously neither had Palmer. Oliver would be alone with Killjoy for the entire trip from the lander to the meeting room. He looked at Jacobs, but knew Killjoy would recognize him. Eldon, sure, but could he trust him enough? "You, tech boy, come here."

The boy got up and walked over to where the three of them were.

"You're going with these two guys," Brandon said. "And I want you to stick with them like glue. Listen to everything that's said."

"Are you crazy?" Oliver said.

"You can trust me," Eldon said. "Let us go alone, as planned."

Brandon looked from one man to the other. "I know, and I do trust you, but I need a third man. It's just how it is."

Oliver shrugged. "Larry, it looks like you've gotten a promotion for a day or two. But, keep your mouth shut at all times."

Larry smiled from ear to ear and nodded his head excitedly. "Wow. I get to meet the CEO of an IPF mother ship. I can't believe this. Wait 'til I tell the guys."

"Nothing," Oliver said. "You say nothing. And you don't tell the guys anything but who you met. This is to be handled as though it's a top secret mission. Understand?"

"I'll keep completely quiet," Larry said.

"I want the meeting room bugged," Brandon said to Larry. He was the perfect person to choose. It would give Larry a purpose. "Can you have that done now?"

Larry rubbed his hands together. "Easy as pie." He removed what looked like a watch and ran over to the control area and opened a drawer. Brandon didn't care what was in there or what he did with it as long as it worked when he was finished. "Jacobs, you're coming with me." He turned back one last time and told Oliver and Eldon, "Best behavior." Before he left with Jacobs, Larry delivered an ear bud for each of them.

"Very short range, but it should be fine within twenty or thirty feet," Larry said.

Brandon inserted the ear bud. "We need transportation."

"There should be a truck in every hangar. Use one of those for now. I have someone coming for when Killjoy gets here," Oliver said.

Larry motioned for Brandon and Jacobs to go downstairs.

Half way to the bottom of the tower, Brandon heard Larry say in a whisper, "Can you hear me?"

"Yes," Brandon said, but there was no response.

"Can you hear me," Larry said again.

Brandon looked at Jacobs who nodded. He turned and yelled up the stairs, "Yes!"

Another whisper came. "Good, then you're all set."

"One way communication," Brandon said. "This should be interesting."

The sun felt extra hot that day. Brandon looked for the lizards as he walked toward the hangar. The wind continued to push waves of blue sand around in a very thin layer over the runway. The air smelled fresh, earthy. By the time they were outside the building, the background noise of the transmitter had faded completely. The next thing he heard was a jet engine run up before takeoff. He jogged to the edge of one of the hangars to watch. Jacobs followed on his heels. Brandon admired the way each piloted jet slipped from the runway and penetrated the air so smoothly. He loved the halo of heat that distorted the air behind the jet, making it look fluid as it moved into the distance. He hadn't been inside an old ground-running aircraft for a long time, but could literally feel what it was like to be in each jet as a passenger. He took a deep breath once the last one lifted into the sky.

"Been a long time?" Jacobs asked.

"It has," Brandon said.

"For me too. I love flying in those things. Ever been in a prop?"

"Once, a long time ago, but I don't remember the feel like I do in one of those," Brandon told him. He gestured to the lander homing in on them from a short distance. "Killjoy's probably asking questions of the tower as we speak."

"Fuck him," Jacobs said.

"We'd better get going." Brandon took the lead. "You don't like the guy at all."

"The truth?" Jacobs said. "They don't give me jobs where I even might like people. I'm continually put undercover around megalomaniacs, neurotics, and schizophrenics. Power does that to more people than you may think."

"The pressure?"

"Perhaps. Sometimes it's the availability of drugs. Simple as that. What I do is locate the problem. Often there are a series of people, all near the top, who are equally crazy. All of them out for themselves, but willing to work together for the big prize."

"Crazy, that a technical term?" Brandon said.

Jacobs gave a little laugh. "Yeah, I guess you could say that."

Even with the cuffs weighing him down, Brandon walked fast enough that Jacobs had to double step every ten feet or so to keep up. Palmer would have had no trouble keeping the pace. "You think he's dangerous?"

"More than you can imagine," Jacobs said. "He's the kind of guy who can fake being on your side so well you'd trust him with intimate details about your lovelife, and then he'd turn on you so fast that you'd swear he wasn't even the same person. These C-47 people don't want to deal with him on any level."

"Well, it's our job to keep that from happening." Brandon slowed and put his arm out to stop Jacobs' advance. "Hold on for a second," he said. A lizard basked in the sun a few feet away. Brandon took two huge strides and then dived onto the ground, grabbed the lizard with both hands, and rolled onto his back.

Jacobs ran over. "How the hell do you do that without firing that weapon of yours?"

"It's all in the way you handle yourself," Brandon said as he pivoted onto one knee. He pulled the lizard to a space between him and Jacobs. "What do you think?" he said as he held the thing out.

"What am I looking for?" Jacobs said.

"It's face," Brandon said. "Every animal on this planet, even this thing, has a round head and a face." He turned it to look at it directly. "Almost human looking," he said, "just like the Mesoans."

"I didn't see them, but I believe you. But what's it mean?"

Brandon let the lizard go and it scurried away. "I'm still trying to figure that out." He stood back up. "Let's go."

As they rounded the hangar to check for a truck to drive to the pit site, Brandon spied Palmer walking toward her cruiser. She must have just finished opening the hangar doors so that she could get out. "Hey, a little late aren't you," he yelled.

Palmer stopped and waited for him to get closer. "The jets are enough of a worry for Killjoy, I didn't want to alarm him with my cruiser in the sky. He shot me down, remember?"

"True, true. So, you heading out soon?"

"He'll land near the refueling station," she said. "I'll be sitting right up there in my cruiser and should be able to see them over there," she went from pointing at her cruiser to pointing in the distance where the road rounded a clump of trees. "Once they pass that way, I'll boot up and head out. He'll never know."

"Smart lady," Brandon said. He reached out and tapped the communicator on her wrist. "Stay in touch, okay?"

"Every hour or so. You have enough on your plate, I'm sure."

"If we get him to stay overnight, what's the flight plan?" Brandon said.

"Oh, we'll come back from time to time. Have to refuel. But I'd like to keep a rotation going as long as he's here." Palmer turned around. "You'd better get going too," she said as she walked toward the cruiser.

A truck had been parked near a temporary office in one corner. Someone, probably ground crew, sat inside the office. Brandon waved to the man and motioned for him to come out. The man came to the office door and yelled, "The tower said you were coming. Go ahead and take it. The keys are inside." He waved and went back inside.

Brandon walked around to the passenger side. "You drive," he said to Jacobs. "I want to get more familiar with the terrain around here."

Jacobs got going right away.

Brandon swung around in his seat and waved to Palmer, although he didn't see her through the cruiser's windshield.

"Forbidden fruit," Jacobs said once Brandon got settled again.

"More than that," Brandon said. "We've run across one another many, many times. You get to know someone. I know it's frowned upon, but some things you can't help."

"And probably don't want to," Jacobs said. "I see the way you two communicate. It's a good relationship you have, mutual respect. Trust me, it's rare."

Brandon looked at Jacobs long enough that he should have recognized it then said, "Thank you." He held onto a safety strap near his head and began to check out the area. Although he had driven there with the others, he was always in a conversation and hadn't focused as much as he normally would have had he been in a combat situation. It was time to change that.

Brandon thought like a soldier. The terrain became a map inside his head. In a combat situation, which they probably would never get into, he could lead men safely from the tower and the hangars all the way to the metal building where the pit was located. He was confident of that.

When they parked the truck outside the pit building, Brandon jumped out and headed inside right away. He knew that Jacobs would catch up.

"Hey there," the guard said. It was the insect-loving man from the evening before.

"You still here?" Brandon stopped for only a moment.

"About to be relieved soon," the guard said. "You look like you could use a bit more sleep."

"Probably," Brandon said. "I'm going in, okay?"

"Be my guest."

Jacobs came through the door and rushed over to Brandon. "Could I get another cup of jasp first?"

The jasp machine sat next to the wall near the hall they were about to take.

"Good idea," Brandon said. "Me too." Holding steaming cups of vaguely coffee smelling liquid, they made their way toward the meeting room. Brandon couldn't help but visualize the two of them walking with their cups held to their chests. "Like a couple of business men heading to work," he said while lifting his cup in a sort-of toast.

Jacobs produced a tight smile. "And a strange business it is."

Brandon laughed. His communicator beeped and he keyed it with a wrist flick. "Heading out," came Palmer's voice. Brandon brought it to his mouth. "Give it hell," he said.

Jacobs said, "I want to apologize for what I did, leaving you inside the lander. I often have to do things that are difficult for me because of my cover, and…"

"No need," Brandon said. "We're both professionals. I fully understand taking orders. Maybe too much sometimes, but there's no need to let it worry us now. I'm here."

"Thank you," Jacobs said.

Brandon smiled at him. "You're off probation."

They walked the rest of the way in silence. When they came to the meeting room where he had been with Oliver and the governmental board, he scanned the area. He knew where guards would be placed, how long it would take them to get inside if there was a disturbance, and which direction they would go once the door was opened. He also imagined where chairs would be as people stood, where he'd have to move to stay low and out of the way, and what the chances of survival were. Brandon then turned to Jacobs and said, "If anything, anything, happens. You run in the opposite direction. You are not trained for this and the best thing for everyone is for you to be safe."

"And not in the way," Jacobs said.

"That too."

# CHAPTER 17

CAPTAIN STARK AWAKENED JAMES the moment Garth Killjoy's lander touched down on the C-47 runway. As James' eyes opened, he caught sight of the blue sand and sharp rocks that lay across the surface of C-47's canyon area. They loomed so much closer than when he fell asleep that he jumped in fear that they might be heading for a crash.

"Easy there," Stark said as he banked the fighter along a mountain range. "We're running through the valleys and canyons so their radar can't pick us up. They have no satellites, you know."

"Yes, yes," James said. "That's why communications end when we're on the other side of the planet. I have been around, you know?" He sat upright in the seat and felt the straps tighten over his shoulders, a sign of restraint. He didn't mean to be snippy even though that's how his words came out. "We've been flying like this for quite a while then?"

"Meant nothing by the comment, sir. It's just difficult to know how much of the technical stuff you understand," Stark said. "We've never flown together. Know nothing about you."

James took a deep breath to hide his frustration. "Don't be concerned about it. What I'm worried about is whether we've been spotted." He wished he had remained awake and watched the progress as they came in. He would have enjoyed the scenery and perhaps felt more comfortable about how close they were to the ground. He lifted his head to the clear sky. "Our exhaust?" he said.

"Should be fine at this distance," Stark said. "It dissipates quickly in this atmosphere. Acton-Kestler filters. My biggest worry is position blue."

James gave him a quizzical look.

"We were ordered to have five fighters and only four were ready. The mechanics had to cannibalize to get the fifth fighter into the air, and it's been having problems with its rudder for the last hour. I hate to put him through this pace," Stark said. "It can only exacerbate the problem."

"Does each fighter have ground troops on board?" James said.

"Multi-use fighters," Stark said. "You won't find many airborne-only fighters around these days. They're too costly and seldom used. Everything pulls double-duty now."

"But they're still fighters, right?"

"GUE Embedded Blast Fighters. Called Gooeys. Yeah, they can do the trick for short blasts of time. Extended battles and they get behind the curve a little. Nothing to fear here, though."

"We're all in danger if there's real trouble, then." James didn't trust Garth and knew it would be a few hours before the fighters were close enough to request clearance for landing. The added concern that sixty people were in danger if anything went wrong bothered him as well. "We should show ourselves before they locate us and get suspicious," James said. "If something happens to position blue..."

"Suspicious, hell," Stark said, "we're intimidating. That's our purpose, isn't it?"

"Of course. That's what Garth wants, but I need to be part of the negotiations down there. I can't piss away time up here. Garth is wrong. The only reason there are five of us is if a problem occurs. Hiding makes that if inevitable."

"I'll think about it. But for now, I'm holding to the ground," Stark said.

James held tight for over an hour, during which time he concerned his mind with strategy and procedure. His biggest worry being if Garth was truly able to get C-47 to sign a contract before he hit the ground or talked with anyone in the C-47 government. If that happened he had only one way out and that was to convince their government officials to tear up the agreement before it could be scanned and transmitted anywhere. He had only talked with Oliver once, but found him to be easily persuaded, the kind of personality that wavered while he looked for a way to keep from having a full-on confrontation. That also meant that Garth could swing him quickly. James put his faith into the planet's governmental board, made up of elders. If he understood the C-47 colony as well as he thought, the elders would slow negotiations down, maybe for days. When he felt as though he had his mind organized and ready, he checked the distance between him and where Garth's lander had set down. "We need to call in," he said as directly and authoritatively as possible.

"My orders…"

"Screw your orders. As soon as we're a bit closer, I want you to clear these mountains and call in. I'll talk with them. They'll listen to me." James found that his tone had climbed up with his statement and decided to lower his voice. Trying to sound calm and in charge, he said, "I'm your superior and you have to do as I say."

"I'm still under orders," Stark said. "Garth said…"

"Jesus Christ, Captain, if you don't listen to me you may not make it out of here at all."

"They don't have the fire power," Stark said, a trace of arrogance in his voice. Then he raised a hand. "Hold on."

"What is it?" James fumbled with his radio dial until he could hear someone else talking. "…this way," was all he heard. "Someone's headed this way?"

Stark held his hand in the air between them, and now shook his head, too. He banked the fighter along a sheer cliff.

James' stomach floated to the side and he felt a bit queasy, reminding him how much of a landlubber he was. "They've seen us. Can't we just come into the open and ask to land now. I have to get down there."

Another pilot said, "They're loaded and coming in fast."

Stark turned to James. "Looks like we don't have much choice now. They have jets in the air. And they've spotted us."

"I told you something was up," James said. "If you would have…"

"Follow me," Stark said over the radio.

He pulled his fighter into a vertical climb perpendicular from the valley floor they were trailing.

James fell into his seat as though shoved by a bully. He closed his eyes. His stomach pushed back and down as he waited for the fighter to level off. It took far too long. How far did they have to go?

His stomach squeezed tighter. He thought he was going to vomit when Stark dropped the nose and leveled off. James' stomach fell back into place, but didn't settle as quickly as the fighter. "You did that on purpose," James said.

"What is your function here," a woman's voice came over the radio.

Stark didn't answer.

James said, "What are you waiting for? Tell her what we're doing. Tell her we just want to land. Tell her I'm on board, the real Peace Coordinator." When Stark didn't respond, James keyed his mic. "This is James Stockwell of the IPF." There was no feedback present in his headset. He couldn't hear his own voice through the speakers. He stopped talking and turned to Stark, "You cut me off. I can hear but not talk?"

"I'm to stay radio silent," Stark said. "Let them make the first move."

"That makes no fucking sense. That's a threatening position," James yelled.

"Gives us the edge," Stark said, obviously repeating his orders directly, something Garth may have told him in private. "They won't fire on us anyway. We'd take them out in a second and they know it. Those little jets are nothing to us."

"Position Blue," the headset said, "having more trouble with my rudder. That last climb did something that…shit!"

Stark slowed and banked left.

James could see one of the fighters spin, pitch upward, then fall. "What's happening over there? Is that Blue?"

"Son of a bitch," Stark said. "It's heading over the side of the mountain."

"Toward the colony?" James wanted to know. "Oh my God," James said. "This is worse than I thought." He stared and pointed as a Shadow Cruiser rose up behind the jets, as though it lifted from the blue sand itself. There was nothing any of them could do. Two missiles blew over the cockpits of the C-47 jets and destroyed the IPF fighter. It burst into a ball of flames, then dissipated and fell harmlessly toward the ground. "No, no, no…," James repeated.

"Clam up," Stark yelled. "I hope they didn't take that as an evasive move."

"How else could they take it?" James said. "That's why they shot it down." He shook his head. "We lost all those men for nothing. I should have known…"

"I don't know what's going on," Stark said, "but they've backed off." He slammed his hand on the console. "Where'd they get a Shadow Cruiser like that?"

James shook his head. "We hired it. But it was shot down."

"I don't think so," Stark said.

"Levels the playing field, doesn't it?" James said. Blood rose into his face and he could feel his cheeks getting red. "You should have listened to me. This is Garth's fault. Come clean. Now's the time."

Stark shook his head. "We're still four against one, with a few mosquitoes as chasers."

James pieced together the situation. He knew exactly where the cruiser had come from, recognized now that it had never been shot down in the first place. And Stark had never known. He probably didn't know about any of the prior flights or attacks. James shook his head. It appeared as though every one of them lived in the dark about the others. No one person seemed to know what the next person did or why. Garth was a smarter man than he thought. James wasted no time. He turned to Stark again. "Hail them. Let me talk with them. Now, God damn-it, now."

The fighter rolled to the left as bullets from the nose of one of the C-47 jets whizzed past. James swore then said, "They haven't backed off, you idiot. Now let me talk with them."

"Might be a bit late to start a conversation," Stark said. "But we can take care of this."

James watched as one of the other IPF fighters knocked out the jet that had fired on them. "Stop it," James yelled. "You'll make it worse."

Even before the jet went down, the cruiser spun into the air like an acrobat performing an impossible stunt, but James knew exactly what was about to happen. Sure enough, the cruiser leveled, rolled to the right, and dropped toward the second fighter just long enough to set off a few rounds and knock it out. The cruiser, just as quickly as it attacked, flipped around and slipped back into position above and behind the fighters. It was like the big dog standing behind the little dogs.

"Hold your fire," James yelled. He shook his head and took a deep breath. "I don't like this at all." They were down to three fighters. Over twenty men had been senselessly allowed to die. If he could jump from his seat he would have. "Multi-purpose fighters my ass." James clenched his teeth for a moment, then released. "There's no way we can compete with that cruiser."

Stark glanced at James. "Who learns to fight like that?"

James didn't answer. "Let me talk with them," he said, holding out his hand in a gesture of resolve.

"Yes, sir," Stark said as he moved his hand to the console and opened the communications link. He told the other fighters to hold their positions. "Evasive action only," he said. He nodded to James. "Go ahead, but you'd better save my ass when the time comes."

"We're here on a peaceful mission," James said into the radio. "That fighter had mechanical problems. We're sorry. It went out of control."

"You fired on us," a woman's voice said.

"A reaction," James said.

"We're waiting," the woman said.

"I'm James Stockwell, IPF Peace Coordinator. Who am I speaking with?"

"Knock off the bullshit and tell us what you're doing here. Your social status with IPF means nothing to us while you're loaded for an attack," the voice came.

"Yes. Fine. I understand," James stammered. He didn't expect such an affront.

Stark gave him a stern look and shook his head in a few tight jerks, obviously trying to urge James to get to the point.

James waved him off. He knew he was fumbling and just needed a moment to get unflustered. He took a few shallow breaths of air. "Okay, straight talk," he said. "The man who landed earlier is trying to cheat you. He's allowing you to assume that you need the IPF to assure your independence, but he's lying. Your independence has already been approved." James knew as he said the words that his own escape from the IPF mother ship might suddenly be in jeopardy. It was a harder decision to make than he thought it would be. But he had to lead with his strongest argument, and that was it.

"So?" the woman's voice came through the headset.

Another woman came online. "If I may," she said, but James knew that she wasn't really asking. He could hear in her tone that she was the one to convince, she was the one in charge, at least for this aircrew. She must have been hailing from the cruiser. "This information could change everything." She waited a moment and James heard her say, "Tower, did you get that statement?"

"Affirmative," came a man's voice. "Recorded and saved."

James had never met Palmer. Garth had Jacobs take care of that part of his plan. But, he was sure it was Palmer who weighed in. She appeared smarter than Garth might have assumed.

"Slow to 200 knots and fall into formation. We'll follow you in. No funny business or you know what'll happen," Palmer said.

So now James knew positively that Palmer had survived the last ditch attack. That meant that Jacobs survived with her. The fact that she was in the air with the jets told him that Palmer, at least, had convinced the planet's government that she was not hostile, which meant that Garth's arrival should already be under suspicion. The question was whether Garth knew that Palmer had survived. James doubted that fact.

So, C-47 knew more than just what Garth told them, even if they didn't have the whole truth—but then no one did. He could only imagine how confusing things could become with no one having the truth, everyone handed their own set of lies. He could only hope that he was closer to the truth than the others, just because of his proximity to Garth's position of power. Plus there were occasions where Garth had let down his guard, needed to brag to someone, and he did it with James. That may have been his mistake, James thought.

The situation also begged for him to wonder what story, or lie, Jacobs may have told the colony? One thing for sure, though, Palmer and Jacobs knew that Garth, or someone with the mother ship, had tried to kill them. That may not go over very well and could be the reason Palmer allowed the IPF fighters to land. She must know that there are troops aboard. Landing would be the best way to keep them under wraps.

Stark flew in at right angles to the C-47 runway. He banked left and leveled off before slowing and engaging the flaps. The two other Gooeys fell into place behind him. He rolled onto the runway instead of making a vertical landing.

James figured that Stark was doing that because landing that way used less fuel. Then his mind shifted gears. He worried that even though Garth might be under suspicion it didn't mean that the C-47 government would believe him either. At this point any and all personnel from the IPF would most assuredly be suspect. They might land only to be put under arrest. He wouldn't get to talk with Oliver or the governmental board. He would lose his chance at producing a deal both he and the colony could live with.

James kept his eyes toward the window and observed his surroundings as the ground appeared to move backward. The planet's scenery had shifted over the past hours from a lush valley of gray-green and brown to the high-mountain dirt and rocks of blue. He glanced at the time. The mother ship would be back in communications soon. Earth Central could appear out of a wormhole any time now. The combination would only complicate the situation, as well as the negotiations. And, as he was learning more and more first hand, few people had the same story about what was going on. No one, not even him, knew all the paths Garth's scheme had taken. He wondered how Garth kept track.

# CRAPTER 18

**"YOU CAN'T DO THIS,"** Garth's voice came through Brandon's ear bud a bit garbled, but intelligible.

"Standard procedure," Eldon said. "You can have your comm unit once we're through with our discussions."

"I'm not recording this. That would be unethical," Garth said. "Do you know who you're dealing with here?"

Brandon gave Jacobs a wink.

"You can't hide arrogance," Jacobs whispered.

The sound of chairs dragging across the floor and people settling into them came through his ear bud. No one else had spoken yet, but Brandon heard some huffing come through. He suspected that Garth wasn't happy at all.

The range of the bug was short. He knew that guards would be outside the far door, but never heard anything through the bug that Larry carried until they were inside the room. It was hard to tell how many there were with all the shuffling around. He didn't try to guess, either.

Garth spoke first. "What about my people? What have you done with them?"

"They are being held until this is decided," Eldon said. "Why did you bring so many with you, anyway? This is supposed to be a friendly communication."

"Council," Garth said. "In case I need to discuss any details."

"You use soldiers and guards as council?" Eldon said.

Garth cleared his throat. "And protection. They won't let me out of the ship without bodyguards. IPF policy."

"Explains things well enough for now," Eldon said.

Everything on the other side of the door got quiet for a moment.

"They staying?" Garth said about the others in the room.

"He's a trainee," Oliver said. The first words from Oliver came out a bit nervous to Brandon, who wished he could see Oliver's face, watch his body language. But that wasn't possible at the moment.

"And he's here in case we need anything," Eldon said.

"Well, I could tell he wasn't a bodyguard," Garth said. "Isn't he a bit young to be a trainee?"

"Never too young to learn. This is a great opportunity for him," Eldon said, obviously taking over the conversation on purpose. Was he as worried about Oliver's reactions as Brandon?

So far, Larry kept his side of the deal by remaining silent in the presence of Garth.

"Let's do this, then." Garth's hand must have slapped the table to get things rolling.

Brandon heard the smacking sound, and wished that Larry would have situated himself centrally, but from the sound of the voices and movements, that wasn't true. The young man must have automatically taken a seat far from the others, polite rather than confident.

"We don't need the others then, do we?" Garth said, obviously talking about the rest of the governmental board.

"Eventually," Oliver said. "But my sign-off is official enough to proceed."

"So, you are taking care of this," Garth said, reiterating his prior concern.

This time Jacobs nudged Brandon to get his attention. "They're a bit too familiar. Sounds like they've talked a few times before now. I don't like it."

"Proceed," Oliver said.

"Good. Here's what's going on—and you'd better listen and react fast—I got word, just before landing, that James Stockwell is headed this way to stop this negotiation. I don't know what's up with him, but he can't be trusted." There was a slight pause. "Well, you'd better check on it now. Send your man here. If he's coming, you've got to stop him. Cut him out of the air. Shoot him down."

"Check to see if it's true," Oliver said.

A door opened and shut.

Brandon shrugged his shoulders to Jacobs' questioning look. He keyed his communicator and said, "Any problems up there?"

"A few troop-carrier fighters. Nothing I couldn't handle," Palmer said.

"A James Stockwell with them?" Brandon asked.

"How'd you know?"

"Inside information," Brandon said. "Out." He nodded to Jacobs. "Should I go in and tell them?"

They both laughed as quietly as they could.

"Are you sure you want this kid in here?" Garth said again.

"Like I said…" Oliver didn't finish the sentence.

"I'm your savior," Garth said in a low, confident tone. "I hate to put it that way, but at this very moment the C-47 colony is in worse shape than ever and soon every pirate, criminal, and shark out there is going to come down to see what you have. You can't possibly protect your planet from all that. Your people are in danger, grave danger if you don't act quickly."

The room fell silent for only a moment before Oliver said, "We are aware of that."

"Good," Killjoy said.

There was some ruffling of papers and zipping sounds from some sort of document holder.

"Paper?" Brandon questioned.

Jacobs nodded. "Paper to start. There are all sorts of secure systems for electronics document signing and approval, but they can all be digitized and faked. A handwritten signature is still the truest way to go. Besides, it's old school."

"Didn't know that," Brandon said.

Just then the door in the conference room opened and closed. "He's right," someone said. "Fighters have been spotted and apprehended."

"Apprehended?" Garth yelled. "Shoot them down. You can't trust them."

"They're landing now sir," the man said.

"Fighters?" Eldon said.

The gopher said, "Gooeys, sir. They must have ground troops loaded with them. But they can pull aerial fighting maneuvers if they have to."

Garth said, "Troops? I told you not to trust him. Not a word James says is true. It's all about personal gain for him."

"And you?" Oliver asked.

Brandon felt a pull on his chest when Oliver confronted Garth. He hadn't expected that to happen and, as it sounded, neither did anyone else. The room fell completely silent for a long time. Brandon could only imagine the looks that were going back and forth at the table, the long stares. Eventually, Larry cleared his throat. Soon after that, Eldon said, "What's going on here?"

A chair squeaked across the floor and Garth's voice escalated, "We had a deal."

Brandon turned to Jacobs with a shocked look on his face. "Oliver? He's the leak?"

"A deal? What kind of deal?" Eldon sounded calm, but completely confused about the turn of events.

"Let's hear it," Oliver said. "What are you able to do? Really?" Another chair squealed across the floor. Once Oliver began to speak the sound of his voice faded in and out, indicating that he paced as he talked to Garth. "We know you were on a secure communications link while coming in. You must have been talking with James at that time." Sound stopped again. Brandon didn't hear Oliver breathing, but could imagine the man taking a deep breath in preparation for his next statement, which came out forcefully. "All this time you're making statements like you're our friend and all this time you're sending fake Peace Coordinators, you're trying to knock out supposed rebels from your own mother ship, and now you're telling us that the fighters were someone else's decision? It suddenly appears as though you aren't in charge of anything up there. Well, we know better than to trust you."

"Trying to knock out?" Garth said referring to Palmer's cruiser.

"Palmer landed safely," Oliver said.

"He's offering up information," Jacobs whispered. "They're in this together. He's allowing Garth to adjust his story."

Brandon held up a hand to stop Jacobs from jabbering. "Just listen," he said.

Garth laughed for a moment and when he stopped he said, "I don't know about Palmer, she's an independent, but we got notice that Jacobs was working on his own to destroy"—things got quiet for a moment and Brandon imagined Garth slyly looking around the room as though he had special information—"your findings, shall we say?"

"Everyone here, with us anyway, knows what's down there," Oliver said. "You can say the words."

"Jacobs is a religious man and doesn't believe in intelligent alien life forms. He was on a mission that we tried to stop," Garth said. "He escaped with Palmer. I suspect she doesn't know his true intentions or she wouldn't have helped him. He's a fanatic."

"You tried to stop the mission by blowing up two soldiers?" Eldon said.

Garth huffed and said, "That wasn't my idea. I just gave the order to stop them. Maybe Jacobs, or maybe James was in it with Jacobs. Those men could have been forced to swallow the explosives."

"He's fumbling," Jacobs said. "I'd love to be involved with intelligent aliens. Fanatic, my ass."

"That makes sense," Oliver said.

"Are you shitting me?" Eldon was incensed. "Jacobs and James? Both?"

"Religious fanatics have grown exponentially violent and dangerous as more of the galaxy has been explored and found empty of intelligent life. It could be true that they want humans to remain as the chosen ones." Oliver stopped for only a second. "Seriously, Eldon, can't you see that?"

"Perhaps some, but to this extent?"

"We're already under attack because of the aliens," Oliver said. "We need the protection. We need the expertise that the IPF has for negotiations." There was another short pause before Oliver added his final lines. "We need to be under protection to maintain our independence. And independence is the only way you'll get to carry out your research. Eldon, you could lose everything you've done."

Brandon shook his head. "Don't do it, Eldon. Don't believe them. Just wait a little longer."

"What do you think they're doing now?" Jacobs said.

Brandon shrugged his shoulders. The feel of the cuffs comforted him. "You?" he said.

Before Jacobs could answer, Eldon said, "I don't like this, but I can't lose this find. I just can't lose it."

More shuffling around the table indicated that Garth and Oliver were sitting again, after their confrontation. Brandon wanted to believe that the whole argument was real, but the idea that it was all put on for his and Jacob's benefit nagged at him. He wondered if Eldon was in on it too.

"I'm glad you've come to your senses. This won't take long," Garth said. "All I need is a quick signature and I can put this through preliminary screening. We'll do everything in our power to help you. We'll start immediately."

Brandon's wrist communicator clicked and Palmer's voice came on. He lifted the speaker near his ear. "Brandon, we've secured three multi-purpose fighters and their crews. That James Stockwell person you knew about claims to be the IPF's Senior Peace Coordinator. He has an interesting story everyone might want to hear."

"Bring him on. It can only make things more fun," Brandon said.

"He's on his way," Palmer said. "I'm heading back into the sky."

"There shouldn't be any problems now," Brandon said.

"I forgot to tell you," she said.

Brandon waited for what felt like a long time before she added the clincher to her communication. "Earth Central has been spotted materializing from a wormhole. They're several days from the IPF mother ship, but their cruisers are only a day at most if they send them out. We could have some interesting company."

"Shit," Jacobs said. "This complicates the issues at hand."

"Sounds like Garth is trying to get them to sign now anyway," Brandon said.

"Well, Big Boy, you'd better stop them don't you think?" Jacobs smiled.

Brandon smiled back. "Roger that." He reached to turn the doorknob on the conference room, but it didn't rotate. "Locked?" he said. "Those sons-of-bitches." With only the movement of his index finger and a twitch of his hand muscle, Brandon blew a hole in the door that took out the knob and all its guts. He slammed the door open. Debris spilled over the floor and onto an empty chair in front of him. "You aren't signing anything," Brandon said.

Garth leaped from his chair. "What the fuck."

Oliver looked upset, but didn't appear as disturbed as Garth. In fact, his expression looked more like relief, as though he wanted to be stopped.

Through the other door, two guards pulled a break-and-entry maneuver by throwing the door wide while standing aside until they could assess the situation.

Brandon knew exactly what they'd do and blasted a hole through the wall and halfway through the guard on the other side. The man collapsed across the entranceway to the conference room. "Step into the open," Brandon said, his arm lifted toward where the other guard would be standing even though all he needed was a finger.

The guard stepped around and behind the fallen man. His eyes widened when he saw the cuffs, and he dropped his weapon without being asked.

"We may have a better way to go," Brandon said. "EC just showed up on the scene."

"Christ," Garth said. He looked squarely at Oliver. "We had a deal." He attempted to get the rest of the room's attention. "He's been feeding me information for months," Garth said. Then he leaned in close to Oliver. "You won't have a life here any longer, mister."

Oliver held out his hands toward Eldon. "You can take me away. Call security," he said to Larry.

"Why in hell would you do this? Now? After all this time?" Garth said.

"I don't think I know exactly," Oliver said. "But I'm doing it." He held out his hands and shook them as he addressed Eldon. "For the betterment of the colony."

Security ran into the room, but Brandon knew that they weren't really trained security by the way they barged in all wide-eyed and confused. "What happened?" the first man said.

"A little redecorating," Brandon said. "Take these three." He looked at Eldon and brought his palms up in question.

"Put them into locked rooms," Eldon said. "Separate ones. With guards."

"Palmer has someone bringing Stockwell here, too. Should be soon," Brandon said to Eldon. "So, who's in charge of the negotiations now? Who's the guy going to talk with?" Brandon had no doubt, if he ever had one, that C-47 wasn't ready for the complexity of what was happening to them because of the aliens, and the more complicated things became, the more their inefficiencies and lack of training showed through. He hoped that Palmer was having a better time of it with the pilots.

Eldon turned toward Oliver, who answered the question. "Get the entire governmental board here. I'll come clean about everything. This has to be done now. We can't wait, not with Earth Central in the vicinity.

Eldon nodded in agreement.

"I'm sorry," Oliver said while being escorted out of the room.

Brandon could see that there was still a lot of admiration between the two of them regardless how much and how often they disagreed. Some sort of professional respect they held to. He understood that.

Eldon addressed the security team warily, obvious that he couldn't tell who to talk with, who was in charge.

"For God's sake," Brandon said. "You," he pointed to the man who, to him, was plainly the leader. "Do as Oliver said. Get the board in here." He glanced around. "And get more men to clean this up. We have a situation that needs action." When the man didn't jump, Brandon lunged at him and the man darted from the room.

Brandon began to give orders to have the doors and walls repaired, to find another conference room, and to get everyone in a room with Oliver before they talk with James Stockwell, the Senior Negotiator supposedly.

When the men who had arrived didn't listen, Jacobs said, "You heard the man. Let's go."

The other men still looked confused until Eldon shook his head at them disappointedly. "Come on guys. Get on board here."

"Sure, Boss," one of them said.

Brandon looked at Eldon. "He works for you?"

"They all work for someone. He just happens to be one of mine."

"You do need protection," Brandon said. He took in the room and ushered Larry and Eldon outside.

"This way," Eldon said, leading them down the corridor only a few rooms away.

Oliver already sat at a table with his hands clasped in front of him, a guard by his side.

Brandon allowed Eldon and Jacobs to enter the room first. He turned to Larry and stopped him from entering. "We don't need a bug at this time, but I want you to stand by. First of all, let them know where to take this Stockwell guy."

"They won't listen to me," Larry said.

Brandon checked with Eldon about that through a quizzical look.

"He's right. There's no real chain of command that easily puts him in charge of anyone. Not for the most part."

"Great," Brandon said. "The tower? Can they communicate with most places around here?"

"Most," Eldon said.

Brandon called Palmer and explained the situation. "I want Larry to have full control, then I want a division of rank. I don't give a shit how they do it, but they'd better have it done in less than half an hour. Can you relay that message?"

"Got it," Palmer said.

"We have a communications room near the lab," Eldon said.

"Too late," Brandon motioned for Larry to carry on.

"If my timing is correct, we have about ten minutes before this IPF Senior Peach Coordinator shows up. So, spill it," Brandon said after closing the door and sitting at the head of the table.

"It's been months," Oliver said. "Garth's got that straight. We first met a few years ago."

"The Colony Conference," Eldon said.

Oliver nodded.

"There's a Colony Conference?" Brandon asked.

"Several," Oliver said. "We feared rumors were getting out. People ran on and off world a lot at that time. Deliveries, other conferences, trade, supplies. It's not so cut and dry like everyone thinks."

"Of course not," Jacobs said.

"What the hell would you know?" Brandon said.

"I've been all over. I told you." Jacobs turned to address Oliver. "What I want to know is why you kept this whole issue of being unsure about the aliens to yourselves. If you had let that information out to the rest of the colony there wouldn't be such an excitement over the aliens. Then, they'd just be another life form," Jacobs said. "It makes no sense."

Brandon waited for the response. He was glad that Jacobs showed up. He looked at things differently.

"A lot of scientists flocked here because of the rumors. We knew there'd be trouble, but we needed the attention, too," Oliver said.

"Oh," Jacobs sat back in his chair. He looked more concerned.

"Oh, what?" Brandon wanted to know.

"This colony isn't self-sufficient at all. It's on the downfall. This lie is all they have to keep them going." Jacobs lowered his head, then put his forearms on the table and leaned over them. When he brought his head up he asked, "How long did you have to survive?"

Oliver shook his head. "I knew Garth was a megalomaniac. I knew he'd rush here. I thought having an IPF Section tied to our independence would not only keep us safe after the rumors, but would give us more negotiation capabilities."

"How many years?" Jacobs asked again.

"Six, seven," Oliver said. "On the outside."

"But if they are real," Eldon said, "we really do need the protection."

"Garth had no idea that he could have been screwed in the long run," Jacobs said. "Your decision here could have saved them while causing C-47 to collapse."

"We were going down either way," Oliver said, more to Eldon than to anyone else.

"Unless the Mesoans are for real," Eldon said. "That changes things." He gave Jacobs a wanting look. "Well? Will you help us?"

"I don't know if I can," Jacobs said.

# CHAPTER 19

**BRANDON STOOD IN THE FRONT OF THE ROOM** with Oliver and Eldon who sat opposite one another near his end of the table, while the rest of the governmental board took the other seats. The older participants shuffled to their places and sat with groans reminding Brandon of his grandparents.

Jacobs slid his chair next to Eldon's. He was there to observe the conversation and hopefully help Brandon decipher the interactions later.

Brandon opened his comm channel to Palmer, knowing that she could at least hear the conversation.

Oliver started immediately once everyone was in place. He bowed his head, "I'd like it to be on record that I'm sorry. I am truly sorry for what I've done. I thought that I was doing the right thing."

"What thing was that, Oli?" a gray haired woman asked. Brandon instantly saw the resemblance and knew how difficult it was for Oliver to face his mother like that, carrying such guilt. Yet, all he'd really done wrong was make a bad decision, albeit one that affected the entire colony.

"I helped to plan this negotiation," he said.

"We know that," the woman said.

"At the beginning, I mean. Remember when I went to that conference for several months? I met Garth there. He had been assigned to Section 204 only a few months before that. His reassignment had come after a long probation period because of his aggressive attacks on a colony in the Lowenthal System. I couldn't keep our discovery to myself. And, well, I was afraid of what might happen to us, to the

Mesoans, if they weren't protected." Oliver rubbed his face and drew his hands back along his hairline. He never looked up at his mother, hadn't made eye contact with anyone at that point.

Brandon's breathing slowed as he watched the agony of the situation fall over Oliver. Every word the man said had to push through his sense of shame. Brandon wondered if he'd be able to do such a thing if he were ever forced to. But that was a ludicrous thought. Brandon didn't lie. Oliver had.

Oliver explained how he feared for the colony's survival under the duress of a galactic system that was based on control. He lifted his head and looked at Eldon. "I know we don't agree often, but I respect you. I wanted you to have this. I wanted us all to have it. At the time I started my conversations with Garth Killjoy we were still excited about the findings. We still believed that they were intelligent, humanlike, beings. I knew we had to protect them. Once we began to doubt that they were for real, I couldn't go back and tell him we changed our mind. I was too deeply into the plan he had for us. I believed I did the right thing." He took his eyes from Eldon and looked at his mother. "That's when I put in for our independence, even though I knew it would be near impossible for us to survive on our own." The weight must have been lifting because his head remained up now. He turned to Brandon, "It's all been one lie on top of the next. The truth is we get help from Earth Central, not much, but enough. We trade when we need to. And we knew that the IPF would be coming along soon anyway. After the mining efforts for C-47 failed, they found that we could supply other natural materials. I feared that the planet would be stripped of all its natural resources. It wouldn't be the first time. So, I wanted our independence to be in the bag. You saw what the mining operation left behind."

"What happened?" Eldon said. "What changed your mind concerning Killjoy a moment ago?"

"Garth," Oliver said. "I got the strongest feeling that he would be worse for us than having no protection at all. Worse than having Earth Central take over. I just knew it. Don't ask me how."

"I could have told you that," Jacobs said.

"I'm not sure I trust you either." Oliver's eyes darted in Brandon's direction, "Him, I trust."

"Okay, okay, let's stop this and get to the real problem," Eldon said. "What's next? That's why we called everyone together, to get the story straight and to figure out our next move. They're bringing this James guy here, this Senior Peace Coordinator, at this very minute. Are we going to talk? Are we going to negotiate or what?"

"We convene," the woman said.

"We are convening," Eldon said. "This is it."

At that moment the door to the room jutted open and Larry stuck in his head. "We have a situation," he said to no one in particular.

"What kind?" Brandon said.

"The troops turned on our people and are heading this way on their own," he said. "They stole several transports. They appear to have taken James Stockwell hostage."

"For God's sake." To Jacobs and Eldon Brandon said, "You two are working with the board here, and will come up with a solution." To Oliver he said, "You are being held under guard for now." He indicated to Larry to have Oliver led away, but when no one moved toward Oliver, he let his shoulders slump. He was exasperated. "Move," he yelled and two men reached for Oliver as he left with Larry and a few other men.

Brandon pulled his wrist close to his mouth, "Did you catch that?"

"Roger," Palmer said. "And I have some information that might help."

"Why didn't you tell me?"

"Your comm unit was keyed the whole time. I couldn't," she said.

He kept walking with Larry as he talked. "Waiting…"

"According to Stockwell, C-47's independence has already been approved," she said.

Brandon stopped dead in his tracks, which caused Larry to stop and two of the others to stumble into him. "You hear that?"

"Yeah. That's good news, right?" Larry said.

"Get back to the conference room or wherever they are now and tell them. They need that piece of information," Brandon said.

Larry spun around and ordered a young woman to deliver the message.

Brandon continued his conversation with Palmer as he walked. "Then could you come down here and help? I'm not good at herding cats, and I hate all this talk. I'm not a talker."

"On my way," Palmer said. "These guys have the sky."

"Out," Brandon said. "So, what happened? Anyone get hurt?"

"A few of the welcoming team," Larry said. "I guess the troops came out shooting. One guy yelling for them to stop, but they didn't listen. I suspect that was Stockwell."

"I'm guessing you're right. Must have been. Well, he's not in charge that's for sure. My guess is that Killjoy still holds all the cards," Brandon said. "Any guess as to where the troops might be entering?"

Larry stopped and swung around to meet Brandon's gaze as though he had asked a crazy question.

"There's only one entrance?" Larry said. "That is except for equipment and shipping, but…"

"Yeah," Brandon said, "you didn't think of those, did you, Smart Ass?"

Larry shook his head but continued toward the front of the building.

After going through the double doors to the expansive lobby, Brandon noticed about twenty men and women in a semicircle with weapons aimed at the front door. "Get them out of here," Brandon said about a few people milling near the jasp dispenser in the lobby. "I want them split up and guarding the other doors."

Larry had taken to his authority well and quickly dispersed everyone, making quick and accurate decisions seemingly based on his personal knowledge of each individual. He delegated well as far as Brandon could tell.

Brandon, ordered the two front desk guards to join him at the door. "Those stunners you have won't do much, but they'll help. Set them on long range and aim for the man in the middle. I'll take the two ends and work in."

"You're going to just kill them all?" one of the guards asked.

The moment he verbalized his concern, Brandon felt a thick ball of something fill his chest. The idea of killing was far outside both guards' comfort zones and Brandon knew it. "I am," Brandon said.

"You can back your stunners off as they get closer so that you don't harm anyone permanently." He patted the man's shoulder. "We only shoot until they stop. Let's hope it's quickly."

Brandon's special training went beyond that of the average military. That's why Earth Central sent him on special assignments. With his cuffs, he could probably take on the entire C-47 colony without trouble. He was a one-man battalion. The guards were only there for show. If the troops heading their way saw only one man it would give them too much hope. Brandon wanted it over quickly, too, and with as few casualties as possible. His only concern was that he didn't have his helmet. It had been lost in the first lander fiasco. His cuffs could stop a bullet, though, so he planned to hold one arm across his face while shooting with the other, like standing behind a tree. His enemy would aim for his chest once he got into the open, but the cuffs' straps would stop anything short of a missile.

He peered out the front and noticed a cloud of blue dust rise from behind the underbrush near the area where he and Palmer had walked the night before. "They're going to circle the area, get ready," he said. He stood over the head of one of the guards, who crouched nervously at the side of the door. "Cross fire," he told them. "Know what I mean?"

Both men nodded.

"They're coming in," Brandon said.

At first a few bullets flew as the troops tested to see how many people blocked the entrance.

Brandon had the guards wait. "You know the saying, 'Not 'til you see the whites of their eyes'?"

The guard at the opposite side lowered the barrel of his stunner and shook his head. "What?"

"It means to wait until they're close before you shoot. That way they have no idea how many we are."

"Oh…"

Brandon shook his head. He said, "Stay ready." He watched and waited.

Eventually someone stepped into the open. When that happened, Brandon knew he had backup. From what he understood, that meant at least twenty-five more men behind him. More of them stepped into view.

The nervous guards fired on the first few men and hit nothing. Brandon could see already that his little plan was relatively worthless since he had no real help. "Step back," he said. "Stay out of my way." He brought his left arm diagonally across his face so that he could peer around it, and so he still had the ability to point with his index finger. Because of the angle of his arm and wrist he could only use low caliber fiber bullets, but they'd do the trick by knocking people out. His right arm, though, was loaded for bear.

Once the guards sat behind the wall safely, Brandon stepped forward and walked straight for the semicircle of troops.

They kneeled and fired on him immediately. But he knew that psychologically they'd weaken if he didn't try to hide. So he walked like a juggernaut into the fray. When he lifted his hand and began shooting, the troops either dropped in their tracks or ran for cover. Familiar sounds came from his cuffs: the pht-pht-pht of the bullets flying and the gulp-gulp of the tiny pneumatic piston. "I can do this all day," he yelled at a lull in the firing.

"Let me go," he heard from a distance. A man came running into the open and stopped as soon as he met Brandon's eyes. He threw his hands into the air. "Don't shoot."

"He's not in charge," one of the men said, but others stood and walked forward.

The man who thought he was in charge glanced from side to side and yelled again. "Stay hidden."

"You," Brandon yelled. He had his right hand pointed directly at the man who yelled. "Tell them to come out," Brandon turned to the person with his hands up. "And you, remove the weapon from under your coat."

The man looked down. "I forgot," he said, reaching down to pull out the membrane pistol and hold it out with two fingers.

"Two fingers. Slow," Brandon said.

About that time Palmer appeared overhead in her cruiser.

Brandon's comm unit screeched and she said, "Thought I'd help." She settled the cruiser to the right of the building, and as she did so the troops came out of hiding, their weapons held over their heads or dropped in front of them.

"Pansies," Brandon said under his breath.

The man in front of him had dropped his membrane pistol and started to walk forward with his hand out. "I'm James Stockwell. I came to help."

"Wait there, Buddy." Brandon kept his finger pointed toward the loud mouth. "What about him?"

"Captain Stark. He's a Garth Killjoy man," James said.

"All I needed to know." Brandon popped Stark with a low power fiber bullet and knocked him out. "Pick him up and bring him along," he said to the troops standing with their hands up. "All the rest of you get together where I can see you." He sidestepped toward Palmer's cruiser. She had enough firepower in the cruiser to clear the entire area for a parking lot.

She ran around to greet Brandon. "You didn't need me," she said.

Brandon held his position as she approached. "They needed you," he said, indicating that he would have taken them all out had she not arrived.

"Did I take your pleasure away?"

"It's my duty, not my pleasure." It bothered him that she would think otherwise.

"May I," James indicated that he wanted to enter the building.

Palmer removed a stunner from her belt and put a bead on James. "You may now."

"I'll get the rest of them," Brandon said. "Don't start anything without me."

"Agreed," Palmer said as she led James away first.

Brandon rounded the others up.

"We were under orders," one of the other men said.

"From your captain here?"

"Yes," the man said.

"Good to know." Brandon didn't need to respond beyond that. He knew they were under orders, but at the moment it was difficult to know who's orders. Although James said it was Garth Killjoy, and that would be his first guess, there was no guarantee anymore. When he got near the front of the building he saw one of the guard's heads poke around the door. "Get out here and help," he said. Palmer had already entered the building with James.

Both guards ran out, their stunners held up and pointing at the troops. The tips of the weapons shook with the nervous hands that held them. The guards kept glancing at one another as though neither knew where the other one was going or who should do what. "We got them now," one guard said with a nervous smile on his face.

"No you don't." Even without weapons, Brandon knew that these troops would be more than the two totally untrained guards could handle. He asked if they had a secure place to put the men and planned to lead them there. "Mean time, one of you get a crew to help the wounded, collect their weapons, and report to me."

"Yes, sir."

At least they moved faster than the governmental board had, he thought. Although not as fast as he'd like.

Palmer stood near the reception desk, oblivious as to where to take James. Brandon had the two of them come with him as he secured the soldiers. It didn't take long. The soldiers were split up and put into rooms next to and running down the hall from the lab. "You don't really have a brig, do you?" he said to the guard who traveled with him.

"In the village, we have a jail. Seldom used," he said. "We're a small colony."

As the man turned to go get more help, Brandon stopped him, "How small?"

"Mainly one location, although we consider it three connected villages, maybe twelve thousand people, mostly scientific experts," he said. "I'm a botanist."

Brandon let him go on his way. He stared for a moment at Palmer who held a stunner on James. "This is going to be tough for them. They're pretty small for independence."

"Oliver had no idea what trouble he was getting them into, did he?" Palmer said.

"He's beginning to."

"Can I say something?" James asked.

Brandon nodded.

"I really can help with their situation," James said. "If they'll let me."

"What's in it for you?" Palmer said.

James took a moment, glanced back and forth between them, and then landed on Brandon. "Home," he said. "I want to be on the ground, for good. I want to be part of the growth of a world, on a more personal level. I'm sick of living on board a mother ship in a corporate setting. But mostly, I want to be outside. Free."

Larry came down the hall flanked by guards for the rooms where the troops had been placed.

Before he swung around to greet Larry, Brandon held James' stare for a long while. He could literally feel the man's passion, his commitment to what he wanted. He believed James, so far. "Let's see how that might work."

James followed Brandon down the hall. "You believe me, don't you?"

"Working on it," Brandon said. Although he did believe James, he couldn't, for the life of him, figure out why. But he did. He sensed it in a way that he had never been able to before, not in any other setting. He wondered what might be going on with him and attributed his sensitivity to the sensitivity and tension of the situation. He had never had his loyalties compromised, and for the moment operated in a capacity other than his Earth Central commission. In fact, he had just wounded several soldiers and captured others who he should have been protecting according to his initial orders. He realized that, like Oliver, he had made a decision without really thinking of the consequences. He looked over his shoulder. Palmer had made a decision too.

He turned a corner and darted to the conference room door. Shoving between the guards that had been placed outside, Brandon barged in. He could tell they had been in deep conversation.

Eldon looked up. "And?"

"I have help," Brandon said. He stepped aside and let James walk into the room.

"You?" James said. "Why are you here?"

Jacobs leaned back in his chair. "I'm helping."

"But you're in operations. You were involved in the first attack," James said. Then he pivoted around as though wanting to see what Brandon's reaction to the information would be.

Brandon didn't react and James turned back to Jacobs who smiled up at him. "They know everything," Jacobs said. "More than you know, I'm sure."

James appeared to take the comment in stride. "Maybe we'll all learn something today." He stepped to the opposite side of the table and sat on the edge of the chair ready to talk.

Palmer and Brandon took seats, too. There were five of them besides the governmental board. A full house, and a lot to cover.

# CHAPTER 20

**"SO YOU BELIEVE ME ABOUT GARTH,"** James started.

"Not yet," Jacobs said.

Brandon agreed with Jacobs but kept his mouth shut for now.

James appeared to be slow, as though he still hadn't taken everything in and simulated it. After blatantly observing each person at the table one at a time as though sizing them up, he stopped at Jacobs and asked with curiosity, "What are you doing here? In this meeting?"

"I'll cut to the chase, but then we're going to talk," Jacobs said. "I'm working for Earth Central Investigation. Been observing Garth's ability to run Section 204. I personally have no ideas concerning his original plan, but I am definitely part of something elaborate that, by the way, you did not have access to, to my knowledge, try to stop in any way, which leads me to believe that you were in on this whole charade to dupe this colony into submission so that you could profit off their discovery." He took a deep breath, leaned forward, and rested his forearms on the table to glare into James' face. "Your turn."

Brandon had no idea why Jacobs would do such a thing, but it didn't matter. He was impressed that James remained unflustered by Jacobs' direct verbal attack. There wasn't time to play games with one another and Brandon got impatient. He tapped a finger on the table and shifted his eyes toward Palmer. She locked eyes with him briefly as if to say, What just happened?

James took his time answering, but did so in such a calm and convincing voice that Brandon leaned in to catch each word. Others at the table leaned in, too. The man had a presence when he wanted to. Good for a Peace Coordinator, bad for Brandon and the rest of them if they expected the truth.

James said, "Garth had already ordered the fighters to follow him. My understanding was that they were only to be used for intimidation if that were needed, but I understand differently now." His chin went up. "I, as the Senior Peace Coordinator, was supposed to come down to talk with you. When Garth canceled my visit, I decided to be aboard one of those fighters. Part of my original negotiation included being allowed to stay here. I make no excuses for that. I hate living in space. I want the same thing now. Nothing's changed when it comes to my interest in staying." He looked at the small group of elders who made up most of the board. "That's why I'll do whatever I can in your defense. You can research my credentials. You'll see that I'm good at what I do and can assist greatly when it comes time for negotiating with Earth Central, the IPF, or anyone else who wishes to work with C-47. Especially," he said with a nod toward Jacobs, "about this amazing discovery of yours."

Jacobs laughed and his face lit up. "You don't know what the discovery is."

James didn't miss a beat. "I know what Garth believes, but I don't know the truth. Aliens," he said. "Intelligent ones? But it doesn't matter. If Garth bet his job on it, it had to be something important, something worth a lot of money. He wanted it all to himself. That's how he is."

"That's what he said about you," Eldon piped in.

James shook his head. "All I want is a place to live and be useful. This discovery is yours. Totally. I'll adjust all contracts to say just that." He glanced around quickly. "You didn't sign anything, did you?"

Palmer interrupted the train of conversation. "The fighters weren't acting like intimidators," she said. "Not when we arrived."

James thought for a second as though the question wasn't expected. "Garth had other plans, as I said. He wanted you to believe that I'd sent them. His plan was to have them all shot down, and possible destroy a lot of you with them. He wanted to be the hero in this."

"I can see that," Jacobs said. "And I'm not surprised. Garth wouldn't care about the lost lives."

"This is all fine and good, but what do we do now?" Eldon said. "For Christ's sake, no one is who they say they are, they're not here for what we thought, and we've got Earth Central on its way to give us independence when we may not be ready for it. The conversation has strayed enough."

"I can help," James said.

"You've said that a bit too often," Brandon noted.

Eldon had his hand to his chin and looked from one elder to another. Something was up. When he turned back he said, "My vote is that we haul this guy away and get a full statement of what he knows and how he was involved. We have security personnel who can do that. Do the same with Garth. And the troops, although I don't expect them to have much information."

"Stark will," James interrupted.

"Stark?"

"He had direct orders from Garth. That's why we didn't answer your first calls. He was ordered to maintain radio silence…all part of the intimidation according to Stark, but I think it was meant to taunt you into firing on us first. The fool was willing to listen to orders all the way to his death bed." He reached toward Brandon and tapped the table. "Stark's the one who opened fire on your people and made the attack on this building. You remember? The guy you knocked out?"

Brandon nodded.

"But we didn't shoot first," Palmer proclaimed.

James said, "That fighter spinning out of control really was an accident. Section 204 has been running lean for far too long and we didn't have enough working equipment for that last fighter. Those men died for nothing."

"So did one of ours," Palmer said.

Eldon raised a hand to stop them from bickering. "We have other things to take care of and this isn't helping." He looked at Jacobs as though he were in charge. "A full report work for you?"

"It does. And I might want to be present, as well," Jacobs said.

"Not this time," Eldon said. "We have other items to attend to and although I hate to admit to it, you're just the person to be there."

Brandon knew what Eldon had in mind. He got up from the table and stepped outside to talk with the guards. "Find a room for this guy and hold him there until we can interrogate him."

"Interview," Jacobs yelled from the room.

Brandon said, "Just hold him."

The guards entered the room and reached for James.

"One more thing, quickly," Eldon said. "As far as you know, is Jacobs a religious fanatic?"

James' face twisted into a quizzical position. "Not that I know of. You won't find that with anyone on board the mother ship. Why?"

"Something he said bothered me," Eldon said, then motioned for the guards to take James away.

Once the door closed, Brandon said, "I know what you're thinking."

"We all do," Jacobs said, "but I'm not sure what help I'll be down there."

"Neither do I, but perhaps you'll notice something we've missed all this time," Eldon said. "We have to try."

Oliver's mother spoke up. "May I suggest we talk with Oliver as well. He would never have done any of this had he not believed it was the right thing to do."

Eldon reached over and put his hand over the woman's hand. "I don't always agree with your son, but I do respect him. And it's not like him to put others in danger. He must have had good reasons. He's been acting strangely for a while now. I'm just sorry I didn't say something sooner."

"Settled then," Brandon said. "When do we go down there?"

"Immediately," Eldon said.

As they made their way toward the lab to suit up, Brandon noticed guards standing at many of the doorways. He acknowledged each man and woman as he passed.

Palmer whispered, "They're running at pretty full capacity, don't you think?"

"It worries me a bit," Brandon said. "Not a professional among them."

"And we're going to be down there again," she said shaking her head. "What if something happens up here?"

Eldon and Jacobs had a conversation of their own going, with Eldon briefing Jacobs on their encounters with the Mesoans. He paused for only a moment and looked over his shoulder to answer Palmer, "It'll be okay."

"You heard?" Brandon said. "I thought you were deep in conversation."

"I hear everything," Eldon turned into the lab area ahead of them.

Jacobs was a bit smaller than Oliver, so they put him into one of the spare suits. From there the group hitched a ride with a transport vehicle and entered the office near the pit elevator. Eldon did all the talking. A man and a woman sat in the office but neither asked about Oliver. Putting on their helmets, Eldon ran through the key code and the four of them stepped inside the small space.

Brandon kept his eyes on Palmer as they dropped. For all the time she spent inside the tiny cockpit of a cruiser, he knew she was slightly claustrophobic. She counted down the time it took for them to be inside each of the compartments. A tiny smile lighted her face as the last airlock door opened into the larger room. He let her rush through first, while he brought up the rear.

Before they sat in the chairs that rested in front of the other airlock, Jacobs announced that he was going to go offline and would remain that way until their discussion ended and they were headed back up.

"Why would you do that now that you came all this way?" Eldon said.

"Eliminates two of the three evils," he said.

"Never thought of that," Eldon said, "but at the same time, how can you interpret body language if you don't know their social structure?"

"If what you told me about your encounters is correct, this is the only way I can stay neutral. Regardless of my lack in background, there are certain telltale signs that I'll recognize. Every species man has run across in the galaxy has certain common reactions whether they are intelligent or not. Intelligent beings may have additional ones, or more refined interactions, but we don't know those nuances anyway."

"It's your call," Eldon said.

Jacobs said, "Let's get over this. Palmer is pretty uncomfortable already."

Brandon sat in one of the chairs and held the plug ready. He had enjoyed the feelings he received the day before and felt eager to experience them again. From his observations the last time they visited the Mesoans, he assumed that Eldon felt the same way. Palmer had become irritated, but from what Jacobs had just observed and from what Brandon already knew about Palmer, perhaps her discomfort was what caused her irritability. It may not have had anything to do with the Mesoans at all.

When the green light went on and the aliens stepped into the room, Brandon relaxed into a state of comfort in anticipation of their interactions. He kept Palmer in his peripheral vision. She wrung her hands and changed sitting positions twice already. She glanced around a lot, as though she didn't even want to look at them.

The Mesoans plugged in and the background noise rushed into his helmet. Then the sound of their voices brought the speakers to life, a whisper Brandon didn't recall hearing the last time he was there. He waited for Eldon to lead the conversation, which went along similar lines as the first time Brandon and Palmer had been introduced to them. The difference for Brandon was that he sensed the answers as well as heard them through the computer translator. Eldon never went deeper with his questions, but Palmer did.

When she first spoke up, it irritated Brandon. Her voice sounded shrill and antagonistic. He wanted to reach out and stop her, but he didn't. He held back, waited to see where she went with her questioning.

"Do you have weapons?" she asked directly and firmly.

The Mesoans became animated and Brandon sensed a definite shift in their demeanor. They made more finger movements than he'd noticed before. The two of them touched and pushed against one another. One spoke. A moment later the translator said, "We are able to protect ourselves."

Although shocked by what he heard them say, Brandon remained sympathetic toward the two of them.

"What types of weapons? Can they kill?" Palmer said in what Brandon felt was too aggressive a manner for such a meeting.

Again the Mesoans touched fingers; their facial expressions changed, some looked painful, others joyful. Brandon didn't know what to make of any of it. He took their movements in as best he could. Then suddenly he felt separated, emotionally, from the two beings in the room, as though they had purposefully pulled away. Palmer's prodding embarrassed him, shamed him.

The translator spoke to them. It said, "We have the ability to kill if we feel that we are being threatened. But more important than that," the translator said, "we are also able to protect ourselves without killing."

"How?" Palmer blurted out. "How can you do that from down here?" Her voice raised to a squeal. She stood. The cord attached between her suit and the translating device sloped down to the floor and back up to her suit. She took a step toward the Mesoans and the cord pulled tighter.

The Mesoans spoke louder too, and more direct. The translator remained tonally even when it said, "There are multiple ways to protect from attacks. First," the translator went silent, waiting. The Mesoans had continued speaking but the translator had stopped. When the translator came online again it said, "A language barrier has been reached. The translator is asking the speakers to use additional words that may be more easily understood. Please wait."

The translator couldn't translate.

Eldon interjected, "I don't like this line of query."

"They're answering," Palmer said. "Or trying to."

Brandon understood that that was her way of saying that they hadn't objected, which made her questioning okay. Brandon, just like everyone in the room except for Jacobs, knew that the translator would inform the aliens of the conversation that the three of them were having among themselves.

The translator came on again. "Subliminal use of sound is one weapon. Technological weapons are another." After a very short pause and a strange sound from the aliens, the translator added. "Those are the ones that kill."

Brandon heard Palmer sigh. "Will you talk with us more? Can I go deeper? We may need your help."

"Can you return? You have exhausted us. We will attempt to gather information that we don't presently possess. There are others we must confer with." The aliens didn't wait for a response. They both unplugged and headed for the airlock.

Palmer unplugged and turned to go, ready to get out of there.

Brandon felt cheated by the conversation, but didn't know why. He followed Palmer. "What did you do back there?"

"I got angry. Really angry. And I wanted answers," she said.

"I didn't like that. Too deep, too fast," Eldon said. "I felt as though we, you, were being brutal."

"I'll tell you one thing," Jacobs said, speaking for the first time. Everyone waited. "They are intelligent beings."

"Judging from their responses, I'm about to agree with you. Except that if they were reading Palmer's emotions like we think they do, couldn't they mimic something she would say? Maybe that's why they didn't have the words readily available."

"Their responses?" Jacobs said. "Remember, I wasn't hooked in."

"Palmer questioned them about weapons," Brandon said. "But I'm more interested in what you saw that told you they were intelligent."

"Yeah, how do you know?" Eldon said.

"The way they interact with one another," Jacobs said. "They weren't grooming, playing, or fighting. They weren't cuing off of you three. From what I saw they were in a conversation between the two of them and were trying to figure something out. I don't know what Palmer said exactly, but the Mesoans appeared to be self-aware, contemplative, and interactive in a way that wasn't mimicking on any level." He waited for a response, then said, "My opinion. So far."

"Don't like the 'so far' part," Brandon said.

"I want to talk with Oliver and each of you, in fact anyone who's been down there. I want to get a better understanding of what's going on. I have an idea that needs to be fleshed out," Jacobs said.

"We can make that happen," Eldon said. "But I'll assign a person to be with you at all times."

"Lack of trust in me?" Jacobs said.

"In humans in general at this time," Eldon told him. "I'd rather be with them," he pointed down, "or with the Ekks, for that matter."

Palmer shoved her way toward the door. "This thing moves too slowly for me."

Brandon reached for her but she shoved his hand away.

Although it seemed like a short time that they were with the Mesoans, over an hour had passed. They took the transport back to the double doors and strolled down the hall to the lab in silence. Brandon noticed that they all appeared to have folded their attentions inward, carrying on private conversations with their own thoughts. He tried to regain the sensations he had succumbed to when the six of them first began their conversation, before Palmer ruined the connection, but couldn't get it back.

After they stripped off the suits, Eldon announced that they should all get some sleep.

Although Brandon agreed, he wanted a few minutes with Jacobs before they put a person on him as Eldon suggested. He had his cuffs over one shoulder and his other hand on the back of Jacobs' neck. "We'll walk together," he said.

Eldon said he'd send someone by Jacobs' room in a few hours and that he could begin his interviews whenever he wished after he had freshened up. Palmer took off in the opposite direction, wanting to check on the C-47 jets before settling in for sleep.

"Your concern?" Jacobs said.

"No concern," Brandon said, "curiosity."

"You want to know what else I think, my theories?"

"Something like that. I want to know what happened down there. You can interview me first if you like, but something definitely changed the moment we connected to the translator." Brandon had to shorten his strides as they walked.

"You've only been down there twice now?" Jacobs said.

"Yep. That was the second time."

"Did you know that the computer translator displays the translation as it's happening? In words?"

"Didn't know that. So, you read the conversation as it took place."

"I did," Jacobs said. "But I wanted to hear it from you, see if it was the same.

"And your theory comes from that?" He patted the back of Jacobs' neck. "Come on, Buddy, I feel like I'm pullin' teeth."

"I watched all your reactions as much as I did theirs. Each person has a general way of carrying him or her self. Do you agree?" he asked.

"I'd say that's true," Brandon said.

"Well that way you each have, it became intensified once the aliens plugged in. More dramatic. I want to know why that is and what happened to you. I think it has something to do with their weapons."

# CHAPTER 21

**"IF THEY HAVE WEAPONS,** you'd think they'd have used them against the miners when they were here. Or against us, for that matter," Brandon said.

Jacobs turned his head slightly toward Brandon as they swung around a corner. "Maybe they did."

"What are you suggesting?"

"That the Mesoans are smarter than anyone may think, that they may be using you for their own gains. That every time you go down there you're subject to their influence unlike anything you can imagine." Jacobs stopped at his door. An extremely serious look came over his face. "This is between us. I owe it to you."

"That's tough," Brandon said. "My training…"

"You can be honest and discreet at the same time as you keep a secret." He nodded once. "You can handle it." Jacobs reached behind Brandon and opened the door. "Get some rest."

Brandon didn't feel like resting, but he had been up a long time. He held his wrist up, "Get that?"

"Every word," Palmer said.

"What do you make of it?"

"Something to think about for sure. I felt calmer the second we get topside. When I recall what happened, I'm surprised at myself. I mean, I'm all about getting the information I need, but I'm not used to feeling that angry while getting it. How about you? Notice anything?" She clicked off.

Brandon did notice something, but he wasn't sure he wanted to discuss it over the comm unit, secure line or not.

"You're not talking," Palmer's voice came over the unit.

"We'll talk later. Do what you're doing and get some sleep."

"Hey," she said. "Jacobs is right, you know. You can handle anything."

"We'd better hope so," Brandon clicked off, "because I might be their weapons technology," he said as he hiked the cuffs up to make them more comfortable on his shoulder.

A bit uninviting the room bore a single cot and bare walls. Brandon lay his cuffs in the center of the room. He kneeled on the floor next to his cuffs and performed a standard maintenance check on them. The fiber bullets lay flat inside their chamber, allowing there to be literally thousands of them, each shot controlled by the amount of pressure he used to inflate them. He still had several dozen short-range missiles and high-power blasters left too. If all else failed, he could torque his stunners up to a point where they'd clear a path within fifty yards. He clipped the chambers closed and checked the pressure valves and connectors. After that he removed the water containers and filled them from a small sink, then reinserted them into the inside of each arm.

When through with his inspection and maintenance, he leaned back on his hands and looked at the ceiling. He took a long, slow breath. As much as he considered the thought that he might be part of the Mesoan's arsenal, he also felt the opposite. Could they control him if he wasn't aware of it? He recalled the sense of concern over the guards at the front of the building. He didn't want them to get hurt. Logically, he knew that wasn't like him. He was a soldier, a specially trained one at that. The mission was the end result, not lives, yet he had felt differently then, even after only one visit with the aliens. And now, after two visits, Brandon sensed a reluctance to strap into his cuffs. The feeling was slight, but he noticed it, and it bothered him. He lay back onto the floor and scooted forward so that he could place his arms over the cuffs. That's how he had learned to sleep while taking outdoor training. Never leave your weapon somewhere without touching it. Stay in contact at all times.

He let his eyes close and in twenty minutes was revived, energized, and ready to get moving again. He sat up and ran his hands down the length of his cuffs. Reluctantly, he strapped them on and left the room.

In the hall, he saw Eldon heading his way. "Get enough rest already?"

"More than enough," Brandon said. "You still look a bit haggard though."

Eldon shook his head and shrugged his shoulders. "Eh, I just show fatigue more than most."

"You coming for me?" Brandon said.

"Only if you were awake. I wanted to know what you thought of Jacobs."

"Seems to know what he's doing, why?"

"He started interviewing Oliver's mom and the board instead of the rest of us. I'm worried that he's searching for inside information. How do we know he's not wanting some part of this discovery for himself? He could be wiggling his way in with the board, getting them to like him, trust him." Eldon displayed suspicion on his face about as bluntly as he did with his words, narrowed eyes, cocked head, pursed lips.

Brandon thought for a moment about what Jacobs had suggested was happening to everyone. Maybe Eldon was being manipulated into thinking this way. After all, the aliens must have known that Jacobs wasn't listening in. "Oh my God," Brandon snapped his fingers, swung around, and headed down the hall. He knew where Jacobs would be holding his sessions. In the last conference room they were in. It was the easiest for everyone to reach.

"What is it," Eldon tagged behind Brandon.

"Just a thought," Brandon said.

Eldon grabbed his shoulder and spun him around. The man was much stronger than Brandon had imagined. "Tell me," desperation plastered over his face.

"What if the Mesoans communicate through emotions without needing the translator at all. I mean, we all notice it, right. Maybe all the sounds, all the words, are just for us."

"That would mean that Jacobs couldn't stay neutral," Eldon said what Brandon was thinking.

"What do you know about psychologists?" Brandon said.

"Besides that I don't trust them?"

"Yeah, besides that."

"They're often more frail emotionally than the people they treat," Eldon said.

Brandon smiled. "Well, some of them. But what I was thinking was that they are secretive. Doctor-patient confidentiality. Plus, he's working for Earth Central Intelligence. What if he knows more about the Mesoans than he's telling?"

"Like what?" Eldon acted perplexed and insulted. "What could he know from one visit that I don't know after thirty?"

"I just think we need to get to the bottom of this," Brandon rounded the last corner.

When he slammed through the door, Jacobs and another man, his escort, sat across from Oliver's mother. Jacobs had both his hands over both of hers. Everyone looked up at once.

"Something's going on here," Brandon said.

"There sure is," Jacobs acknowledged. He turned back to Oliver's mom and said, "Marie, I appreciate your honesty. Please, don't worry about this. I'll take care of everything."

He stood and his escort stood with him. Marie slipped from her chair and out the rear door where she halted for a moment. "Shall I send someone else in?"

"Not yet," Jacobs said. "Give me five."

She closed the door and Jacobs motioned for Eldon and Brandon to take a seat.

"What do you mean you'll take care of everything?" Brandon said.

Jacobs stared into Brandon's eyes. "It must be your training."

"What? What's my training have to do with anything?" Brandon said.

"I'm not sure what to say or what to do. Neither of you can be trusted completely." He cocked his head toward Brandon. "Perhaps you more than him." He asked Eldon, "How many times have you been down there?"

"Twenty, thirty. I am the Chief Scientist on the job," Eldon said.

"Alone? Ever?"

"No. That wouldn't be wise," Eldon said. His lips pursed. "I've wanted to, though. I've almost done it."

"That wouldn't be scientific though, would it?" Jacobs said.

"What's this about? Are you questioning us now?" Brandon said.

Jacobs turned to his escort. "You taping all this?"

"Every word, sir, just as you asked."

"You are then," Brandon said.

"Let me explain. There is an emotional thing that happens between people called transference."

"When someone next to you is angry and you pick it up," Eldon said.

Jacobs nodded. "Yes. Exactly."

That statement proved Brandon's theory. "Then you were affected. We can't trust you either. If they're manipulating us, you've been infected..."

"Hold on for a moment," Jacobs said. "You're right to an extent. I was affected, but once I left their presence — or more exact, once they left our presence — I recovered more quickly."

"So, we'll recover eventually?" Brandon shifted his position slightly.

"Recover from what? They aren't manipulating me." Eldon started to stand.

Brandon reached for him and Eldon sat back down. "Explain further," Brandon urged Jacobs.

"A combination of subliminal suggestion, through either what they say or how they say it—I don't know which because I wasn't plugged in—and direct emotional transference. You," he pointed to Brandon, "you know what I'm saying."

"How do you know that?"

"Of all those who have been down there, you have remained closer to your habitual self than the others. Oliver, I've found out from his mother, has gone through stages of change. Eldon, here, is struggling with the hidden messages, whatever they are. As a scientist he needs to produce proof, but as a man, and when his emotions are triggered, he can go off in either direction." Jacobs sat back and waited for his words to sink in.

Eldon's eyes got bigger, as though he was going to explode.

Brandon put a hand on Eldon's arm. "I've changed the least?" He wanted further explanation.

"From what I can tell," Jacobs said. "I'm a little worried about Palmer, though, running around out there with the aggression she's porting through." He turned again toward Eldon. "Who else has been down there?"

"Only a few others. Not for the same reasons as us though, mostly maintenance, equipment installation, that sort of thing. Not all of them had contact. I'll get you a list."

Jacobs nodded his head slowly while keeping his eyes on Eldon. "Can you give me a few minutes of your time today?"

"What's up?" Brandon said.

"I can work Eldon through this. I can appeal to his left brain, if you will. Understanding what's going on gets you half way or more toward recovery," Jacobs said.

"Recovery?" Brandon didn't like the sound of that.

"Yes, recovery." Jacobs puffed his cheeks and let out a blast of air. "Get me that list, would you Eldon? And while he's doing that, you and I are going to talk," he said to Brandon.

Eldon got up from the table and left the room.

"Is he safe?" Brandon asked.

"I believe so," Jacobs said. "The Mesoans have made no outward attempt to harm anyone that I can see." He reached toward Brandon, but didn't touch him. "So, how are you feeling?"

Brandon clenched his jaws and blew air out as though he'd taken a deep breath. He emptied his lungs, wondered what to say, how to put into words how he felt. He glanced away.

"Take your time."

"Okay. Look," Brandon said, "I'm feeling soft."

"I didn't expect you to say that."

"I know. Me either. I thought that if they were going to use me as a weapon, they'd want me more on the edge. Like Palmer, maybe. I don't know. Just a thought. Look, I'm sensing that I don't want to hurt anyone. It's not like me, not totally. I mean I'm not a killing machine, but lately it's felt a bit unnecessary or something."

"But you did go out firing earlier, from what I understand," Jacobs said.

"It's my duty. Although, I did use low-power membrane bullets. A last minute decision. Most of the men were just knocked out." Brandon perked up. "That's it, isn't it? Training. I've been brainwashed once already, so it's more difficult for these, these Mesoans to break through that wall." Brandon smiled at the idea. "In a way, it's made me stronger."

"You could say that. In this situation perhaps," Jacobs said. "But I'd say you have the right idea. That's why you've held to your personality. I suspect Eldon's commitment to his scientific methods has helped his stability, too. Not so with Oliver."

"What's up with him, anyway?"

"Let me explain. When you get scared, you get calm. That's how you clear your head so that you can make good choices in battle. Palmer, by the looks of it, gets pissed off, angry. She flies off the handle."

"You got that right. She gets passionate," Brandon confirmed. "I like that word better."

"Eldon buckles down and buries his thoughts into his research, switches automatically to working like a scientist."

"And we're back to Oliver," Brandon said.

"He gets help." Jacobs stared at Brandon as though waiting for him to get the point.

"Each time he met with them the need escalated until he was desperate," Brandon said.

"He searched for someone who had opposite qualities to himself. That's what felt safe to him. He needed someone who would do anything to save the Mesoans. The only problem with that was that he chose Garth, a man who doesn't want to save them the same way Oliver does, or the way the Mesoans might have hoped. Garth wants them for his own gain. He'll save them all right, but then turn around and exploit them."

"The Mesoans don't know that, though," Brandon said.

"No. I suspect all they get from Oliver is that they'll be safe. I'm not so sure they have weapons, so to speak. They didn't appear to know the term. So I began to think about it," Jacobs said. "If I were an alien and never needed weapons, how would I interpret the word? How would I protect myself?"

"Manipulation. Making someone do what you wanted of them," Brandon said. "Not persuading, but making."

"And the method they might use to do such a thing is, in their words, 'subliminal'."

"What about technological?"

"I think you're right about that. They gathered that understanding from you—after all they have technology too—and applied it to the question. I really don't think they can manipulate in specific ways, so you have little worries there. But, they can excite your deeper emotions. Palmer's, deep-seated anger, for example, becomes outward aggression. Your empathetic nature, the part of you that you try to hide, comes out a bit stronger."

"I'm starting to understand."

"Good. I knew you would. So, here's what we have to do: we're going to work together for a while, and I'm going to teach you to become aware of what's going on with them more quickly so that you can adjust. It's a conscious thing. Your training will allow you to implement the stages easily."

"I'm good with that, but what about the others?"

"Eldon won't be too bad. His exposure is what's broken him down. I think it might take a bit longer with him, but he'll come around. Oliver will take months, I'm afraid, but judging by his latest turn against Garth, I could be wrong there. There's always the possibility that overexposure allows a person to get used to their emotional transference, dulling the effect and perhaps even reversing it after a while. Whatever subliminal messages they're sending may be coming to the surface, too. I don't know for sure at this time, but I'll figure it out."

"You're liking this?"

"For once, Brandon, I'm using my training for good. I don't have to hide. I don't have to work with idiots. I more than like this, I love it." Jacobs beamed.

"It suits you," Brandon said. "Okay, let's get to this. He shrugged his shoulders to feel the weight of the cuffs. You want me to take these off?"

Jacobs looked at the man beside him. "No. You're safe."

Brandon and Jacobs went through the five steps needed to recognize an emotion physically and consciously so that Brandon could adjust to the Mesoans' influence. By creating rules and operations, Brandon would be able to intellectualize each emotion that came through and actually choose which ones he wanted to accept and which to reject. As Jacobs suggested early in their conversation, Brandon found the steps not only easy to complete, but comfortable and natural, and could relate the activity to his advanced military training.

Jacobs stood at the end of their work and reached to shake Brandon's hand.

"Who's next?" Brandon asked.

"Palmer. She's been exposed the least amount of time."

"Then Eldon and Oliver?"

Jacobs shook his head affirmatively. "Like I said, they'll take longer, but we'll get it done."

"One thing, Buddy. What about all these soldiers and James and Garth? We have a growing situation on our hands, and not much time to fix it."

Jacobs looked at the man beside him, his escort and now helper.

"They're all being interviewed by different staff members as we speak," Jacobs said. "We'll pull everything together and go over it for flaws, then make a determination from there."

Brandon shook his head. "A lot of shit to go through. You up for this?"

"More than you might understand," he said.

Brandon left the meeting and headed back to his room to go over his new method of operations. On his way, he saw that two men walked with Palmer.

"What the fuck is going on?" she said when she saw Brandon. "I can't shake these guys."

He shooed them away with a hand wave and the men stopped advancing with Palmer and went the other way. Brandon thought that the word got around pretty quickly for a place with only a few comm units. "It's nothing," he said.

Palmer leaned her head against Brandon's shoulder as they walked. "What's happening to me? I can't seem to calm down for some reason."

"Get any sleep?"

"Not a wink. I kept thinking about the weapons those aliens said they had. I wanted to scour the planet looking for them, but it made no sense. I don't get it."

Brandon slowed and reached to open the door to the conference room. "You'll understand in a moment." Inside he said to Jacobs, "Would you like me to stay?"

"I have it from here," Jacobs said.

Palmer looked from one to the other several times. Brandon waited for her. Finally, she said, "I want him to stay." It wasn't a request, that's not how Palmer worked.

Jacobs accepted gracefully by motioning for the two of them to sit.

Palmer yanked the chair back with an effort that made as much noise as possible. "God damn it," she said. She plopped down and swung toward Brandon. "I'm getting worse."

"I know, Sweetheart, I can tell."

Palmer breathed heavily. She looked crazed.

Brandon put an arm around her shoulder and she melted into his chest like butter to heat.

Jacobs didn't look happy. "She's bouncing a bit uncontrollably at the moment."

Palmer's voice squeaked out a "Help me," before she burst into tears.

Brandon glared at Jacobs who took a deep breath. "I can do this," he said, but Brandon wasn't convinced yet.

# CHAPTER 22

**ALTHOUGH, FROM TIME TO TIME,** rushing or yelling sounds from the hall outside the conference room turned therapy office interrupted the conversation, Brandon found that the few hours they spent together proceeded smoothly. With Brandon beside her, Palmer's emotions bounced back and forth between calm and angry, but not half as far as they could have. He'd seen her at her most vulnerable and her most angry, although not without reason, and not within a few minutes of one another.

Jacobs performed the perfect balance of teaching and listening. Brandon had never witnessed such an act of pure mastery in a very original situation. After all, a few hours earlier Jacobs beliefs about what had occurred below were completely theoretical. The more he inquired and probed, the more he appeared to understand and solidify his analysis as well as his chosen treatment. On occasion he addressed Brandon directly, telling him that what he told Palmer might work as an alternative method for him, too, to stay centered. To reject the influence of the Mesoans.

The escort sat so still it was like he was afraid to be noticed, and Brandon ignored him hoping that he wouldn't feel put on the spot for any reason.

"No drugs?" Palmer joked at one point.

Jacobs laughed. "You're feeling better all ready," he said. "But to answer your question, not all psychologists rely on drugs. In fact, in this situation it's not a chemical imbalance we're dealing with. All you really need to understand is your own reactions and how to counteract them by reasonable choice. Logic."

"Understand them physically," Brandon said, as half question and half statement.

"For the most part understanding starts physically, yes," Jacobs said. "I was surprised at Palmer's quick acceptance of the Mesoans' influence until now. Through our brief conversations, I see that she had already been going through a stressful internal struggle, only partly due to the closed space. Because she was unsure and wavering internally, the Mesoan's emotional push, shall we say, was easy to take on."

"Her stress about us?" Brandon asked.

Palmer leaned into him. "That's only a small part of it," she said.

"Oh?"

"I compromised my integrity. That's what's been bothering me," she admitted to them both.

"I would never ask you to do that," Brandon said.

"No, no—" Jacobs started.

But Palmer didn't let him finish. "It wasn't about our relationship. It was about this job." She glanced around the room indicating all the events that had taken place in the past days. "I knew something was up, but I wanted the money. I don't often ask a lot of questions. I mean, a job's a job, but I'm usually much more thorough, especially when things don't feel right from the start. Faking a mission has the feel of underhandedness written all over it. I thought I shoved the idea out of my mind but, of course, that can't happen." She reached toward Jacobs and let her hand fall short of his by only an inch or two. "You protected me on several occasions."

Jacobs nodded. To Brandon he said, "I'm sorry. Had I known you'd have left your seat…"

"No need. If it were my choice, I'd have wanted Palmer safe, too." Brandon fully understood that Jacobs had a job as well. He got back to business right away. "So, this internal struggle is what made her vulnerable, just by being in close proximity to the aliens?"

"And listening," Jacobs said. "Don't forget the subliminal part."

"Well, I feel better now that I can intellectualize the events and my feelings," Palmer said.

Jacobs shook his head. "It's not about intellectualizing; it's about awareness and then setting up methods to adjust to a change, combat the feelings if necessary, and use a practiced method to get back to center."

Brandon shook his head. "Everything you said is foreign except to 'use a practiced method'."

"Where I can make a decision that is true to myself. I got it." Palmer slid her chair back and touched Brandon's arm for him to get up with her.

"Get rest," Jacobs said. "That'll help relieve any additional stress. Try not to think about this for now. Wait until you're fresh. Can you do that?" He looked tired as well. "Can you help?" he asked Brandon.

"I'll stay with her until she gets some sleep."

Jacobs nodded and sat back in his chair. He asked if the man next to him could find him some water. "Or better yet," he said, "some jasp."

"Richard," the man said. He had a crooked smile, but a pleasant one. "Yeah, I can do that."

Brandon and Palmer walked out of the room in front of Richard. When he stepped into the hall he let out a huge sigh. "Unbelievable," he said.

"It had better be believable or we're in bigger trouble than we thought," Palmer said.

Richard laughed and moved off in the opposite direction than Brandon and Palmer were going. "It does feel unbelievable," Palmer said. "This whole operation is crazy. Sometimes it makes sense and other times it doesn't...on all sides."

"Let's discuss it later. I agree with Jacobs, you need rest."

"I know, but it's creepy to think that those things down there were able to control me so easily. And look what they've done to Oliver. I mean, the way Jacobs talked in there, Oliver is hardly the same man."

"I know. Even I was taken over for a short while, I have to admit."

Palmer lowered her eyes to meet his. "I've only seen you relinquish control a few times. Always in the face of duty. You're a loyal person."

"Enough of that," he said as he led her to her chamber. After closing the door behind them, Brandon removed his cuffs. Once they were off he had the sense of missing a part of himself, which actually made him feel better. His attachment to his weapons might not be natural for someone else, but they reminded him that he was stable and centered. A flag letting him know when things were and weren't going right.

Palmer lay on her bunk and reached for Brandon's hand.

He slid his cuffs and himself closer so that he could rest his legs on top of the cuffs and lean his back against the side of the bunk. In that position he laid his arm next to her body and took her hand. She a bit vulnerable, he felt glad that he was there to help her through it.

As soon as Palmer's breathing indicated that she had fallen asleep, Brandon slid his hand from hers and stood. He reached down and keyed her wrist communicator so that it was open at all times. This allowed him to monitor the room while she slept and to know when she awoke. He figured that he could give her several hours minimum, which gave him time to think, poke around the complex, and collect as much information as he could. He put his cuffs back on and left the room to find Larry. It didn't take long. The young man stood on a short ladder while rigging an audio link inside one of the makeshift prison cells. Brandon stepped inside the small room where there were five IPF enforcers and three armed men from C-47. "A bit crowded isn't it?"

"Not much choice," Larry said as he slid a piece of equipment into the ceiling and screwed it down. "Now, you guys," he said, addressing the enforcers, "this has a beacon on it. If you even try to tamper with it, we'll know."

The men didn't say anything, but Brandon could tell that they got the picture. "Leave guards, too," he said.

"Will do," Larry saluted.

"No need for that," Brandon said.

Larry grabbed the ladder and followed Brandon out of the room. "You wanted me for something?"

"Yeah, just what you're doing. You were ahead of me. So, are you recording everything, too? You have someone to monitor these rooms? How're the interviews going? That sort of thing."

Larry appeared happy to be helping out. He lifted a hand and peeled a finger down with each statement. "We're recording everything; we have three men monitoring the rooms; we have guards posted; interviews are going well; and I'm going behind each interviewer to rig the rooms permanently. Nothing's going to get past us."

"I noticed that unit you put into the ceiling wasn't portable," Brandon said.

"Cannibalized from their lander." Larry lowered his eyes for a moment. "We don't have enough equipment, so I've been jerry rigging and stealing all I can. Some of the rooms will have computers set up."

"And the beacons?"

"Simple circuits. I have a few of my buddies making them," Larry said.

"You're not set up for this at all are you?" Brandon said.

"We're well equipped for scientific research, for farming, and for protecting ourselves, but no, we're not prepared for this. Should we have been?" Larry said.

"It appears so." Brandon saw Larry's expression change and put a hand on his shoulder. "You're doing a great job here."

Larry recovered slightly and went back to his work. "Where to next?" he asked one of the men with him.

Brandon didn't wait for the answer because he didn't care what Larry's next job was, he cared only that he find Jacobs. The man had looked pretty tired before he left with Palmer. And if there were one thing Brandon could recognize it was battle fatigue.

There were guards at most of the doors in the building, which meant that if any one group of soldiers tried to escape, there'd be plenty of firepower to stop them. Even though C-47 wasn't manned by trained soldiers, there were enough of them to handle the job against the unarmed IPFers. As he headed down the last passageway toward the therapy room, he noticed Richard in the other direction, "Hey, wait a minute," he yelled.

Richard turned and smiled his crooked smile when he saw Brandon.

"How come you're off duty? Jacobs taking a break?"

"Dismissed," Richard said. "Jacobs left with Eldon."

"With Eldon? Dismissed? Weren't you in the same room as me?"

"They order—"

"Where they going?"

Richard looked away and didn't say anything.

"What the hell?" Brandon said. "Just the two of them?"

"As far as I know."

"Christ almighty. I've got to get to them." He gave Richard a look of disappointment. "Next time, stick with him. That's your job, isn't it?"

"Yes, sir."

Brandon jogged toward the lab hoping to catch them before they suited up, but he got there too late. And by the time he dressed quickly and reached the office near the pit they had already gone into the first elevator. "Let me in there," he said to the operators.

"Can't go until we disinfect the chambers after they come back."

"What?"

"We disinfect all the chambers," the man repeated in a tone that questioned whether or not Brandon had heard him the first time.

"Eldon and Jacobs, right?"

"Yes," the man said.

"Did they seem chummy?"

"Chummy? How so?"

"Were they in a good mood?"

The man shrugged and looked at the woman who sat beside him. "Serious, maybe?"

The woman nodded in agreement.

"They didn't say much. But nothing seemed out of the ordinary," the man said. "Sorry I don't have more to offer."

"How long do you think they'll be down there?" Brandon asked.

"Usually an hour or two."

"Did Jacobs look tired?"

"I'm sorry, but…"

"You didn't notice. I understand. This is routine for you," Brandon said.

"Not exactly. Usually they don't go down twice in one day. And…"

Brandon urged him. "Now you're talking. What is it? Come on?"

"Eldon asked that we let the Mesoans know that it was urgent. They don't always agree to meet, you know."

"I didn't know. But telling them that it's urgent is only going to scare them. What were they thinking?"

"Don't know, sir."

"Rhetorical," Brandon said. He turned to leave and swung back before he went out the door. "Do you have radio contact with Larry?"

"The tower," the man said. "They'll relay any message to Larry. We know what's going on back there even if we appear to be disconnected."

"I've got to tell you that I'm surprised by that, but nonetheless I want you to let me know the second they begin their return. Got it?"

The man nodded and so did the woman.

"The second."

"I promise," the man said.

Brandon rushed out and took a single person carrier back to the main building. He worried about why Jacobs and Eldon would even go down there together. To warn them? Of what? He heard a moan come from his wrist communicator and brought it to his ear. Nothing but deep breathing. Palmer slept hard.

He made his way back to the lab, removed the suit, and sat down at one of the benches to think. What might happen if the Mesoans got really scared? How would that come through emotionally? He didn't like the directions such a situation might go. Eldon wasn't out of the woods at all and Jacobs had never been under the full influence of the aliens. How would he react? Or was he going to observe again? That wouldn't help the Mesoans to feel any safer.

Brandon needed Palmer's help on this one. Something was happening that he just couldn't understand. He continued to think that if it were his choice he wouldn't have gone down there at all. So, what was up?

Brandon got up from his stool and began to pace in the empty lab. As he passed the benches, he ran his hand over any equipment that sat near the edge. All he could come up with was that the Mesoans were like scared rabbits. If he understood Jacobs properly, the more frightened the Mesoans became, the stronger the emotional push. He had no reference point as to what that could mean. How much influence could they even have? If they were scared, like any soldier who allows himself to become frightened, they'd lose control. He stopped and tapped his forehead with a finger as he repeated the thought: they'd lose control if they were frightened. Not good.

A moan came from his wrist communicator and he looked at the time. He left the lab to go to Palmer's room. She was just sitting up as he entered.

"You left me?" Palmer accused.

Brandon skipped to the point. "Jacobs went down to see the Mesoans with Eldon."

Palmer rubbed her face and pulled her hair back. "I probably look awful."

"Did you hear me?"

Palmer moved to the sink and ran water over her hands then rubbed her hands over her face. "Let me think," she said while toweling off.

"I don't like it. Jacobs was in no condition…"

"He didn't know that."

"How could that be?"

"Adrenaline pushed him forward." She cocked her head and stared for a moment. "This is probably the most exciting thing he's ever done. That'll carry him forward for a while. I doubt it was anything but study, research."

"What about Eldon?"

"Now that's another story. But Jacobs had no one else to take, did he? Eldon was his only choice." Palmer didn't appear to be too concerned with the situation.

Brandon stopped cold while she talked. "If we could just know what was going on."

"There must be a way," she said. "I should have taped it myself. Maybe Larry?" She opened her door and bolted down the hall until she ran into a guard. "Can you get hold of Larry?"

Brandon was right behind her.

The guard called for Larry and shoved a handheld communicator toward Palmer. "Are there recorders in the suits?" she asked.

"No. Why?"

"I wanted to review the conversation from down there."

Larry's voice came back. "That's easy. The computer they use in the pit ports to Eldon's research computer. I'll be right there."

"His research computer?" Brandon shook his head. "Why didn't we know that?"

"We do now," she said.

"So, what are you thinking?"

"I don't know yet."

It didn't take long for Larry to march the two of them to Eldon's office and open it using his security code. "There you go," he said.

"Hold on, Cowboy. You've got to start this thing. I'm sure you've got to sign in," Brandon said.

"Not if the room is secured," Palmer said while starting the computer. "Aaaannnnnd here we are." She stood back and told Larry he could go.

Brandon leaned to look over the screen. "They're all here. Every visit." He sat down. "Are you ready to listen again?"

"No," Palmer said while pulling a second chair next to Brandon's.

"No? Then what'd we come down here for?"

"To look at it. Let's run it through the translator." She reached across him and punched a few keys. The translator opened and she ran one of the conversations, at random, through the device with the mute on. "Let's see," she said while using the computer to locate and separate the aliens' speech from the human speech. "Do you see that?"

"The background," Brandon said. "I see it. Noise, isn't it? My speakers had a fairly constant white noise present, didn't yours?"

"They did," she said. "But there isn't any noise on our end, only theirs." She punched a few more keys, "Let's separate their voice from the background noise."

"Should I take it off mute?"

"God, no. Not yet. Let's enhance the noise signal first then send it through the translator."

"The translator? You don't think..." Brandon waited for Palmer to finish his statement.

"If so, we'll be able to read it onscreen." Palmer increased the amplitude of the background noise until the signal had the appearance of a speech pattern. With a few more keys punched, the translator did nothing more than produce typed words that matched the visual of the sounds. Over the screen came, I will protect you from harm at all cost. It is what I most want to do. My life's purpose is to keep you safe. You are my brothers.

Palmer started the translation at the beginning again. "Now you can take it off mute."

Brandon pushed the volume key and heard Oliver's voice over the speakers, then Eldon's voice came on. "They're feeding our words back to us using our own voices and simultaneous to our conversation."

"Subliminal messages in our own voices," Palmer said, "not emotional." She took her eyes from the screen to look into Brandon's eyes. "Those are the most powerful. I suspect that the messages go back and forth between Oliver and Eldon's voices. That could be why they irritate one another and yet respect one another. They more or less have the same purpose."

Brandon pushed back from the desk. "But they have two different approaches. Now I'm even more concerned for Jacobs being down there with Eldon."

"Let's translate more of this and get it on a chip drive," Palmer said.

Brandon stood from the chair. "Can you do that? I need to be there when they come up."

# CHAPTER 23

**BRANDON WORE NO SUIT** as he stood ready at the elevator door. He did wear his cuffs, though. The moment the door opened he stepped inside. Eldon stood over a crumpled Jacobs pummeling his helmetless face. Brandon yanked Eldon out of the way and threw him from the elevator.

Jacobs was conscious, but bleeding from the nose.

"You okay?" Brandon said.

Jacobs laughed.

"Good enough." Brandon helped Jacobs stand.

One of the operators, the woman, had a stunner pointed at Eldon who stood stoically, his eyes blank and staring.

"This has happened before," the man said.

"And no one saw it important to tell me?" Brandon said.

"They knew," the woman shook her stunner at Eldon. "It's been a long time, though."

Brandon asked Jacobs if he could walk on his own and when he got an affirmative he grabbed hold of Eldon again. "I need transport for three."

"You're not going to call anyone for help?" the woman asked.

"The man I need to talk with is here," Brandon said, indicating Jacobs.

The other operator called for transport and nodded. "Here in a minute."

"This is just all routine for you two, isn't it?" Brandon said to the operators.

"Not really, but you seem to have things under control, and according to what we've heard there's not much that'll stop you anyway."

Brandon had to laugh at that one. "You people just want to live peacefully don't you?" He didn't need an answer, so he guided Eldon out of the office. Jacobs brought up the rear, although a bit slower than he normally moved.

Once the transport dropped them off, Brandon guided Eldon to the lab and helped him strip off the suit. Jacobs found some wipes and cleaned up his nose the best he could. The bleeding had stopped. Bruises appeared around his cheeks and one eye.

"You look like shit," Brandon said. "Why didn't you get some sleep like you suggested for us? I mean, what were you expecting to learn from going down there?"

"I wanted to see what the Mesoans would do."

"About what?"

"If they felt that there was real danger," Jacobs said. "All the information so far indicates that they're worried. The next step could have turned their fear into fight or flight. I needed to know what we were dealing with."

"Find out?"

Jacobs rubbed his nose. "Looks that way, doesn't it?"

Eldon sat on a stool against the wall. He held his head low as he said, "I'm sorry. That wasn't like me."

Brandon and Jacobs turned their attention to Eldon. "He's coming out of it," Jacobs said. "Some kind of trance almost. Pretty powerful. That I didn't expect."

"I kind of went off for no reason. I just felt as though what you were doing wasn't right, that you were dangerous? You're so secretive." Eldon rubbed his head and neck as he talked.

Brandon asked how he was feeling.

"Better. But I don't like him going down there and not participating. That's dishonest," Eldon said.

"Fear of the unknown," Jacobs said.

"Dishonest," Eldon repeated. "It's not unknown if you're keeping things from us on purpose."

Brandon saw in Eldon's body language that he was passionate about what he said. His jaw locked into place and his eyes narrowed as he looked at Jacobs. While keeping an eye on Eldon, Brandon reach out and put a hand on Jacobs' shoulder. "They're somehow recording everyone's words and feeding them back subliminally. They're scared and are manipulating everyone they can into protecting them just like you guessed, but I suspect it goes much deeper."

"How do you know what they're doing?" Jacobs said in a whisper, as though Eldon couldn't hear.

Brandon pointed toward Eldon. "His tapes of the conversations. Palmer figured it out."

"They wanted you to be down there again," Eldon said to Brandon.

"He's right. I read it on the translator. They asked for you by description," Jacobs said. "You must be on to something. They want your firepower."

"So, I am their technology," Brandon said.

"You and Palmer." Jacobs thought for a moment. "Now what do we do?"

"We start by putting him somewhere safe," Brandon said. Reaching for Jacobs' suit, Brandon remembered what the operator at the pit office had said about this happening before. "The suit being repaired..." he said to Eldon.

The man shrunk down in his seat. "Oliver did the same thing to me once. He said that he had the strongest feeling that I was prying too much; that my interest was more than scientific."

"Was it?" Jacobs said.

Eldon turned his face away.

"Fame? Money?" Jacobs inquired.

"I'd be the one who discovered them," Eldon said. "Humans have been going everywhere in the galaxy looking for intelligent life, and this is the first time. We are so close. I admit, I wanted the credit."

Jacobs shook his head. "Let's go. I want to hear the messages the aliens are sending." He stood to go. "So, subliminal meant sound not just emotion. Didn't think of that."

"You broke into my lab. I should be allowed to see what you discovered," Eldon said as he stood to go as well.

"Not this time." Brandon found a guard in the hall and instructed him where to take Eldon. It was strange how easily the C-47 men and women had accepted him as their leader. The whole place was so passive. He mentioned his concern to Jacobs who blew it off. "That's the case with a lot of scientific communities. All they really want is to do their research. With a new planet, there's plenty of that needed. These days, colonies, for what it's worth, are made up of more scientists than anything else. They're here as much to explore as to settle the planet." He gave Brandon a sideways glance. "You've been on enough of these planets, I'm sure. Haven't you noticed before?"

"Mission critical. If it doesn't have to do with my mission, I let it go." He tapped his head with a finger. "Focus. That's what allows me to do my job."

"Every time you point toward yourself, I worry that damned weapon you're wearing will go off," Jacobs said.

"It's happened before, but never with me."

"It's that touchy?"

"It's that loaded," Brandon said. "Here we go." He opened the door and let Jacobs walk in behind Palmer who bent close to the screen of Eldon's research computer.

"It's hard to believe that Eldon never thought to look at this," Palmer said without turning around.

"He loves going down there. He trusts them. Why would he suspect anything?" Jacobs said.

Palmer turned to answer him and said, "Whoa! What hit you in the head?"

"Eldon, actually," Jacobs said.

"He did a nice job for a wimp," she said.

"Get on with it," Brandon said. "Jacobs needs to get some sleep pretty soon or he won't be worth shit to us."

"Sure," Palmer swung around and hit a few buttons. "I can only imagine that Eldon's research was all about Eldon and had very little to do about the Mesoans. That must be why he never suspected that they would be doing anything like this. He was asking the questions and taking down the answers. That's all."

"Pretty one-sided," Brandon said.

"Most scientists are like that in my opinion," Palmer said. "Now listen." She turned to the computer for a moment and out of the speakers came Oliver's voice. We are brothers of the world. I must protect my brothers from everyone who could do them harm. I will find those who can help me and let them help me. We are brothers of the world. She poked the mute button and turned around. "Most of the messages are similar in content, and repetitive. Sometimes in Oliver's voice, sometimes Eldon's. I'll check for our voices later. I'm sure they're in there."

"Amazing," Jacobs said.

Palmer had her hand perched over the keyboard. "Not as amazing as this." She pushed a few keys and Eldon's voice said, The other man is bad. He is hiding something from me. He wants to do me harm and he wants to harm my brothers. He must be stopped. He must be killed. Destroy the man. I must kill him before he can do harm. She turned it off.

Brandon watched the screen as it indicated the signal that matched the sound. "Not good."

"I'll say." Jacobs looked worried. "He would have killed me if you hadn't stopped him."

"That's not the worst of it." Brandon pointed to the computer screen. "If I'm reading this correctly, that wasn't subliminal. The amplitude equaled normal speech. They were telling him directly. Ordering him. And he obeyed."

Palmer nodded in agreement.

"It didn't show up on the screen down there," Jacobs said. "All I read was a conversation about the dangers that we were experiencing up here. I asked Eldon to explain, roughly, the situation with Garth. I hoped that they'd see how their fear had brought about trouble instead of relieving it," Jacobs explained. "I thought the honesty would get them to reciprocate, get them to trust us."

"Didn't work." Brandon turned his attention to Palmer. "They could easily rewrite the interface so that some messages bypassed the terminal. What's their technological level? Do we even know? Both terminals in that room are ours by design." Brandon rattled off his thoughts. When he looked at Jacobs for an answer to any of his questions, the man just shook his head.

"Talk about secretive," Palmer said. "I don't think Oliver or Eldon know the answer to that question either. I've been all over his computer and find dozens of crazy theories concerning the possibilities." She patted Brandon's arm. "Several revolved around the feasibility that they were feeding back learned reactions based on the emotional connections they made with Oliver and Eldon. There's a definite leaning toward not wanting to accept that they are intelligent, so they almost never ask questions about technology. It's noticeably avoided."

Jacobs had a hand to his chin and stared into the corner.

"What?" Brandon said.

"Either of you have any idea how the air chambers got installed on their end?"

"No, why?" Palmer bent to listen to him.

"They'll do everything in their power to protect their people, wouldn't you?"

Brandon shrugged, accepting the idea as it stood.

"Their airlock looks human-made." He looked at the two of them as though expecting them to follow his thoughts. "An open hole would allow their air to escape, killing all of them, wiping out the only humanlike, intelligent life form in the galaxy. What's that worth to them, and what's it worth to us, or more precisely to Oliver and Eldon and C-47?"

Palmer shook her head. "I don't think we could imagine."

Jacobs said, "Consider if you two were the only contacts with a race that was able to destroy all of humanity how would you feel? What would you be willing to do to stop it from happening? Stop that kind of destruction? It's not your lives now we're talking about. It's every last man, woman, and child in the human, or in this case the Mesoan race?"

No one spoke.

"That's what we're talking about." Jacobs scratched his head and ran the same hand tenderly across his bruises. "I'd have me killed too. You can't blame them. We have total power over them."

"But if they'd just talk with us straight, we could help," Palmer said.

"We don't know how many of them we already killed when the mining company created that hole. We have no idea how it feels to teeter on the edge of extinction." Jacobs asked, "Would you trust a race of people who came in and killed the first hundred people they ran into?"

"It was an accident," Palmer said.

Brandon said, "They wouldn't know that."

"When they read Oliver and Eldon's energy, the first time, wouldn't that tell them?"

"Yeah," Brandon said with a little laugh. "I can imagine that to Eldon they suddenly felt like lab rats and to Oliver they felt like an economic breakthrough for the humans. From that, they'd assume we were parasites."

"And they wouldn't be too far off the mark," Palmer said. "Look what's been done already."

"Exactly," Jacobs said. "Seeing that Oliver was the easiest to manipulate, they picked on him to focus their survival plans. They couldn't know how sloppy and inexperienced Oliver was about such things. How he might misinterpret their true needs and replace them with blind selection. They also would have no idea how much more self-serving people like Garth would be. How could they?"

Palmer said, "I get it. There are thousands of ways this could have gone. But what do we do now?"

"I don't know," Jacobs said. "I'll sleep on it."

"What'll we do in the mean time?" Brandon said.

"Keep everyone away from those aliens for now."

"That's a given," Palmer said.

"Why don't you two check to see what's happening with Earth Central and the IPF ship? EC is usually pretty quick to take over. All they have to do is suspect something's out of order. Once they find out who's down here, how many troops and fighters, they'll want to investigate. My guess would be that Earth Central will find a few discrepancies in procedures or paperwork and halt all previous rulings."

"That would include C-47's independence," Brandon said.

Jacobs nodded. "It could, but at this point, I don't know if that would be a good thing or a bad one."

"I know how these guys will take it," Palmer said.

Jacobs got up from his chair. "A lot going on. I'd better talk with their council."

"Governmental board," Brandon corrected.

"Same thing to me. They act like a council. You see how they interacted with Oliver and Eldon. It's time we flesh this government out. It's starting to look like a crazed and manipulated Oliver was running almost the whole place. And with Eldon as sidekick." Jacobs waved for Brandon to follow him. "One of you, come with me."

"Still a bit unstable?" Brandon said.

Jacobs shook his head. "For support. I think they trust the uniforms or something."

"I'll go," Palmer said, "and meet up with you at the tower."

Brandon locked the lab door behind them and watched as Palmer and Jacobs walked down the hall. Guards wandered everywhere in the building, well not really guards, but C-47ers with guns. Brandon wasn't too sure if that was the safest place to be for any of them, but there it was.

He took a truck from the pit building to the tower, traveling slowly through the canyon watching for Ekks or lizards or any other animal. He did notice the birdlike creatures flitting around some of the bushes, but it appeared as though not much else hung around. It could have been the sound of the vehicle. If the Ekks were afraid of loud noises there was a case to be made that other indigenous animals would be too…including the Mesoans, he thought. The drills must have been unbelievably loud down there, vibratory, all adding to the fear that it was the end of the world for them. Would he do what they're doing? He probably would. He stopped the vehicle and turned off the engine. Holding his wrist communicator up he keyed it and said, "Palmer, could you check something for me?"

"Sure, what do you need?"

"Can you find out why the mining company really left? What were the circumstances?"

"I'm just dropping Jacobs off now. I'll see what I can find out."

He keyed twice to indicate he was through talking. Not a sound came from anywhere around him except for the fluttering of wings every once in a while. He stepped out of the truck and stood still. He took a deep breath and looked to the sky. From where he stood, only a few clouds stood above the blue hills, which rose on either side of him. Brush protruded from the ground about as often as rocks. A breeze whipped up. The air settled at about seventy degrees, even in the direct sunlight. A cool day.

Brandon enjoyed the quiet. He thought more clearly. He knew that once he reached the tower, it would be activity and noise again. Was he getting to be more like the Ekks? No, every creature understood the sanctity of silence, he thought. He took a short walk and spent a moment touching the blue sand, inspecting a bush, trying to get a better look at one of the birds. As he got closer, he got a clear view of the tiny round head similar in shape to the Ekks. He heard something stir to his left and glanced over. One of the birds lay on the ground dead, while a second one tore at its flesh, pulling off small pieces of meet with a jerk of its head. Brandon leaned in closer and the live bird turned toward him with its teeth bared, protecting its meal. Like the Ekks, they were cannibalistic. He held that thought and stood slowly.

Brandon got back into the truck and drove toward the tower. He didn't like where his thoughts were headed. Before he reached the tower, Palmer called on his communicator. He said, "Go."

"It appears that the miners built the airlock," Palmer said. "Then they left, but not before having some pretty unbelievable internal problems."

"What kind of problems?"

"Murders," she said. "Arguments. Many of the men refused to go back into the pit to work."

"They wouldn't have put in the translator. They wouldn't have had the time to run that kind of experiment. Not a mining outfit, anyway," Brandon suggested.

"Probably not, but if they created a hole into the aliens' world and got bombarded with the emotional explosion that would have occurred with those deaths, there's no telling what happened even if they couldn't hear anything."

"Who said they couldn't hear?" Brandon said. "They wouldn't have worn suits if they didn't know what they'd done. They'd be open to whatever the aliens said."

"That means that the aliens would have to be capable of some pretty fast manipulation of sound. Wouldn't they have to know the language to do that?"

"Universal sounds," Brandon said.

"What the hell is that?"

"You know how when you're listening to music, or to someone mumbling, you try to pick out words? Maybe it's like that? Or like 'ouch' appears in most languages. Crying, or other sounds of distress. It could be that the miners' brains heard what the Mesoans' emotions expressed, but also their cries. We decipher the words the way we want to. The emotional impact could apply an additional effect to what we think we hear." Brandon kept the communicator keyed. "They must have two sets of vocal cords? One for speech and one for the subliminal material?"

"They were starting to trust us," Palmer said. "Us. That's why they wanted us back. Not for our weapons. We were neutral and they could feel it. We are who we are. We had no alternative motive. When Eldon brought Jacobs back without us, they got scared again. They were telling us the truth."

"That means that they have technical weapons, you know. If they didn't mean our weapons, they meant theirs." He paused for a second. "Here's something else to consider." He held off for a moment, rethinking what he was about to say to Palmer.

"What else," she pushed.

"I think they may be cannibalistic."

# CHAPTER 24

"**WHAT THE HELL DO YOU MEAN** by that?" Palmer shouted.

"The Ekks are cannibals and so are these little birds I found hanging around in the bushes out here. The lizards probably are too. Isn't that clear enough?"

"What lizards?"

"Lizards? You choose to focus on the lizards? Okay. I'm talking about the critters you see out on the runway. Don't tell me you haven't noticed them when you're out there," he said.

"I think so, but I haven't studied them like you apparently have."

"I'm just observant of my surroundings, or I try to be."

"Yeah, you keep reminding me. Well, look, Mr. Scientist, if what you're saying is true then you're suggesting that our buddies in the pit are interested in eating the occupants of C-47?" Palmer said. "Do you really believe that?"

"Not yet. So far, from what I understand, they only eat each other. That's how they dispose of the sick or dying, or those that have accidents and can't fend for themselves. I'm still trying to figure it out."

"But they showed us pictures, and we look like them. That might be good news if they have a food production problem. And I can't imagine them not having one if they're literally trapped in some kind of underground, air-tight prison." She paused long enough for Brandon to pull up next to the tower and shut down the engine.

He stood outside the truck talking with her while gazing out beyond the runway.

"Why wouldn't Oliver and Eldon come up with this theory? It was easy enough for us," she said.

"Yeah, well, you've seen what state their thinking is in. They should have checked on that background noise too, but they didn't."

"Point well taken."

"Look, I'm at the tower. I'll get back to you."

"Over and out for now," Palmer said.

Brandon took the stairs two at a time. He strutted inside but no one turned around to look at him. They stayed busy. "What's going on?"

All five of the men and women stopped and turned to face Brandon. One of the women he recognized from the last time he'd been there slapped her knees with both hands. "We'd like to know what's going on ourselves."

"I don't know what to tell you," Brandon said.

"We've been told by a number of people that you guys are in charge while we're in this code red situation, but we don't know who you are or why we're trusting you. I'm fine with declaring the planet under martial law, but aren't you the two from the first lander who came in loaded with explosives? Why would we want to trust you now? Hell, why would we trust anyone who came from the IPF mother ship? Everything they send down here is either loaded with bombs or soldiers." She opened her mouth to continue, but Brandon interrupted.

"Hold on for a second." He stepped into the center of the room and looked around at each one of them. "You're right. And I've got to tell you that I don't fully understand what happened either. And I definitely don't like that we've been handed a whole planet's worth of colonists to protect and care for. On our own, I might add. But I do take this very seriously and am more than willing to explain what I do know."

"Then let's hear it," the woman said to nods from the others.

To the best of his ability and understanding, Brandon ran through what he knew about the situation, most importantly how Oliver and Eldon had been manipulated by the Mesoans. He also acknowledged that it was Oliver who first turned things over to him and Palmer, and that he probably wasn't in the best of mental states.

"If he turned the protection of the colony over to you while under the influence of the Mesoans then what authority holds us to that?" The woman looked to be the oldest among the group, sun wrinkled around the eyes and mouth, articulate, not afraid to speak out. They were lucky they had her.

Brandon lowered his eyes from hers. "None. But it's done and we're it. I'll tell you one thing, you people couldn't protect yourselves if you wanted to. You're not trained." He glared at her, waiting for a rebuttal.

After looking around at the others, the woman shook her head. "Okay. So far I can only assume, from where I'm sitting, that you've helped us remain safe. We all heard about the way you walked out of the pit building straight into gunfire. That's enough proof for now." She turned back to her console and the rest followed suit.

"Your communications capabilities are almost non-existent, yet you heard about that?"

"Gossip travels faster than logic," she said over her shoulder. "So, what do you need from us?"

"An update."

"Earth Central is headed for the IPF mother ship, presumably to take over," she said. "It's about time. All they've done is attack us. Peace Force, my ass. We know they want access to what we found, and we've no doubt it's for their own purposes."

"I can't imagine how it stayed a secret as long as it has," Brandon said.

One of the men to his side said, "We don't get out much." The rest of them laughed at his joke, but Brandon knew that it was funny only because it was so close to the truth.

"That I can see," Brandon said. For once he felt accepted. "So, what's their premise?"

"Don't know. We tapped into their communications and that's all we know," the woman said.

"Can you open a line for me?"

"Yes, sir," one of the others said while holding out a headset with a mic attached.

Brandon put the headset over his hear. "I'm ready."

Through his earpiece, Brandon heard, "This is Captain Jan Hollis."

"First Lieutenant Brandon Lockhardt here," he said. "Following the A.C.T. ruling of 3290-A, I would like to know what premise you have to acquisition the IPF Section 204 Mother Ship."

The woman's voice came on. "What gives you the authority over the planet's government officials to request such information?"

"Martial law," Brandon said. He shrugged his shoulders and looked at the woman he had been talking with. He figured she wouldn't mind if he used her words. They made sense even if martial law hadn't been officially called.

"Very well. We have Falsified Documentation, Avoidance of Appointed Duties, Relinquishment of Control to a lesser official, and a few others. I'll leave out the rumors of sending a fake Peace Coordinator to the planet's surface until we do our interrogations. Which reason would you like?"

"Do you plan a hostile takeover or peaceful one?" Brandon pushed.

A laugh came through the speaker. "We are on orders, First Lieutenant Brandon Lockhardt."

He knew what that meant. They'd complete a takeover by whatever means were necessary. He clicked off the mic. "Hail the IPF mother ship," he said.

"Will do," the man pushed a few buttons and turned to Brandon, "All yours."

"Garth? James?" the voice came.

"This is First Lieutenant Brandon Lockhardt."

"Shit. Look, we're in trouble here. Earth Central is not happy. There are more reports out of order than in order, all our key personnel are down there with you, and our enforcers, the few left up here, have taken over control. They're going to oppose Earth Central. What'll I do?"

"Who is this?"

"Oh, it's Jason. James put me in charge, but I've never had to deal with anything like this before. How do you stop a military force like our enforcers? Who do I believe? What choices…"

"Slow down, Jason. I need more information before I can recommend anything." Brandon knew that the entire tower of people listened in. He saw the concern on their faces. Earth Central wasn't known for being gentle in such situations, but they probably didn't know that. They reacted to the fear in Jason's voice, no different than what had happened between the Mesoans and the four of them who had gone down to talk. The only thing Brandon could do at the moment was to keep everyone calm and thinking clearly. He snapped his fingers and whispered for someone to get Palmer there. Then he went back to Jason, running through simple security maneuvers. There wasn't much to go on, though. He guessed that the enforcers took over precisely because Jason didn't and not for any kind of revolutionary reasons. "Where are you and can you get me to talk with whoever is in charge?"

"I've locked myself in my chambers and I'm not going out there. You've got to tell Garth what's going on and tell him to get back here. This is his fault. His lies."

Brandon shook his head and yanked the headset off. "Jesus, can't we reach anyone else on that damned ship besides this guy?"

"He's overriding the circuits," someone said. "Must have some technical knowledge."

"Great. I probably just wasted time talking with him about security maneuvers."

"If he's not listening and he won't leave his chambers, then what?" the woman said.

"Earth Central will have an easy time of it." Brandon hung his head. "Cancel that call for Palmer. There's nothing we can do for now."

"At this point, does it even matter who's in charge up there as long as we're okay down here?" the woman said.

"At this point, perhaps not. But things will change once that's sorted out up there." Brandon paced a few steps, then back. "We're next."

"Will they attack us?"

He thought for a moment then smiled. "You've given me an idea." He pointed to the man who had given him the headset. Stay in touch with Jason so we know what's going on up there, at least through his eyes. And keep monitoring EC the best you can. Information is precious in these situations. Any lines that are open will help us stay on top of things. Got it everyone?"

"They know when we open a line," someone said. "They'll want answers, too."

"Pretend you can't hear them; deliver weather reports; I don't give a shit. Just make sure you're collecting information."

There were approvals from all five of those in the tower.

Brandon pulled his comm unit to his lips. "Palmer?"

"I'm here. You want me to go somewhere else now? I got to tell you, I'm tired of being a yoyo."

"Get to the governmental board and run the paperwork for martial law. We're in charge," he said.

"I'm not sure they'll do that."

"It's either that or Earth Central will be here next, and you know that won't be pretty."

"Martial law will slow them down, but it won't stop them."

"You'll think of something before then." Brandon waved at those in the tower as he headed for the stairs. "Hold on a sec." He swung around to the others. "You guys are in touch with Larry?"

"He's using everything we have to monitor those soldiers, but we can reach him," the woman said. "We could use a few of those," she added pointing at his wrist unit.

Brandon lowered his hand. "I'm beginning to see how people can miss what's right before their eyes. Call Larry, every soldier down there has either a wrist communicator, a shoulder unit, or one in their helmet if they came for battle. They're short range, but that's all we need."

"Good call," one of the other people said.

Brandon headed down the stairs. Back to Palmer, he said, "Get Larry to adjust your communicator so that we're on an open channel instead of this private one."

"I don't like that idea."

"Then get a second unit or we're out of touch except through a proxy, and that never works. Besides, you need to talk with the tower for background on what's happening between the IPF and EC. You'll need that information for your plan."

"There you go again calling it my plan when I don't have any plan."

"Get the paperwork done. I'm on my way." Brandon thought that he was a bit harsh once she clicked off, but he was on a mission and there was no time for tactful interaction. He fell into get-it-done mode. Why he considered her feelings at all while in a battle situation was still a bit new to him. And that's why they frown upon getting involved with someone you're working with, he thought: an interruption in how smoothly you can proceed.

He jumped into the truck and headed back to the pit building.

The sun glanced off the mountains and created a blue glare, while the late afternoon clouds appeared to have a green tint. He wished there were more time to sit and stare and enjoy the beauty, but that wasn't about to happen any time soon. He'd like to take a good hike, too. And, he thought, where the colonists live must have more vegetation than this rocky and sandy gorge. Judging by the flyover he and Palmer had made days ago, there were some beautifully thick areas he'd like to explore. He let his mind wander while driving with the understanding that he needed to rest his thoughts if he wanted to use them to focus later. Overtaxing his body in any way could jeopardize the circumstances they were in, whatever circumstance that was at the moment. Brandon swung the truck up to the front of the building, jumped out, and rushed inside.

"Hey, how you doing today?" one of the door guards asked.

Brandon shook his head. "Fine." He walked past the desk and through the first set of doors. It amazed him how nonchalant and unaware the colonists appeared to be.

He met Jacobs coming down the hall who asked, "What is it?"

"These guys act as though nothing's going on. Do they have any idea how insane that is?"

"They're actually having fun with this," Jacobs said. "It's probably the most adventure they've had since the colony first arrived."

"But don't they see the dangers?"

"Not at all. This is all you know, so it's normal that things would be, well, dangerous most of the time. They don't have any experience like that. They can't really fathom the immensely tight position they're in." Jacobs walked with Brandon toward the conference room. "Although, I have to say that their governmental board has a better feel for it, they're not totally aware of the ramifications either." He glanced at Brandon. "But they don't have to be. We're aware enough for all of them. Come on, you have to sign some papers."

In the conference room sat the governmental board along with Palmer and, to Brandon's surprise, Eldon. "Why not have Oliver here, too," he said.

"He's taking this a little harder," Jacobs said. "Eldon's much easier to work with at the moment and I think he's stable enough as long as he's not exposed to them for a while."

"I'm still processing the whole thing, though," Eldon said.

Brandon turned to Jacobs, "I'm surprised you're not worried."

"I know what I'm doing," he said.

"I'm with the doc here. Where do I sign?" Brandon wielded the pen and signed the paperwork that put him and Palmer and, he noticed, Jacobs, in charge of C-47 under martial law. Of course they didn't have an army to actually use, but he'd figure that out eventually. In the meantime, there would be no argument from Earth Central when one of them conducted communications.

Outside the room, the four of them walked down the hall together while Brandon explained how he believed Earth Central would react to their predicament, until he recalled what James had told them. He stopped and the others halted a few steps in front of him. When they turned around he said, "Your independence is already on record."

Jacobs cocked his head. "That's right. Isn't that what James said when we had him in the conference room?"

Larry rounded a corner before Brandon could answer. "Hey, good to see you guys together." He stopped among them, a fellow tech beside him held a bag up. Larry reached into the bag and pulled out a comm unit. "Most of the soldiers had shoulder units, but a few had wrist units too. I didn't fuck with the helmets. It would take too long and I think we have what we need now."

"Those in charge have multiple units," Brandon said.

Larry looked up at him. "Well, I tagged them so you'd know who's who."

"Thanks, but we can tell by rank...most of the time," Brandon said.

"Anyway, these are all open lines. It may get a bit busy from time to time, so it won't be as efficient as you might think. And...that's why I'm giving you these." He pulled out additional units and handed them to Jacobs and Eldon. "Now the four of you can have a private conversation if you want."

"Couldn't you put a switch on these things instead of handing us two?" Palmer said.

"Fastest way," Larry said. "I thought that was important."

"It is," Brandon said. "You've done well."

Larry rushed off to his next project as soon as Brandon nodded at him.

The four of them looked at one another for a moment. "These aren't much use while we're together," Eldon said. "Unless we leave them open and hear ourselves twice, once with a short delay."

Brandon swung around and hollered for Larry to come back.

"Now what," Palmer said.

"Eldon," Brandon said. Once Larry got close to them again, Brandon told him, "I need you to delegate your duties for a short while and come with us."

"Sure," Larry turned and made a call to one of his buddies then twisted back around. "Where to?"

"Eldon's lab," Brandon forged ahead of the group.

"Are you going to let us in on your plan there, Big Guy?" Eldon said.

"Brandon talked over his shoulder. "You could get on my nerves if you wanted to."

Eldon threw up his hands.

"I think I know what he's up to." Palmer reached and put a hand on his shoulder. "You're a detailed thinker. You're right about that."

Inside the lab, Brandon waited for Palmer to pull up one of the conversations with the subliminal soundtrack.

Larry's eyes widened. "That's what's been happening?" He dropped into the seat beside Palmer and put a hand to his head. "Who all's been affected?"

"You don't want to know," Palmer said.

He shrugged. "So what do you want from me?"

Palmer turned to look at Brandon.

"I want you to program the translator to delay the signal long enough to remove the subliminal message. Or put in some kind of filter that will eliminate the message from the start. Can you do that?"

"Sure. I can have Arnie reprogram it," Larry said. "Arnie handles a lot of the software," he explained.

"Folks," Brandon said, "the next conversation we have with those pit-boys will be a bit more in our favor."

# CHAPTER 25

**IT FELT LIKE MINUTES TO BRANDON,** but hours passed while he and Palmer strategized with Jacobs and Eldon. He didn't know if he liked the idea of interviewing the Mesoans this soon after they influenced Eldon to attack Jacobs. Even with the translator adjusted, another confrontation didn't seem to be a good idea, and he said as much. "Besides, if emotional transference is still part of the pie, we can still be influenced. All we've done is take their double whammy and split it into a single whammy."

"What else do we have?" Jacobs pointed out.

The four of them sat around a table in what appeared to be a breakroom. A pot of jasp sat along one wall near a sink and cabinet. Cups and napkins, a local substance used as a sweetener, and what amounted to synthetic milk rested on the cabinet as well. They were the only ones in the room that accommodated five round tables and twenty-odd chairs. Occasionally, someone from C-47 stopped in to pour a cup of jasp and then leave.

Palmer got up from the table and headed in the direction of the jasp.

"Get me a cup while you're up," Jacobs said.

"Thinking." Brandon explained to the others what Palmer was doing and why she didn't go for the jasp.

Eldon got up from the table. "I'll get you a cup, he told Jacobs." He tapped the table near Brandon's hand. "Want one?"

"Sure."

Palmer made a few more swings back and forth before she put a hand to her chin and sat back down.

Eldon held two cups of jasp in one hand and one in the other. "Want any," he asked Palmer before sitting across from her.

She shook her head then laid out her idea. "We send James and one of the enforcers down there with a scripted conversation. He's a Peace Coordinator. We'll give him enough leeway to pry some answers out of them."

"Everything will be taped on Eldon's computer," Jacobs said. "I can see this working. I suppose we could even put a bud in his ear so we can be part of the conversation without concern of emotional transference. Keeps us at a safe distance."

"Why the enforcer, the soldier?" Brandon wasn't on board yet.

Jacobs answered instead of Palmer. "As a marker. We set up heart and respiratory monitors to make sure they're both reacting the same way. If they deviate, then they're somehow accepting the messages differently. Since they can't get the subliminal messages—because we are canceling them out—we get to detect how detailed and honed the Mesoans' emotional transference works."

Palmer cocked her head. "Sounds good to me. I just didn't think anyone should go down alone."

Brandon had to smile. Palmer had the big picture, but dropped off at the details. He wasn't going to mention it to her, though.

Eldon used the wrist unit he'd been given to contact Larry and requested that someone bring James into the room. It didn't take long.

James appeared calm as he entered. A young man held a gun to his back.

"Dismissed," Brandon said. "Boy, that's got to make anyone nervous. He didn't look old enough to know where the trigger was."

"I have enforcers who will listen to orders if you put me in charge," James said. He continued to stand next to the table. "I suppose you've decided to accept my proposition. I told you I could help."

"Sit," Brandon said. "You know damned fool well we're not putting you in charge."

"But after the interrogation...I thought..."

"Interview," Jacobs said with a bit of annoyance in his voice.

"Either way, I thought you knew where I stood." James looked around. "Then why did you bring me here?"

"We haven't had time to review all those little talks you guys have been having," Brandon said. "So, why don't you give us the short version."

"I did. But here it goes again. Garth is crazy and wants to run this whole place so that he can sell off your proposed aliens to the highest bidder and be on his way. I mean, he might want to stick around for a little while. He likes to manipulate people. But for the most part, he just wants the money, where I'm looking for a home. I know how that must sound, but it's true. I hate living in that mother ship and I just want a life on a planet where I can be part of a team." He leaned forward and let both of his forearms fall across the table in front of him, his hands outstretched as though pleading. His eyes went from one person to the next. "I mean this. I don't care if you have me digging in the fields or running your government, I just want to be at ground level."

Jacobs nodded at Brandon.

"We'll see," Brandon said.

"What do you mean by that?" James said.

"We have a mission for you. It's very specific, and we're going to walk you through it step by step. There will be moments where you will have the opportunity to do what you want, though. Do your negotiating thing. Be the Peace Coordinator you say you are. We want some specific information from this, though, and you're going to get it for us." Brandon looked to the others to be sure that he put it well enough.

"Shall we take him to my lab?" Eldon said.

"First, is there a particular soldier you think you can trust to go with you?" Brandon asked.

"We call them enforcers," James said.

Brandon winked at him.

James laughed a little nervously. "Not Stark. He's got strict orders from Garth. I'd watch him closely if I were you."

"Duly noted," Brandon put a hand on Eldon's shoulder as they all walked toward the door. "Have someone round up the lowest ranking enforcer they can find and bring him to me. Let him know that we've been placed under martial law and that I'm the commanding officer, that I work for Earth Central. That should be enough to gain some loyalty."

"As long as Garth didn't get to him first," James said. When everyone looked at him, he added, "Trust me. That's how he is. He uses everyone equally. Even I fell for it."

"That doesn't surprise me," Brandon said.

"Why would you say that?" James asked.

"You want something badly enough, it makes you vulnerable. And you want something badly." Even as he said the words, Brandon felt the sting of them lash back at him. He wanted Palmer badly and couldn't help wonder if that put him, and the rest of C-47, in jeopardy. He didn't like feeling vulnerable.

They ushered James to the lab where Eldon made the arrangements for him to be wired to several monitors he collected, along with sensors and meters, from a corner workbench. Another guard brought the low-ranking soldier they asked for. Finally, a call was put through to Larry about the progress on the software, and soon after the call a skinny kid showed up to implement what they needed.

"Arnie," he said before sitting down. "Hey, Eldon," Arnie waved.

"Hey."

In hushed tones, Palmer explained what was going on. Brandon heard her say, "I want to be able to record and hear the subliminal messages on a separate screen on the computer. I just don't want these two to hear it," Palmer indicated James and the enforcer.

Eldon and Jacobs were attaching sensors and setting up the monitors on the two men.

"I want a key on the translator cable, too," Palmer said. "I want to hear everything James says. Mister," she yelled over to him, "you're going to tell me what you're feeling, hearing, and seeing. Same with you..." she snapped her fingers toward the enforcer. "Your name?"

"Suren," the man said.

"Suren, it is," she said, "but you're only going to talk with the aliens when your mic is keyed to do so. Got it?"

"Aliens?" Suren looked surprised and a bit unnerved. The dark line of his single eyebrow peaked in the middle.

"Don't worry about it. We'll be fine," James said to him.

"But nobody said anything about—"

Brandon stood for a moment and Suren came around at attention. "This is an important mission to the safety of the C-47 colony. You are expected to complete that mission in full. I will write a report detailing your actions and recommending you for advancement once this situation is under control. Do you understand?"

Suren saluted, "Yes, sir," and turned back to James.

"Key the mics," Palmer repeated.

They both nodded their heads.

"I'm impressed," Jacobs said to her. He looked over at Brandon questioningly.

"I'm not," Brandon said. "This," he emphasized, "is the woman I have come to know." He hated how his words sounded, as though he'd come to love her and not just know her. Of course that's exactly what he meant, but his fear that everyone else in the room heard that in his voice bothered him.

Eldon patted Suren's chest. "He's set. We're ready."

The six of them walked to where James and Suren dressed in the environmental suits used to travel down to the Mesoans. Arnie rigged a switch in the translator cable, and afterward they made their way to the pit office.

"You two again?" the operator said when Jacobs and Eldon walked in.

"We're not going in," Jacobs said, even though that was evident.

After a few formalities, Brandon reminded Suren of his duties and Palmer reiterated what she expected of them. Once inside the first elevator, Brandon let the operators know to watch for anything funny when the two men came back out. He pointed toward the door. "We'll be back in the main building, but should return before they get back up."

"Just in case, then," the man said.

"Yeah. In case we're late." With that Brandon and the others made their way back to Eldon's lab. They arrived about the time James and Suren entered the chamber where the Mesoans were to meet them.

"We're here," Palmer said. She had an ear bud in her right ear. The main speaker crackled but appeared to work fine.

"I didn't like the trip here very much," James' voice came over the speaker. "I'm already nervous. Can you tell?"

Eldon sat at a different console and nodded. "That's okay. We can create a baseline from any point." He turned to Brandon. "Suren appears to be calm so far."

"He'd make a good soldier. I think we made the right choice."

"We're hooking up to the translator, but the aliens haven't arrived yet," James said.

"Then don't hook up. They like a few minutes to settle in," Eldon said.

"Roger that."

Even without being there, everyone in the lab knew when the Mesoans showed up. Not only did both men draw a quick breath, both their hearts began to beat faster.

"I never noticed this happening when we were down there," Eldon said.

"Probably wouldn't," Jacobs said. "I'm surprised you didn't monitor this through your suits."

Eldon looked at Jacobs sternly. "First of all, we are lucky to have the few suits we have. A lot of equipment was left behind when the mining operation closed down. And secondly, our reaction wasn't what we were hoping to record. That wasn't our purpose."

Jacobs pointed quickly toward the far corner of the lab as though the Mesoans were in the room. "They controlled your purpose. That's why you don't have much information."

"Hey," Eldon got up, but Brandon swung around before he could move toward Jacobs. "I don't know why I feel like this. I'm sorry," Eldon said.

Jacobs said, "How do you feel?"

"I'm angry."

"Reaction based on the situation. If you imagine being down there, which is easy while monitoring James and Suren, you take on the stance you last held. Interesting," Jacobs said.

"We're going to plug in now," James said over the speakers.

Jacobs motioned for Eldon to sit. He whispered, "You can control it. Now that you're aware. Practice."

Eldon nodded positively and got more comfortable in his seat.

"They plugged in," Palmer said. She handed Brandon an ear bud while shaking her head as though she couldn't believe what she was hearing.

Brandon brought the bud to his ear and heard the distinct sound of the translator alternating between the voices of James and Suren. "We are not safe. We are not safe," the aliens were saying in their subliminal voices. But through the speakers everyone heard, "Who are you and where are the others?"

"I feel unsafe down here," James said before keying his voice through to the translator. "I am a Senior Peace Coordinator for the Intergalactic Peace Force and have come to learn more about your culture and to find common ground for us to live by."

Brandon heard through the ear bud, "I must protect them. Their lives are in danger. I want to protect them all."

Palmer shook her head and had a quizzical look on her face. Her hand perched over a volume control. "It's getting louder," she said. "Eldon, what do the monitors say?"

"No change. Once their heart rates increased when the aliens arrived, they stabilized. Their breathing stabilized too. But you say their subliminal conversation is getting louder?"

"The Mesoans are looking a bit nervous to me," James said. "I can't be sure, but they don't appear comfortable in their seats and they continue to look at one another. Their hands and fingers continue to move, too."

"Getting louder," Palmer said, turning the dial down.

"We must leave now," the voice in the ear bud said.

Brandon put a hand over Palmer's hand for a moment. "Kill him. Kill him," he heard. "They're scared to death," Brandon said.

"Can we hear?" Jacobs said.

"Not yet," Palmer said. "They must realize they're not getting through to James and Suren. They're fear has escalated."

"Yes, in fact they're so fearful, I don't think James is going to get through to them with anything he says," Brandon said.

"James," Palmer leaned close to a mic. "I want you to tell them what we've done?"

"Are you serious?" James questioned.

"Absolutely. Tell them that we've isolated their subliminal messages and that it was the only way for us to level the playing field so that we could have a reasonable talk. You're the pro. Convince them that we mean them no harm. We want to help, but can't help if they continually try to manipulate us," Palmer said.

"Like Garth."

"Whatever you say," she said, "just get them to calm down. They're off the charts up here."

The next thing Brandon heard was James explaining about the subliminal isolation. He did just what Palmer had suggested only with an elegance of words that impressed Brandon.

"Subliminals are dropping off," Palmer said.

"They still look nervous," James responded.

"Keep at it," Palmer said.

Brandon jerked his chin toward Eldon. "Steady as she goes," Eldon said.

Arnie tapped his foot. He stood over Eldon's shoulder. "Can I go?"

"No," Brandon said. "In case something goes wrong."

"What can I do?"

"You're staying." Brandon watched as the signal for the subliminal message decreased. He didn't have time to argue the point.

"Something's happening over here," Eldon said.

Palmer stood. "What is it?"

James' voice came through the speaker, "I don't like this. I'm not happy down here."

"Suren?" Brandon said.

"Suren's pulse is rising pretty fast," Eldon said.

"But he's not talking," Jacobs said. "Brandon, talk with him. Calm him down."

Brandon took the mic and said, "Suren, this is Brandon. You need to focus on your breathing. Slowly. Your heart rate has increased. Can you slow it down? Are you feeling all right?"

Jacobs motioned for Brandon to continue talking. He whispered, "I don't care what you say, your voice keeps him occupied." He aimed his next order at Palmer. "Get them out of there."

"But we're not finished," she said. "We've gotten nothing."

"Get them out," Jacobs said again.

James' voice was loud. "Jesus. I hate this place. It's not safe. It's not safe."

Brandon saw that Palmer had the volume control for the subliminal messages all the way up and all he could hear was a low tone. When he looked at her, she shrugged.

"Get them out," Brandon said. He got up from the table and pulled the bud from his ear. "Get them the hell out of there now."

"The aliens have disconnected, but are coming toward us," James said.

Palmer gave the order. "Disconnect and get out of there," she said. "Can you make it to the airlock?"

Nothing came through the speaker except for heavy breathing. Then some rustling sounds as though furniture was being moved. "Go," Suren said.

"Oh no, oh no," James panted.

"Where's Suren," Palmer yelled into the mic.

"He's in there. He's holding them back."

"Do not close that airlock door until he is there with you," Brandon said.

"I have to," James said.

Brandon held still for a moment, then keyed his mic and said calmly, "Retreat maneuver, soldier."

James' voice came again. "He's in. He's in. What did you do?"

"It's okay," Suren said. "The door is closed."

Eldon stared at Brandon. "What was that?"

"He's trained to hold off the attackers until everyone else, in this case James, is safe. A retreat maneuver tells him to save himself regardless of others," Brandon explained.

"So, he would have stayed to hold them off, but by calling a retreat it's okay for him to run?" Eldon said. "I thought soldiers had a 'no man left behind' attitude."

"That's about it, except that James was already out of danger, so no man was left behind."

"How'd you know he'd make it inside the airlock? He could have been stuck there," Jacobs said.

Palmer answered for Brandon. "He counted how long it took for the airlock to close. He probably knows how many steps it is."

"Seven," Brandon said.

"Details," Palmer said.

"Well it saved Suren's life, didn't it," Jacobs said.

"We'll see," Palmer said.

Nothing but the sound of breathing came through the speakers.

"We'd better get down there to greet them," Jacobs said.

"I'm staying here," Eldon said.

Brandon headed for the door. "Arnie and Palmer are staying too." No one in the room questioned his authority.

# CHAPTER 26

JACOBS STEPPED PAST BRANDON to meet James and Suren, who were laughing with one another as the door opened for them to exit.

"What's all this?" Jacobs said, asking the question Brandon had not been able to form just yet.

James, with a grand smile across his face said, "I don't know."

Brandon shook his head, allowing his thoughts to purge the situation again. He stepped next to Jacobs and said, "Soldier?"

Suren responded immediately. "I was so scared, sir. But once we were about three-quarters of the way back, I saw how ridiculous it was. I mean they moved about as fast as, as…"

"Turtles?" Brandon said.

"Yeah. And I held them off with almost no effort. But I was scared out of my wits. It made no sense," Suren said.

Brandon motioned toward Jacobs. "So what happened? Why are they hysterical?"

Jacobs stared at the two of them. He was in deep thought as though completing a difficult math problem in his head. Then he finally turned to answer Brandon. "Ever been scared by a sibling who jumped out from a dark hall?" In a moment, he threw his arms out with his hands wide and fingers spread, "Boo!"

Brandon jumped, then smiled and shook his head.

"See what I mean? Once you realized there was no real danger, you found it funny. Multiply that times ten, at least. Without the subliminal words to carry their deeper message forward, the emotional data switches over to logic more quickly, which levels you out again. In fact, it pushes you in the other direction." He smiled about as wide as James and Suren. Finally, he said, "They're harmless." He shook his head. "All they can do is manipulate through the subliminal messages, but when we take that away, all they can do is say boo. Granted, they say it emotionally, which has a greater impact at first, but that's only until we get used to it."

"But I was scared," James said. "I mean, out of my head scared."

"Me too," Suren said.

"But you didn't want to kill anyone? Either of you?" James said.

"No," they said simultaneously.

"Why would we want to do that?" Suren asked.

"That's the message they pushed through," Jacobs told them. "We read the subliminal message on the computer."

"So they were only able to scare us," James said again.

"This time. But they can only scare you from jumping out at you for the first few times. After that it doesn't work. Once you're ready for it..." Jacobs waited for someone else to answer the question, but no one did. Everyone in the room knew exactly what he was saying.

"Makes sense," Brandon said. "So now we can talk with them?"

Jacobs looked pretty satisfied about the situation. "I think so. But let's give them some time to think things over. They need to calm down. While they're doing that, let's see what information we can gather about our other growing situations."

"I do feel out of the loop," Brandon said.

James laughed.

Brandon turned on him. "What?"

Suren said, "Palmer's still connected and we heard her give a yahoo. She said, 'We got them on the run, now.' It just struck us as funny."

"Tell her we're on our way," Brandon told Suren instead of using his wrist unit.

"She heard you."

After regrouping and updating themselves on all other activities, James lowered his head. "I'm sorry. I still haven't helped much. That situation down there didn't work out well at all, and so far it sounds as though Earth Central is about to clear the decks. If they take over Section 204, they'll clean house and bring in all new management. We'll all be gone."

Jacobs agreed. "Regardless of the shared responsibility measures that Earth Central longed to put into effect once the human race spread itself thinner and thinner throughout the galaxy, it still rules with a firm hand. You should know that, being in your position. And the fact that your own military arm, your enforcers, forced their hand at the mother ship, I can see how EC might step in."

"We need to help them," James said.

"Help them how," Brandon interjected. "Do you mean go up there and help them hold their position? That's not going to happen. EC has every right. According to Captain Jan Hollis, who is heading the takeover of Section 204, they've got proof for Falsified Documentation, Avoidance of Appointed Duties," he nodded toward James, "Relinquishment of Control to a lesser official, and she didn't go on from there, but I understand there's plenty more screw ups than that."

"I had full authority to place Jason in charge." James shook his head in despair. "I didn't know he'd break down so easily. I really thought he could handle it. I believed it."

"Well, it hardly matters. There's nothing I can do short of break the law. If I lift a hand to help at this point it puts C-47 into the fray. We become an extension to Section 204." Brandon shook his head. "There's nothing I can do."

"It's not anyone's fault that Section 204 is so screwed up." James face became stern and serious. "Except maybe Garth's."

Jacobs tapped the table as James took a moment to contemplate the situation.

Everyone in the room, some standing, some sitting, some sipping at cups of jasp, knew that James needed the quiet. He took a deep breath. "C-47 is independent."

"We don't have the paperwork to prove it," Palmer pointed out.

"Once the paperwork is issued it can't be repealed without all parties being involved. So," James said, "paperwork or not, this planet's colonies are independent from the system. You can share goods and services, you can explore, you can even create a separate section to colonize another planet. And, you own your discovery."

"All we have to do is pay taxes to EC," Eldon said. "I don't know if you've noticed, but we're not in any position…"

James smiled. "A small price to pay."

"All well and good," Brandon said, "but what's any of this have to do with Section 204 of the International fucking Peace Force?"

"Join with us and Earth Central will have to back off," James said.

"Not if they find you a threat," Palmer said. "I don't care how independent we all are, if we've taken up arms, and you have, then EC has a right and a duty to intercede."

James leaned forward. "How can that ship be a threat to anyone at the moment. It's in total chaos up there. Half their damned enforcers are down here for Christ's sake."

"If we join hands, what's that mean in regards to who's in charge. You and Garth suddenly become Kings?" Eldon said. "You sell off our discovery just as we're beginning to understand how to communicate with them? You run our government?"

"He has a point," Brandon said.

James looked at those who sat or stood around him and answered slowly. "We sign away all our rights to rank, order, and control to your government. We resign." His head shook along with his hands as though he had just gotten a chill. "You own us, instead of the other way around."

"In exchange for what?" Eldon said.

"You let me stay here," James said.

Brandon had to get the suggestion straight, as though he'd heard it wrong. "You're willing to give up everything?"

"I've got to believe that you'll treat me fairly, in lieu of what I've already done. That you'll see that I have talents and that you'll let me use them. But I don't need to be in charge. I don't need to own your discovery," James said. "That's not what I want."

"Good try," Eldon said. Then he pointed out the real challenge. "If only you were truly in charge of Section 204. But you're not."

"Garth," Brandon said again. "It comes back to him."

James said, "I can sway him to sign if you can draw up the papers. If he signs over his rights as the superior entity, then C-47's in charge of Section 204. Then you have the authority to do something about all of this, including Earth Central's move on us and them."

Palmer laughed out loud.

"What?" James said.

"We're operating under martial law, which means that Brandon, here, will be King Shit." She looked around. "I just find that funny." When no one else laughed she said, "Fine, then I'm the only one."

After a unanimous agreement, there was only one thing to do. Deliberation with the C-47 governmental body took only a few minutes. After all, they were gaining protection just as they'd wanted, plus wouldn't be under the authority of the Section 204 staff. They knew they'd have complete control back once everything had been sorted out, even though they appeared to know that they were in over their heads. Since Oliver had always been the leader in the group and he was out of the way for the time being, the board moved quickly on Eldon's suggestion.

James' plan appeared to be on course until Garth was called in to resign his position.

"Why would I do that?" Garth said as he stared at James as though he'd kill him if he had the chance. They had been deliberating the finer points of the agreement and were stale-mated on the final one, his resignation.

"It's okay," James said. "Don't sign." He stared Garth down.

Brandon glanced over at Palmer who stood in the corner of the room with an ear bud cord hanging from her head.

Palmer yelled from across the room. "The news on this end is that Earth Central has issued verbals for Section 204 to stand down." She listened for a moment then lifted her head. "They've refused, of course. Looks like you're in for a removal from post anyway," she said. "Earth Central's only a few hours from your ship."

"I know people," Garth said. "Once I'm allowed to talk with Earth Central, this whole scenario will turn around and you will be on your ass," he said to James. He waved a hand across the air between them. "These people can't make it without our help. They need us, which means that they'll sign over everything for our protection. You fucked up. You could have been in charge here. You still can if you let me go. I'll smooth everything out up there and leave you alone."

James made no effort to argue. He just smiled and sat quietly.

Before long, Garth couldn't contain himself. "You know I'm right."

"They're already independent," James said. "You never told me. So how do you expect me to believe that I was part of the deal? I wasn't. Not when you promised me this post and not now." He slapped the table. "You can't stop lying, can you?"

"So," Garth said, "that can be changed. I can fix all that." He wasn't giving in. He wanted control and Brandon could see it in his demeanor. But he also saw something in James. Confidence. James had something up his sleeve, a final card to play. And it must have been a good one because when James leaned over the table he had an even larger smile on his face than when he left the elevator a few hours earlier. "I'm going to negotiate with Earth Central concerning the aliens. C-47 will have plenty of money and support once their findings are explained in full. What they have here is the most important discovery in history. They don't even need Section 204. I could let Earth Central destroy it. You'd have nothing. The way I see it, Section 204 needs C-47."

Garth fidgeted but stayed in the same position as though feigning self-control. "They still can't govern themselves. I've talked long and hard with Oliver. Where is he, by the way? You can't sign these papers without him."

"All we need is a majority and we have that," James said.

Jacobs said, "Oliver is under psychiatric surveillance and has been relieved of his post temporarily anyway."

Garth gritted his teeth and was about to say something when James drove his point home. "We have statements from every one of your cohorts concerning your orders." He pointed to Jacobs. "And he's from Earth Central Intelligence and has documentation that will make it impossible for you to get out of this unless you know the Presidential Staff in full. Personally." He shook his head slowly as though he enjoyed his next statement immensely. "We've got so much on you that you'll never get out of prison, let alone be in charge of anyone or anything ever again."

Garth's shoulders slumped and his eyes darted from side to side. "I can't go to prison," he said. "Don't do that. Please."

"Under the laws of an independent colony, we can hold you as long as we wish and in any manner that we wish," Eldon said.

James relaxed and turned slightly in his seat, allowing Eldon to go on.

"We don't even have a prison to put you in," Eldon said.

Brandon watched as Garth turned from manipulative tyrant into an agreeable servant. The transformation reminded him of what Jacobs had said, that Garth was crazy. As Garth signed the paperwork, Brandon couldn't help but wonder what they would do with him once everything was settled, if it was settled, but knew that he'd have to be watched for a long time. He hoped that Jacobs would be involved. He was beginning to like the man.

"It's done," James said, but as he reached for the paperwork, Eldon stepped beside him and swiped it from the table.

"Step one," Eldon said.

Brandon reached out.

Eldon reluctantly handed the paperwork over. "Only until the conflict subsides," he said.

Brandon didn't answer. He told the guards to remove Garth and take him back to his room.

Garth went quietly.

"You enjoyed that a bit too much," Brandon said to James.

"He's been beating me up for years. But it's done. I feel redeemed." James stood to go. "It's not over, though. We've got to pass this information along to Earth Central."

"Not so fast," Palmer said. "I have a plan."

"It's about damned time," Brandon said.

Palmer shot him a look that was both surprised and loving. She was back in form.

"We're listening," Eldon said once Garth was out of the room.

Palmer looked happy to take center stage. She pulled the ear bud from her ear and let it rest at the end of the cord over her shoulder. "First thing we do is rig the translator down there so that Eldon can continue his research. This time for real, and without disruption from the subliminal feedback. I figure Larry can wire us and the aliens remotely."

"Shouldn't researching the aliens be done after we're clear?" Jacobs said.

"Knowledge about what we really have could be essential at the moment. Earth Central can't be convinced of its importance unless we have some solid, undeniable evidence. And we're going to get it. Next is for James to handle the negotiations with Earth Central just as he's suggested. I want the governmental board sitting beside him, though, and Jacobs, who can hand over reports on Garth and his underhanded manipulations. We should have plenty to add to a report once you go through the statements we've received," she said.

"That's a lot of data," Jacobs said.

Palmer smiled. "You can handle it." She pursed her lips as though she was ready to explain her favorite part of the plan. "We're going to protect Section 204."

"Yes," James said pulling his hand into a fist and pumping it. "I hoped you'd say that."

Palmer shot him a glance.

"What?" he said. "Section 204 did nothing wrong. And if Earth Central attacks them some very good men will be hurt, maybe killed." He looked around as though for approval, but didn't get it. "I take it you two will be hand-carrying the agreement we just signed?"

"What about here?" Brandon said. "I can't leave. Who would I hand the place over to?"

"You're not going," she said.

"But you said we," Brandon said.

"We as in C-47."

"I thought you said their landers couldn't break atmosphere? And their ground fighters can't for sure, they're not designed for it," Brandon said. "You can't go alone."

"There's Garth's lander," Palmer said.

"What will we have if you get into trouble?" Brandon said.

"Understood," Palmer said. "I'll take some of the soldiers after you explain to them what's happening and that you're in charge," she said. "They'll take orders from you." Before anyone could give a rebuttal, she went on. "I'll take the pilots from here with me." She looked around. "And for backup, you'll send two of the fighters behind me. Not Stark, according to James here. It'll be enough to hold Earth Central until we transfer digital copies of the paperwork to the EC mother ship and they have time to verify signatures and get to Hollis."

"Sounds like you'll be cutting it close," Brandon said. "You really think Section 204's enforcers will let you through? And even if they do, you know that EC could take days to go through verification of digital documents, and that's with our cooperation. I don't like it."

"Me either," Jacobs said. "Even after questioning and a short Q and A from me, we might pick the wrong fighter pilot to follow you."

"My plan," Palmer said. "It goes my way."

"I should be able to find someone to take over here," Brandon said. "Then I can go with you. You'll need my firepower anyway."

"You're staying," she said. "We've already established that." She held out her hand to take the signed agreement.

"Even if you stop Earth Central. We'll be caught between them and Section 204. Plus, we still have negotiations to handle between all parties," James said. "It'll be days before that can happen and you know it."

"Maybe," she said, "but it'll go a bit faster if you go with me."

"Oh, no. You can't do that. You promised that I'd stay here." James backed away from her. "If I go back, you'll leave me there. They'll need a strong leader and with Garth gone and Jason useless, who'll they have? It'll be part of the negotiations, I know it." He shook his head and drew his arms close to his body. "Take someone else. I don't care who."

"Final negotiations will have to be done here," she said. "On the planet that it affects. They've done it that way for hundreds of years. They'll want to inspect the Mesoans, review governmental documents, and finalize a cooperative agreement concerning the discovery. You'll be back, don't worry about that," she said.

James appeared worried, but relinquished. "Don't cheat me," he said.

"We're not Garth," Eldon said. "We wouldn't know how to have a hidden agenda even if we wanted to." He turned and nodded his approval for Palmer's plan. "Let's get to it. Time is bearing down quickly."

Brandon nodded too. "Once I explain the situation, the soldiers will be more cooperative. They're used to taking orders and won't mind helping out as long as I have Garth's signature. So, I'll need a copy of that before you go."

"Naturally," Palmer said. "We make several copies and spread them as far and wide as we can."

# CHAPTER 27

WITH SECTION 204 IN A DECLINING ORBIT, there were hours when it was out of direct line of sight communications. Not the most efficient situation, but C-47 didn't have the money or the technology on planet to build and launch satellites to take care of the problem. Colonization had become more and more slipshod as habitable planets were discovered.

Brandon stood next to Palmer. Her lander had been loaded with the C-47 pilots and as many soldiers as there were seats left. "Watch what you're doing," he said in a low tone. "You'll be out of communications range in a few hours. Let me know what you find as soon as you can."

"You know what I'm going to find," she said as she reached out to touch his biceps through the cuffs. She let her hair fall around her face as she leaned closer and kissed him. "Who cares about appearances," she said then kissed him again more passionately.

Brandon held her close. "Don't get into any trouble. I'm duty bound here. You have no backup."

"Trust me," she said as she pulled away, "you'd just get in my way."

Brandon shook his head and smiled up at her. After she pulled away, he watched her enter the lander through the side door. She moved with confidence and attitude, both of which he found endearing and sexy. He checked his emotions. What would he do if she were in trouble? Would he let both C-47 and Section 204 go down in smoke just to help her? Would he jeopardize his commission? He didn't have the answer to either question and hoped like hell that he wouldn't have to find out any time soon.

It didn't take long before her lander and the two fighters were off the ground and on their way to the Section 204 mother ship. He laughed to himself thinking about how much of a pain in the ass James was about to become for her. His arrogance was difficult to hide no matter how well he did his job. Maybe that was part of the job description when hiring for IPF ships, he thought. "Asshole."

Brandon regrouped with the tower long enough to let them know what was going on. He asserted that they needed to keep him informed with all progress. "Especially if anything appears to be wrong for any reason," he ordered.

"We'll keep an eye on them," the woman said. "And an ear," the man sitting next to her said with a little laugh.

"You're good people," Brandon told them before he wandered down the stairs and out to the truck idling outside. He climbed into the passenger seat. "Let's go," he told the driver.

Back at the pit building he ran into Larry holding a cup of jasp in the makeshift lobby. "Everything quieting down?" Brandon acknowledged.

"Finally."

"You've done a nice job keeping everyone in communications," Brandon put a hand on the hand unit clipped to his belt and shook it.

"Tower communications," Larry said.

"Yeah."

"I'm just sorry we have to rig everything so half-assed. How'd the adjustment to the translator work out?"

"Perfectly. But let me ask you something else."

"Sure." Larry listened.

"How bad a shape is this colony in? Your weapons look to be about as poorly taken care of as your communications. Most colonies start out with a whole lot more ability to protect themselves. Something go wrong along the way?"

Larry stared at Brandon for a moment. "You might want to talk with Eldon since Oliver's out of the picture for now."

"I'm talking with you," Brandon said.

"Is it an order? I can't sidestep a direct order," Larry said, "even if I'm sworn to secrecy, which, by the way, is almost nonexistent around here. Still, I promised."

"Okay," Brandon said, "it's an order. What's going on?"

Larry stepped closer to Brandon and lowered his voice. "I only know what I hear and what I see, but since the mining company left we've been using their equipment, at least for a while, to stay in touch with the aliens, as you know."

Brandon nodded. "I got that part. Go on."

"We actually bought the equipment. Bet you didn't know that. It took a lot from us." Larry stared into his cup. "That's not all."

"I didn't think so."

"Remember, I don't know any of this first hand, but I do know that everything we had before the alien discovery was fine, it ran smoothly. Economically, governmentally, and scientifically. After the discovery things tightened up: food, farming equipment, repairs, even the landers."

"They used to work?"

"When we couldn't afford equipment, we began to cannibalize them," Larry said. "Most of us didn't really notice until we couldn't get what we needed anymore. Everything's gone down the drain."

"Like Oliver was handing over the whole planet just to protect them," Brandon said. "Just like he handed over his governmental duties."

Larry nodded. "You should really talk with Eldon. I'm sure he knows more about this than I do. And he probably has facts instead of rumors."

Brandon smiled and turned to go. "Look, this was a private conversation, okay?"

"Don't need to tell me," Larry said.

Brandon spent the next few minutes looking for Eldon, until it dawned on him where he'd be. Rather than go to the pit, he rushed to the lab. Jacobs and Suren sat side-by-side staring at the computer. Each had a headset on and their eyes plastered to the screen. "Eldon's down there alone isn't he?" Brandon said.

"He insisted," Jacobs said.

"Doesn't anyone around here have any balls?" Brandon yelled, "No one should go down there alone."

Jacobs swung around in his chair. "Don't give me your shit until you have asked the right questions."

Brandon gave him a quizzical look.

"I cleared it. The man's a scientist. He has a very logical brain. Understanding is the highest form of interaction with him and once he understood what those guys were doing, he was able to segment it in his brain, separate it out so that it didn't affect him." He turned back to the screen. "Frankly, I'm impressed by the man's mental capabilities."

"It still wasn't a smart thing to do. You took a chance that you were right," Brandon said. "Besides, you said he insisted, which indicates you couldn't stop him."

"He insisted and I complied. We both made a decision," Jacobs said. "Look, my friend, no matter how worried you are, I am an expert in my field, too. I did the right thing." He pulled an ear bud from the table and held it out to Brandon. "Go ahead and listen."

Brandon lifted the bud to his ear and held it close. Eldon was in a calm conversation with the aliens. He asked about their social structure and got clear, precise answers. "What's going on here," Brandon said. "Are they not transmitting emotional data any longer? Where's the subliminal track?" He pointed at the screen where an almost smooth line ran across it.

Jacobs keyed his mic and said, "I sense they're getting tired. They're taking longer to get to their answers."

"Either that or my questions are becoming more difficult. I don't get the sense that they're the experts on all aspects of their life down here," Eldon said. "But they are the diplomats, so to speak. Anyway, I hate to stop now, just as we're getting started. And after all this time. There's so much to learn."

"I think it best," Jacobs said.

"I hear you," Eldon said.

"You tape everything," Brandon said.

Suren nodded.

"One question," Brandon said.

"Shoot," Jacobs said.

"Are they cannibals? Like the Ekks?"

Jacobs smiled widely. "No," he said in a quiet voice. "I am glad to say that they are not. Although we haven't even touched on how they find nourishment."

"What have you discovered?" Brandon said.

"Tons," Suren blurted out. He appeared to be enjoying his new job. "It's unbelievable. Fascinating."

"The short story is that they have a crude, mostly mechanical based technology. They used to have more than that, but when the atmosphere of C-47 began to change and they were forced underground, their ability to maneuver depleted their ability to evolve technologically. Eventually all their transports and electronics, what little they appeared to have, were gone and couldn't be replaced. They had an underground transportation system and began to seal it off from topside. They continued to expand, but only for a short while, and only so far."

"That's too bad," Brandon said. "It must have been difficult for them."

Jacobs smile never left his face. "On the contrary. It allowed them to evolve spiritually."

"Spiritually?"

"Not through a sense of a god, like humans, but through a closer sense of who they are. They already had a second set of vocal cords. Dormant ones at the beginning. They had little else to do so they learned to use them. One problem," he shrugged. "Or at least it was a problem at the beginning. The second set worked rather automatically. They couldn't lie any longer."

"Wow," Brandon said, surprising himself.

"Wow, indeed," Jacobs said.

"Why didn't they tell Oliver and Eldon before now? Before we showed up?"

"You won't believe it if I tell you."

Brandon knew the answer before Jacobs said the words. "They never asked, did they?"

"They never asked," Jacobs confirmed. "Oliver was so susceptible to their subliminal messages that he probably didn't even hear, or register, the overt conversation. Eldon received both, but from what I can tell he couldn't separate them. He wasn't even sure what was said and what was subliminal. It took Palmer to ask the question and get the automatic answer." Jacobs turned back to the computer. "You won't believe this unless I show you." He opened another window on the computer and pointed out the conversation they had had.

"Look," he said. "They never said those words out loud. It was subliminal all the way once she asked about weapons."

"But we all heard it," Brandon said.

"You sure as hell did," Jacobs said. "And it registered."

"They can't control the subliminal message at all?"

"We're finding the extent of that answer now. It appears that they have some control, but because of their evolution they seldom monitor that control. All of this is to say that if I'm correct, they may come in handy."

"You want their help in the negotiations," Brandon said. "Isn't that cheating?"

"It's using the tools you have available to solve a difficult challenge," Jacobs said. "I trust you don't have any aversion to that?"

"You're the shrink. If you say it's fair, it's fair." Brandon started to leave then turned back around. "If the miners broke into their catacombs, why didn't they claim the discovery?"

"A sad story, I'm afraid. I don't know exactly, but I can imagine that breaking through meant that an enormous emotional pulse pushed through the aliens as the breach killed hundreds of them. Uncontrollably, their subliminal larynx, that's what I'm going to call it for now, copied and threw back the miner's fear that came from the emotional pulse."

"The snowball effect."

"Good analogy. The aliens' fearful emotions drove into the hearts of the miners, plowing them over like a giant snowball. When the miners reacted verbally, the aliens threw their words back at them again. This probably escalated quickly. According to what Eldon and Oliver told me during our talks, the miners thought the aliens were monsters of some kind. They refused to go back down. They returned angry, hurt, violent. That might be where it all started because Oliver and Eldon went down to see what had happened. By that time, the aliens had sealed the breach. I think it was Eldon who realized what they might have on their hands and convinced Oliver and the governmental board to make a quick deal with the miners before they realized what they'd actually discovered down there."

Brandon shook his head. "Unbelievable. Then Oliver and Eldon were both bombarded by the alien emotions, but only Oliver took it on as his own."

"Well, in all fairness, Eldon is a scientist who has searched for life since he arrived. His curiosity may have gone wild, but his approach to facts kept him in check. Oliver, on the other hand, was in a position to do something about the situation. If you think of it this way, both men protected the aliens in the only ways they were able too."

"Eldon wouldn't let anyone else down there to do the research. That's all he could do," Brandon said. "And he held tightly to it, I remember."

"But Oliver had much more potential."

"And he abused it."

"Let us not forget that he was under the influence. Abuse is a harsh word for someone who was doing his best to protect another race."

Brandon agreed. "How's he doing, by the way?"

"It's going to take a while. If we can get the Mesoans to help, it might go more smoothly."

"Sounds like they're cooperating."

Jacobs shrugged. "So far, but we're taking it slowly."

Outside the lab they heard people running. Jacobs raised his eyebrows.

"I'll check on it," Brandon rushed over and opened the door to witness a mix of IPF armed enforcers and C-47 armed citizens headed right for him, a mob in the making.

"Told you I saw him go in there," one man said.

"What's the rush?" Brandon said.

"Last word from your pilot friend said that Earth Central started firing on them," the man in front said between breaths.

Brandon shot into action. He parted the group and jogged down the hall. "They can't do that. C-47 has their independence."

"We do?" a man next to him asked.

Brandon ignored the question and pushed on down the corridor. As he rushed along with a line of followers, he considered his options, the ones he'd hoped he wouldn't have to weigh in. His primary thought was how to protect Palmer, but with the IPF mother ship heading into a no communications orbit, it meant hours before he could get there even if he left right away. By then Palmer and the two IPF fighters could be captured...or blown from the sky. He clenched his jaw at the thought.

In the lobby, he found Larry again. "Too much of that jasp and you won't have a stomach," Brandon said.

Larry poured it out. I just got here. I've been working.

"No explanation necessary. I need your help," The situation had escalated and all he could think about was Palmer's safety. He had to clear his head. But he also needed Jacobs. "One of you, go back and get Jacobs. Now," he yelled at the men who'd followed him.

"What do you need," Larry said.

"I need to communicate with Palmer," Brandon said.

Larry looked at his watch. "You can for another few minutes, but it'll be a shaky signal."

"I need to talk with her for the next few hours," Brandon said staring into Larry's face.

The young man looked like a boy for a moment, then his expression changed and a man's smile spread across his face. "One of the fighters," he said.

Brandon didn't even ask what Larry meant. He saw that Larry knew exactly what he was going to do. Brandon looked around at the group. "Larry's word is gold," he told the man closest to him. "Do whatever he asks."

Before he made it to the front door, Jacobs ran into the lobby with Larry in tow. "You're not going anywhere," he said. "We need you here."

Brandon halted. He felt torn in two. He still didn't have a clear plan. The cuffs weighed heavily on his shoulders as did the responsibility of C-47's safety. But Palmer needed him. As Jacobs walked slowly toward him, Brandon noticed that Suren had followed. "Suren, you will select a commanding officer to operate on my behalf while I'm gone. Jacobs, you are in charge, but will take close council with Suren's chosen officer."

"Brandon, don't do this. It's not good for you and not good for us."

"Palmer's in trouble," he said.

"Then hear me out," Jacobs said.

Brandon waited, not because he didn't want to go, but because his responsibility to his station still battled with his love for Palmer, and as that battle waged he had no energy to move.

Jacobs stepped closer. "We have little choice. In order for us to complete a negotiation with all parties, we'll have to do it there." He pointed toward the sky.

"But EC will have control of the IPF mother ship, they'll have already..." Brandon didn't even say the words.

"Even if you took the fastest ship, you couldn't get there in time," Jacobs said. "Palmer is a professional. She can do this." His voice eased. "You know it's true."

Something inside Brandon told him that Jacobs was right. "I've got to try," Brandon said as a last resort.

"We may have to act swiftly, but you'll do more than try, my friend. We're all going, including our new friends." Jacobs stared, waiting for a response.

Getting his wits back, Brandon said, "Who will hold this place together?"

Jacobs looked around. A mix of IPF soldiers and C-47 men and women crowded into the room. "They're independent. Put it back into the hands of the board. Not much can happen in a day or two, and it leaves you free to go."

Brandon knew when someone was thinking clearly and Jacobs made all kinds of sense. "Will they come with us?"

"If they know what's good for them," Jacobs said. "We may be their only way of staying protected. Eldon will nurture our relationship and not allow anyone, not even Earth Central, to take over. I think with our new way of talking with them, they've become extremely less dangerous. For us, that is."

"As long as we can't hear their subliminal voices," Brandon said. He motioned toward Larry. "Can you rig communicators that can delete the subliminal messages in some speakers but not others?"

Jacobs smiled broadly. "Now we're talking about a plan."

Many of those in the lobby looked confused, but it didn't matter. All Brandon wanted was for Larry to understand what he needed.

"Arnie can do it," Larry said.

"I don't have much time for this," Brandon said. "I want to be on that IPF fighter and on my way in less than an hour."

Jacobs swung around to address Larry. "I need to talk with Eldon before he gets back here."

"Easy to do," Larry said as he reached for a communicator.

Brandon put a hand on Jacobs' shoulder. "You really think the Mesoans will join us? That will make for quite a display. There'll be no concern over whether they're real or not."

"Yeah," Jacobs said, "this could be one hell of a little discussion."

"Earth Central can be quite aggressive when it's in their interest," Brandon said. "What if things turn sour?"

"They're already sour for Palmer." Jacobs shoved against Brandon, driving his shoulder into the cuffs. "These things may come in handy up there."

# CHAPTER 28

**"THE OTHER PROBLEM,"** Brandon said to Jacobs as they headed for the pit office, "is James."

"How so?"

"He's going to think we've changed our mind. No matter what we tell him, he'll think that we're cheating him. That he's not going to get to stay on C-47," Brandon said.

"I've thought of that and have ordered up specific paperwork providing him with a permanent job here. The details of that job have been left open to interpretation, but his life on C-47 will be secured."

"If they made it alive," Brandon said, even though he didn't want the words to be mentioned out loud. Didn't want to jinx their trip.

"Have you ever found a situation Palmer couldn't handle?"

"Not yet."

"Trust her. She trusts you. After all, she left you with all this."

"The easy job," Brandon said. "And soon, I won't have it anymore."

"She doesn't know that."

"True."

Eldon waited for them at the pit office. Oliver's mother sat beside him. She wore an environmental suit.

"What's this about?" Brandon didn't like the turn of events.

"I'm going," Oliver's mother stood and held out her hand. "Mary."

Brandon shook her hand. "Down there or up there," he said indicating direction by adjusting his chin toward each place, a slight cock to his head.

"Both," she gave him a wide grin. The wrinkles around her eyes and lips appeared deeper with the smile. But her eyes were soft, knowing.

"I'm not sure this is the best thing."

"You put us back in charge. You can't stop me."

"Word gets around fast, but it hasn't been done yet," Brandon said. "I could change my mind."

Her grin looked firm. "There's no time to argue the point. Let's get on with this."

Eldon stood. "We waited for you in case either of you wanted to go down with us, but it looks as though you're not suited up, so that answers that."

"She's not been briefed," Jacobs said.

"I'll be with her," Eldon said.

"And I've been briefed often enough and long before you arrived," she said.

"Suren?" Brandon wanted to know where he was.

"He's taping everything from the lab computer for now, while Larry's working on a portable translator. Arnie's working on the software with him," Eldon said. "Really, I think this is the only way they'll even consider doing what you've asked." He addressed his comment to Jacobs.

"Go with your instincts," Jacobs said.

"We'll be right here," Brandon said.

"You'd better be," Mary said. "I'm going to tell them that the big guns are going to go with us for protection." She nodded, "That's you." Again the grin, which was beginning to ease Brandon's worries.

"I think they'll remember you as soon as they connect emotionally," Eldon said to Brandon.

"I thought they weren't doing that anymore."

"Oh, they still make the connection, they just don't push with it. Much more subtle, but much more pleasing in the long run. You'll like it." Eldon turned to go into the elevator. Once inside, the two of them leaned and swung around to look out. "But they can push when they want to," Eldon warned.

Brandon and Jacobs watched as the doors closed and Eldon and Mary slipped helmets over their heads.

"This makes me nervous," Brandon said.

"Me too," Jacobs said.

"I thought…"

"We're taking a lot of this as it comes. I thought you knew that," he said.

Brandon let out a heavy breath. "I'll take battle over this any time."

"You may get your chance."

The wait for Eldon and Mary felt long though it was only around forty-five minutes. It was still later than what Brandon had hoped and he complained a few times to Jacobs.

"We're already running a bit rough," Jacobs said. "I figure the longer they're down there, the better chance we have that the Mesoans will fully understand how important this is to all of us, especially them." He turned to talk to Brandon face to face. "You have to remember that their first contact with humans was when the mining crew broke into their house and killed a hundred people or so."

"Not purposefully. They should know that now," Brandon said.

Jacobs shook his head. "You military people. You've killed so often that you've forgotten how much of an impact it makes on normal people. And, yes," he said looking directly at Brandon, "I consider them normal people at this point." He paced the area in front of Brandon looking up every once in a while as though conducting a training session. "If someone broke into your house and killed your family, would you be so easily swayed when they told you it was just a mistake?" He stopped to look into Brandon's face, but Brandon knew the question was rhetorical. "Would you believe they didn't mean it? Would you hand over enough information for them to wipe out the rest of your neighborhood or, in this case, your entire race?"

Brandon held his tongue. "They'd better hurry," is all he said.

In a few more minutes, one of the operators interrupted and said, "They're on their way up."

"And," Brandon said.

"There are four bodies in the airlock."

Brandon closed his eyes. "My God, I hope this is the right thing to do."

"Me too," Jacobs had turned back to his more serious self.

Brandon wished he could take Jacobs comment lightly, but thoughts of Palmer flooded his mind. He wanted to be on his way, and they still had the drive to the airstrip, the flight time. Bringing the aliens was beginning to look like an excuse for him to run to Palmer's side and he wasn't sure he liked that part of him showing up so blatantly.

The long journey for the four of them to reach the pit elevator drove Brandon and Jacobs' wait over an hour just for this segment of the plan. Brandon was itchy to get going, but well aware of the need to stay calm. He normally wouldn't be in such a hurry. As a soldier, he'd learned to sit and wait for days if he needed to. But with Palmer in potential danger, he found his emotions weren't so easily managed. For a brief second he wondered if his meeting with the Mesoans had opened a space inside him that had never been opened before…or was it Palmer who had opened that space months ago and he hadn't noticed before?

When the doors to the elevator opened, a sense of excitement filled his chest. He knew it wasn't from his thoughts. There was something new and adventuresome about it. He bowed to the aliens as they made their way slowly from the elevator. Their hands were touching and moving. Mary held the shortened elbow of one, while Eldon did the same with the other.

Brandon had the sense that he wanted to embrace each of the Mesoans, as though they were long lost friends or family. He recalled the sense of warmth he had felt the last time he was with them, the sense of peace. He acknowledged his feelings to Eldon and Mary forgetting that they were disconnected and couldn't relay the message.

The aliens bowed their heads as though in response, and Brandon noticed a knowing smile cross each of their faces.

"Let's go," he said.

A truck waited outside for them and everyone loaded inside quickly and fairly easily since Eldon and Mary were helping the Mesoans. Rather than go through the building, Brandon suggested they use the equipment bays, which would get them outside quickly and on their way to the airstrip. He lifted his communicator from his belt and called the tower, telling them to have Larry meet them at the strip.

So far everything moved forward at a slower pace than Brandon would have liked, but at least it moved forward. On occasion, he glanced back at the aliens dressed in environmental suits. The sense that came from them was not only that of adventure but curiosity. They had taken a huge risk and, at the moment, he couldn't figure out why. Preservation? "Everything all right back there?"

Eldon yelled over the rush of the wind and the engine, "We're fine."

Mary leaned over and rocked back and forth as though she were trying to ease the concern of the aliens.

Brandon couldn't help but think of his own mother doing the same thing to him as a child. What was it about women, mothers in particular?

When they rounded the last corner, Brandon brightened to see a dozen men and women at work near the IPF fighter, giving it the once over. But where were Larry and Arnie? Where was the equipment they needed, the translator?

The truck stopped and Brandon leaped out and ran over to the group where he asked about Larry. One of the men stepped around from the back holding an electronics unit, a black box with a few lights and knobs, but mostly plugs, over a dozen of them. The person beside the man carried an equal number of cables with the male portion of the plugs on one end and either ear buds or headsets soldered to the other end. It was a hodgepodge of equipment that Brandon hoped would work. "The translator?" Brandon took the black box from the man.

"Yeah. And here," he let loose a strap attached to the bottom of it. "We'll attach this to one of their backs," he pointed to the Mesoans, "and you can plug the cables in whenever you're ready."

As the Mesoans got closer, Brandon noticed the crew staring. A few stepped back, unsure of what to do or say. The man who handed him the translator appeared to be a bit nervous, but pointed at the plugs, which were different colors. There were two plugs at the very top and then two rows more under those. "These top two are for them," he pointed to the Mesoans, taking a moment to look into their helmets. He broke his stare and said, "These two rows are for everyone else. Larry said to tell you that the red and green plugs, starting from the left, have one signal only. The yellow and blue ones have two signals. He said you'd know what he meant."

"I do," Brandon said. "Mics?" He pointed at the bumps located near the speaker end of the cable.

"Exactly," the man patted the box. "Oh, and it has an internal digital recorder that'll capture everything."

"Smart man," Brandon said. "One last question. Power?"

"Enough battery in that thing for a month," the man said. "That's why it's so heavy."

Brandon took the unit over to one of the aliens, the male, and plugged a feed-through wire from the ear bud into the red plug at the far left. And plugged both the aliens' cords into place where they belonged. He explained that he was about to strap the unit onto the environmental suit and that there would be some tugging as he tightened it down.

The Mesoans' hands had been together continually, moving their fingers in their strange tactile language.

From the unit came the sounds of the alien language then the translation. "We are ready. And we are glad you are with us."

Their words were very simple, yet carried much emotional weight, and Brandon couldn't help but wonder if the weight came from him or them. He realized this was going to be a very strange communication between peoples. "I'm glad as well," he said.

Mary held out a hand. "Hook us up."

Brandon disconnected his cable and connected Mary and Eldon before they entered the fighter together. Six of those who had been checking the fighter out for flight took seats inside as well. "Backup," one of the men said.

Brandon followed the others inside and disconnected from the translator. "So, who's flying this thing?"

One of the IPF pilots twisted and peered back into the fighter's interior. He raised a hand and yelled to Brandon. "I'm taking this ride," he said.

"Let's get going," Brandon said as he slipped past Jacobs to get into the copilot's seat.

"You know what to do over there in an emergency?" the pilot said.

"Done it a thousand times," Brandon said.

"Crenshaw," the pilot said, holding his hand toward Brandon.

"Brandon."

Crenshaw reached up and flipped the power switch on, then the override for engine safety. He cranked up the engines then waved out the window for the ground crew to disconnect external power and move out of the way. He looked over at Brandon then twisted to look behind him. "Everybody strapped in?"

Jacobs yelled forward that they were ready back there.

"My favorite part," the pilot said as he pushed the throttles forward.

Brandon reminded himself to keep an eye on the pilot as well as the backup, since they were IPF enforcers. The last thing he needed at this point was funny business. He slipped his headset on and listened as the woman from the tower gave the wind velocity at different altitudes. Apparently the canyon caused some hefty wind shear at times. Knowing what shifts were going on would help the pilot as he maneuvered out of the area. There was a bit of low-level turbulence as they climbed. But, once that was over, Crenshaw pushed the ship into full throttle and they were on their way.

"How long before we're at an angle that we can contact Palmer?" Brandon asked.

"Estimate, about two hours," Crenshaw said. "In a hurry?"

"Always," Brandon said, which wasn't true until recently.

Jacobs kneeled down behind the center console and looked out the windshield. "If we fly at a steeper angle we'll get to communicate with them faster won't we?"

Crenshaw leaned back in his seat and turned his head slightly, not enough to look at Jacobs, but enough to appear as though he was listening. "True, but then it'll take us longer to get there. Which is it?"

"We're fine," Brandon said. "If I can't do anything either way, I want to reach them fast. Listening to them get shot at isn't going to help them."

"Good point," Jacobs said. "But I still don't think there's much to worry about."

"Even a little much is too much," Brandon said holding his thumb and forefinger close together. Then he thought of something else. "What about Earth Central's mother ship?"

"They came through between planets. It'll take them a while to get close to the action. By my estimates, the best course is the one we're on. These poor planets don't have the resources to make this easy as you can see," Crenshaw said.

Brandon looked at Jacobs. "You think IPF will let her inside?"

"Originally they wanted to join with C-47, but at this point we don't know who was privy to that information. Garth handed out more stories and promises than any ten people."

"But with James returning…"

Jacobs nodded. "Yeah, I think they'll help. Since Earth Central made the first move against Palmer, the IPF enforcers will most likely see them as allies. Especially with James on-board. That was a good call." He turned to Crenshaw. "Your thoughts?"

"Sounds like you know more about this than I do," Crenshaw said.

"Palmer has the plan," Brandon assured them.

"She does that," Jacobs said. "By the way, we're going to give the whole true story to the Mesoans back there. We want them to realize how essential this negotiation is going to be."

"Have at it," Brandon settled into his seat once Jacobs returned to one of the jumpers and strapped in. Staring out the side window, Brandon let his thoughts go and almost drifted off. His body had calmed. At one time he wondered how the Mesoans were doing, but didn't ask. He let it ride. He let everything ride. And before long, they were in communications range.

Crenshaw reached down at the center console and hit a button.

"We're stable," Palmer was saying.

Brandon hadn't even heard Crenshaw talking. But now he came fully alert. He keyed his mic. "Are you inside the IPF Mother Ship?" Brandon said.

"Brandon," came Palmer's voice, but the way she said his name was familiar and comforting, not for him but it sounded as though it was comforting for her.

"Yeah, Babe, it's me." His response sounded strange to him, his tone, but he blew it off as relief.

"What about the colony?"

"Tell you later. What's your story?"

"James has some talents," she said. "The IPF enforcers are going to let us in. They've also run a few maneuvers to keep the Earth Central ships busy."

"So you're still being attacked by EC?" Brandon asked.

It took a moment before Palmer came back on. "Sorry. Evasive maneuvers. So, yes, they're still putting a few shots in. But we're doing fine and should be inside momentarily."

"We're a few hours behind you. So, what's next?"

"Plan B," Palmer said, then she laughed.

"Not funny."

"I have a feeling that even once we're inside, Earth Central's going to want to take over. That means they may not want you to get close enough to join us. Although James and his silver tongue may be able to convince Hollis, nothing can go down until some diplomat shows up. I think we're going to have our hands full keeping everyone at arm's length."

"We'll get in," Brandon said. "We have the two Mesoans with us."

"What?"

"Plus Eldon and Oliver's mom, Mary. According to them, that's enough to make a deal and sign off on it."

"Do you really think that was a smart move? I mean the Mesoans. What about their, their…abilities?" Palmer said.

"Under check. Jacobs believes that they'll be able to help. They're being briefed on the whole situation as we speak. Under complete supervision."

"Jacobs is there too?" She let out a long breath. "Hold on. We're approaching the bay doors. I'm going off line with you for a little while. Once we're safe and inside, I'll contact you again."

Crenshaw acknowledged her last message. "Won't take long," he said to Brandon.

"This thing go any faster?"

"Not unless you get out and push," Crenshaw commented.

"I like a smart ass."

"Then we'll get along." Crenshaw maintained his angle of ascent and as soon as he thought it possible, he hailed the Earth Central Mother Ship. He reached over to Brandon and whispered. "Galactic Module 18 Senator McMasters."

Brandon fumbled with the mic. "Senator McMasters?"

"I've ordered my people to hold IPF Section 204 under Earth Central Military Law until this situation is resolved. There are just way too many conflicting stories going around. If you have any influence on them, you'd better employ it now."

Brandon leaned back and cocked his head toward Crenshaw. "No hello, how you doing with this guy." He turned back and keyed his mic. "First Lieutenant Brandon Lockhardt here. Got your message loud and clear. Tell your fighters to lay off the attack and we'll attempt to comply. Can't do much until I get there."

"No attempt to it. When they get inside, they're taking over. Guns down, hands up. All of you."

"Jesus, the guy's worse than me." Back on line, he said, "Do my best, but I'm not in charge there. You're shooting at the guy in charge."

"Get us in there," the Senator said.

Brandon didn't answer him right away. He waited for Palmer, which didn't take long. After explaining what McMasters had ordered, he held on for a response.

"He tried that with us too," Palmer said. "He knows we have James with us, but we couldn't tell him for sure what was going to happen so he maintained his attack. It was feeble, though, like he was just putting on the pressure. What is it with all the intimidation tactics? Anyhow, Section 204 helped, like I told you. But, we're inside now and all I see are enforcers with guns. They're everywhere. I have a feeling that James isn't as good as I thought there for a while."

"What's next, then? We're coming in fast," Brandon said.

"And so is Hollis," she said. "I have a feeling things might get a bit ugly."

# CHAPTER 29

**BY THE TIME BRANDON ARRIVED** with his delegates from C-47's old civilization, Palmer had gone off-line for good. He had no idea what to expect. At least Section 204 hadn't fired on them. The bay doors opened and, as always, the open chamber inside looked deserted to Brandon, which reminded him of entering a dead ship, something he'd only done a few times, but wasn't a good memory at all. Everything before him appeared to be in order. Tools had been secured to the walls, equipment had been docked in place. Nothing appeared unusual except for a few stains here and there. Ground crews were always good at keeping their bay spotless or he wouldn't have noticed the stains. Perhaps they were in a hurry for some reason, or the upheaval made them less conscientious.

Palmer's Shadow Cruiser sat to one side, near a few IPF fighters and two Earth Central fighters, which looked like later models of the IPF fighters. The IPF ships were a bit scraped up, on one a wing panel was opened and looked gutted inside. The EC ships definitely looked better cared for, buffed and polished.

Under radio silence, Crenshaw brought their fighter in like a pro, swinging it around so that it pointed out toward space when he touched down, ready for the next run. Crenshaw's piloting skills caused Brandon to wonder why they made such a big deal out of Palmer's expertise. No sooner did the question arrive, the answer came through. Garth required a pilot who didn't know about all the internal turmoil, had no connection to anyone who worked for him. And probably someone who was expendable had his little plan not worked. That last thought irked Brandon.

It was literally impossible to keep every government, every colony, every space station under wraps in a space as large as the galaxy, even for Earth Central. That's why all the different modules had been created. They were basically spheres of space, like states or counties, each with its own local government, as it were, but backed by Earth Central's federal umbrella. Parcel those modules into Sections and create an infrastructure of military on one end and the peace force on the other, and Brandon started to admit to himself how things could get corrupt pretty fast. A little individual control could go a long way in making someone rich enough to leave the system.

As far as corruption went, well, Brandon knew it was there, but had seldom come face to face with it in his line of work. Until now. And at the moment, he couldn't tell which side was more corrupt. Which meant that he didn't know whose side to be on, so he decided to be on Palmer's until further notice.

As soon as the bay doors closed behind them, it wasn't ground crews who rushed the ship, but Earth Central military. In a fleeting moment, he felt as though he was home, but then realized that they were rushing him. "Stay in the ship and don't open any doors yet," Brandon yelled back to everyone.

"What's wrong?" Jacobs snapped out of his harness and rushed toward the cockpit. He leaned over the center console and saw what was happening outside. "Not good," he said.

Brandon keyed his mic. "What's the military assaulting my ride for?"

"You are to stand down and surrender your weapons," someone said.

"By whose authority?"

"Senator McMasters. He said that he talked with you already."

The man on the other end didn't quite sound confident to Brandon, so he pushed him a little. "Not what he told me," Brandon said.

The speakers went dead.

Brandon turned to Jacobs. "He's thinking about it. What do you suggest?"

Jacobs patted Brandon's chest and straightened his collar. "You're an Earth Central man aren't you? That's what your rank says."

"Assigned to IPF Section 204 like you," Brandon said. "So, I'm essentially working for them." He shot Crenshaw a glance. "Until they tried to kill me."

"I'm guessing they don't know that," Jacobs said. "So, take us in. Under guard."

Brandon keyed his mic. "Look, I'll save you some trouble. I have a group of prisoners here. And a few Section 204 enforcers helping me." He winked at Crenshaw. "I've also got a top secret, ah, discovery that I can't let out of my site. Something I found on C-47. "Let me get these guys to a cell and we can talk this out."

"Senator McMasters is on his way. Come on out and you can talk with him when he arrives." The man still sounded a bit unsure of himself, something Brandon counted on at the moment.

"Get Eldon and Mary to put their helmets back on, visors down on all four of them," Brandon said. He keyed the mic. "We're preparing the prisoners. So, where's my first pilot and her crew?"

"We've got them under wraps until McMasters arrives," the man said.

Brandon climbed into the rear and saw six soldiers sitting in the back. He turned to Crenshaw. "Select one other soldier to help us and strip the rest of their rank. They're under arrest until we need them."

"Yes, sir," Crenshaw said.

Brandon put a hand on Jacobs shoulder. "Sorry, but you're one of them for now, until I figure something out." He stepped back to the front and grabbed the mic. "Could you tell your guys to back away until I get clear of the ship? Don't want any mishaps."

"No funny business," the man said.

Brandon leaned down and looked around quickly. None of the EC soldiers had cuffs. They all held either machine guns or stunners. He wondered what the stunners were set at, but didn't want to guess.

When the others were ready, Brandon took a few long strides to the rear of the fighter. "Opening the doors," he said just before pushing the button. As the rear ramp lowered he yelled out, "Earth Central First Lieutenant Brandon Lockhardt escorting prisoners, please stand aside." He saw that the soldiers outside stood ready but did not advance. He motioned for Crenshaw and the man he'd selected to usher the others down the ramp. They moved slowly, the four dressed in environmental suits setting the pace from the center of the small group.

"Get on with it," one of the soldiers said.

"We have some injuries," Brandon said. "We'll take it as it comes." He noticed the soldiers twisting to see the four center figures. They probably wondered why the suits, and why they didn't look quite normal. But he had no time to come up with a story for them.

As he led the party, he noticed that the stains he had seen earlier were bloodstains, not oil as he had thought. So, it was a hostile takeover. His heart sank. He wondered what they'd done with Palmer and James. He looked over at Crenshaw, who must have known the soldiers who had taken over the IPF ship when it appeared to be vulnerable.

Crenshaw winked slowly to indicate that he'd also noticed the situation.

The EC soldiers advanced on the small group as they got closer to the debriefing room door.

Brandon stood to the side as Crenshaw and his partner led the others into the room. He stepped between Crenshaw, who was the last to enter, and the EC soldiers. "I can take it from here," he said, hoping that his rank would allow him at least this one privilege. But it wasn't that easy. When one of the soldiers continued forward Brandon had to shove against him, puffing out his chest, with his rank insignia, into the man's face. "This is my job," he said. "I've been working for Earth Central on this for a long time. I'm going to debrief these guys and I'll call you when I'm going to take them to the brig." He looked around at the men. "Don't worry, I know where the recording equipment is." Then he closed the door.

"Now we're trapped in here," Jacobs said.

"Yeah," Brandon said, "not a whole lot better is it?"

"I can't believe they let you in here with us alone," Crenshaw said. "And they didn't bat an eye at our uniforms, as though two of us would take in our cohorts."

"Jesus," Brandon said.

"What's that," Jacobs said.

"These guys aren't very impressive either now that you mention it. You have to wonder how much training any of them gets anymore. And no cuffs? I didn't know we were that elite."

"I'm surprised they didn't try to disarm us and take in our prisoners on their own," Crenshaw said.

Jacobs shook his head. "The more mankind spreads out into the galaxy, the thinner the fabric of our control, I suppose. My guess is that they gave C-47 their independence to get them off their back. With no real mineral deposits the colony doesn't have much to offer, present company excepted, not even in the way of taxes. Earth Central probably looks at them as a burden."

"We pay enough taxes now anyway," Eldon piped in.

Brandon saw that Jacobs was about to comment on Eldon's observation and held out his hand to stop him. "No time for a debate. We have other problems facing us."

"What do you think will happen when they find out about you-know-who over here?" Eldon said.

"We might want to keep that question handy as we go down this road. But my guess at the moment is that it depends on who finds out. There may be a different answer for the IPF than there is for McMasters and his staff," Jacobs said.

"Is everyone crooked?" Brandon shook his head in disbelief.

"Everyone wants something, and when it looks like it's close at hand, they are a bit unpredictable. Will they go for it? Won't they? You never quite know unless they've been in therapy with you for the last six months." Jacobs indicated Crenshaw and his men. "If they were here during the Section 204 takeover and saw it as a way to get more out of the system, they may have been a part of it."

"And we could have been killed by those goons, too," Crenshaw said. "Right now, it looks like we've got a chance, at least."

"Nonetheless, my suggestion is that we trust no one," Jacobs said.

"Maybe what Garth was doing by handing out different stories to everyone actually kept a kind of balance in order," Brandon said.

"Honesty may have done it better," Jacobs said, "and he wouldn't have run into as many discrepancies."

A knock came to the door that led into the heart of the mother ship. "You're done in there. Unlock this and come on out."

"On our way," Brandon yelled as he made his way over to the door. When he arrived, he shrugged to everyone, pushed the unlock button. "Let's see what happens next. Just protect our friends there. This isn't their battle." He grinned and said, "Open."

As the door began to slide over, someone on the other side shoved their way into the room. Three more men behind him held machine guns aimed into the group. The tallest man, nodded toward Brandon. "Off with the cuffs and drop all your weapons. We'll take it from here."

Brandon stepped in front of the door. "I'm the senior officer here. And I was told I'd have access to the ship until my prisoners were…"

"Hollis is in charge and she said that you're going with them," the man said. He shook the end of his machine gun at Brandon. "Now, off with the ammo."

Brandon continued to look forward. "Change of plans, men." Just as a grin came over the soldier's mouth, Brandon, without lifting his arm, pointed his finger at the man in charge and blasted him away. Blood splattered the wall, and before either of the other two could move, he blasted them away as well. He swung around. "Like I said, our plans have changed." He ushered everyone toward the rear door after shouting close and locking the one that led into the ship. "Back to the fighter."

"Is it safe to go back out there?" Eldon's voice shook like his lips.

Brandon glanced over his shoulder, gave Eldon a quick grin, and said, "I'll just give them the finger." He held up his cuffed hand.

Mary said, "He's the expert."

Brandon came out the door right behind the others and saw that Crenshaw and his selected partner stood to either side of the door with their guns held out as though they still escorted the prisoners. It looked like the soldiers inside the bay didn't know about the latest orders Hollis had put down, nor did they hear the shots from the debriefing room.

Brandon plowed through and around the group. He counted the soldiers inside the bay. There were seven at the moment: five below with them and two above on the catwalks. With no warning, Brandon lifted both arms into the air and took out the two soldiers on the catwalk. He could see out the corner of his eye as Crenshaw made the order to protect the aliens. His troops turned on the five soldiers inside the bay.

Crenshaw had stripped them of their ranks but not of their weapons, which came out the second Crenshaw said the word.

Quickly, those wearing the four environmental suits were huddled into the middle of gunfire between the IPF enforcers and the Earth Central soldiers. It didn't take long for the IPF to down the five bay guards who weren't ready for such an onslaught.

Brandon scoured the area, watching every door that led into the bay. As a soldier opened a door to enter, Brandon pointed at him and took him out. Near the ramp, he said to Jacobs, "I'm going after Palmer, get these guys out of here. I should never have chanced this. I was wrong."

"We can't leave you," Jacobs said.

"No choice," Brandon said, "I'm not going."

As the ramp rose into place, Brandon yelled inside, "I'll get the bay doors opened." He took out several more soldiers who rushed into the bay area. Once the engines started, he ran for the observation deck instead of the debriefing room. He blasted a soldier coming through the control room door, then ran up the stairs two at a time. At the top of the stairwell Brandon took out several men, visually located the emergency oxygen masks in case the door didn't automatically seal when it closed, and then took out the controller who also wore an Earth Central uniform. "This isn't going to look good on your resume," he said to himself as he slipped a mask over his face. He shoved the soldier he'd just shot off of the control panel. Then, over the sound of the air lock alarm, he went through the sequence of buttons to open the bay doors for the fighter to get out.

C-47 loomed blue and green, innocent and curious beyond the doors. For a brief moment, he wished he were on the ship with Crenshaw. There was a chance that either Palmer had already been killed or that he'd never make it to her. Thinking about it wouldn't help though, and he knew that.

He had never said anything to Crenshaw about maneuvers, but noticed that the fighter didn't rocket straight out of the bay and into open space. It dropped under the mother ship. A single evasive move that would allow him to avoid whoever handled their warheads. If he chose to leave at the right time, and travel in the right direction, it would take a few milliseconds before the weapons officer for the mother ship would locate and fire on him. If they were lucky, the

Earth Central soldiers were cocky enough to believe they didn't need anyone on weapons. Brandon smiled, "Smart man." Under the mother ship would be the safest place for Crenshaw to be at the moment. The safety of the Mesoans was in his hands now.

"Plan B," Brandon said with a smirk. He shrugged his shoulders to get the cuffs comfortable and bent his head down, ready for his run toward the brig where he hoped to find Palmer, James, and the men who had come with them.

He heard shuffling as more soldiers made their way up the stairs toward the control room. He crossed the expanse and sat in a chair opposite from where the soldiers would expect him to be, looking out the bay windows. Sure enough, when they ran into the room they faced the windows, stopping dead as though confused.

"Over here," Brandon said. As they swung around he blasted them away, pht-pht-pht. He headed down the stairs two at a time again. He'd knocked out fourteen or fifteen soldiers so far and there were only two fighters in the bay, so that meant that there may be another fifteen to eighteen EC soldiers left. But, if McMasters were on his way, there'd be more coming. He checked the time and figured he had an hour, maybe two at the most, depending when McMasters decided to make the trip.

Taking the hall by ducking into one doorway after another wasn't very fast, but he couldn't risk walking down the center of the corridor as though there was nothing to worry about. His armor would only protect him so well. Halfway down the hall, Brandon turned right toward the aft quarter of the ship where the brig was located.

He heard feet running down a side hallway and waited until they turned the corner then, pointing both index fingers at them, took them out. It was almost too easy with the cuffs.

He was too deep into the ship when he realized that he'd forgotten to close the bay doors. That meant that McMasters could dock whenever he arrived. "Shit," he said under his breath. Brandon jogged to the next turn and blasted through a closed door. Not far now, he thought.

When he turned the last corner, he stopped. Palmer and James were in front of him, but so were five of the leftover, to his count, twelve EC soldiers. Only one was a woman, and he guessed it was Hollis.

She said, "It appears as though we have a checkmate."

# CHAPTER 30

"NOT IF YOU INCLUDE THEM," Brandon said, pointing behind her.

Hollis didn't move a muscle, but her men did, and the second their attention was off of Palmer and James, Brandon took them out using low power membrane shells: small holes but quick deaths if done correctly, and he knew how to do it well. He also knew that any soldier worth his salt wouldn't think to kill the hostage, but would turn their guns on the enemy, in this case him. And that's just what they did. Using both hands, Brandon pointed at the two men closest to Palmer and James. A small hole in each of their heads produced a bead of blood, and the two soldiers crumpled to the ground.

Brandon raised his arms to cover his face and heard bullets hit his cuffs. A slight concussion shoved his arms back, but his head was saved. Then the onslaught stopped. He lowered his arms enough to see, and retaliate if necessary, but Palmer had knocked out one of the soldiers, backed from the others, and held the confiscated machine gun on Hollis and the other two.

"I wouldn't move," Palmer said. "Drop them."

Hollis told her soldiers to comply after Brandon pointed his finger at her forehead.

"Glad to see you know what I can do with these. Now, call in your men and tell them to come empty handed." Brandon advanced. He told James to pick up one of the machine guns and to cover the soldiers with Palmer.

James' hands shook, but he picked up the weapon and held it toward the soldiers Palmer already had in check.

As Hollis made the call, Brandon backed her into the cell where Palmer and James had just been pulled from. "The others?" he asked.

"Our crew came willingly," Palmer said, "no casualties. I knew you were on your way."

Brandon smiled. "Trust in her man."

"Maybe," she said as she locked Hollis and her two men inside. "Down there are the others." She turned to James, "You can get them out. Then we want to talk with whoever is able to control the IPF enforcers."

"That would be me," James said.

"You'd better be sure of that statement," Palmer threatened. She swung around at the noise of rushing soldiers. "Here they come."

Brandon took one side of the cell door while Palmer took the other. The soldiers would see Hollis and her men inside and focus on them long enough for him to make an impression. He doubted they'd be empty handed. Sure enough, the men came around the corner, stopped as soon as they saw Hollis, and Brandon lifted his arm to fire.

The man in front said, "Wait," and raised his gun over his head.

"Too easy," Brandon said to Palmer.

James showed up a moment later with the IPF soldiers. He looked to Brandon for approval. "I sent some of our guys around behind them," he said pointing at the EC soldiers. The rest are releasing our staff. I'll keep Jason locked in his room until I find out what happened to him and why he turned the place over so easily." James took a step toward Brandon.

"Stay there," Brandon said. "Never get between prisoners and their captors."

"Yes, sir," James said. He turned, "I'll make sure the captain and his crew are back in control of the ship, and get with the board. Should have operations back to relative normalcy pretty quickly now that there's no fear of Earth Central taking over."

Brandon let the IPF enforcers take over the capture, while he reached for Palmer's hand and headed back down the hall. "I want five men to come with us," he said over his shoulder.

"Where we going?" she said.

"I'm going to see where Crenshaw and our friends are. Maybe they can swing back around." He glanced over his shoulder quickly enough to see that five enforcers followed closely behind him, just as he'd ordered.

"You still want to do this here?" She didn't sound like she approved. "Can we trust anyone?"

"I want to get it finished. Here. There. I don't give a shit. Over, is what I'm looking for."

Silence from Palmer was acceptance.

When the seven of them reached the control room to the landing bay, several other IPF enforcers had already arrived and were carrying bodies out. Brandon reached for the mic, twisted a dial to the right frequency, and hailed Crenshaw.

"Crenshaw here. That didn't take long. You know somebody?"

"Two finger army," Brandon said. "What's your location?"

"Five meters, I'd say."

Brandon laughed. "Man, you are my kind of soldier." He told Palmer how Crenshaw had dropped out of the bay and that he never left the underside of the ship. "He's still there."

"I'm glad you're happy," she said.

Brandon couldn't help but smile. "Bring her in."

"Will do, but the Senator's coming in fast. He's got a Shadow Cruiser like your friend's. I'm surprised you haven't heard from him," Crenshaw said.

Brandon checked the other channels. "Oh, yes," he said into the microphone. "He's hailed us a couple of times." He turned to the men in the room. "Two of you guys go get Hollis. I need somebody to talk to the senator. Palmer, you're going to figure out what she's going to say to McMasters to get him to think we're safe."

"You think I'm going to do that?" she said waving her hands in front of her face.

"Please. Is there really time to argue about this?"

"I'll do it, but you'd better ask nicely next time."

"I promise. And can someone get James to come to the debriefing room. This meeting may happen fast."

Other enforcers left the room.

Brandon paced for a short time, turned and watched as Crenshaw brought in the fighter. C-47 had slipped out of view except for a halo of atmosphere visible along the lower right edge of the door opening.

"Can we trust these guys?" Brandon indicated the IPF enforcers even though they were within listening distance.

"I think that was my question a moment ago," Palmer said. "And if I had to answer it myself, I'd say that I don't think we can trust anyone at this point, not even the Mesoans. Do we really know what they want from all this? Are we pushing something onto them?" Palmer shook her head as though she didn't believe any of it was really happening. "I'm rather surprised they agreed to come along. Makes me nervous about their agenda."

Brandon trusted her observation, and knew that he had to be on alert at all times. That was except for the Mesoans. He had connected with them at a deeper level and knew that all they wanted was protection. They didn't want money, power, not anything that humans appeared to covet. Their greatest desire was to be left alone. He envisioned them as ancient gurus sitting in a cave on a mountaintop, but in this case it was in a cave under the surface. They had their spiritual practices and didn't want to engage in the world any longer. He saw no reason why he couldn't help them have that. C-47, Eldon, could do their research; after all the aliens were the first intelligent life ever found in the galaxy. The implications were huge. Maybe human kind could learn from the experiences of the Mesoans. Maybe all these criminal acts between humans could be countered by a new vision. He shook his head at the thought.

Palmer stood next to him and reached over him to push the button that would close the bay doors. "What is it?" she said in a whisper.

"I don't know. Somehow, I feel like we have more to learn from them than they have to learn from us."

"Earth Central?"

"No," Brandon said, "the Mesoans. I was thinking about the Mesoans."

"You believe that's true even after what they did to Oliver? You see what shape he's in. That wasn't good."

"Self-preservation," Jacobs said as he came through the door with Crenshaw. "We scared them and they threw it back at us."

"Well, now that we can't hear their subliminal messages maybe things will go more smoothly, maybe we'll figure all this out," Palmer said. "That's up to Eldon. Where is he, by the way."

"He and Mary are in the debriefing room with the Mesoans. We were asked to wait there until James showed up since he's still in charge of the ship," Jacobs said, "and appears to be rather busy getting things back to normal." He turned to Brandon, "So, go on with your conversation. I find it interesting."

"In a minute. First, Crenshaw, get down there and find James. Tell him I'm putting you in charge of the IPF enforcers for now. All he has to do is assign someone from the board to handle things while he's with us."

"I suspect I can do that until the commander is freed and back in service," Crenshaw said, "if he isn't already. I'm not the ranking officer, you know."

Brandon nodded. He understood. "I can live with that as long as you trust him."

"You can trust me," Crenshaw said.

"Good enough."

Crenshaw left the room.

"I don't get you," Palmer said to Brandon. "You're trusting everyone."

"Not much of a choice as I see it." He turned back to Jacobs. "I was going to remind everyone that they still have an emotional affect when they want to, but as long as we hear no evil, as it were, we're safe from their fears to a certain extent."

"Evil is a rough word," Jacobs said.

"I don't think so," Palmer said. "And you shouldn't either. Have you looked in a mirror lately?" She turned back to Brandon. "You think it's enough that they can't use subliminal messages on us?"

"I do."

When the soldiers brought Hollis she resisted taking the mic until Brandon held his index finger to her cheek. "No more pretty," he said.

Her jaw clenched, but she hailed McMasters.

"Why didn't anyone get back to me?" he said. "I was about to turn around."

"We had a little scuffle and some broken equipment." She kept her eyes on Brandon's hand. "There were no technicians with us, so we had to fiddle with things. It's working now."

Palmer smiled at her.

"Good thing," he said. "I'll be there in fifteen."

"Roger that," Hollis said. She handed the mic back to Palmer.

"Good girl," Palmer said.

"You want us to take her back to the brig?" one of the soldiers asked.

Palmer smiled at Hollis. "No. She's our greeting party."

In fifteen minutes the EC cruiser settled into the bay. Palmer and Brandon stood behind Hollis as they shoved her out the door alone. "Be good," Palmer said.

She advanced as Senator McMasters and about twenty soldiers filed from their cruiser. Hollis escorted them toward the debriefing room while Brandon and Palmer ducked out and ran down the hall to the interior door to the room. There were still bloodstains on the wall and floor from when Brandon blasted the EC soldiers. He felt a spike of worry run through his chest as he recalled that as an EC soldier himself, he could easily get put into prison for a long time for firing on his own men. Was his present situation even an exception? Probably not in McMasters' eyes. He could claim that he was still working for the IPF, but then, he'd shot a few of them, too. Christ, he was in trouble from all sides.

When Brandon and Palmer entered the debriefing room, McMasters stood alone with Hollis just inside the bayside door. They stared across the debriefing table at the two colonists, Jacobs, and the aliens. Brandon knew that the IPF soldiers had come up behind the EC guards and disarmed them. It would have been easy since no one expected any problems.

"What's this about?" McMasters said.

At that moment, James shoved between Palmer and Brandon.

"James?" McMasters said, "I thought you were planet side. That was one of the discrepancies in the paperwork. If you're here, then you did send the fighters."

"Sir. It's good to see you again." James looked around for a moment. "Yeah. I was down there when the orders were put through, which proves that I didn't do it. You can check the flight logs. Garth is still down there. Either way, I have several people who have come forward about how Garth coerced them into doing things they knew were wrong, including submitting an entry that I ordered the fighters to attack C-47." He nodded toward Jacobs. "I believe Intelligence Agent Jacobs can attest to that."

McMasters looked over. "So, you're Jacobs?"

"Sir," Jacobs said with a nod.

Senator McMasters shook his head. "I expected my people to be in charge, but since you're back and appear to have things under control...," he turned slightly.

"You're not leaving," James said.

"You can't hold me," the senator said.

"There are a few things we have to deal with," James said, "and you're authority in dealing with these issues is necessary."

Brandon had not seen James so adamant and aggressive.

McMasters' eyes narrowed. "What do you mean?"

"I want the paperwork transferred for C-47's independence from the system before we talk," James said.

"McMasters nodded and turned to Hollis," Take care of it," he said.

"Under guard," Palmer said, and two enforcers flanked Hollis as she left.

"She'll cooperate," Senator McMasters said.

"We'll make sure," Brandon said.

McMasters obviously checked Brandon's Earth Central Rank Insignia. How many casualties...on both sides?"

"We'll copy you from our report," Brandon said.

"Someone's going to have to account for this, you know?" the senator said.

"I know that, sir."

James apparently had several items of concern that he wanted taken care of before anyone talked about, or with, the Mesoans.

To Brandon, McMasters didn't appear to be surprised when the aliens were exposed, or surprised that there were aliens at all. Unless McMasters controlled his emotional presentation, the man must have known about the Mesoans. But he sure didn't let on.

James advanced on the senator at one point and asked him point blank if he had prior knowledge of the "findings on C-47 after the mining operation failed."

Coolly, McMasters said, "Not one bit."

Brandon didn't believe him, and he suspected that James didn't either, but neither of them said anything.

Finally, with all the preliminary items out of the way, and an official IPF transcriber in the room, everyone sat down, including the Mesoans who settled into place with help from Mary and Eldon. The Mesoans' hands intertwined and their fingers moved as though their intercommunication never subsided.

There had to be two witnesses on every side of an agreement, and Hollis remained as one of them along with another soldier pulled from the group that came in with Senator McMasters. Jacobs and Eldon would witness for Mary, and Crenshaw and another IPF enforcer witnessed James' signature.

All was in order.

Brandon plugged the headset cords into the translator. McMasters, Hollis, and the other EC soldier got dual sound, while Mary, Eldon, Jacobs, and James were plugged into the mono side. After plugging his cord in, he plugged in Palmer's. "We're ready," he said.

Stepping around the translator and the Mesoans, Brandon went to settle into a seat when James said, "You aren't needed for this. Neither is Palmer. I'm sorry."

Brandon opened his mouth to speak but Mary stopped him with a wave of her hand. "We are better served if you help in getting the IPF ship back into order. There must be something you can do out there."

Brandon felt rejected, but relieved at the same time. He unplugged the cords belonging to him and Palmer, let the headsets lie on the table, and excused the two of them.

"I don't believe that," Palmer said once they were outside the door.

"It's okay, I trust most of those in the room," Brandon said.

"But we've been a part of this for a long time."

Brandon took a deep breath. "I suspect we're going to be part of the conversation.

Palmer turned away. "I hadn't thought of that."

\*   \*   \*

Three days later Brandon and Palmer were called into the C-47 governmental boardroom. They had had three wonderful days together exploring the hills and valleys of the planet, while staying in a private suite in the colony's settlement. Once they were away from the pit and the natural landing strips, the flora and fauna became more colorful and interesting. The colony actually had shopping areas like most planets, as well as restaurants. There was a big difference between living among the community and in what amounted to an industrial park. But the honeymoon was over and Brandon knew it.

He and Palmer came into the room ready to take their knocks.

Around the table sat Mary, Eldon, James, Jacobs, and Oliver, whom Brandon was surprised to see. Mary smiled and welcomed them as they came in and sat down. "You have done a lot to help us over the last week or so. And we truly appreciate that."

Brandon lifted his eyes and held his chin up. He had not worn his cuffs since he and Palmer began their time together, the vacation they had wanted, but now felt naked without them. "I see you've asked James to be on the board with you," Brandon said.

James smiled, but it was Jacobs who spoke. "He was crucial in our negotiations with Earth Central, which have lasted these last few days. There are more things to discuss, and we're confident that he's on our side."

"We've made great strides," Eldon said.

"Still going down there alone?" Brandon asked.

"No," Eldon said. "I've gotten over that need." He had a grand smile across his face. "In fact, they've allowed me, and a guard, into their caverns. They're unbelievable."

Jacobs reached out to stop him. "There's time for that conversation later."

"There is?" Brandon said. "Aren't we leaving?"

"Still in a conversation about whether joining with IPF Section 204 is a good thing for C-47. We have a few more items to consider," James said. "But we have made some decisions in light of your little killing spree."

"I was doing my duty," Brandon said. "Although for a while it was difficult to know who the enemy was."

"Yeah, I can attest to that," Oliver said. "At one point, I was part of the problem."

James looked to either side at Jacobs and Mary, Oliver and Eldon. "We've gone through the records several times and it appears as though no matter who you were shooting at, you were protecting the people of this colony, and that's what the military is for, to keep civilians safe."

"But the senator said that someone had to—"

"Garth appears to have been the bad apple," James said.

"That's it?" Palmer said. "You're pinning most of this on Garth?"

"As the senator said, 'Someone has to take the fall'," James said. "And we had so much on Garth that he wasn't going to see daylight for a long time anyway. Starting with using a prisoner as a decoy." James shook his head. "He's a bad man and I, for one, don't feel as though we've done anything wrong."

Brandon felt Palmer's hand reach for his under the table. "Go on then," she said.

"Truth is, we assume that McMasters and Garth were communicating regularly. There were traces of messages, but no entire links. We think that's why things went relatively smoothly. That and the subliminal messaging the aliens sent through."

"All's fair…" James said.

Mary interrupted. "Tell him what we've done. Enough of the background. There'll be time for that." Her face lit up.

"There will?" Brandon said, for the second time, wondering what they were going to do about him. "If I'm off the hook, I'll have to put in for new orders."

"We've requested. Or, more correctly, the Mesoans requested that you stay on as their bodyguard if they feel they need you," Jacobs said. "He let out a loud laugh. You should see your face right now."

Brandon shook his head in confusion. "Bodyguard?"

"Our security team needs training, too," Mary said. "Earth Central, through our good friend Senator McMasters has agreed to assign you to C-47 for the next few years. He may have gotten the sense that we knew about his connection to Garth, but only the Mesoans can attest to that," she said with a smile.

"Don't look so shocked," Jacobs said. "You get to choose your own team to work with and everything."

"Crenshaw?" Brandon said.

"Up to James at the moment. He's still operating from a dual position until we decide what to do with Section 204," Jacobs said.

"We can make those arrangements," James said.

Brandon felt as though he'd dropped into the best luck he'd had for years until he felt Palmer squeeze his hand. "Wait. Could I be assigned somewhere near Palmer's next job location instead?"

She pulled his hand closer to her.

"Done," James said, "because we'd like for her to stay on for a few years also. The IPF still owes you quite a sum for completion of your last assignment."

"But they already paid me," Palmer said.

James leaned forward. "Overtime," he said.

Brandon couldn't believe his ears. He looked over and Palmer had her eyes closed as though she couldn't believe it either.

"What can I say?" she said.

"Then it's final," Mary said. She stood. "We owe you two a lot for what you've done. Everyone on this planet owes you."

"And I owe you even more than they do," Jacobs said.

Brandon let go of Palmer's hand and reached his arm around her shoulder and pulled her close. "Payment accepted. Paid in full."

## ThE END

**IF YOU ENJOYED THIS NOVEL, TRY OTHER SCI-FI AND FANTASY TITLES BY TERRY PERSUN:**

*Revision 7: DNA*

*Cathedral of Dreams*

*Doublesight*

# MORE GREAT SCI-FI/FANTASY READS FROM BOOKTROPE

*A Kingdom's Possession* **by Nicole Persun** (Young Adult Fantasy) A slave girl inhabited by a Goddess, loved by a Prince, hunted by a King. The beginning of an epic saga.

*Dead of Knight* **by Nicole Persun** (Fantasy) King Orson and King Odell are power-stricken, grieving, and mad. As they wage war against a rebel army led by Elise des Eresther, it appears as though they're merely in it for the glory. But their struggles are deeper and darker.

*The Water Sign* **by C.S. Samulski** (Science Fiction) In the post-diluvian world of the future many children find themselves lost in the fog of war.

*Ouroboros* **by Christopher Turkel** (Science Fiction) In a dystopian future, Thomas the assassin is about to face the job of his career — and his life.

*Changeling Eyes* **by L.A. Catron** (Fantasy) An epic tale of loss, self-discovery, revenge, and magic. The first book in the Aesir Chronicles.

*Seducer Fey* **by Cullyn Royson** (Fantasy) When Celtic mythology meets genetic engineering, youth and charisma can be bought.

Discover more books and learn more about our new approach to publishing at **booktrope.com**.

CPSIA information can be obtained at www.ICGtesting.com
Printed in the USA
LVOW05s2231110813

347350LV00001B/5/P